★ ★ ★ ★ ★

Reviews for
*Murder at the
Universe*

Lambert's wry turn as an accidental
house detective puts Craig's erudite
whodunit solidly on the map.

—*Publishers Weekly*

An entertaining insider's look at the
hotel business by a first-timer.

—*Library Journal*

More than just a crime novel, *Murder
at the Universe* is an entertaining satire
of the modern hospitality industry.

—*Calgary Sun*

The compellingly readable story weaves
together ideas about family, love, alcohol
and the real cost of a job…reading about
it is entertaining, from the meet-and-greet
right up to the guest departure experience.

—*Vancouver Sun*

★ ★ ★ ★ ★

Craig has kicked off his series with a
bang, a big bang of a book ... wonderfully
clever and well executed.
—*Crimespree Magazine*

Editors' Choice: A mysterious tale of intrigue.
—*EnRoute Magazine*

Best in the West this month!
—*Western Living Magazine*

Craig takes readers on a raucous, quick-paced
murder mystery through the glamorous halls
of the fictional Universe Hotel in New York.
—*Los Angeles Confidential*

Hit List: ... this is kind of like an episode of
Survivor in five-star accommodations.
—*Wish Magazine*

A page-turning read that keeps you
guessing "whodunit" until the very end.
—*Where Magazine*

Check in to a delightful and deadly hotel.
—*The StarPhoenix*

★★★★★

A FIVE-STAR MYSTERY

OTHER BOOKS BY DANIEL EDWARD CRAIG

Murder at the Universe
(Midnight Ink, 2007)

Murder at Graverly Manor
(coming in April 2009)

DANIEL EDWARD
CRAIG
A FIVE-STAR MYSTERY

MURDER

—————— AT ——————

HOTEL CINEMA

MIDNIGHT INK
WOODBURY, MINNESOTA

FIRST EDITION
First Printing, 2008

Cover design by Ellen L. Dahl
Cover photo © Image Source/Punchstock

Midnight Ink, an imprint of Llewellyn Publications

Cover model(s) used for illustrative purposes only
and may not endorse or represent the book's subject

This is a work of fiction. Names, characters, places, and incidents are either the product of the author's imagination or are used fictitiously, and any resemblance to actual persons, living or dead, business establishments, events, or locales is entirely coincidental.

Library of Congress Cataloging-in-Publication Data
Craig, Daniel Edward, 1966-
    Murder at Hotel Cinema : a five-star mystery / Daniel Edward Craig.
—1st ed.
        p.   cm.
    ISBN 978-0-7387-1119-5
 1. Hotels—California—Los Angeles—Fiction. 2. Hollywood (Los Angeles, Calif.)—Fiction. I. Title.
PS3603.R353M85 2007
813'.6—dc22

                                                    2008000623

Midnight Ink
2143 Wooddale Drive, Dept. 978-0-7387-1119-5
Woodbury, MN 55125-2989

www.midnightinkbooks.com

Printed in the United States of America

FOR MY SISTERS AND BROTHERS,
Ben, Robert, Bonnie, Lisa, and David.

A Splashy Affair

Opening night at Hotel Cinema.

I stood on the periphery of the pool deck under the shadow of a palm tree, enjoying a moment of peace in the warm summer air. Floodlights from the balconies above illuminated famous faces and beautiful people everywhere, the jet set of Hollywood. They were crowded around the deck, spilling out of the cabana rooms, wall-to-wall in the restaurant, gathered around the deejay booth in the lounge. What a change from three days ago, when the city inspector had arrived to find little more than a construction site. By some miracle—or perhaps money exchanged hands—Antonio Cavalli, the hotel's owner, had finagled an occupancy permit. When he made the announcement, an enormous cheer had erupted from staff. Panic quickly followed. Hotel Cinema was finally about to open, and only seventy-two hours remained to prepare for a full house and a star-studded opening party.

Yet somehow we made it. Now, catching my reflection on the surface of the swimming pool, I detected a glimmer of satisfaction in my eyes. There was even a trace of—what was it again?—oh yes, happiness. Or at least the memory of happiness. Perhaps my trepidation in coming to Los Angeles had been unjustified. This was my third opening, the first as general manager, and each time it was a harrowing experience rife with impossible deadlines, delayed furniture, incompetent contractors, overbearing owners, and harried employees. And all this even before the guests arrived with a whole new set of challenges. Yet the camaraderie among staff, the satisfaction of seeing the hotel buzzing with guests, made it all worthwhile. Much work remained—only 65 of 124 rooms were finished—but the hardest part was behind us, and Hotel Cinema, with its contemporary, ultra-stylish décor, was destined to be the hottest boutique hotel in Los Angeles.

And then my moment was gone.

Tony Cavalli spotted me across the pool and lumbered over. "You wanna know the truth, Trevor?"

I was quite sure I didn't.

"I think she's gonna no-show. Something must have happened at check-in to piss her off. Did one of your employees look her in the eye?"

"That's a myth, Tony. Nothing happened at check-in."

"What if she hates her suite? Maybe she found a pubic hair or something. Isn't she supposed to be a germaphobe?"

"She's the first guest to stay in that suite, Tony. I did the final inspection myself, and it's immaculate. And she's not a germaphobe. You shouldn't believe what you read in the tabloids. Give her time. She'll be here."

He glared up at Penthouse Suite 1, which occupied the northeast end of the U-shaped building and overlooked the shallow end of the pool. He tugged at his black goatee, eyes blazing, fueled by his manic personality and, I suspected, copious amounts of cocaine. Tall, his black hair receding in the front and long at the back, he looked stylish tonight, almost handsome, his round belly and bullfrog neck concealed under a tailored black Versace suit with elaborate swirls of purple stitching on the lapels. His shirt, like his teeth, was impossibly white, reflecting a soft orange glow from the concrete fire basins that lined the pool. Undoubtedly, his girlfriend—Liz Welch, the hotel's frosty, much-lauded interior designer—had dressed him.

"I'll kill her if she doesn't show. You know that conniving bitch Moira called to try and weasel out? She said Chelsea's 'exhausted.' Know what it means when a publicist says that? She's been partying so hard she looks like a train wreck. 'Not a goddamn chance,' I told her. 'I planned this entire party around her. I put her name on the invitations. She better show, or I'll fucking sue.'"

I contemplated telling Tony that Miss Fricks had called me from her suite a couple of hours ago but decided it was better to keep him in the dark. If he found out she had called to complain, he would insist on knowing every detail. I was tired of listening to him blame my employees for everything that went wrong and take credit for everything that went right. I glanced up at the penthouse suite again. The balcony was dark, its sun chairs hidden behind smoked glass underlit by soft red lighting. The sliding glass door was open, and the wind had coaxed out the diaphanous curtain, whipping it around in the breeze. A light was on in the living room.

"I don't see much life up there," I said.

"What if she passed out?" He checked his watch. "It's 11:10. People are getting antsy. We're gonna lose them. Think I should call Moira again?"

"Give it a few minutes. If she doesn't come down, I'll go up there myself."

Officially, the party had started at eight PM, but this being Los Angeles, our servers had stared at one other across an empty room for the first hour. Meanwhile, hotel guests had begun arriving to check in around noon, and by nine PM every available room was occupied. The first party guests began to trickle in around that time. Mortified to be the first, they drifted into dark corners and sipped cocktails until the trickle swelled into a steady flow. By ten PM, the time Miss Fricks was expected, the lobby, restaurant, lounge, and pool deck were overflowing.

I wasn't surprised she was late. Reputedly, she had once shown up for a photo shoot a full three days after call time. Tonight's appearance had been negotiated in excruciating detail by Moira Schwartz, her snarling pit bull of a publicist. Tony, who worshipped Chelsea, a twenty-seven-year-old former Mouseketeer, and hoped to one day call her a close friend, had set the date months ago based on her availability. When it became apparent that construction wouldn't be completed in time, he sent out invitations anyway and then rode herd on Fratelli Construction, owned by his second cousins, griping over their slow pace and shoddy workmanship. The moment he acquired the occupancy permit he had chased them off-property, leaving the daunting task of completing unfinished guestrooms and public areas to chief engineer Al Combs and his team of two.

Moira had refused to commit Chelsea beyond a fifteen-minute appearance. The contract stipulated that she would be escorted through the lounge and onto the pool deck by Tony, where she would pose for one official photo. Should she feel inclined, she could mingle with guests; otherwise, she could retire with her entourage to the VIP section in the back of the lounge. Our hope, of course, was that she would stay and socialize, that she might stay until closing like she had at nightclub openings in Vegas and South Beach. Moira had demanded the penthouse suite as part of the agreement, along with an adjoining room for herself and one for Chelsea's actor-boyfriend Bryce Davies, who always stayed in a separate room. The three were scheduled to leave for a three-month shoot in Lima, Peru, the following day, and Moira said it would be more convenient to go to LAX from the hotel in the morning, even though Chelsea lived nearby in Bel-Air. Moira also negotiated limousine transfers, meals, incidentals, and a bottle of Jack Daniels to be waiting in Chelsea's suite for arrival—no flowers, no gift basket, no chef's creation, just Jack Daniels.

The fee for her appearance came to the tidy sum of $150,000.

Initially, Tony had balked at the price, insisting I step in when Sydney Cheevers, official supplier of stars to LA parties, refused to negotiate with Moira. I understood why when I had my first encounter on the telephone. "Do you have any idea what a photo of Chelsea is worth these days?" Moira barked. "If that harebrained publicist of yours does her job, it'll be printed in every tabloid, every entertainment magazine, every fashion rag in this country. It'll put your little hotel on the map." Ultimately, Tony caved out of desperation. After several disastrous attempts at breaking into the film business—as screenwriter, director, and producer—he had concluded that his only hope of being accepted into Hollywood's inner circles was to own a hot hotel. If André Balazs of Standard Hotels could date Uma Thurman and Jason Pomeranc of Thompson Hotels could call J Lo a close friend, then Antonio Cavalli could have stars fawning over him too.

And so far his plan was working, save for one small detail: his $150,000 guest of honor was a no-show.

"Why won't she come down?" Tony whined. He began to pace back and forth, teetering precariously on the edge of the pool.

"Antonio Cavalli, there you are!" A tall, well-preserved man with permed blond hair and orange skin, who looked vaguely like Barry Manilow, burst through the crowd, grabbing Tony by the shoulder and spinning him around. "How's it hanging, you handsome devil?"

"Marlon Peters, you fucking homo! How the hell are ya?" Tony opened his arms and gave him a man-hug, slapping him hard on the back.

"Congratulations on this fucking *fabulous* hotel," Marlon purred.

Tony's eyes lit up. "You like?"

"It's incredible, almost too hip for me. And *look* at this crowd. I feel like I'm backstage at the Teen Choice Awards. But the name? *Hotel Cinema*? How bourgeois."

"See, I've always thought of hotels as a soundstage," Tony explained. "Guests come to stay, and while they're here, they basically star in their own movie. You follow? Problem is, employees too often act like *they're* the stars. It's all about how beautiful they are and how much you should tip them. My hotel is different. Our guests are the stars. Employees are crew and supporting cast." Tony clutched Marlon's shoulder and swept his hand across the crowd. "Each day, a hundred different movies will play here. Drama, romance, comedy, action-adventure, chick flick, hard-core porn—you name it. Whatever our guests need—props, styling, beds, catering, crew, and supporting cast—we'll provide it to ensure a flawless performance every time. Hotel *Cinema*. Get it?"

"Oh, I get it all right," Marlon said with a bemused expression. "You just better hope there are no tragedies." Taking notice of me, he looked me up and down as though about to introduce himself, but reconsidered when he saw my nametag. He turned back to Tony. "Well, you've done a *fabulous* job hiring staff. I checked in an hour ago—Morris and I thought we'd spend the night rather than risk another DUI—and they couldn't have been more hospitable."

"I only hire the best," Tony said, puffing his chest. "And I treat 'em real good." His eyes darted toward me. "Right, Trevor?"

"Absolutely," I said. Tony could take credit for a handful of hires— relatives or friends or relatives of friends or friends of relatives rang-ing in skill levels from moderately benign to hopelessly incompetent. As for treating staff "real good," he expected us to fall to our knees when he entered the room. At thirty-two years old, he was several years younger than me, yet he knew little about running a hotel or, it appeared, about business in general. His biggest assets were his family's money, which seemed to be in short supply, and his aggressive behavior, which seemed to have no limit. Yet he was my boss, and I am a professional. If Tony wished to take credit, I wasn't about to deny him the right. As obnoxious as he could be, I knew he was driven by a tyrannical father and, like me, the fear of failing yet again.

"Clearly everyone underestimated you, Tony Cavalli," said Marlon, lifting his champagne glass to toast him. "You're a genius hotelier."

Tony beamed. "This is just the beginning. I intend to make Cavalli Hotels & Resorts a major international chain—comparable to W Hotels but much, much better."

I took the opportunity to sidestep away and do a quick tour of the hotel. I searched the crowd for Shanna Virani, the hotel's brassy director of sales and marketing, but couldn't find her. My mother was here somewhere, having insisted on flying down from Vancouver for the opening. Earlier I had watched her work the crowd like a seasoned politician, boldly introducing herself to world-renowned directors, talk-show hosts, and supermodels. "Hello, I'm Evelyn Lambert," she would say, informing them she worked as head nurse at a hospital in a suburb of Vancouver. She considered her vocation equal to or more important than that of most of the people present; in her opinion, the film and television business was frivolous. As a head nurse she saved lives, comforted the sick, helped cure disease. In fact, it was a nurse who detected a lump in her breast that a doctor had over-looked, resulting in a lost breast but a saved life. People responded to her politely but weren't particularly interested. Yet she was having a marvelous time.

Unable to find Shanna or my mother, I made my way back to the pool deck and peered up at the penthouse suite again. This time I detected movement in the living room, flickers of shadow and light behind the sheer curtains. A small thrill ran through me. Chelsea Fricks was one of Hollywood's hottest stars. Her face adorned current issues of *Vanity Fair*, *Details*, and *Glamour*. She was relentlessly pursued by paparazzi, who sold photos of her and Bryce to tabloids for top dollar. Each week a new rumor appeared in the headlines: CHELSEA ADOPTION SCANDAL! CHELSEA IN & OUT OF REHAB ON SAME DAY! CHELSEA A RACIST! Her latest movie, *Blind Ambition*, had premiered a few weeks ago to rave reviews. Already there was Oscar buzz over her portrayal of real-life Stephanie Greene, the American diving champion who had won a gold medal in the 1996 Olympics despite suffering a degenerative eye condition that made her blind. In my career, I've met movie stars, heads of state, billionaire philanthropists, royalty, rock stars, and CEOs of major corporations. Few people faze me anymore. Yet once in a while someone gets through, makes me quiver with anticipation, renders me a stammering fool. Why Chelsea Fricks, a spoiled, bad-ass party girl with a volatile temper and a reputation for erratic behavior? Perhaps I sensed a sensitive, vulnerable person beneath the brash exterior. She was a nice girl from a suburb of Portland. Her fame had been explosive and overwhelming. Like others who followed her antics, I rooted for her. I hoped she would triumph over her demons.

"Hey, Trevor!" Tony pushed his way toward me and grabbed my arm. "I know how to get her down," he said, breaking into a devilish grin. He pointed to a floodlight on the deck. "She loves the spotlight, right? Let's smoke her out!"

Partly wary and partly amused, I watched him lug the floodlight toward the edge of the pool, bumping into people with his backside, wheeling over toes, and prompting cries of protest. At the edge of the pool he circled the floodlight to calculate the best positioning, his body hunched over, arms swinging back and forth like Quasimodo. A circle of light hit the fifth floor of the east wing of the building. He guided it along the row of balconies until it lit up the penthouse suite. Chuckling to himself, he muttered, "This'll get her out. This'll teach her not to no-show my party. Heh heh."

Through the illuminated curtain I could make out two figures in the living room. Their movements seemed to become animated, as though, aware of the spotlight, they were performing for the crowd. I craned my ear to hear their voices but they were lost in the din of music and voices around me.

Taking notice of the spotlight, a number of partygoers stopped talking and directed their attention to the balcony. Employees were under strict instructions not to reveal that Miss Fricks was residing in-house, but Tony had been bragging about it all night. Over the course of the evening I had observed people sneaking glances at the suite, hoping for a glimpse of the enigmatic guest of honor. Now, a tremor of anticipation ran through the crowd. They assumed this was part of the show. Chelsea would step onto the balcony, give an Eva Peron-like wave and air-kiss, perhaps regale us with a song from her soon-to-be released album, and then step onto a platform to be magically transported to the pool deck. People gathered along the edge of the pool and regarded the penthouse suite, faces flickering in the light of the fire basins. The pool looked like a great phosphorescent iceberg, having been treated with a biodegradable blue dye for the party. At its bottom, the Hotel Cinema logo rippled with the water.

I wondered what the party would look like from the heavens. A glowing blue pool surrounded by stylishly dressed men and scantily clad women clutching cocktails with manicured hands, heads craned in the same direction. I lifted my head and scanned the clear black sky lit up by hundreds of stars, some so faint they were barely perceptible, others so bright they might be planets. The moon, large and luminous, outshone all other entities—much like Chelsea Fricks.

Next to me, a tall, full-figured woman in a snug silver dress flicked a cigarette butt into the pool. I watched it soar through the air like a miniature jet, hitting the water and sizzling out in a plume of smoke. I cast a disapproving look in her direction and recognized the hotel's publicist, Katherine "Kitty" Caine. Like others, she was watching the penthouse suite in anticipation. A buzz was traveling across the crowd, and people were spilling onto the deck from the lounge and restaurant.

Yet the spotlight remained empty.

Tony lifted his fingers to his mouth and whistled. "Hey, Chelsea!" he shouted. "Come on out! We're waitin' for ya!"

There were chuckles in the crowd, murmurs of excitement. The movements inside the suite seemed to gain momentum. I heard a female voice shouting, followed by a scream. Wearing only a black bra and panties, a young woman rushed onto the balcony. The crowd cheered. How very Chelsea! She leaned over the railing, looking down at the pool as though gauging its distance. She scrambled onto the railing, teetering on top, prompting gasps. Glancing over her shoulder, she let out a shriek and leapt off the railing. Her arms flailed in the air as though she were trying to flap her way to the pool, then came together in a clumsy dive. She struck the surface and disappeared.

The splash sent the crowd stumbling backward. Immediately, they rushed forward again. They peered into the pool, waiting for Chelsea to surface. There was absolute silence.

"It's a prank!" Kitty Caine shouted in her Texas drawl. "A publicity stunt for *Blind Ambition*!"

There were sighs of relief, groans of disapproval, cries of outrage. Someone began clapping, and others joined in.

Yet Chelsea didn't surface.

I rushed around the periphery of the pool, nudging people out of the way as I searched the water. I knew something the others didn't: Chelsea had landed in the shallow end. Near the center of the pool I spotted her. She was closer to the deep end now, several feet beneath the surface. Fumbling for the two-way radio clipped to my belt, I rasped into the mouthpiece, "Trevor to Comm Center. Call 911 immediately. Emergency on the pool deck. I repeat, call 911!"

The reply came instantly. "Ten-four, Trevor. Calling 911 right now."

I tossed down the radio, kicked off my shoes, and pulled off my tuxedo jacket. Across the pool, I caught a glimpse of Tony Cavalli staring into the water with a lascivious grin. Chelsea had been under for at least thirty seconds, yet he still expected her to surface and take a bow. Others were shifting on their feet, becoming antsy, yet no one made a move to rescue her. It crossed my mind that Kitty might be right, that it was a publicity stunt. What better way to draw attention to her movie than to dive off the balcony of her suite? People were hesitant to risk ruining designer clothes and coiffed hair only to be the butt of a practical joke. I stared at Chelsea's morphing body in the murky blue water. An image of Nancy came to me. How many times had I imagined her breaking the surface, gasping for air, thrashing about in the raging sea surrounded by wreckage, struggling in vain to keep from drowning? How often had I wished I had been there to save her?

I dove into the pool.

The water was startlingly cold. I opened my eyes. The blue dye stung like iodine, blurring my vision. I spotted Chelsea's pale body floating a few feet away and kicked toward her. Purplish liquid swirled around her. Reaching for her arm, I pulled her toward me. Her head swung in my direction, green eyes open. Wrapping my arms around her torso, I planted my feet on the bottom and pushed upward.

The crowd cheered as we broke the surface. I heaved Chelsea over my shoulder and swam to the edge of the pool. I expected her to struggle, to break free, to climb onto the edge of the pool and take her bow. But she lay limp in my arms, not choking or gasping for air.

A dozen hands reached out and pulled her from my arms. Her eyes stared back at me, almost accusingly. She disappeared into the crowd.

Ignoring the proffered hands, I placed my hands on the edge of the pool and pulled myself out. A houseman hurried over with a towel. I mopped my face and dried my eyes. Looking down at my shirt, I saw a large red stain on the front. Blood? I covered it with the towel and stooped down to pick up my radio.

"Is there a doctor here?" a woman shouted. "This woman needs medical attention!"

There were murmurs among the crowd.

"I played a doctor on *House*," said a man to my right. "Does that count?"

No one laughed.

I tried to pry my way toward Chelsea to offer assistance but stopped when I saw Artie Truman making his way through the crowd. "Hotel security!" he shouted. "Let me through!" The hotel's security director was a former Los Angeles Police Department officer and certified first-aid attendant.

Above me, I heard a cry of anguish. A pale, black-haired woman was leaning over the railing of the room next to Chelsea's suite, her face horror-stricken. Moira Schwartz, Chelsea's publicist.

Bryce Davies' curly blond head appeared next to her. "Oh fuck. Hold on, baby! I'll be right down!"

They disappeared.

I lifted my radio. "Trevor to Comm Center. Is an ambulance on the way?"

"Affirmative. Has Artie Truman arrived on-scene?"

"Yes." By now, hundreds of people were crowded onto the deck. "Paging all security staff," I breathed into the radio. "We need everyone off the pool deck *now*." I began herding people back inside. In the lounge, faces were pressed against the floor-to-ceiling windows, anxious to see what was going on. I went back to herd in more people and caught another glimpse of Chelsea where she had been set down on a white towel. There was a large, red welt on her forehead, likely from striking the bottom of the pool. Her long, honey-colored hair was splayed around her. She looked like Botticelli's Venus having decided to lie down for a nap. Her head was turned away, neck unnaturally twisted. A circle of dark liquid was seeping into the towel under her—blood. Artie was squatting over her. Suddenly, her chest heaved. The crowd cried out with joy, but then realized the motion was from Artie's attempts at CPR. Turning away, I guided a sobbing woman inside, doing my best to comfort her.

As we reached the doorway, Bryce Davies appeared. "Out of my fucking way!" he shouted, shoving me aside and rushing past.

Moira Schwartz was right behind him. "Move, people! Move!" she screamed.

I turned and watched Bryce push his way through the crowd. He grabbed Artie by his shirt and wrenched him off of Chelsea. "What the fuck you doing, man?" he cried. "Leave her alone, you perv!"

I hurried over and gently pulled Bryce out of the way. "It's okay," I said. "He's our security director. He's certified in first aid."

Bryce turned to me and lifted his fist, eyes fierce, but let it drop. He turned back to Chelsea and fell to his knees. "Don't die, Chelsea baby!" he cried. "Don't leave me! I love you. I'm sorry … I'm so sorry."

Moira stood motionless behind him, her face in her hands.

"Out of the way!" a security officer shouted from behind. "Emergency personnel!"

Two paramedics rushed toward us, followed by two LAPD officers.

The crowd cheered.

Artie stood up and backed away to make room. Spotting me, he came over.

"Is she going to make it?" I whispered.

He shook his head. "She's already dead."

2

Wakeup Call

Back in November, when Shanna Virani called about the general manager position, I was dozing on the sofa in my living room in Vancouver, Canada, my hometown. I ignored the phone, as I had done for weeks since the hangups began. It rang again and again, until I couldn't stand the shrill sound anymore and picked it up.

"Yes." I waited for the click.

"Trevor, is that you?"

"Who is this?" I didn't have to ask; the regal British-Pakistani accent was unmistakable.

"It's Shanna, silly. You sound strange. You're not still hiding under the bed, are you?"

"Maybe."

She let out a great sigh. "You poor dear. I know you've been through a dreadful time, but it's been four months. It's time to return to the land of the living. Remember that boutique hotel I told you they're renovating in Hollywood? It's set to open this spring—and guess who's the new director of sales and marketing."

"You? You're kidding."

Shanna had managed sales departments in five-star hotels around the world—Four Seasons, Mandarin Oriental, Ritz Carlton, St.

Regis—and could get a job anywhere. When her fiancé, Willard God-frey, died after a hit-and-run last year, he left her the Universe Hotel in New York. Soon after, she surprised everyone by selling the hotel and moving to Los Angeles, where her son and daughter from a pre-vious marriage were attending UCLA. "That place is a money pit," she explained to me later. "I sold it to avoid bankruptcy." She couldn't stand being idle, and I knew she would resurface in the hotel indus-try somewhere in LA. But a small, unknown, independent hotel? It seemed an odd fit for the worldly Shanna.

"You sound disappointed," she said, sounding disappointed her-self.

"No, I'm happy for you, Shanna. Congratulations."

"I'm thrilled. I started a couple of weeks ago, and so far it's been fabulous. The owner, Antonio Cavalli, has given me free rein to run the sales and marketing department as I wish. He's been searching for a general manager for several months now, but he can't find the right fit. I told him I know the perfect candidate."

So this was why she was calling. "I'm not interested, Shanna."

"Darling, this job is made for you. Tony wants a manager with classic hotel training. This hotel is part of the rejuvenation of Old Hollywood. It's right on the Walk of Fame, a few minutes' walk from Grauman's Theatre and the Kodak Theatre, home of the Academy Awards, and a W Hotel is going to be built down the street. It's quickly becoming the new 'It' neighborhood. The hotel is going to be ultra-contemporary and uber-stylish. When it opens, it will be crawling with celebrities."

I laughed. "That doesn't exactly sound like me."

"That's the point. Tony refuses to make the mistake of other design hotels—hiring hipsters more interested in partying in the lounge and hobnobbing with stars than in delivering great service. He wants someone who won't get caught up in the scene. Someone like you!"

I shouldn't have answered the phone. I didn't want to play this game. It was too much effort. Shanna was too much effort. I wanted to place the phone down and go back to the sofa and resume watching my friend the resident hairy-legged spider trap unwitting insects in her web and suck the life out of them.

"If this is such a great opportunity, why don't you be the GM?"

"Me?" Her accent grew more pronounced. "You know I can't *stand* operations. Just the thought of having to worry about tedious things like employee morale and workplace safety and guest complaints makes me go cross-eyed. That's your domain. Besides, Tony wants someone young and fresh-faced, not a tired old has-been like me."

Shanna was in her early fifties but could easily pass for forty. Petite and voluptuous, she had a prominent nose, high cheekbones, and a stormcloud of black hair. She could lie about her age without batting an eye, shooting as low as she thought she could get away with, which often correlated with the lighting in the room.

"This hotel is going to be five-star all the way," she persisted. "I know you refuse to work for anything but."

"I refuse to work in *any* type of hotel, Shanna."

"Don't tell me you still blame the hotel business for Nancy's death? How ludicrous. It was your decision to cut your vacation short. You could have refused. And it was her decision to take that earlier flight."

"I don't blame anyone anymore. I'm over it."

"Honestly?"

"Yes."

"Good. Have they found out anything more about what happened?"

"There's nothing more to find out. It was an accident, a random tragedy, that's all."

"What about that girl who disappeared? Any news on her?"

"Can we not talk about this, please? When I'm ready to go back to work, I'll let you know. But I plan to pursue a far less demanding career—a greeter at Wal-Mart or towel-folder at Linens-n-Things. Why are you so desperate to bring me on board, anyway?"

"Don't ever call a woman desperate, my darling, particularly one of *un certain âge*. I'm merely excited by the prospect of working with you again. You have too much talent to waste. The hotel business is your calling. What happened to your ambition to become a general manager? Your last job as hotel manager lasted what, three days?"

"That's not fair. You know what happened."

"All I'm saying is you're not going to walk into a GM position at a 1,000-room, five-star hotel. You'll have to start at a smaller hotel. And if you don't act soon, you'll be lucky to get a job parking cars at HoJos. You won't find a better opportunity than this. And this is an *opening*, Trevor. I know how you love openings."

"I hate openings."

"Remember what you told me after we opened the Universe?"

"That I'd never open another hotel as long as I live."

"That nothing was more exciting."

"Or hectic. Or all-consuming. I need order in my life right now, Shanna, not chaos."

"No one can bring order to chaos like you. The hotel has only 124 rooms—how difficult could it be? We'll have lots of time to explore this fantastic city."

"Isn't LA full of smog and shallow people?"

"That's what makes it so wonderful! Vancouverites are far too healthy, always climbing mountains and eating overpriced organic foods. You must be miserable there. New Yorkers are just as insufferable, always trying to prove their intellectual superiority to compensate for pale skin and sagging bodies. There are none of those pretenses here. The people are blessedly, unapologetically superficial, tanned, toned, cosmetically enhanced, surgically preserved, and gorgeous. And the weather is divine. You must be drowning in all that rain."

I wandered to the window and peeked through the blinds. To my surprise, the sky was clear and blue. I slumped onto the sofa, sinking deep into the pillows, and pulled a blanket around me. I looked up to the ceiling for my spider, but she wasn't around. Maybe a predator had trapped her in her own web and eaten her. I was completely alone now. Was Shanna right? Was this the opportunity I needed to stop wallowing and start living again?

"What's the owner like?" I asked.

"Tony? He's brilliant. His father, Giancarlo, has become fabulously wealthy importing fine classical art and sculpture from Italy. He lent Tony the money to build the hotel, but it's Tony's baby. It's the family's first foray into the hotel business, and they're already talking about expanding. Tony's made it clear he's not interested in getting involved in day-to-day operations. He'll be very hands-off. He's a brilliant, brilliant man."

Though my head was clouded with the effects of months of sleeping pills and anxiety medication, I was alert enough to recognize Shanna's use of repeated adjectives.

"So he's a moron," I said.

She sighed. "I can't lie to you. But what he lacks in brainpower, he makes up for in energy and enthusiasm. His weak areas are your strong points, so you'll make excellent colleagues. We could use some of your honesty and integrity here—those *Universal values* Willard Godfrey used to hold so dear. Why are you being so difficult? We need you here, Trevor. *I* need you. This is an incredible opportunity to make a name for yourself. In Hollywood, hotel managers are revered, absolutely worshipped. They're celebrities in their own right."

I felt a tremor of excitement, a feeling I hadn't experienced in months. It scared the hell out of me.

"So?" she persisted. "What do you say? Are you in?"

"I don't think so," I said, turning on my side and hugging a pillow. "I'm just not ready to go back to work."

There was an edge to her voice now. "Christ, Trevor. Enough is enough. Your mother is sick with worry."

I sat up. "You talked to my mother?"

"When you didn't answer for days, I—"

I groaned. "She's probably on her way over with an army of therapists."

In the days after the crash, my mother came to visit every day, observing me from across the room with pitying, tearful, prying eyes as though I were a sad movie she couldn't turn off. Unable to stand the scrutiny, I told her to stop coming. She resorted to calling every day until I asked her to stop that too. That's when the hangups began. At first, I thought they were random calls. Then I began to suspect they were Mom checking up on me. On the fifth or sixth call, exasperated, I shouted into the phone, "Mom, will you *please* stop calling me?" The calls stopped for a while after that. Then, in October, they resumed. Mom had me on suicide watch. I stopped answering the phone.

"We're worried about you, Trevor," said Shanna. "We don't think you've dealt with …"

A small thump drew my attention to the front door. Was Mom here already? Pressing the receiver against my chest, I tiptoed to the door and peered through the peephole. In the hallway I saw my neighbor, an elderly widower with a veiny, bulbous nose and perpetual scowl, waiting for the elevator. My knee bumped against the door. He turned in my direction. I leapt away, flattening myself against the wall.

"Trevor, are you there?" Shanna's voice called from the receiver.

My heart was pounding. Why was I so scared? Did I think he was going to pull out an Uzi and Swiss-cheese the door? Oh God, I'd become paranoid. Borderline schizophrenic. Heading toward insanity. How long had it been since I'd left my apartment—days, weeks, months? Or had I gone out earlier today? What day *was* it?

"Trevor? Hellooo?"

I lifted the receiver. "I'm here."

"Goodness, I thought I'd lost you. My, you're becoming an odd young man."

I wandered into the bedroom. On the nightstand next to my unmade bed was a small felt box. It had been sitting there for months. In the hallway, the elevator dinged and the doors rumbled open. Was Shanna right, was I becoming odd? Undoubtedly. Still, I was suspicious of her motives.

"Shanna, why do you want me to move to LA?"

She was silent for a moment. "I could use some company, Trevor. I thought you could too. We both lost loved ones in the past year, and … I thought we could help one another."

I heard the elevator doors glide shut.

"I'm flying up on Monday with an executive recruiter. He's anxious to meet you. We're staying at the Opus. Will you commit to at least one short meeting?"

"Fine. One meeting."

"Marvelous! I'll call you when our flights are booked."

I nodded, not saying anything, as if she could see me.

"Bye for now, darling. I can't wait to see you."

"Shanna, wait."

"Yes?"

"What's it called? The hotel."

"Hotel Cinema. Isn't that fabulous? I've already come up with the tagline. Want to hear it?"

"No."

"High Drama in Hollywood."

★ ★ ★ ★ ★

A few days later, in the early morning before the sun made its appearance, I trudged along the sands of English Bay, so close to the water that the waves lapped at my shoes. At the center of the bay I stopped to face the ocean. Reaching inside my pocket, I pulled out the felt box and turned it over in my hands. I pictured the ring inside, simple and elegant and expensive, furtively bought in Opéra Garnier while Nancy was in the hotel room resting. I watched the roiling black waves until the sun hit the back of my head. Drawing my arm back, I flung the box as far as I could into the ocean depths.

Then I turned to make my way home.

3

Like a Moth to a Flame

"You *idiot*, Moira! How could you leave her alone like that? You knew she was unstable."

"Screw you, Bryce. She's *your* girlfriend."

"Not anymore—thanks to you."

I was positioned in the lobby, in the neutral zone between the restaurant, Scene, where Moira Schwartz was perched at a table near the entrance, and the lounge, Action, where Bryce Davies was padding around like a caged animal. Although visibly distraught, Moira was taking a more businesslike approach to her grief than Bryce. Having demanded a laptop from the front desk, she was typing furiously on the keyboard, stopping occasionally to fire an insult at Bryce or simply to raise her middle finger.

Fortunately, save for hotel staff, they were the only guests in the lobby. In the three hours since the police had arrived, party guests and hotel guests had been questioned and asked to leave the property or go to their rooms. Only Bryce and Moira had not been permitted to return to their rooms. The detective in charge had dispatched orders for them to remain on-property until he questioned them personally. Neither was pleased.

Meanwhile, a half-dozen LAPD personnel were milling about the pool deck. To my dismay, Chelsea Fricks' body still lay there, draped in a white plastic sheet, in full view of guestrooms. Light flooded the deck as if a late-night movie shoot were taking place. More police officers were in the penthouse suite, while others were going door to door interviewing guests and inspecting rooms. Unable to fathom why a simple act of foolishness was being treated like a full-scale homicide investigation, I demanded to speak with the detective but was politely told to be patient and stay out of the way.

Outside, four police cars and an ambulance blocked both ends of the short, U-shaped driveway leading to Hollywood Boulevard, their flashing ambers attracting a burgeoning crowd of reporters, paparazzi, fans, and the curious like movie premier searchlights. Artie Truman and four doormen, now on overtime, were struggling to control the ornery crowd, refusing entry to all but registered guests and employees. Staff members, accosted by media as they arrived and departed, were under strict instructions not to comment. Tony Cavalli was nowhere to be found, having left for a party in Beverly Hills with his entourage the moment the LAPD arrived. I had tried Kitty Caine's cell phone several times, looking for advice on how to handle the media, but she wasn't answering. I had last seen her stumbling around drunk in the arms of a tall, distinguished man with a large Adam's apple. Shanna's cell phone went straight to voice mail, and my mother was either out on the town or asleep.

Which left me alone with Bryce Davies and Moira Schwartz.

Like the captain of a sinking ship, I considered it my duty to ensure all passengers were safely off-property or in bed before I could abandon ship myself. Even if I wanted to leave, I couldn't; the detective wanted to speak with me.

But as I crossed the lobby, a swishing sound reminded me I was still wearing my soggy tuxedo pants, the jacket buttoned over my shirt to conceal the red stain. My hair felt stiff and smelled of chlorine. Knowing it would be a while before the detective got to me, I took the back service stairs to B2, retrieved a new suit from the dry-cleaning rack in the housekeeping office, and showered in the men's locker room.

Upon my return to the lobby, I saw that the detective still hadn't appeared. I watched Bryce Davies, tabloid heartthrob and star of prime-time drama *Modern Loving,* navigate the translucent bead curtains and white leather furniture of the lounge. He grappled at a cube chair like a blind man and sat hunched over with his head in his hands. The soft violet lighting above him cast a phosphorescent glow on his blond hair. I made my way over and attempted to console him, but he was despondent. As I walked away I heard him croak, "Scotch." Happy to provide some comfort, I went to the bar and retrieved a bottle of Chivas Regal and a rock glass filled with ice.

Moira Schwartz was similarly unapproachable, in part because she had been on her cell phone from the moment she took residence in the restaurant. Her words echoed across the lobby, making it impossible not to listen.

"Patrick? It's Moira from the Moira Schwartz Media Group. Chelsea's dead." Her tone was world-weary and slightly irritated, as though she were reporting that Chelsea had missed her flight. "Moira *Schwartz*, Chelsea's *publicist* ... Who do you think—Chelsea Clinton? Chelsea *Fricks*, for Christ's sake ... Yes, I *know* what time it is. I thought you might want to know, being a freaking *journalist* ... You think I'd joke about something like this? ... I know, it's devastating ... Some new designer hotel in Hollywood ... It's been a difficult time for her. She was depressed. I guess she couldn't take the scrutiny anymore.

How would you feel if you couldn't pop a zit without it being plastered over every magazine in the country? … Looks like she climbed onto the balcony railing and—"

"She didn't fucking kill herself, Moira!" Bryce hollered across the lobby, rising to his feet and banging his fists together like a boxer. "She *fell*. It was an accident."

Moira pressed the phone against her chest. "When people fall, they don't break into a swan dive, jackass."

"How would you know? You were in your room, probably watching lesbo porn, when you should have been looking after her."

"I was on the phone. *I* had just checked in on her. Where were *you*? In your room smoking crack?"

Charming. I shot a nervous glance at the front desk. Simka, night agent, was busy on the phone, head lowered, discreetly observing Bryce through her blond-streaked hair. Next to her, night manager David Woo sifted through registration cards, eyes bulging as he pretended not to listen. I needed to get Moira and Bryce off-property before the arguing came to blows.

"If she jumped, it's your fault!" Bryce cried. "You put her up to it, didn't you? Another desperate publicity stunt? It backfired this time, didn't it? You killed her, Moira. You killed my girl!" He collapsed onto the floor and curled into a fetal position, convulsing with sobs.

Before I could come to his aid, Simka hung up the phone and bustled over. Kneeling before him, she placed her hands on his back and caressed him—fulfilling a dream of thousands of adoring fans.

"Gotta go, Patrick," Moira said behind me. "I need to get this release on the wire. If I don't get the real story out, God knows what kind of crap will show up in the news. I'll copy you." She put the phone down on the table and resumed typing, either unaware of my presence or ignoring me.

I cleared my throat.

She looked up. "What?"

"I'm sorry to disturb you, Miss Schwartz. I'm Trevor Lambert, the hotel's general manager. We spoke on the phone?"

Her expression registered no recognition.

"I—I wanted to check in with you. Can I bring you anything while you're waiting?" Up close, I was surprised to see how young she was. By her combative nature and shrewd negotiating skills, I had assumed she was in her thirties or forties, possibly even her fifties. She could be no older than thirty. She was about the same height as Chelsea, although at least twenty pounds heavier. Surrounded by the bohemian glamour of the restaurant, perched on a gold Louis XV chair upholstered in red leather, she looked out of place in her old-fashioned black ruffled dress. Had she paid more attention to her looks, she might be attractive. Her dyed black bob looked slept on, and her pale skin and black lipstick gave her a sinister, goth-like appearance. A pair of worn sandals sat on the white sparkled tablecloth next to a silver candelabra.

"What I *need* is my room," she bellowed in a deep monotone. Her dark eyes bored into me. "Can I go back now?"

"Unfortunately not. I do apologize. If you need privacy, you are welcome to use my office behind the front desk."

She let out a sigh and picked up her cell phone again, dismissing me. "Ian, is that you? It's Moira with the Moira Schwartz Media Group. I'm sending a release out shortly, but thought I'd give you the heads-up. Chelsea's dead … she killed herself."

As I made my way out of Scene, I heard someone cough. I turned to see a stylishly dressed man in his late twenties emerge from the pool deck. Hands on his hips, he scanned the lobby, eyes closed to two slits, as though in search of someone. Short, handsome in a swarthy way, his hair mussed to perfection, he was dressed in faded jeans and a white belt with a large silver buckle shaped like a star. Assuming he was a party guest who had wandered in from one of the cabana rooms, I marched over.

"Good evening, sir," I said. "Are you a registered hotel guest?"

He looked Italian. One of Tony's relatives? They had been everywhere tonight. His shirt was open, revealing a silver medallion resting on a bed of black chest hair.

He gave me the once-over. "Nope. I'm Detective Stavros Christakos. Are you Trevor Lambert?"

"I am." I held out my hand. "Pleased to meet you, Detective. I've been wanting to talk to you." His grip was firm, almost painful. Greek, not Italian, I realized.

"And I've been wanting to talk to you," he said, his voice resonating through the lobby. "But first I need to talk to those two characters." He gestured with his chin toward Moira and Bryce.

"Of course," I said. "Your officers will be leaving soon, I trust?"

"They're taking the body away now."

At that moment, two paramedics appeared, carrying a gurney draped with a white plastic sheet.

Moira stood up and let out a small cry, covering her mouth.

Bryce rushed toward the stretcher. "Chelsea baby, don't leave me!" he cried.

The detective hurried over to intercept him. "Mr. Davies, please. I need you to stand back."

"Let me see her!" Bryce cried, struggling to get past the detective. "I gotta see her one last time. I want to say goodbye to my baby!" The night doorman held open the door, and the gurney was whisked through. "I love you, Chelsea girl!" Bryce called out. Then he crumbled to the marble floor. "Oh baby, I'm so sorry! I didn't mean to hurt

28

you. I love you so much!" He covered his head with his hands, his body rocking with sobs.

Simka dutifully hurried from the front desk to attend to him.

Over in Scene, Moira was staring at the exit, eyes wide. After a moment, she lowered herself into her chair and resumed typing.

I followed the detective out the door.

The appearance of Chelsea's body had caused a huge uproar in the crowd. Artie and his doormen, assisted by four LAPD officers, struggled to keep people at bay as the gurney was whisked to the waiting ambulance. A paramedic pulled open the back doors, and a lanky, long-haired man in the crowd reached out and yanked the sheet, exposing Chelsea's white feet and red toenails. This prompted cries of outrage. An officer whacked the man in the arm with a club, and he cried out in pain, stumbling backward. Hurriedly replacing the sheet, the attendants slid the gurney into the ambulance in one swift motion and slammed the doors shut. The driver fought his way to the front door and climbed in. The ambulance rolled into motion, lights flashing. Cameramen, reporters, and fans chased it down the driveway. A female reporter reached for the door handle and tried to wrench the door open but was clubbed away by a police officer. She howled in pain.

The ambulance sped down Hollywood Boulevard.

★ ★ ★ ★ ★

When I returned to the lobby, the detective was in Scene interviewing Moira. Bryce was in the lounge with a blanket over his shoulders, sipping scotch. Simka had returned to the front desk and was fielding phone calls while keeping a close eye on Bryce. I looked through the windows to the pool deck and was relieved to find it empty. I asked

David to radio the night cleaners to hose it down and to drain and refill the pool.

A half-hour later, Moira was sent home, and the detective went to the lounge to interview Bryce. By then, the effects of several weeks of sleep deprivation were beginning to catch up with me. To keep awake I busied myself in the lobby, arranging and rearranging the dizzying array of pillows on the numerous divans and ottomans there. The heat of the fireplace—a three-foot flame lit by ethanol gas in a rectangular glass box that occupied the center lobby, a nod to the fire that destroyed the original building—made me sleepy. I sat down to rest and felt the weight of sleep descend. But I could hardly allow myself to sleep in view of staff and guests. I heaved myself to my feet and went to the front desk to assist with the phones, which had lit up with the news of Chelsea's demise.

At four thirty AM, the detective finished up with Bryce and sent him on his way.

"Come with me," he said, leading me to the pool deck along with a tall, balding man in uniform, whom he introduced as Officer George Gertz.

A crisscross of yellow police tape blocked entry to the deck. Officer Gertz removed the bottom strip, and Detective Christakos, although short enough to walk straight through, made a show of ducking underneath. I stepped onto the deck and breathed in the cool morning air, instantly more alert. The sweet scent of Encyclias wafted from the planters around the pool. The sky was dark. The fire pits had been extinguished, but the area was brightly lit by the floodlights around the pool and on the balconies above. Yellow police tape ran the periphery of the deck, blocking access from the cabana rooms. The pool water looked black. Cocktail napkins floated on the surface like miniature rafts. The stench of stale booze and cigarettes drew my attention to the bar, where the cocktail tables were littered with ashtrays, empty glasses, and debris. A number of chairs were overturned.

"I told the cleaners they can do their thing once we're done here," the detective explained. He led me to the northeastern corner of the pool below the penthouse suite. "You were out here when the incident occurred, right, Mr. Lambert? Tell us what you saw."

He was talking too loudly for my comfort; every cabana room was occupied, lights out. Speaking in a loud whisper, I recounted what I had observed. The detective eyed me closely as I spoke, eyes following each gesture, head unmoving. Next to him, Officer Gertz scribbled furiously into a notepad.

"So she jumped?" the detective surmised.

"It appeared that way."

"She didn't fall?"

"Fall?" I shot a nervous glance at the balcony. Could she have climbed onto the railing, only to have it collapse from under her? My thoughts went back to the battles Tony had fought with Fratelli Construction. Could they have overlooked a critical bolt, an integral screw? Imagine the uproar if the hotel were liable for her death. But no, Al Combs had inspected every room himself, balconies included, and he was thorough and meticulous. Then the housekeeping department had given them a final deep cleaning before Ezmerelda Lopez, executive housekeeper, also a stickler for detail, inspected them. I personally conducted the final inspection of every room, including the penthouse suite, before it was put into service. Nothing would have escaped our scrutiny. I could see from where I was that the railing was solid. The balcony walls, composed of smoked glass and secured by thick, round metal beams, were strong enough for six large men to stand on. "Impossible," I said.

"Why impossible?"

"If she fell, she would have landed here." I walked directly below the balcony. "To reach the pool she would have to leap."

"You think she was playing some kind of prank? She jumped into the pool for attention?"

"I'm quite sure that wasn't the case."

The detective narrowed his eyes. "What makes you so sure?"

A light flickered on in a room on the fifth floor, and a woman stepped onto the balcony in a hotel bathrobe.

"Can we talk about this inside, Detective? We're disturbing our guests."

He gave a quick shake of his head. "A few more minutes. Why don't you think it was a prank? That's what everyone else seems to think."

I lowered my voice. "Miss Fricks came down for a swim shortly after she checked in."

The detective's eyes bulged. "Chelsea was *here*? In the pool?"

I nodded. I related the events that occurred around six that evening, when I was obliged to take aside Sydney Cheevers, the high-strung event promoter Tony had hired to attract stars to the party. All afternoon she had been storming about the hotel, hollering at staff like a fiercely competitive soccer mom.

"Listen, Sydney," I had said, "you're doing a terrific job, but I need to ask you to treat my staff with more respect."

Apparently I hit a nerve. "What? *What?*" she roared, pawing at her mane of fiery red hair. "I've been busting my butt trying to get this disaster zone ready while *your* employees have been milling about like heavily sedated government workers, and *you* have the audacity to tell *me* to treat them with respect? Some of the biggest names in Hollywood are coming tonight, all because of *me*." Her voice broke. "I've sacrificed everything for this party, *everything*. If you people fuck up, it's *my* reputation on the line. If you think I'm going to…"

At that moment Chelsea Fricks had floated onto the deck, causing a collective gasp among the employees and contractors present. Only Sydney, her back to the pool, didn't see her. Her shrill voice faded as I discreetly watched Chelsea veer past the Pool Closed sign, either not seeing it or choosing to ignore it, and set down a pink inflatable air mattress. Her bathrobe fell from her shoulders. I looked away, reestablished contact with Sydney's raging eyes, and quickly sneaked another look. Chelsea Fricks was standing on the pool deck in near-naked splendor with only a tiny black two-piece bikini covering her petite, curvy body. A perfectly shaped leg extended to dip her toe in the water. As if the Virgin Mary herself had appeared, everyone on the pool deck—housemen, technicians, decorators, bartenders, chefs, servers—stopped what they were doing and stared. Able Al Combs, stooped over a concrete fire basin, slopped fuel over his work boots. Chelsea stood on her toes, lifted her arms, arched her back, and did a perfect swan dive into the pool, causing barely a ripple in the water. Al hurried off with the fuel can, mopping his bald head with a handkerchief.

Hearing the splash, Sydney spun around. "What the hell? Don't tell me someone just dived into the pool!" Spotting Chelsea's shape gliding like a dolphin underwater, she stormed to the edge. "*Hel-lo-o?* Can you read? The pool is fucking *closed!*" She spun around to me. "Who the fuck does she think she is? Get her out *now,* Trevor."

"Relax, it's okay," I said, taking her arm and trying to lead her away. "Let her have a swim."

"*Okay?*" she shrieked, yanking her arm away. "Some brainless bitch decides to go for a swim in the midst of setup for one of the biggest parties of the year, and you think it's okay? She's lucky we haven't treated it with dye yet. She'd emerge looking like a great blue whale. I want her out *now.*"

I locked eyes with her, speaking slowly and calmly like a doctor talking a patient down from a psychotic episode. "Trust me, Sydney, it's *okay*. She's a *VVIP* guest. Do you understand? A *V-V-I-P* guest." I was reluctant to utter Miss Fricks' name, even though everyone present was fully aware of her presence. "I'm sure she'll be out in a few minutes."

Chelsea reached the shallow end and came up for air, wiped her eyes, and kicked in the other direction.

"Oh my God," Sydney whispered, clutching my arm. "It's her."

"Yes."

At the other end of the pool, Chelsea hopped onto the edge and reached for the mattress, blew air into it, pulled it into the water, and climbed on top, drifting toward the shallow end.

Suddenly aware that everyone was staring, I lifted my hands and signalled for them to get back to work.

Sydney marched to the pool bar and grabbed her purse. "We've got to get a picture of this. Chelsea Fricks in your pool on the first day of operation. This is *priceless*."

"Oh no, you don't," I said, stopping her. "I'm not sure where you've worked before, but around here we don't go around snapping photos of our guests. We respect their privacy."

"She's a paid employee. We have a signed contract."

"For a fifteen-minute appearance and one photo." I took Sydney by the arm to guide her away.

"When I returned a few minutes later, she was gone," I told the detective, who had been listening with rapt attention.

He nodded, scrunching his eyes, thinking hard. "Describe what she was wearing again?"

"A black two-piece bathing suit. It was tied on the sides with strings. Why do you ask?"

He broke into a grin. "Bet she looked hot!" He reached out to slap me playfully on the arm.

"Detective, the woman died only hours ago."

"Don't get all huffy now. I'm just kidding around. So what's the point of this story?"

"It couldn't have been a prank. She knew she was jumping into the shallow end."

"So then why did she jump?"

I felt like I was being tested, like Detective Christakos knew the answer and wanted to know how much I knew. "I can only assume it was suicide," I said in a hushed voice. "Moira Schwartz seems to think so too, although Bryce Davies appears to think otherwise. What did they tell you?"

"Moira Schwartz is too concerned about Chelsea's image to be a reliable witness. And Bryce is too coked out. Did it look like she was being chased?"

"Chased?" I closed my eyes and replayed the scene in my head ... Chelsea racing out to the balcony ... scrambling onto the railing ... glancing over her shoulder. A chill ran through me. It *did* look like she was being chased. My eyes snapped open. "I suppose it's possible. Why—?"

"Did you hear anything before she jumped?"

"I heard shouting. And she screamed. But it was hard to tell who was shouting. It was noisy out here. You're better off asking whoever was in the suite with her."

"So there *was* someone in the suite at the time?" the detective asked. "You saw the assailant?"

"Assailant? Surely you don't think ... Isn't this a simple matter of suicide?"

"If you were going to kill yourself, would you jump off the *fifth* floor into a *pool*?"

"Well, Chelsea Fricks was not like other people. Maybe she wanted to go out with a splash." I lowered my voice further. "Detective, I've encountered my share of famous actors in my career. Some of them are nuts."

"Not all," he said, sounding defensive.

"By all accounts, Chelsea Fricks was." I was about to tell him about her nasty phone call when the sound of a patio door drew our attention to one of the cabana rooms. A straggly haired, skinny man in boxer shorts appeared.

"Mornin'," he greeted us in a gravelly voice.

"Good morning, sir," I called out. "I'm very sorry to disturb you. We were just about to leave."

"No prob. Couldn't sleep anyway." I saw the flicker of a lighter and the red glow of a cigarette. He crossed his arms and smoked, observing us, his face obscured in the shadows. His arms and torso were covered in tattoos.

I flipped through the guest list I kept stored in my head: Cabana Room 115, Mr. Dan D. Lyon—a pseudonym, of course. I turned to the detective. "Can we finish this conversation inside?"

Detective Christakos was staring at the man.

"Detective? Do you mind?" I hastened toward the door, beckoning the two policemen to follow.

Officer Gertz complied, but Detective Christakos lingered, arms crossed, observing the man closely.

When he finally caught up with us in the lobby, I whispered, "You don't think he had anything to do with it, do you?"

"Is that Tommy Lee? Did you see him, Georgie? It's Tommy Lee, isn't it?"

Officer Gertz nodded. "I interviewed him earlier. Awesome guy."

"How cool is that?" The detective turned to stare out the window. "I *love* that guy! Think I should interview him again, Georgie? Just to be safe?"

"He didn't see anything. He was in the john when it happened."

"Too bad. Maybe I should introduce myself anyway, give him my card. He might want to jam someday." He broke into garrulous laughter.

"Are we done here, Detective?" I said impatiently. "It's late. I'd like to get some sleep."

He turned to me, his face darkening. "Let's go to the penthouse suite."

Officer Gertz stayed behind while the detective and I headed for the elevator. We stepped inside, and I stood in front of the Opti-Scan panel, waited for the beep, and pressed the fifth floor. The elevator lurched into motion.

"Tell me about this fancy security system," said the detective.

"It's called the Private-Eye Opti-Scan System. At check-in, we take a digital snapshot of your iris using a handheld device like a barcode scanner. The image is stored in our database with your profile, and an exact match is required to open the door of your room."

"Oh yeah? Why not fingerprints?"

"Privacy issues, mostly. Travelers are reluctant to give fingerprints due to their use in law enforcement. We researched several biometric options, and iris technology offered the greatest convenience, safety, and security. Private-Eye Corporation says this technology is going to be the next big thing. It'll be used at work, at home, and for retail and online shopping. A number of airports and banks use it in Europe."

"Sounds like you spent a whack of dough."

"Considering the high profile of our guests, Mr. Cavalli decided the price tag was justified. I'll ask security to print off activity reports for the elevator and penthouse suites."

"Artie Truman already gave them to me, along with activity reports for the adjoining rooms," the detective said, patting his pocket. "He also gave me guest lists and let me review camera footage in the security office."

"Did you discover anything unusual?"

He studied the scanner, ignoring my question. "So the system is fault free?"

I nodded. "No two irises are identical. According to Private-Eye, it never lies."

"These elevators don't seem too state-of-the-art," he said, suddenly antsy. "How slow can they be?"

"They survived the fire that destroyed the motel that occupied this site in the 1970s. They were found in reasonable working condition, and Mr. Cavalli decided to keep them."

The elevator let out a groan, as though protesting having been awoken from its thirty-five-year slumber, and jolted to a stop on the fifth floor, pausing briefly before the doors burst open.

"After you, Detective," I said.

The elevators were located at the curve of the horseshoe-shaped building. To the left, a hallway led to the rooms of the west wing, with Penthouse Suite 2 at the far end, occupied by Tony Cavalli and his girlfriend Liz. We headed right, following a narrow corridor lined with lush red carpet. Suede-like fabric covered the walls, and amber sconces provided moody lighting. To the right of each door at eye level was a stainless steel Opti-Scan panel. At the center of each door, a gold star covered the peephole to emulate a star's dressing room.

The detective slowed to a halt and turned to me. "I was speaking with your front office manager earlier, a Miss Valerie Smitts. What a knockout! She told me about an incident with the scanner at check-in?"

I nodded, trying to draw him down the corridor to the suite where we could talk in privacy, but he wouldn't budge. "Miss Fricks arrived around five thirty PM with Moira Schwartz and Bryce Davies in a limousine arranged by the hotel, followed by two bodyguards in a separate car. When Valerie took Miss Fricks' eye scan, it wouldn't register. The matter was quickly resolved when Miss Fricks removed her colored contacts."

"Her eyes aren't green?"

"They're brown. Valerie escorted the guests to their rooms without further incident. Miss Fricks sent the bodyguards home when she got to her room."

"Lots of movie stars stay here, right?"

"We just opened, but that's our hope," I whispered.

"Georgie had a little chat with a gorgeous young blond thing in this room," he said, voice booming as he jabbed his finger at the gold star fastened to the door of Room 505. "Her name on the register said Betty Rubble, but her ID said Jessica Simpson. Think we should knock on her door, see if she's up?"

"No, I don't."

"George said this place was crawling with celebrities when he got here. Who else is here?"

"With all due respect, Detective, what does this have to do with the case?"

"I might have to do some more interviews. But only if they're hot!" He broke into more garrulous laughter.

"Can we continue?"

At the end of the hallway, two LAPD officers stepped aside to let us into Penthouse Suite 1. The door was double-bolted open. I hesitated, suddenly apprehensive. Only hours ago a young woman had ended her life here. Taking a breath, I followed the detective down the short hallway, past the dining room, and into a large, open living room furnished with sleek, contemporary furniture: a bright orange curved sectional sofa, a gunmetal glass coffee table, and a stainless steel lamp that arched over the room from the back of the sofa. The suite was in disarray: chairs overturned, dishes smashed, broken glass scattered across the kitchen floor. The sheepskin carpet was spotted with stains, and a large crack ran across the center of the oval coffee table. On the table sat the bottle of Jack Daniels we had sent up, with Tony's obsequious note beside it unopened. The bottle was almost empty.

"Look at this place," I said. "Couldn't your people have taken more care?"

"It was like this when we got here, my friend. It was probably much worse before your maid started cleaning up."

"A room attendant was up here?"

He nodded. "Stupid broad tainted the scene. She vacuumed the glass from the carpet, erasing all the footprints in the process. Then she took off before we could question her."

"You're kidding. Who?"

"George said she was Mexican or maybe Filipina. Short, a bit heavy, black hair."

"That narrows it down to about half the housekeeping department."

"Name is Esther or Elizabetha or something." He pulled a sheet of paper from his pocket and unfolded it. "Here we go: Ezmerelda Lopez."

"Our executive housekeeper is no 'stupid broad,' Detective. She's one of our best. She insisted on taking care of this suite personally, so it makes sense that she was up here around eleven PM."

The detective studied the activity report in his hands. "According to this she came back around eleven thirty, around the time Chelsea took the plunge. When my guys got here, they found her in the kitchen sweeping up. She claimed to have no idea Chelsea had just jumped off the balcony." He narrowed his eyes. "What's an executive housekeeper doing cleaning rooms, anyway?"

"This is a small hotel. We all pitch in where necessary. Ez is extremely hands-on."

"She should have kept her paws off this suite. It won't make this investigation any easier."

"Who else came up here?" I asked, peering at the report over his shoulder.

"Moira Schwartz came in through the adjoining door at 22:15 and stayed for twenty-one minutes. Bryce Davies came in next, at 22:45, and stayed until 23:02. Then Mrs. Lopez came in at 23:07." He tapped the report with a stubby finger. "This 'system bypass' at 23:12—Artie tells me access to the suite from the adjoining rooms was canceled. Any idea why Chelsea would lock Bryce and Moira out?"

"Privacy, I can only assume."

I thought back to her phone call and considered telling the detective. Sounding flighty and erratic, Miss Fricks had complained about being missed for evening maid service and ranted about the employee who had come to fix her leaky bathtub faucet earlier—chief engineer Al Combs—accusing him of acting "all creepy" around her. Shocked and disconcerted, I apologized profusely and assured her I would address the matter at once. I called Al to my office immediately. He seemed genuinely taken aback by her allegation, and I quickly decided he had been falsely accused by a spoiled, paranoid star. Instructing him to refrain from further contact, I sent him home for the night.

Now, I furtively scanned the report. Al's entry was recorded at 20:11. An exit, presumably his, was logged at 20:35—minutes before Miss Fricks called. The next activity, the system bypass, took place almost two hours later, and there was no further activity from Al. I decided there was no point in mentioning the complaint, since the incident had taken place hours before she jumped.

Detective Christakos lifted his eyes to regard me, long lashes drooping, then lowered them to the report. "We've got an 'exit' at 23:14 and again at 23:18, but it doesn't say who. Why does the system identify entries but not exits?"

"Ask your colleagues at the fire department. The scanner is required to access rooms, but to exit rooms and stairwells, you simply punch the red exit button beside the door. That way, if there's a fire, no one is trapped inside."

He frowned at the report like a schoolboy facing a difficult exam. "The next activity after Mrs. Lopez is Chelsea herself, who enters at 23:20. Which means one of these exits at 23:14 and 23:18 is her and one is Mrs. Lopez."

"A safe bet."

"Then Lopez comes back in at 23:36. That's the last activity before my guys arrive. Chelsea jumped sometime around 23:35, either before or after Mrs. Lopez arrived. Why'd she come back?"

"She would have come to tidy the room around eleven PM. Miss Fricks was probably still in the suite, so she came back a half-hour later."

The detective seemed to accept this explanation. "Have a look around. Tell me if you see anything unusual."

"*Everything* is unusual. This suite was immaculate yesterday."

"Maybe she was warming up for her debut as a rock star."

"Rock stars don't trash hotel rooms anymore. Times have changed. They can't get away with bad behavior without it being all over the tabloids."

I wandered into the bedroom. Designer clothes spilled out of two large suitcases set on luggage racks in front of the bed and were strewn across the carpet, as though a group of girls had held a dress-up party. The bed was neatly made and turned down, its top sheet pulled back into a perfect fold—undoubtedly the work of Ezmerelda. Spread out on the duvet was a short red cocktail dress. I stared at it. Chelsea would have looked stunning in it. I remembered standing at the closet in the spare bedroom at my mother's house the day after I received news of the crash, staring at Nancy's clothes: two identical dresses, one rose colored and one baby blue; a V-neck cashmere sweater; three vintage T-shirts she insisted on keeping on hangers; a garish, burnt-orange bridesmaid dress she couldn't bring herself to throw away. A half-hour later, Mom had discovered me standing in the closet, swaddled in Nancy's clothes. She coaxed me out.

Tearing my eyes from the dress, I wandered into the bathroom. A wall of glass separated the walk-in shower and infinity bathtub from the long glass vanity. Beauty products, utensils, and small appliances were scattered across the counter. I picked up a cotton ball smeared with flesh-colored makeup and tossed it into the toilet. An open lipstick container had fallen into the sink, leaving a streak of red on the glass bowl. A dripping sound drew my attention to the bathtub. I reached for the faucet to turn it off, but the leak persisted. Hadn't Al been up to fix it last night? I made a mental note to ask him to have another look. On the floor beside the bathtub lay a heap of wet towels. Why would she bathe, put on makeup, and lay out a dress, only to leap off the balcony? It was useless to speculate, I told myself. Nancy's death had taught me that some mysteries go unsolved. The search for an explanation only caused pain. A plane falls from the sky. An actress leaps from a balcony. Bad things happen to good people, often inexplicably. For the sake of our own sanity, we must accept tragedy at face value and move on. I left the bathroom.

On my way back to the living room, I ducked into an alcove furnished with a desk, filing cabinet, and bookshelf. I noted a small crack in the plastic shade on the Bourgie table lamp and made a mental note to report it to housekeeping. On the desk sat a MacBook, three books, and a ringed binder that looked like a movie script. The top book was entitled *Bleaching America: The OBA's Heroic Struggle to Cleanse America*. Curious, I picked it up and turned it over, assuming it was an environmental book. A handsome, square-jawed man with hooded eyes stared at me from the back cover. The caption read, "Dwight Reed, President of Operation Bleach America." I gasped. The OBA was a notorious association of extreme right-wing conservatives whose mission was to halt immigration and deport illegal immigrants. I had seen Dwight Reed on FOXNews and CNN several times. Last year he was assassinated in Houston by masked gunmen representing the National Immigrant Solidarity Front. Why would Chelsea be reading this trash? I looked down at the next book: *Ignorant Immigrants*. The third book: *Why White Is Better than Black*. Was Chelsea Fricks a racist?

The detective clamped his hand on my shoulder, making me jump. "Find anything interesting?"

The book fell from my hands. "Are these hers?" I asked, stooping down to pick it up.

He didn't answer. Guiding me into the kitchen, he pointed at the tiled floor, where a trail of brownish-red droplets led into the living room as though someone had slopped coffee or red wine. I followed the trail. The droplets turned to splotches on the sheepskin carpet.

I squatted down for a closer look. "Blood?"

He pointed toward the balcony door.

Heart pounding, I went to the door and slid it open. Blood pooled on the balcony floor, and more was smeared on the glass wall. I turned to the detective. "My God, what happened here?"

"You tell me."

The detective watched as I circled the suite and tried to piece things together. In the kitchen, a broom rested against the counter next to a pile of glass. Likely Ezmerelda had been sweeping up when she was interrupted by police. Crossing into the living room, I noticed a thin layer of powder on the cracked coffee table. I crouched down to inspect it. "Drug residue?" I said, looking up.

He nodded. "Impressive."

"Someone did a rush job of wiping it clean. Definitely not Ezmerelda. Did you find any drugs?"

The detective gave a faint shake of his head.

I went to the closet by the front door and opened it. Guests frequently neglected to clear the in-room safe before checking out, and occasionally drugs were left behind. The safe was open and empty. I returned to the living room.

"Maybe she cut herself," I said, mind racing. "She dropped a glass on the floor and stepped on it. Her foot was bleeding. She was high, running around the room. She saw the spotlight outside and dove into it like a moth to a flame. That's it, isn't it? That's what happened."

"I hope you're a better hotel manager than a detective."

I threw my hands in the air. "Why are you asking me, anyway? Isn't this your job?"

45

"I'm curious," he said. "Your cut foot theory sucks, but your perspective as the hotel manager is unique. I've learned a few things already. You've been in this business awhile, right?"

"Since I was eighteen."

"But you're not from here. You're Canadian?"

"Now I'm impressed."

"Artie told me." He marched into the kitchen and gestured to the knife block on the counter. "Notice anything missing?"

Five knives of varying sizes were sheathed in the block. The largest slot was empty. I did a quick search, pulling open drawers and cupboards, the dishwasher, even the refrigerator and oven, but couldn't find the knife.

"A knife is missing."

"You carried her from the pool. Did you notice anything unusual about her body?"

I remembered the swirls of purple liquid around her, the gashes in her back and abdomen, the blood on my shirt, the circle of blood on the towel beneath her body. "She'd been stabbed?"

"She had three gashes on her body, one on her stomach and two on her back."

"Someone chased her around this suite with a knife?" I said, incredulous. "She jumped off the balcony to save her life?"

He raised an eyebrow but said nothing.

"Did you recover the knife?" I asked.

He shook his head. "We searched every inch of this suite, Moira's room, Bryce's room—every room in this hotel—maid closets, janitor closets, everywhere. It's gone."

I fell onto the sofa. "She was murdered?"

Again he didn't answer. He wandered over to the massive piece of contemporary art that covered the wall opposite the sofa and studied it. Entitled *Apart*, it depicted a stick man and woman standing with backs to one another. The woman's arms were crossed. The man was covering his face with his hands. A heart, cracked through the middle like the coffee table beneath the painting, was floating in the air between them. Drawn in crude brushstrokes with a crayon-like material as though by a child, it seemed obvious and amateur to me. But there had to be something to it that I couldn't appreciate. Liz Welch had acquired it for $35,000.

"Ever been married, Trevor?"

I was silent for a moment. "No. Not really."

"*Not really*? You're either married or not, my friend."

"No, I've never been married."

"Been in love, though, right?"

I decided to use his own evasive tactic. "Are *you* married, Detective?"

"Call me Stav." He left the painting and lowered himself to the sofa. "Nope. Never have been, maybe never will. Not for lack of trying." He laughed. "I've proposed to maybe a half-dozen women. They all turned me down." He was contemplative for a moment. "Last night I met my future wife, Trevor. My buddy Gustavo got us into this swanky party in Hollywood Hills. This girl was sitting by the pool all by herself smoking a cigarette. She looked like she needed company, so I sat down with her. Her name was Cappuccino."

I almost burst out laughing. "Cappuccino?"

"We talked for two hours, Trevor, *two hours*. It was amazing. She's young, but super smart and extremely mature for her age. She's from some remote island—I can't remember the name—and she's got this sexy, exotic accent, and beautiful brown skin the color of..." He stopped, pressing his fingers against his forehead.

"Coffee?"

"Yeah! Like coffee! She's in the biz too, so we had a lot to talk about."

"She's a cop?"

"No, no. The force is only my day job. I'm an actor."

I stared at him. "You're an actor."

"I guess 'aspiring actor' is more accurate. I'm only getting serious about it now. You won't have seen me in anything. Not yet. Unless you saw that Scope commercial with the lady on the bicycle? I played the cop. No lines, but boy was I a handsome devil." He grinned, and then his face grew serious. "I've made a commitment to myself to dedicate more time to my craft. I just started an audition class. Don't worry, it doesn't interfere with my police work."

"Of course not," I said, my confidence plunging. The designer clothes, the exposed chest, the vintage police medallion, the star-spotting—it all began to fit the new picture. He's an actor. Only in Los Angeles.

"Cappy's done well," he said. "She's been in a few movies-of-the-week, a dozen commercials, and two TV pilots. I think I recognized her. She's got a heavy accent, but she does a flawless American accent too." He looked at me. "You think I fall in love all the time, don't you? Well, I don't. Only once every few weeks." He chuckled and heaved himself from the sofa. Stepping around the glass in the kitchen, he pulled open a cupboard door and withdrew two glasses. "You got a mini-bar somewhere?"

I pointed to the armoire in the hallway. "There's a full bar in there. Be my guest."

He opened the door and let out a whistle. "Don't know how you stay sober with all this booze around. Mini-bars in every room, full bar in here." I expected him to select scotch or tequila, but he pulled out a bottle of Bailey's Irish Cream. "Care to join me?"

"No, thanks."

"Suit yourself." He poured several ounces into a glass and slugged it back, gasping. "Had the worst taste in my mouth. Needed to kill it with something."

"There's mouthwash in the bathroom," I said.

"Not nearly as effective. Or as pleasurable." He refilled the glass and carried it into the living room, swirling the drink with his finger. "Around midnight, I was working up the courage to ask her for her phone number. I was feeling pretty confident she was going to give it to me. Her friend kept coming out to talk to her, this short, fat, annoying thing with braces, and Cappy kept sending her away. She was totally into me. Then she got up and excused herself, said she was going to the bathroom, and I was thinking, yeah, okay, this is where she disappears. But before she goes, she gives me this long, sensuous kiss that gives me an instant boner and tells me to wait. I didn't see her again."

"She left?" I asked, feeling bad for him.

"*I* left. I got a fucking call. Some harebrained actress hurled herself off the balcony at a fancy-ass hotel in Hollywood. On my way out I couldn't find her. The place was packed. I'll probably never see her again." He sighed and gulped at his drink.

Now I understood why he was dressed for a party. "I'm sorry," I said.

"Yeah, well, it's not the first time. My job gets in the way of leading a normal life."

"I know the feeling."

There was a long silence.

"This probably has no relevance," I said, "but Miss Fricks called me last night just after nine PM."

He blinked. "Oh yeah? Why?"

"She complained about turndown."

I saw a twinkle in his eye. He opened his mouth to say a bad joke about having the same complaint, but reconsidered. "Why would she care about turndown?"

"She said the maid missed her room. Now that I see the state of this place, I understand why she wanted someone up here so badly. Ezmerelda hadn't disturbed her because her privacy sign was out. Guests do that all the time—place the privacy sign on the door and then complain when their room isn't serviced. Of course, if a maid ignores the privacy sign and enters the room, there's hell to pay. You can't win. Hotels are a funny business. You can never—"

The detective held up his hand. "Spare me. What else did she say?"

"I apologized and assured her I'd send a room attendant up immediately. She said no, not now, wait until she left for the party. I asked her what time she planned to go, to which she replied, 'Whenever I fucking feel like it' and slammed the phone down."

"Ouch!" The detective threw his head back and laughed. "My God, these celebrities! I don't know how you do it, Trevor."

"Better than criminals."

"I'm not so sure." He drained the rest of his Bailey's. "That's it? That's all she said?"

I hesitated, eyes grazing the messed-up room. "Yes, that's it." I stood up. "I called housekeeping and told them to go up around eleven PM, assuming she'd be at the party by then."

"Good to know," said the detective.

Feeling a wave of fatigue, I looked at my watch. "It's almost six AM. Are we done now? I have a meeting in two hours." On our way to the exit I asked, "Is this place clear for cleaning? It's reserved for another guest tonight."

"It's clear. Just beware, the blood might upset your staff. And people talk. I need you to keep this information confidential. The media will have a heyday if they find out."

"Not to worry, I'm of the same mind."

In the elevator, the detective let out a roar of a yawn. "I'm going home to catch a few Zs. I'll be back in a few hours to interview any employees I missed last night, starting with Ezmerelda Lopez and your maintenance guy."

"Al? Why him?"

"Four people visited Chelsea's suite last night: Al Combs, Moira Schwartz, Bryce Davies, Ezmerelda Lopez, and then Ezmerelda Lopez again—in that order. I've interviewed two of them, now I need to talk to the other two."

"But why Al? He was in and out long before anything happened."

"All the same, I'd like to speak with him. If it's okay with you."

His tone was patronizing. "Of course it's okay with me. But I need you to respect my guests and go easy on my staff. I have a hotel to run."

"And I have a death to investigate," he said, indignation flashing in his eyes.

I made a mental note to ensure I was present during those meetings. I didn't think Ezmerelda or Al had anything to hide, but they were both shy and reserved. Being subjected to questioning by this bullying detective could be traumatizing, and I needed them focused on their work.

"Detective, what do you think really happened last night?"

He pondered the question. "I'm not sure yet. But I know this was no accident and no prank. Chelsea Fricks was murdered."

"Why would someone want to kill her?"

"Murders are committed for three reasons, Trevor: love, money, and drugs. In this case, I have a sneaking suspicion all three were involved."

4

Facial Validity

"Isn't it about time you went home, Trevor?"

Night manager David Woo observed me with an expression of concern as I made my way across the lobby, my legs wobbling from exhaustion. I peered at him over the desk, trying to focus on his black-on-black uniform. Beside him, Simka was a similar haze of pink and grey.

"Is past six AM," she said in her thick Russian accent. "We take care everything. You go home."

Home. I tried to recall where home was ... the place where I slept ... a sparse one-bedroom apartment ten minutes away in Whitley Heights ... second floor, shrouded in leaves ... an empty balcony overlooking the alley. After six months, it still didn't feel like home.

"I better stick around," I said. "The morning shift will arrive soon, and I need to brief them." I went to place my hand on the front desk but missed it and stumbled, almost cracking my head on the granite top. "Maybe I should lie down for a few minutes," I said.

Artie Truman hurried over from the front door, as fresh and alert as when he arrived twenty-four hours earlier. "I'm going to head home, if that's all right," he said. "Raj just got in. I'll be back at three."

"Have things settled down outside?"

"Are you kidding? They're heating up." He pulled me aside. "Is someone going to talk to the reporters? They're getting ornery. I'm no pro when it comes to this stuff, but I think someone needs to speak up on behalf of the hotel. A lot of things are being said."

There was a layer of stubble on his face. I touched my own chin and felt the same. "Like what?"

He lowered his voice. "Like Chelsea was murdered."

"Christ. I hope you squelched that talk."

"I haven't said a word, just like you told me." He looked over both shoulders. "I was in the penthouse suite, Trevor. I saw the blood. Something bad happened up there."

"Listen, Artie," I said, gripping his arm, "until the LAPD says otherwise, it was a prank gone wrong. Understand? Do you realize how explosive this could be?"

He scratched at his stubble. "That's why I think someone needs to go out there."

★ ★ ★ ★ ★

It was beginning to get light outside. Over a hundred people were gathered in clusters on the driveway and on the street in front of the hotel. Some chatted and sipped coffee, others lounged on the grass and sidewalk. No one paid attention to me at first. I had no intention of giving a statement, certainly not without consulting Tony Cavalli and Kitty Caine—though I had misgivings about their ability to handle the situation astutely. I envisioned Kitty bursting out the front door and crying out in her Texas accent, "Come on in, y'all! Come see where Chelsea Fricks died!"

I walked over to the security supervisor, Raj. "We're going to have to push these people back to the street."

He gave me an apprehensive look. "It's all we can do to keep them this far back."

A sun-baked woman in her mid-forties with straight black hair like Cleopatra eyed us from behind the velvet rope. "Excuse me!" she called out in a raspy voice. "Judy Wasserman from KCAL 9. Are you the hotel manager?"

"Yes, I am," I said. Not wanting to engage her, I turned back to Raj. "I'll give you a hand. Let's—"

"Guys!" The KCAL woman whistled to a crew on the sidewalk. "Let's go! The manager's giving a statement!"

A mad rush of reporters, cameramen, and crew charged in my direction. I stepped back, alarmed. A dozen microphones, Dictaphones, and cameras were thrust toward me.

"Stand back, please!" Raj called out as two other doormen hurried over to assist.

"I'm sorry," I said, holding up my hands. "You must have misunderstood. I'm not giving a statement. I do, however, kindly request you to respect hotel property and—"

"Please state your name and title," a reporter from *Entertainment Tonight* shouted.

"I—I'm Trevor Lambert, General Manager. I need to ask—"

The KCAL reporter raised her hand. "Mr. Lambert, is it true that Chelsea Fricks leapt to her death from the roof of your establishment?"

"The roof? No, it was the balcony of her penthouse suite. She—"

"What message would you like to send to Chelsea's fans?" asked a reporter with *Inside Edition*.

"Well," I said, searching for the appropriate words, "I suppose I would like them to know that we at Hotel Cinema are deeply saddened by this accident."

"Accident?" said a heavyset man from *Spotlight Tonight*. "She didn't jump?"

"Well … we're, hmm … we're not entirely sure what happened."

Several reporters fired questions all at once.

"Was it a prank? Did she pull a Lohan?"

"Was she drunk? Were drugs involved?"

The KCAL reporter stood directly in front of me. "What a beautiful hotel," she said.

I smiled. "Why, thank you."

"I'd love a tour," she said, fluttering her eyes.

"Maybe some other time. We're a bit distracted today."

The crowd laughed.

I started to breathe easier. Just a few more words to appease them, and I could go back inside and track down Kitty Caine to issue a proper statement. The crowd seemed pleasant enough, consisting mostly of harmless entertainment reporters who wrote fluff pieces to glorify celebrities—not hard-nosed journalists digging for scandal or disaster media digging for heartbreak.

"How does it feel to have one of the world's most beloved actresses die under your care?" asked Cleopatra from KCAL.

Under our care? My lips tightened. "As I said, we're devastated. But Hotel Cinema accepts no—"

"So Chelsea *fell* off the balcony?" said the *Spotlight* reporter, scribbling onto a notepad.

"Oh no, she didn't fall," I said, not liking where the questioning was heading.

"Someone pushed her?"

"Was it suicide?"

"Enough," I said, horrified. "I refuse to comment."

"Was she murdered?" the KCAL woman blurted out.

The group fell silent.

I opened my mouth and shut it again. How could I possibly leave this question lingering in the air? "No," I said firmly. "Miss Fricks was not murdered. It was an accident. That's all I can say. We at Hotel Cinema intend to extend our full cooperation to the investigation. We feel—"

"Investigation?" shouted the *Entertainment Tonight* reporter. "Then foul play *was* involved?"

"Oh my *God*! Chelsea Fricks was murdered?"

"How awful!"

"Who did it?"

The crowd surged forward. Shutters clicked. Digital cameras beeped. The camera lights were blinding. Panicked, I did what any reasonable manager would do: I retreated into the sanctity of the hotel.

★ ★ ★ ★ ★

Activity was beginning to pick up as the first guests trickled into Scene for breakfast. I went from department to department and took aside staff to brief them on the previous night's events and how to respond to inquiries, instructing them to be gracious and compassionate but to say as little as possible. Then I went out to check the pool deck. A handful of guests were seated at tables around the pool bar, gazing at Penthouse Suite 1 and murmuring to one another. I greeted them cordially but kept moving, not wishing to engage them. I was in no condition to be interacting with guests; I desperately needed rest, even for only an hour.

At the front desk, David and Simka had been replaced by Valerie Smitts and Janie Spanozzini. I stood in Valerie's line, hoping she would be free next. Less than an hour remained before the operations meeting. I couldn't possibly miss it in light of last night's incident. Who was this man dominating Valerie's time? Until now, I'd had unfettered access to staff. From now on I would have to defer to guests. He was wearing white board shorts with graffiti graphics, flip-flops, and a tie-dyed shirt—hardly appropriate attire for the lobby of a luxury hotel. I reminded myself I was in Southern California, where beachwear was acceptable virtually everywhere.

Janie was finishing up with her guest, a heavyset, short man in high-waisted khaki pants and a pink golf shirt. "No *praw*-blem!" she said, flashing her big teeth, her shrill voice and Bronx accent reminiscent of Edith Bunker. "Bye-bye now!"

The man thanked her and left, rolling his eyes as he passed.

Janie was one of Tony Cavalli's hires, one of two nieces who had wiggled into the pre-opening offices, fresh from New York, and informed me that Uncle Tony had promised them jobs. By then I had realized that Tony intended to treat the hotel like a family employment agency, and I was intent on thwarting him. At twenty-one and twenty respectively, Janie and Bernadina were undeniably attractive, but their natural looks were camouflaged by big hair, heavy makeup, and tight, glittery clothing. Although I knew in an instant they weren't the right fit, I invited them into my office for a courtesy interview.

Bernadina came in first. "So if I understand correctly," I said, glancing down at her résumé—eight lines of text and six butterfly decals—"you've never worked in a hotel before—or even held a job?"

"I worked in the school canteen once. But that didn't work out."

"Did Tony mention what kind of job he promised?"

"Um ... consigliere?"

"You mean concierge?"

"He said somethin' about a chef position."

"Chef concierge? Have you ever been to Los Angeles before?"

"When I was fourteen we went to Disneyland."

"Do you know what a chef concierge does, Bernadina?"

"Makes recommendations and stuff?"

"A concierge requires intimate knowledge of Los Angeles: the best restaurants, the arts and culture scene, tours and activities, the city's most exclusive nightclubs."

"Me 'n Janie are going out clubbing tonight. I got a fake ID. We'll know the scene by tomorra."

Janie was next. "I see you have some hotel experience," I said. "Assistant manager at a Sheraton Four Points at La Guardia?"

"I wasn't *exactly* assistant manager. I helped the manager lots and stuff. It was a pretty fancy hotel."

"The Sheraton Four Points? Really. Your résumé says assistant manager."

"Did I forget to put 'to the'? Oops."

As soon as they left, I picked up the phone to call Tony. "What am I supposed to do with them?" I said. "They're nice girls, but they have no relevant experience and no identifiable skills. Do you have any idea how high the expectations of our guests will be?"

"You be nice to my nieces!" Tony growled. "They're quality girls. Ain't Bernie a knockout? And Janie's got a great pair of tits. Not that I ever looked. Heh heh."

"We're not casting for a porn shoot, Tony. This is a luxury hotel. I refuse to hire them."

"You have no choice! In ten years I'm going to have an international chain of five-star hotels, and these girls are going to be running them. You better give them good jobs! Janie's got experience. Make her assistant director or something."

"Assistant director? Of what? Hair extensions?"

"I'm talking about movie-set roles."

"Can we please lose the movie-set roles? It's confusing to staff, and it's going to confuse our guests."

"No way! It's part of our branding."

Unbeknownst to Tony, I had already instructed staff to revert to standard hotel-industry lingo and to use the movie-set lingo in his presence only.

"I refuse to give a manager title to someone with no relevant skills," I said. "Staff will revolt. How can we expect her to make major decisions?"

"I said give her a title. Don't let her make any decisions." He coughed. Even Tony realized how ludicrous this sounded. "Fine, give her a job as a production coordinator."

"You mean front desk agent."

"No, I mean production coordinator!"

"Tony, these ladies have no experience."

"But isn't that perfect? You won't have to unteach any bad habits. They're like empty vessels."

"You got that part right."

"Don't get smart, Trevor! Remember what I told you. You're not casting for a hotel, you're casting for the movies. Looks are more important than anything else. You can teach a beautiful girl to be smart, but you can't teach an ugly girl to be beautiful. I didn't spend millions of dollars on this production only to have you cast it with a bunch of mutt-faces. Janie and Bernie, they got facial validity!"

I cringed. "Please stop using that term. It's distasteful. Hotels in this city have been sued for discrimination for hiring only attractive employees."

"Am I going to have to start looking for a new general manager?"

"Christ, Tony, will you please stop threatening to fire me?"

There was dead silence.

"Okay, I'll find a place for your nieces, and I'll make sure they get excellent training. Satisfied?"

"One of the twins is coming to see you too. Enzo's been moping around the past few months. He's jealous because his brother Lorenzo's getting married. They're sons of my Uncle Bruno. My father promised Enzo a job. I'm thinking production assistant to start out."

"Bellman?"

"Production assistant! He wants to get into sales, so maybe you can move him to a distribution manager role in a few months. I'll be honest: he's not the brightest kid, but he's got—"

"Don't tell me, facial validity."

"He could be a movie star—if he could act his way out of a paper bag."

When Enzo showed up for an interview two days later, I discovered he was even more of a sleazeball than Tony. Knowing I'd face a fight with Tony if I refused to hire him, I asked Dennis Claiborne, human resources manager ("casting director" in Tony's lingo), to call him in for a second opinion. During the interview I dropped by Dennis's office to pick up a file. When I greeted Enzo, he stammered a response and became flustered. I dismissed the behavior as further proof of his stupidity, but Dennis suspected something more sinister was afloat. Probing deeper, he exacted a confession: this was not Enzo but his twin brother Lorenzo. Enzo, having realized how badly he bungled my interview, sent in his smarter brother as a stand-in. When I informed Tony of the ruse, he was furious. I thereby managed to thwart at least one disastrous hire.

Now, I stepped up to the desk to get Janie's attention, but she was too distracted by Valerie's guest to notice. By her bug-eyed expression, I surmised he was very good-looking or famous—or both. I sneaked a sidelong glance at him. Matthew McConaughey? Star-spotting didn't come easy for me, since I rarely went to movies and never read enter-tainment magazines or tabloids. Janie circled around Valerie and reached out to borrow her stapler, even though her own stapler was in plain view at her station. She didn't take her eyes off the man. Her water balloon-like boobs were bursting out of her black bra (which should have been white) and pink shirt (unbuttoned too low).

"Good morning, Janie," I said to get her attention.

"Treva! How are ya?" She left Valerie's station and returned to hers.

I whispered, "A friendly reminder to use the guest's name at least three times in all interactions. And watch the slang, okay? Say 'my pleasure' not 'no problem,' and 'goodbye' not 'bye-bye.'" I smiled to soften the reprimand. It was the hotel's first day of operation, after all, and she was undoubtedly nervous.

"You got it, Treva," she said, squeezing her eyes shut as though committing a complex procedure to memory. When she opened them, she sneaked another peek at Valerie's guest.

"Janie, I need a room to take a quick nap in. Can you help me with that?"

She shook her head. "Sorry, we're sold out." Her hoity-toity tone implied I was a tramp off the street. She scrunched up her face. "You don't look so good. Rough night? You potty it up or somethin'?"

"I haven't slept all night."

"O-oh. Why, becuzzuh Chelsea Fricks drownin' in the pool?"

I cut a swath through the air with my hand and lowered my voice. "Please refrain from mentioning last night's incident, Janie. Pretend it never happened. An out-of-service room is fine. All I need is a bed. Just click Rooms Management, select Out of Service, and click Search."

She looked at me as though I had asked her to reconfigure the computer system. The situation appeared to be hopeless.

"Aren't you supposed to be shadowing someone?" I said.

"Beth got called up to a room to help a guy with the Internet."

"You mean a gentleman?"

"I dunno," she quipped. "I never met him." Another glance at Valerie's guest.

"Janie, are you chewing gum?"

She stopped in mid-chew. "That not allowed?"

"Of course it's not allowed. This is a hotel, not a roadside diner. Please remove it at once."

She reached into her mouth, retrieving a wad of pink gum and pressing it into her palm. "I'm tryin' to quit smoking and it's, like, totally stressing me out. Nobody smokes in this city. I feel like a lepa. Gum keeps me from clenchin' my jaw so hard my teeth are gonna fall out." She looked down at the screen. "This computa is really weird."

Exasperated, I looked over to Valerie, who now had a phone on each shoulder and was typing madly into the computer. She appeared to be rearranging the man's entire travel schedule.

"Sorry about this," her guest said in a Southern drawl. "I asked your concierge, but she said she isn't allowed to make changes to flights. Something about privacy concerns."

"Is that so?" said Valerie with a bemused smile. "I'm terribly sorry, Mr. Balboa. She must have misunderstood."

I looked over to the concierge desk and saw Janie's sister, Bernadina, sitting alone, her face barely visible behind a shroud of curly black hair. She was checking her teeth in a pocket mirror.

Looking back at Valerie's guest, I flipped through my internal guest list. Balboa, Rocky, Room 521. Another pseudonym, of course. It was hotel policy to address guests by their alias everywhere on-property.

Janie Spanozzini's talon-like fingernails tapped the keyboard like a preschooler on a toy piano. She wasn't even looking down; she was staring at Mr. Balboa. Her phone was ringing.

"Do you remember our three-ring rule?" I asked Janie.

She looked down at her fingers. "I'm only allowed three?"

"I mean the phone."

"Oh yeah. Hold on a sec, 'kay?" She reached for the phone. "Front desk, Janie smoking—I mean speaking." She listened for a moment and then slammed the phone down. "Loser," she muttered under her breath.

I was too exhausted to protest. "Please just assign me a room, Janie."

"Looks like Room 314 is available." She reached for the iris scanner and waved it in the air like a Safeway cashier. "You need me to scan you?"

"No, I have master access. Don't forget to check me into the system. And put me down for a 7:45 wakeup call."

"Sure, no problem." She scribbled the time on her gum-wielding hand. "PM, right?"

"AM."

"Like in a half-hour?"

I grimaced and nodded.

"Sleep tight, don't let the bedbugs bite! Bye-bye!"

As I backed toward the elevator, Valerie gave me a helpless look and mouthed the words, "I'm so sorry!" I smiled to assure her I was fine.

Meanwhile, Janie moved in on Mr. Balboa, flicking her hair back and jostling Valerie aside.

5

Let's Wait and See

Paris.

July, the height of tourist season. We're staying at the lavish Hotel Le Meurice across from the Louvre. It's late afternoon and we're starving, but one look at the prices—*mon dieu!*—and we opt to order more wine. The tower of hors d'oeuvres the waiter has presented with great flourish will tide us over until dinner. I ask for two more glasses of Bordeaux. They're $48 each, but I don't mind. I want this moment to be perfect.

In Europe, life has never been simpler or grander. Barcelona, Rome, and now Paris—in mornings I follow Nancy through art galleries, museums, and cathedrals; in afternoons she follows me through grand hotels, landmark hotels, and contemporary hotels. Nights are occupied by mutual interests: intimate dinners in outdoor cafés, long walks, making love as the moon rises and again as it sinks.

She is watching me with her big brown eyes. Her long, lustrous hair cascades over her naked shoulders. I am performing for an audience of one, an adoring, enraptured audience, regaling her with a tale from my supply of hotel stories about eccentric guests, temperamental celebrities, misbehaving businessmen. Nancy loves to hear the stories, although she was never as enamored by the industry as I; her time as a duty manager at the Universe was brief. My story concludes, and I'm rewarded with laughter so raw it sends her into a fit of coughing. When she recovers, I do an impression of the waiter: his formal comportment, his bad English, his flirtatious manner. She giggles, nervously sneaking glances at him.

Our wine arrives.

Nancy has rescued me from my internal panic room. Employing tactics she used to win over irate guests—empathy, compassion, quiet confidence—she found her way in. First she passed by the window. Then she knocked on the door and called out my name. Undaunted, she charged the door, setting off alarm bells, compelling me to retreat into full lock-down mode. Then she used bolt-cutters to break the deadbolts, a sledgehammer to smash the handle, a wrecking ball to knock the door down. She took my hand and pulled me out, showed me how to bask in the sunshine of requited love. I asked her to move to Vancouver with me. I found my home.

The ring comes alive in my pocket, rattling in its box, demanding attention like the magical ring in *Lord of the Rings*. As we clink glasses, the words burst from my mouth.

"Nancy, will you marry me?"

Her smile vanishes. I see a flicker in her eyes. Like a screen switching from light summer movie to film noir, her expression changes from joy to—what is it, fear? Heartache? Everything is wrong—the script, my lines, her reaction, the prop. How could I have forgotten the ring? I want to start over again.

She opens her mouth, searching for words. "Trevor, I—"

The ring stirs again. "Wait," I say, digging into my pocket. I will go down on my knee this time, take her hand, declare my undying love. But it's not the ring, it's my cell phone. We rented it for outbound calls; only a handful of people have the number. I pull it out. It vibrates in my hand.

"Answer it," Nancy says, looking relieved by the interruption.

It's the general manager at the Fairmont Waterfront, where I accepted a job as hotel manager prior to our trip. The director of rooms has fallen ill. He's short a director of food and beverage and a front office manager. It's peak season, and a convention is due to arrive. Can I start a few days earlier?

I glance at Nancy. Her gaze is fixed on her wine glass.

"But I'm still in Europe," I say.

"I wouldn't ask you if the situation weren't dire. Could you fly back tomorrow?"

"*Tomorrow?*"

A delta of lines forms at the corners of Nancy's eyes. She contemplates the tower of hors d'oeuvres between us, gourmet morsels provided as compensation for pricey drinks. She looks tired now, as though hit by a sudden wave of the fatigue that has plagued her these past weeks.

In the end I acquiesce. I set the phone on the table.

She lifts her head. "You're going back to work."

I open my mouth to explain, but she holds up her hand. She turns to gaze into the lobby, where a tall, distinguished man in a tailored suit is conversing with an unhappy American couple. Everything about him—his posture, his clothes, the way he cocks his head to one side in empathy—tells me he is the hotel manager.

"Will you come back with me?"

She shakes her head. "My grandmother is expecting me."

"You two can spend time alone now," I say softly. "You can rest." I reach for her hand.

She doesn't pull away but balls it into a fist. Without taking her eyes off the hotel manager, she sips her wine.

"The last thing I want to do is cut our vacation short."

"You don't have to explain. I understand."

I reach in my pocket for the ring. "As I was saying …"

She gives a quick shake of her head. Her eyes grow distant.

"You don't want to …?"

"Let's wait and see."

The hotel manager is shaking hands with the American couple. All three are smiling. The matter has been settled. As he walks off, his face bears a faint grimace.

The next morning she wakes up feeling ill again. She waves off my concern, blaming the wine. Her fingers are swollen. Her face is pale. We embrace at the entrance to the hotel. The manager is there, as though he never left. He asks how our stay was.

"*Magnifique*," replies Nancy in impeccable French.

She is taking the Eurostar to London, and then a train to Oxford, where a car will take her to her grandmother's house in Salisbury, minutes from Stonehenge. Her white cotton dress is decorated with purple fleurs-de-lis. She looks fragile, yet more beautiful than ever. As she climbs into a taxi, I make her promise to visit a doctor.

The taxi rolls away. I wave, but she doesn't turn around.

Let's wait and see.

6

Celebrity Phobia

I wake up with a start, shivering. A red light blinks like a distress signal in the distance. I roll over and reach for Nancy's warm body. I feel cold, dead air. Hard plastic. Not a blanket or sheet.

I sit up in alarm. Where am I?

A sliver of light shines through a gap in the curtains. Daylight. The leaf of a palm tree presses against the window. The red light above: a fire detector. A hotel. My hands pad my body. I am wearing a dress shirt and suit pants. Outside I hear shouts, engines revving, the slamming of doors, murmurs of conversations. In New York I often woke to similar sounds. The block where I lived on Tenth Avenue was a favorite of film crews. Is a movie being filmed outside?

I remember the party. Hotel Cinema.

In the hallway, I hear the familiar sounds of room attendants calling to one another in Spanish. A vacuum cleaner whirs. Someone knocks on my door. "Housekeeping, good afternoon."

Afternoon? As my eyes adjust, I see how stark the room is. No television, no paint on the walls, no phone for a wakeup call.

The door opens, and a dark, round figure appears. "Oh! So sorry!" she cries, pulling the door closed.

I think of Ezmerelda, then Chelsea Fricks, and suddenly it all comes rushing back.

I jump out of bed and shower quickly, drying myself with paper towels and pulling on my suit. As I leave the room, I check the room number: 314. I'm quite certain it's reserved for a guest arrival tonight.

★ ★ ★ ★ ★

Shanna Virani was waiting in my office. "Where on earth have you been? I've been worried sick."

"I slept in. I can't believe it's one PM. I feel sick about it."

I squeezed past her and went to my desk. The administration offices, located behind the front desk, had none of the style and glamour of the public areas. My office, the largest, barely had room for three people to meet in. Having moved in only two days earlier, I hadn't had time to settle in. The freshly painted ivory walls were bare.

Perched on a club chair in an all-white Chanel business suit and white patent-leather pumps, Shanna made up for the lack of glamour. Her wavy black hair was perfectly coiffed, her nails manicured, her fingers, wrists, and neck accessorized: gold rings and bangles, a black bead necklace. Behind her, through the window that overlooked the corridor, I could see human resources manager Dennis Claiborne at the photocopier, sneaking peeks at us over his shoulder, likely wanting to see me but too afraid to interrupt and face Shanna's wrath. In New York, staff had given her the nickname Queen of the Fucking Universe for her imperious attitude, and it seemed the reputation had followed her to LA.

"It's not *entirely* your fault," said Shanna. "Janie Spanozzini forgot which room she assigned you. We knocked on every unoccupied room in the hotel but couldn't find you. Either you were shacked up with Betty Rubble or you mistook a broom closet for a guestroom."

"I was in 314."

"That crappy little room? I'm sure we knocked on it."

"I must have slept through it." I sat down at my desk and booted up my computer.

Shanna leaned toward me, fingers splayed on the desk, eyebrows arched in an inquisitive expression. Her diminutive figure, heavy makeup, and over-hairsprayed hair reminded me of a child model, a middle-aged Pakistani JonBenet Ramsey. I felt instantly guilty at the thought—she would be mortified. She was expecting the scoop on last night's incident, but I didn't want to talk about it. I was angry at myself for sleeping in, for *hours,* and needed to bring myself up to speed at once, to check my calendar, go through email, and run my daily reports. Only then would I be ready to face the day.

"How's occupancy?" I asked, waiting for the software to load.

Shanna sat on the edge of the desk, threw her head back, and let out a dramatic sigh. "*Major* relocates."

"Like how many?"

"With Penthouse 1 out of commission, I'd say a dozen at least."

"We've had *no* cancellations? Even after last night?"

"To the contrary, darling. The reservation lines are going mad. Overnight, Hotel Cinema has become the Graceland for Chelsea Fricks."

I whistled. "I hope Al gets more rooms completed today." Clicking open the property management system, I began running my morning reports. The printer jerked to life.

Shanna was staring at me. "Trevor, did you see the news this morning?"

"There was no television in my room. No toilet or phone either, for the record."

"Chelsea's death is on every news program, every radio station, every tongue in this city, probably across the country, maybe around the world. The media has gone into an absolute frenzy. I thought you had come in really early when I saw you on KCAL 9."

I looked up. "How was I?"

She hesitated, carefully choosing her words. "You looked, well … a tad haggard. Like you'd been up all night."

"I had!"

"Why did you say 'I refuse to comment'? It came across as harsh. You looked angry and a bit pompous, if the truth must be told."

"Reporters were badgering me! I was gracious and cordial until they launched a barrage of accusations and innuendo. They were ruthless. How haggard did I look?"

"Don't be upset, darling. I know how vicious they can be. They've surrounded the hotel like a pack of starving wolves."

"They're still out there?"

"Did you think this was going to go away overnight? It's just the beginning."

"What do they want from us? It's not like her body is still here."

"They need something to fill the nonstop live coverage. You should see it out there. Mobs of grieving fans are lining the street. Reporters are arriving by the vanload and setting up camp on our lawn. Our poor little flower garden, planted only two days ago, has been trampled. We've become a stop for city tours and star tours. Police have had to close down Hollywood Boulevard three blocks in either direction. I can't believe you slept through it all."

"I was a wee bit tired." I picked up the reports from the printer and began flipping through them. "What happened to you last night?"

She hopped off the desk and smoothed her white jacket. "I left early."

"Tony was pissed when he couldn't find you."

"Screw Tony. He harassed me about it this morning." Her attitude toward Tony had changed dramatically in the past few months. There was no more, "He's brilliant, just brilliant."

"He was storming around the hotel looking for you this morning," she said, walking to the full-length mirror on the wall to spruce her hair. "Truth is, I couldn't stand being around all those pretentious people."

"I thought you'd feel right at home."

"Not around pretentious twelve-year-old supermodels. I left at eight."

"*Eight*? How could you know what the crowd was like? No one arrived before nine."

"I saw the guest list. That was enough."

Dennis Claiborne was still lingering in the hallway. Shanna gestured for him to scoot with a flick of her hand, and he scampered down the hallway. He was one recruit I couldn't blame Tony for. Shanna and I had hired him based on his impeccable credentials—Ritz Carlton, Marriott, W Hotels—but he was quickly revealing himself to be a busybody and a gossip.

"You've been talking about this party for weeks, Shanna. Why didn't you stay?"

"Oh, I don't know." She was silent for a moment, and then said brightly, "I went to a late movie with Bantu and Eliza."

It seemed an odd night to make plans with her son and daughter, but I was happy to hear they had found time for her. "How are they?" I asked.

"Wonderful, absolutely wonderful."

Employees were gathering in the hallway, lined up at my door. I stood up. The reports would have to wait. "I'm going to call a staff meeting. I need to brief everyone on what happened, how to respond to questions, and who to talk to if they're feeling distraught."

"Done."

"You held a staff meeting?"

"After chairing the operations meeting for you, I called an executive committee meeting, followed by a general staff meeting." She blew on her nails. "Done, done, and done."

I felt a rush of gratitude, followed by shame. "I'm grateful, Shanna, but I should have been leading this charge. How are staff handling things?"

"Quite well, under the circumstances. The lead-up to last night's opening had them so charged up practically nothing will dampen their spirits. They're shaken, naturally, and a few are deeply disturbed, but they're trying to remain positive. I drafted a list of guidelines for handling media, guest, and public inquiries and reviewed it at the meeting. All media inquiries are to be directed to you, me, or Caine Public Relations. I assured them this matter will be handled with the utmost sensitivity and tact."

"Perfect. Now if you'll excuse me, there's a small army of staff waiting."

"Not so fast," she said, blocking the door. She reached out to close the blinds, and the employees outside vanished from view. Placing her knuckles on her hips, bracelets jangling, she implored, "What happened last night? The consensus is she staged a publicity stunt for *Blind Ambition* and broke her neck. Is that true?"

"I'm really not sure."

"Don't be coy with me, Trevor. I heard you witnessed the leap. Staff say you spent hours with the detective. Did she pull a Lohan?"

"What's a Lohan? A reporter used that term this morning."

"Don't you remember when Lindsay Lohan jumped off the balcony into the pool at Hotel Roosevelt? It would be just like Chelsea to try and one-up her. Ever since Lindsay beat her out for that Hayley Mills role in *The Parent Trap* they've been archrivals. Needless to say, hotel management was not impressed."

"And we are?"

She slumped into her chair. "I'm sick about it. The poor girl was only twenty-seven. She was so talented, yet she surrounded herself with the wrong people. Enablers. Bryce Davies used her. Moira Schwartz exploited her. She was going through a rough patch. And the media scrutiny was relentless. She probably still hadn't recovered from that horrid scandal in Rome."

"What scandal?"

"A word of advice, Trevor: if you want to succeed as hotelier-to-the-stars in this town, you need to keep up on celebrity news. A few months ago, a hotel employee took photos of Chelsea sunbathing topless at the hotel pool and leaked them to the tabloids. He also broke into her hotel room and took photos of various, shall we say, 'highly personal' items. Chels was outraged and humiliated. Since she got back from Europe she's been on an exhausting publicity junket for *Blind Ambition*. Critics have raved, but box-office sales have been disappointing. Add to that the DUI charge, the fact that her debut CD hasn't even been released and is already being panned, and the falling-out with her parents, and how could the poor thing be expected to cope? Today she was supposed to fly to Peru to shoot another movie, a semi-pornographic Incan epic co-starring Colin Farrell and Orlando Bloom. I guess it will never be made. Now *that's* a tragedy."

"You make it sound like you and Chelsea were intimate friends."

"In a way, I feel like I knew her."

"Reading *Us*, *People*, and *Spotlight* will do that."

"I read those magazines purely for research purposes, darling. If we're going to pander to celebrities, we need to know their likes and dislikes."

"Like their favorite brand of toilet paper? If the two of you are soul mates, I'm surprised you didn't stick around to meet her."

"Oh no, I could never. I'm terrified of stars. I love to read about them, but I couldn't possibly ever meet one. I would simply die."

"You're afraid of celebrities?"

She pressed a hand against her chest and breathed in. "It's not a laughing matter. It's not that uncommon an affliction. I looked it up. It's called celebrity phobia. I didn't realize I had it until I ran smack into Jessica Alba in the dairy section at Bristol Farms a few months ago. I was panic-stricken. I dropped the carton of eggs I was holding. She stooped down to help me clean up, and I fled."

I smirked. "Did you tell Tony this before he hired you?"

"I was determined to get over it. What better way than to take a job at a hotel that would be crawling with celebrities? I realize now I may never recover. The prospect of being surrounded by famous people last night was unbearable. If I met Chelsea Fricks, I would have fainted."

"Remind me not to ask you to do any celebrity meet-and-greets." I got up and sneaked a peek through the blinds, feeling guilty for keeping staff waiting. The hallway was empty. I turned to Shanna. "Why do you say Bryce Davies used her?"

"You don't watch *Modern Loving?* He plays a troubled street youth whose social status skyrockets when he falls in love with a New York senator's rebellious daughter. I swear he's playing himself. Season five just ended, and he's sleeping with the senator now. His character is universally despised, whereas Chelsea's appearance on the show as the daughter, just one season, is legendary, like Farrah Fawcett's stint on *Charlie's Angels*. Since she left, her film career has taken off. Did you see her in *White Slavery?* Helen Mirren robbed her of that Oscar. She's bound to get one for *Blind Ambition*. Sadly, it will be posthumously. Thanks to Chelsea, Bryce is far more famous than he could ever hope to be on his own. His attempts to break into film have been total flops. Did you see *Notoriety?*"

"Never even heard of it."

"Exactly. What about that *Three's Company* movie?"

"I heard it was bad."

"Deplorable."

"Was their relationship violent?" I asked.

Shanna frowned. "Not as far as I know. I'm sure Bryce envies her success, but I don't believe he's ever abused her. Why do you ask?"

"Just curious."

"You know something."

"I don't know anything, Shanna."

"Trevor."

"I just don't think it was a publicity stunt." Knowing Shanna wouldn't leave until I told her everything, I recounted some of what I had seen: Chelsea's early evening swim, her leap from the balcony, my conversation with the detective. I left out the blood stains, the stab wounds, and Detective Christakos's remarks—anything that suggested foul play.

Shanna's eyes were riveted. "Tony Cavalli killed her," she breathed.

"*What?*"

"He lured her to her death with that spotlight."

"You can't blame Tony. How could he know she would leap off the balcony?"

"Then she killed herself."

"I didn't say that."

"She was pushed."

"Christ, Shanna. You're worse than the reporters outside. Chelsea wasn't pushed. I saw it happen. She climbed onto the railing and jumped. I don't think it was a prank because she knew she was jumping into the shallow end. That's all. Let's leave the rest to the police. Now, if you don't mind ..."

While Shanna stood looking stunned, both hands wrapped around her neck as though having difficulty breathing, I sat down at my desk and clicked open my Outlook account. The email messages began piling up: 20, 40, 80, 120, 160, and still going. I began scrolling through them, determined to get some work done before venturing out to deal with staff and guests. Most were internal, as mundane as the Daily Flash report, others more unusual, such as the inquiry from Ezmerelda Lopez about what to do with the contents of Miss Fricks' room. "Pack the items and lock them up," I typed back. "I'm sure a friend or family member will come by to pick them up." I needed to go see Ezmerelda as soon as I was done here. There were messages from media requesting interviews, condolences and threats from Chelsea fans, inquiries from guests and clients about the status of bookings, and messages from colleagues asking for the inside scoop. The total reached 273 and was still downloading. I had no assistant to screen messages and phone calls. Tony made me choose between an executive assistant and a human resources manager, and I had opted for the latter. Now I wondered if I had made the right choice.

"Trevor, what on earth are you doing?" asked Shanna.

"I'm checking my email."

"Today might call for a change in routine. Many people have been looking for you."

"Such as?"

"Your mother."

"God, I forgot she was here." I stood up. "We were supposed to have breakfast."

"Not to worry. I ran into her in the lobby this morning. She didn't expect you to make it in light of last night's incident. She says she's quite enjoying her stay. I can't believe you put your own mother in the fitness room."

"It was her idea!" She had turned her nose up at my apartment, and by the time she decided to fly down for the opening, the hotel was booked. She insisted I book her at the Four Seasons Regent until my counterpart quoted a "special industry rate" of $325. When I took her on a tour of the hotel and told her the fitness room wouldn't be open for a few days due to delayed equipment, she had suggested staying there. It made for a fantastic guestroom—1,200 square feet, full bathroom, infrared sauna, floor-to-ceiling windows. A houseman rolled in a cot, but she insisted on sleeping on an exercise mat, surrounded by barbells, weight benches, and exercise balls.

"Do you know if she's there now?" I asked Shanna.

"She went on a tour of Paramount Studios with some producer she met at the party." Shanna's lips parted into a smile. "The little tart."

I recalled her introducing me to a handsome man at least ten years her junior last night, Bruce Leonard. "He's in 'the biz,'" she had said, air-quoting the words as though employing a term used only by industry insiders. By this time, she had consumed a few cocktails. "I'm so proud of my son," she gushed, "managing this trendy little hipster hangout." I was glad Shanna wasn't there. She had banished words like "trendy," "hip," and "sexy" from staff vocabulary. "If you have to use these words to describe yourself, you just aren't," she explained at yesterday's general staff meeting. "And if I hear anyone utter the odious word 'funky' in reference to this hotel, I'll sentence you to a week of cold-calling from my icebox of an office."

An email from Kitty Caine popped up on my screen. "So Kitty finally surfaces," I said, scanning. "Looks like we have an emergency PR meeting this afternoon." I read the message aloud, exaggerating the publicist's Texas drawl. "'Tony and I are comin' down at four to discuss our publicity campaign surroundin' the death of Chayle-say Frakes. See y'all then.'" It was signed, "Kindest regards, Katherine Caine. Caine Public Relations. *Putting the Spotlight on Your Business.*"

"Publicity campaign?" said Shanna. "What on earth is she talking about? We won't be wading into this cesspool of sensationalism. We should issue a brief statement expressing our condolences and leave it at that."

"My sentiments exactly."

"Speaking of insufferable people, a detective was asking for you. Burly, bossy little Greek guy?"

"Detective Christakos."

"All morning he was dragging staff into the boardroom, lining them up against the wall, and firing accusatory questions. He really upset a few of them."

I jumped to my feet. "Damn, I wanted to be present. Who did he upset?"

"Al was ghost-faced afterwards, but he refused to talk about it. Ezmerelda Lopez hasn't stopped crying."

I slammed my hands down on the desk, making her jump. "That son of a bitch!" Grabbing my suit jacket, I charged out the door.

★ ★ ★ ★ ★

Ezmerelda wasn't answering her two-way radio. I went down to B2, two levels below the main floor, and searched the housekeeping office, laundry room, staff lounge, and accounting offices, but nobody had seen her in the past two hours. At the storeroom I stopped to ask Olga Slovenka, inventory and supply attendant, who was standing at her window with a fierce look in her eyes.

"I'm looking for Ezmerelda. Have you seen her?"

She looked me up and down, her expression severe. "No see!" She lowered her eyes.

"Is everything okay, Olga?" I asked.

"No problem," she replied, unconvincingly, in a thick Polish accent.

"If you see her, please tell her I need to speak with her urgently."

"Okay, I tell."

Olga was another of Tony's forced hires, but unlike the relatives she was hardworking and experienced. She had worked as a house-keeper in the Cavalli household for almost twenty years until she was fired three months ago—by Tony's four-year-old daughter, Emily. Emily decided she didn't like the way Olga made her bed and staged a hunger strike when Tony tried to reinstate her. Feeling guilty, Tony promised her a job at the hotel. "She's an ogre," he told me, "so keep her away from guests. She'll scare them. Facial validity clocks some-where in the negative." Her English vocabulary was limited to about twenty words, usually blurted in imperatives, and smiling seemed to involve great physical pain. She was getting too old for the physical demands of cleaning rooms, yet she was organized and officious, the perfect fit for this back-of-house role as storeroom attendant.

"Is there something you want to tell me, Olga?" I asked.

With a long-suffering sigh, she unlatched the door and stepped aside, pointing inside the storeroom. "Go! See!"

Puzzled, I stepped in and looked around. The room was immacu-late. To the immediate right, three housekeeping carts were parked in perfect rows, loaded with supplies. Directly ahead, rows of shelving were neatly stacked with pillows, linen, bathroom amenities, irons, toilet paper rolls, boxes of tissues, iPod docking stations, boom boxes, and other items a hotel guest might request. There was no one in sight and nothing out of the ordinary. I turned to Olga inquiringly.

She jabbed her finger toward the mini-bar supply room in the far corner.

Crossing over to it, I put my ear to the door and listened. I heard a sniffle. Stepping in front of the scanner, I pushed open the door.

The room was dark. "Hello?" I called out. I heard another sniffle. The bare bulb in the storeroom behind me illuminated a portly shape hunched over on a case of wine. "Ezmerelda? Why are you sitting in the dark? What's wrong?" I flicked on the light.

She lifted her head. Her beatific, round face was wet with tears. "He tink I kill her!"

I crouched down before her. "What? Who?"

"The detectib! He tink I kill Mees Freaks."

Twelve years had lapsed since she immigrated from Mexico at twenty-one years old, yet Ez still spoke broken English with a heavy accent. Her skills as head of housekeeping more than compensated. Shanna and I had worked with her in New York, where, as assistant director of housekeeping, she was hardworking and highly respected. When it was time to recruit an executive housekeeper at Hotel Cinema, I only had eyes for Ezmerelda. After much cajoling, I managed to convince Tony to pay to relocate her family—husband Felix and two young children, Bello and Bella—and she started on May 1. She was a tireless worker with zero tolerance for dust and dirt, firm but fair with her thirty-five employees, proud, and—until now—irrepressibly optimistic.

"Surely not," I said. "What makes you think that?"

She wiped her eye with the back of her hand. I surveyed the shelves above, searching for a box of tissues. They were loaded with mini-bar snacks, trays of soda, boxes of Pringles and chocolate bars, and cases of miniature bottles of alcohol and liqueurs—but no tissues. I dashed out of the room and grabbed a box of Kleenex from one of the housekeeping carts, ignoring Olga's reproachful glare. I pulled the door closed and sat on a case of Voss water, handing Ezmerelda a few tissues.

She dabbed her eyes. "He ask so many question."

"What kind of questions?"

"He say, 'Why you in suite so late? What you doing? Why you clean room? What you hide?'"

That sounded like Christakos, all right. "What did you say?"

"I tell him I go to suite at 11:10. I knock on door. No answer. I tink Mees Freaks at party, so I go in. I call out hello. Nobody answer. I start tidy up. The suite is very messy. How someone make so many mess in such short time? She is there five hours and room looks like cyclone."

"I know, I saw it."

"I am dusting the desk when Mees Freaks come in from bedroom. She scare me so hard, I knock lamp on floor."

"The Bourgie lamp? That was you?"

She nodded slowly, eyes filled with shame. "I'm sorry. I ask Al to replace it. I will pay."

"Don't worry about it, Ez. What happened then?"

"She ask me why I don't knock. She say, 'Why you snooping?' I tell her sorry, I only housekeeping, I only be cleaning. She tell me get out, come back when she goes to party, half-hour maybe."

"Then what?"

"I go," Ezmerelda said with a shrug. "I leave the cart in hallway, come back here, talk with Olga, fold towels, wait. I don't want to go home before I tidy her room. Half-hour later, I go back up."

"That was around 11:35?" I said, recalling the activity report.

She nodded. "Twenty minutes later I'm sweeping the kitchen when Artie burst in with police, scares me half to death. Artie tells me Mees Freaks jumped off balcony. I am so shocked. A policeman tell me get out, wait outside. I am so upset I take cart, bring back here, go home. I cry all night." She lowered her eyes.

"I'm sorry, Ez," I said, taking her hand and giving it a squeeze.

She gave a small cry and pulled her hand away. "Why the detectib ask me so many questions? My husband, my kids, my family in Mexico. So many questions."

"He's just doing his job. He asked me lots of questions too."

"I am so sorry for to cause trouble."

"You haven't caused any trouble."

She looked up again. "Can I ask question, Trevor? Why was blood on carpet? I see glass and think Mees Freaks cut her foot. I vacuum up right away."

I hesitated. "I'm not sure."

"The detectib ask me what happen to the knife on counter."

"You never saw it?"

"It was there when I inspect room. Now it's gone." Her eyes grew wide. "What happened to Mees Freaks?"

"I honestly don't know. But I need you to keep quiet about what you saw, okay? Have any staff been up to Penthouse 1 today?"

She shook her head.

"Good. I'm going to call an outside company to come in and clean it."

"But I already clean."

"You cleaned the penthouse suite?"

She nodded. "I come in early. The stains come out, no problem. I put her tings in my office." A fearful look came over her. "Did someone kill Mees Freaks?"

I regarded her for a moment. I didn't want to lie to her, but the detective had made me promise not to divulge details. I shook my head. "No one killed Miss Fricks, Ezmerelda. It was some kind of bizarre accident. I'm sure the police will determine what happened soon. In the meantime, you have nothing to worry about. I promise." I put my arm around her. "I need you to pull yourself together and get back to work, okay? Your staff need you right now. *I* need you. We have a full house tonight. There are rooms to clean, surfaces to polish, germs to kill." I stood up and held out my hand for her.

She burst into tears. "I afraid to go out there," she said.

"Afraid? Why?"

"Everybody looking at me, talking, saying bad things."

"That's ridiculous. Nobody would think for a second that you had anything to do with what happened. I want you to wipe away your tears, hold your head high, and walk out there with poise and dignity. Okay?"

She nodded slowly. "I try."

"Do more than try. Come out swinging. Can you do that for me?"

She dabbed her eyes and broke into a smile. "Sure I can."

"Great." I reached for a bottle of Moët & Chandon champagne from the shelf. "What do you say we break this open and toast the opening of Hotel Cinema? We can crack open a box of Oh Henry's, break out the Pringles, have a party! But *shh*! Don't let Olga hear. She'll want to join us, and she'll hog the champagne."

Ezmerelda giggled. "You crazy."

"Just a sip?"

"No way, José! I have work to do." She stood up, suddenly all business, pushed the door open, and flicked off the light by force of habit as she bustled out.

The door swung closed, leaving me alone in the darkness. I placed the champagne bottle back on the shelf and sat down, suddenly understanding why Ezmerelda had holed up here. It was warm and safe and dark, far removed from the challenging day that waited outside. Ezmerelda's account did little to reassure me that something sinister hadn't taken place. In a period of fifteen minutes or less, between the time Chelsea told Ez to leave the suite and the time Ez returned, something had happened that left blood all over the suite and a dead woman in the pool.

But what?

I decided Al Combs was next on my list.

Glancing at the snacks around me, I realized I hadn't eaten since dinner last night. I grabbed a Kit Kat, a can of tamari almonds, and a Sprite and squirreled them out of the storeroom. Olga was sweeping the spotless floor. I wished her a pleasant day. She only glowered at the loot in my hands.

★ ★ ★ ★ ★

Able Al wasn't in his office down the hall. I called the operator and had him paged, and he called back to say he was in Room 311. Taking the back stairs up to the third floor, I headed down the corridor to the west wing of the building and found the door to 311 propped open. Al was in the living room before a large hole in the drywall, a sledgehammer in his hands. The furniture was covered with plastic.

"What are you doing?" He was supposed to be completing rooms, not destroying them. "Isn't this room scheduled to go into service today?"

Al ran a huge hand over his glistening bald head. "The delivery guys put a dent in the wall while installing the headboard. I had to replace the panel, but it's turned out to be a bigger job than I anticipated." His black Lacoste shirt and work pants were covered with drywall dust. The strain of the past few days, since Tony sent the Fratelli Construction crew packing, was showing in his pale blue eyes. I had lured this gentle-natured giant from Hotel Mondrian with a modest salary increase and the promise of free rein over the maintenance department, but he got much more than he bargained for. Not only was completion of remaining rooms left to him and his two shift engineers, but he soon discovered that Fratelli's workmanship was slapdash and shoddy. Rico, Stephen, and Al had been working around the clock to repair deficiencies and finish rooms.

"Don't worry," he said. "Valerie says the guest is coming in late. I'll make sure it's ready in time." He lifted the sledgehammer over his head and heaved it at the wall.

A cloud of dust flew toward me. I stepped back. "Exactly how late?" I asked, staring at the hole, now double in size.

"Midnight," he replied, lifting the sledgehammer to strike again. "Come here, I need to show you something." He set the sledgehammer down and yanked at a chunk of drywall until it came loose, tossing it on the floor. He pointed inside the hole. "Check this out."

I peered inside. It was too dark to see anything.

Al pulled a flashlight from his tool belt and shone it inside.

In the midst of the building's internal organs was a thick wooden beam, black, charred, and eaten by fire. "A fire?"

"Thirty years ago."

"This beam is from the original building? They didn't replace it?"

He shook his head. "The Fratelli bozos bolstered it with a two-by-four." He pointed to a piece of lumber fastened to the back of the beam with a large metal bolt. "They should have replaced it. They were either too lazy or too cheap."

I massaged my jaw, feeling it tighten. "I hope this is the only one."

"It's the third one I've found so far," Al said, pulling a handkerchief from his back pocket and running it over his forehead. "Looks like they preserved the old beams wherever they could. The entire foundation of this building could be rotten, Trevor. It may look pretty on the outside, but it's a mess on the inside. I don't know what Mr. Cavalli was thinking, hiring those Fratelli hacks. What construction company with a grain of integrity would use fire-damaged beams as foundation?"

I stepped back and surveyed the room, suddenly fearful the walls and ceiling would cave in. How was I going to break it to Tony that his treasured hotel had major structural problems? Maybe he knew already. Maybe it was his call. From the moment Shanna called me about this job, everything had been a rush. A rush to sign my contract. A rush to get to LA. A rush to hire staff. A rush to secure bookings. A rush to open. My spirits deflated. No amount of attentive service or optimism could save a poorly built hotel.

"What do we do?" I asked Al, deferring to his expertise.

"I'll do what I can to stabilize this one," he said. "I asked the guys to go room to room and look for other weak areas. But it's going to take us away from finishing other rooms. We already lost the entire morning, so we're really behind."

"What happened to the morning?" I asked, anxiety mounting.

"I had to spend some time with that detective. Then Rico and I went out front to fix the hedge and clean up the gardens. Have you seen it out there? They built a shrine on the hotel's marble sign like it's a headstone and surrounded it with flowers, photographs, cards, and candles. We didn't feel right clearing it away, so we left it as is.

I didn't want to linger there for long. People were harassing us for information. A reporter from KCAL 9 was following me around with a cameraman. It freaked me out."

For such a large, imposing fellow, Al could be painfully shy. "How many rooms can you get into service today?" I asked.

"Three at the most, maybe as few as two."

"Al, we were counting on five at least. We're oversold by a dozen rooms." I pressed my hand against my temple. Hotel rooms are perishable inventory; every night one goes empty means lost revenue. Guests who had a guaranteed reservation but couldn't be accommodated were relocated to another hotel that we were obliged to pay for as compensation. Sometimes guests were so irate they never returned. "Can you bring in an outside contractor?"

He shook his head. "Mr. Cavalli says it's not in the budget."

"Get as many rooms completed as you can, okay? I know you're working a lot of hours. I promise I'll make it up to you."

"I don't mind, Trevor. I just wish I could do more."

"How did it go with Detective Christakos?"

Al visibly tensed up. "Fine," he said. He went back to work, pulling drywall from the periphery of the hole.

"Did you tell him about the complaint?" I asked.

He didn't respond.

"Al? Did you discuss Miss Fricks' complaint at all?"

He stopped working and turned to me. "Why would I tell him, Trevor? Her story was totally fabricated. Don't tell me *you* told him?"

I shook my head. "I didn't think it was relevant. It's not, is it? I mean ... you were up there hours before ..."

Al's lips quivered. "I told you last night: I did nothing inappropriate or creepy," he said, staring into the hole. "I got called to her room to fix her bathtub faucet around eight PM. I knocked but nobody answered, so I let myself in. I called out her name a few times and then headed for the bathroom. I was surprised to see her in the bedroom, listening to music and trying clothes on. I said hello. I was courteous and professional, like I always am. I barely even looked at her. A few minutes later I left."

Suddenly I remembered the dripping faucet. "Did you fix the faucet, Al?"

He turned to me and blinked. "I did my best."

"Well, it's leaking again. You better have another look." My eyes moved to Al's enormous hands. They were shaking. If he had behaved inappropriately, it wouldn't be the first time in history a hotel employee crossed the line. Whether delivering luggage or room service, making beds, or fixing a faucet, hotel employees got closer to famous people than most could ever hope. Occasionally it led to inappropriate behavior. But Al wasn't the type. I had known him for only a few months, but his work references had been impeccable. Both Shanna and I interviewed him for the position. I recalled our conversation afterward, discussing the pros and cons.

"Think he has a family?" I asked Shanna. The chief engineer job would be all-consuming, at least for the first few months, and a wife and children might interfere.

She rolled her eyes. "He's thirty-two, single, buff, and lives in West Hollywood. You do the math."

If Al was gay, Chelsea's accusations were all the more ludicrous.

When he resigned from Hotel Mondrian, the general manager, Alyson Parker, called me in tears. "I could kill you for stealing him," she said. "Able Al is the best damned chief engineer I've ever had."

"You went home when I told you to?" I asked him now.

"Not right away. I had to finish up a few things first."

I nodded, observing him. He looked hurt. "What did you and the detective talk about?" I asked.

"I told him the same thing I told you. He asked if I saw or heard anything unusual, and I said no." He lifted the sledgehammer again.

"Then there's nothing more to discuss, is there?"

"Nope." He let the sledgehammer fall, causing an explosion of drywall powder.

I looked at the gaping hole. "Haven't you done enough damage already?"

"Damage? I'm *fixing* this."

"Of course." I backed toward the door. "Carry on, then."

7

Putting the Spotlight on Your Business

Back at my desk that afternoon, I was flying through my email when the lovely Valerie Smitts appeared at my door. "I hate to bother you, Trevor. Mr. Cavalli is here for you."

I looked at my watch. 3:58 PM. Time for the PR meeting. Damn.

"Tell him I'll be out in a sec," I said. "Don't let him come back here. This is a Tony Cavalli-free zone."

She flashed a knowing smile. "Got it."

I watched her swish away. One day, I thought, I'm going to ask that girl out for dinner. But first I would have to fire her. With a sigh, I returned to my computer and opened a message from Alyson Parker, general manager of Hotel Mondrian. "Heya Trevor," she wrote. "Heard the news about Chelsea. UNREAL. She used to be our regular gest until you stole her. NIGHTMARE. Let's hope your service isn't so bad it drove her kill herself! Ha Ha. Gallows humor, hey? I know things are probly crazy, just wanted to say I'm thinking about ya. Call me if you need a simpathetic ear or want to go for lunch. Smiles, Alyson. PS: I hear you're relocating—we've got a few rooms left so keep us in mind."

I glowered at the screen, picturing Alyson seated smugly at her desk, surrounded by a cast of thousands compared to my skeletal crew, gloating over the tragedy that had befallen her newest competitor. Clearly she was still bitter about Al. I had met her once, at a LA Convention and Visitors Bureau meeting, and she was friendly and forthright and attractive, a tall, thin blond with dark eyebrows—the type my mother would choose for me but I wouldn't go near. What adult writes "Ha Ha" and "Smiles" like a nine-year-old girl? She was an atrocious speller—imagine, a hotel manager who couldn't spell the word "guest"! And she had the audacity to ask for our relocates—as if we would send them to the Mondrian. Hotels sent relocates to inferior properties to ensure guests came back.

I fired off a terse reply: "Thank you for your concern, Alyson. All is well at Hotel Cinema. Our 'gests' are loving the hotel. Sincerely, Trevor." The moment I pressed Send I felt guilty. Why was I being so snarky? The stress was getting to me. I continued scrolling, forgetting that Tony was waiting. More media inquiries, a guest complaint about the mayhem outside, spam, a note from a heartbroken eleven-year-old Chelsea fan, a message entitled "Your Giong to Hell for Kilin Chelsea." Judging by the spelling, this last one could have come from Alyson Parker. A wave of remorse passed through me. I reached for the phone. It had been ringing nonstop all afternoon, and I had learned to tune it out. Just before I lifted it, it rang again.

"Good afternoon, Trevor Lambert speaking."

There was dead air.

"Hello?" I said. I was about to hang up when I heard the sound of labored breathing. A hangup. I pressed the phone to my ear, listening intently, and detected a tiny, almost inaudible gasp. I shuddered. Since I decided Mom wasn't behind these calls—a while back I received one while she was in the same room—they had taken on an eerie slant, like I was being contacted by another world. Now Mom was at Disneyland or Universal Studios or some other place where people didn't have suffocating workloads. "Mom? Is that you?" No response. If not my mother, then who? I hadn't received a hangup in weeks, and they were always at home, at odd hours, never at my office during daylight.

"Who is this?" I demanded. "What do you want? Why do you keep calling me?"

The breathing stopped.

Just hang up, I told myself. But I couldn't. There was something *familiar* about the breathing. All at once I was filled with dread. I dropped the receiver as though it had burst into flames.

Almost immediately it began ringing again.

I snatched it up. "Why are you tormenting me like this?"

"Ouch! Trevor, is that you? It's Alyson from Hotel Mondrian."

"Alyson? I'm sorry. Did I just hang up on you?"

"No. Are you okay? You sound spooked. Things must be really bad there."

"Things are just fine, Alyson. I'm sorry about the email."

"No worries. I do know how to spell 'guests,' by the way. I'm just a notoriously bad typist."

"I see."

"How's Able Al? I finally found a replacement last month—stole him from Sofitel. He couldn't give a reference because they didn't know he was looking. Now I know why. Turns out he's not mechanically minded. Ironic, no? I asked him to adjust the temperature on the mini-bar in my office, and he dismantled it entirely and can't figure out how to put it back together. He's so fired tomorrow. *God* I miss Al. Is he doing okay?"

Al's anguished expression came to me ... unfairly accused of inappropriate behavior by a paranoid guest ... working exorbitant hours as he struggled to get rooms done ... completion of the hotel dumped in his lap ... its rotten foundation. It was a good question—how *was* he doing? Probably not well. What if it was all too much, and he decided he had made a mistake in leaving the Mondrian? We would be screwed.

And here Alyson was, circling like a vulture. "Al couldn't be better, Alyson. Don't even think about trying to lure him back."

"I wasn't, I promise! I'm just curious about how he's making out. I hear you're still under construction."

"Who told you that?"

"I heard it on the news—KCAL 9, I think. As I said, feel free to send any overflow our way."

"That's kind of you to offer," I said. "I'll be sure to keep you in mind."

"I'd love to pop by sometime and see the hotel. I've heard great things. Maybe we could have lunch."

"Why don't I call you when things settle down? Thanks for calling."

"Hey, wait! You going to give me the inside scoop on what happened to Chelsea?"

"If you've seen the news, you know as much as I do."

"*Come on.* There's gotta be a juicy tidbit you can divulge. GM to GM? I promise not to tell anyone. Did she pull a Lohan?"

"I really don't know what happened, Alyson."

"Nothing untoward happened, did it? Like somebody pushed her or something?"

"Absolutely not."

"Aren't you a tight-lipped little devil," she said good-naturedly. "Hey, can I ask you something?" She hesitated. "Was Al Combs around when Chelsea, you know, jumped?"

"What a strange question. Why do you ask?"

A shadow passed over my desk. Tony Cavalli was towering over me, dressed up in a white three-piece suit and a pink, open-collared shirt. His receding hair was slicked back and oily.

Valerie Smitts was standing behind him, hands pressed against her cheeks, mouthing the words, "I'm so sorry!"

"Alyson, I've gotta run," I said into the phone.

"Where the fuck is my revenue forecast?" Tony bellowed.

"Uh-oh," said Alyson. "Sounds like an owner to me. Is that Cavalli? Tell him I think he's an asshole. Thank *God* he's got a bar of his own. Maybe he'll stop terrorizing Sky Bar."

"Uh, thanks very much for the market intelligence, Alyson," I said, holding my index finger up to Tony. "Glad to hear things are going well at the Mondrian. Talk soon!" I placed the phone on the hook and stood up. "Sorry, Tony. I got caught up in work."

"Where the fuck have you been all day?"

"I was up all night. I fell asleep and missed my wakeup call."

"You were *sleeping* on the first day of operation. During a *crisis?*" His eyes were fierce.

I was tempted to blame his harebrained niece but resisted. "I apologize, Tony. There's really no excuse. It won't happen again."

He opened his mouth to retort but realized I hadn't argued. I had accepted full responsibility and apologized—a simple, effective tactic for defusing irate guests. "Let's go," he said. "We're late."

★ ★ ★ ★ ★

The hotel's four meeting rooms were located on the second floor: the Pre-Production Suite, the Production Suite, the Post-Production Suite, and the Screening Room. All were approximately 1,200 square feet in area, with retractable walls to allow expansion into larger rooms. Each was equipped with a fifty-two-inch plasma screen television mounted on the wall, video conferencing facilities, and a large screen for viewing dailies and previews. The public relations meeting was held in the Pre-Production Suite overlooking the pool deck.

Shanna Virani and Kitty Caine were seated at opposite ends of the boardroom table, as far away from one another as the table permitted, separated by twelve high-backed throne chairs and a granite tabletop. Kitty sprang from her chair as I entered and jiggled toward me with arms open wide, breasts bouncing.

"Hiya, handsome! Great to see y'all again!"

"Good to see you too, Kitty," I said, breathing in cigarette smoke infused with mint perfume.

Spotting Tony behind me, she rushed to hug him next. "Why, Antonio Giancarlo Cavalli, look at you all dressed up in a three-piece suit! You look like a gangsta. My, how this sexy little goatee has grown in!"

Tony stroked his goatee and grinned. "You like?"

"*Love. It.*"

I sneaked a glance at Shanna, who poked two fingers in her mouth in a gagging gesture. Shanna had disliked Kitty even before they met, in part due to how she was hired: without our consent, after Tony met her at a fundraiser she had organized for homeless cats and was impressed by the star power she attracted.

"She's never represented a hotel before," Shanna had protested. "She won't know the travel media."

"Doesn't matter," Tony retorted. "She represents stars, and my hotel is going to be a star."

When Shanna met Kitty in person, she was appalled. "She's everything I abhor in a woman: blond, loud, and Republican," she told me. "She's got so many fake parts she's practically a Fem-Bot."

"How can you tell?" I asked.

Shanna looked down at her own chest and sighed. "The breasts of a fiftyish woman don't touch her chin. We're lucky if they stay above our bellybuttons. *Not* that I'm that old."

"She seems really ebullient."

"If by ebullient you mean irritating, then I agree. With a name like Kitty, she's a former drag queen or porn star. A lot of girls come to Hollywood with dreams of being a star, only to fall into the porn industry. The poor thing's real name is probably Mary-Jo Smithers."

In spite of her flirty, syrupy tactics, Kitty had generated an impressive volume of pre-opening media coverage for the hotel and could share credit for the solid advance bookings, the month-long wait for a dinner table in Scene, and the "who's who of Hollywood" crowd anticipated at Action. Whereas Sydney Cheevers was responsible for getting the stars to show up, it was Kitty's job to ensure media captured arrivals and departures on film.

"How you holdin' up, gorgeous?" Kitty asked Tony, pulling his head toward her bosom and patting his head.

"I'm devastated," Tony said, nuzzling against her chest. "We were very close."

"I know you were, poodle."

Shanna's left eye bulged almost imperceptibly. There was some question as to whether Tony had even met Chelsea. His devastation was more likely related to having been deprived of parading her around like a new bride.

Tony sat down with Kitty, and I joined Shanna.

"What a gorgeous li'l boardroom!" Kitty burbled. "I tell you, Tony, you nailed every aspect of this li'l boutique hotel!" Reaching into her red pleather purse, she withdrew a notepad covered with red fur and a red-and-white striped pencil. "Shall we git down to business? I must say I'm still in shock. Who would have thought that Chelsea-Friggin'-

Fricks would chuck herself off the penthouse before a thousand party guests?"

I didn't bother to point out that about 350 had attended the party, and no more than 100 had witnessed her fall. Kitty was prone to exaggeration—an occupational trait.

"It's devastating," I said, shaking my head.

"Heartbreaking, really," said Shanna.

"A tragedy," said Tony. He turned to Kitty with a glint in his eye.

"*Such* a tragedy," Kitty echoed. The corner of her mouth twitched. She let out a screech of laughter like a chicken squawking, then tried to compose herself, but Tony erupted next, throwing his head back, jowls rippling, which set her off again.

Shanna's lips tightened. "I can't imagine what you could find funny," she said, her British-Pakistani accent sharpening. She splayed her perfectly manicured nails before her, waiting for them to finish.

"I'm sorry!" Kitty cried, pulling a tissue from her purse and dabbing her eyes. "We don't mean any disrespect. Tony and I talked things over this morning and said all the proper things one says in these situations. We really are deeply saddened." Another giggle bubbled inside her, but she fought it down. Averting her eyes from Tony, she adopted a grave expression. "Chelsea"—*Chayle-say*—"was a talented actress. Hollywood is gonna miss her bad. But she was messed up, a greedy and connivin' little witch, always starvin' for attention. I refuse to waste tears over that girl. Truth is"—she turned to Tony, who was eyeing her thirstily—"Chelsea's death is the best dang thing that could happen to this li'l boutique hotel."

"Damn right!" Tony cried. Then his expression grew stern. "But stop calling it that, Kitty," he grumbled. "It's degrading."

"The *best* thing?" I said, leaning forward. "How so?"

"*Everybody's* talkin' about Hotel Cinema," said Kitty. "When that little vixen took her final swan dive, history was made. You can't *buy* this kind of publicity."

"This isn't the kind of publicity we want," Shanna said, eyes darting from Tony to Kitty and back again. "We don't want to go down in history as the hotel where Chelsea Fricks killed herself. What kind of positioning is that? People want to feel safe and secure in a hotel."

"Any publicity is good publicity," Tony growled. "Right, Kitty?"

"Well, not exactly," Kitty said. "Shanna's partly right, we don't want to be cast in a negative light. That's why we're gonna use this incident to maximize our exposure in a *positive* way."

"Exactly how do you propose to put a positive spin on a tragic death?" I asked, mystified.

"Of course we'll do it extremely tastefully," said Kitty.

Shanna's eyes grazed Kitty's pouffy hair and low-cut dress. "Undoubtedly."

Tony became delirious with excitement. "Everybody's been calling Kitty—*People* magazine, *Us Weekly*, *Spotlight*, *Entertainment Tonight*, *Hard Copy*, *CNN Entertainment*. They want the inside story, and they know we got it. Kitty knows all the key people."

"Come on," I said. "A young woman just died, and you want to exploit it? I find the notion completely distasteful. Tony, I thought Chelsea was your friend."

Tony furrowed his brow. A sheepish look came over him. He opened his mouth to respond but couldn't think of anything, and turned to Kitty.

Kitty planted her knuckles on her side. "*Well*, excuuuse me for not feelin' sorry for Chelsea Fricks," she snapped. "Might I point out that *she's* to blame for what happened, not us? Her little stunt could ruin this hotel if it weren't in our capable hands. Nobody can blame us for tryin' to turn it into a good thang."

"*Exactly*," Tony chimed in. "Chelsea pulled a bonehead stunt while she was *my* guest of honor. I paid 150,000 big ones for her to kill herself in front of the biggest wigs in Hollywood? Fuck that. She did it to attract attention to her movie, to sell tickets! I'm not about to let my business suffer because of her."

"It's hardly suffering," I said. "The reservation lines have been ringing off the hook. Besides, what makes you think it was a stunt?"

"I was right beside you when it happened," Tony said. "She couldn't just step out on the balcony and take a bow like a normal person, she had to do something that would make headlines."

"Stupid girl," said Kitty.

"No one knows for sure why she jumped," I said, looking to Shanna for support. She was unusually quiet. Did she agree with them?

"*I* know what happened," said Kitty. "I talked to Moira Schwartz less than an hour ago. She says Chelsea was depressed. Bryce was pissin' her off, as usual. Her schedule was insane. She couldn't take it anymore. Moira did everything she could to help her. She even asked Tony to allow Chelsea to back out of the party, but—"

"Hey, hold it right there!" Tony shouted. "I did no such thing!" He sneaked a nervous glance at me. "I never ... if I had known she was going to ..." His words trailed off.

I tried to reconcile Moira's suicide claim with the trail of blood, the knife wounds. Would Tony and Kitty be so eager to exploit her death if they knew she was murdered? *Love, drugs, and money*, Detective Christakos had said. All the ingredients of a tabloid typhoon. We were better off hunkering down and waiting the storm out.

"Exactly how credible is Moira?" I asked. "She seems a bit bizarre to me."

"Moira Schwartz is just as credible as any other lyin', cheatin' skank of a publicist in this town," Kitty replied. "Present party excluded, *bien sûr*. I've known that uppity little you-know-what for three years, since she moved from New York. She was twenty-three at the time but even then she looked like a middle-aged cadaver. We were in the same crisis communications class at SoCal. She was doing PR for a toothpaste company—Rembrandt, I think. One night durin' class she whispered to me that she had met Chelsea Fricks at some club—Prey, I believe it was—and helped her escape the paparazzi through the back door. 'Chelsea's going to be my client, just watch,' she told me. Chelsea wasn't so huge back then, but she had left *Modern Loving* and was getting more famous by the day. A few weeks later Moira tells me Chelsea hired her to plan her twenty-fourth birthday bash in Vegas. I was so jealous I wanted to rip her tits off. When Moira Schwartz wants something, she gets it. It's the New York Jew in her. The party got Chelsea's mug in every darned magazine on the planet, and the two have been inseparable since."

Shanna, who had been leaning toward Kitty with the wide-eyed, guilty expression she had when she read tabloids, snapped to attention. "What does this have to do with our current situation?" she said. "We're in a crisis, and we need to decide how to move forward."

"All I'm saying is if anybody knows what happened, it's Moira. She and Chelsea were like sisters—Moira being the homely, butch sister." Kitty gave a mean-spirited cackle. "Moira acts like her, wears her discarded clothes, albeit badly, sometimes even pretends she's her. It's creepy. Kind of a *Single White Female* thang goin' on, if you ask me. If Moira says it was suicide, it was suicide."

I thought of Moira's pale, fleshy skin, her dark clothes and black hair. She didn't seem to be trying to emulate Chelsea. "Why is Moira so convinced Chelsea killed herself?" I said.

"*Well*," Kitty said dramatically, "Moira says she still hadn't recovered from the episode with that hotel employee in Rome who took topless photos of her sunbathin' in the privacy of the hotel pool. He broke into her room and took pictures of her panties, every beauty product you could imagine *except* CoverGirl—even though she was the new face—medication for genital herpes, face lotion for post-cosmetic surgery, and a black dildo the size of a zucchini. Not that any of this should have been a surprise to the public—the girl had so much work done she was starting to look like the bride of Frankenstein—but apparently she was *devastated*. Moira thinks she saw that spotlight Tony was shinin' in the window and thought it was God beckoning."

"I'm telling you to shut up about that spotlight," Tony shouted. "You're my publicist, for God's sake."

"It was the perfect finale for Chelsea, wasn't it? She wasn't the type to wash down a bottle of Vicodin with vodka and go quietly. She went with a splash."

Shanna plucked a hair off the shoulder of her white suit and flicked it away. "Kitty," she said icily, "explain to me again how you propose to put a positive spin on the tragic death of a beloved movie star?"

"I got a plan!" Kitty announced, opening her notebook. "First we need to appoint a spokesperson."

Tony raised his hand like a schoolboy. "I can be spokesperson."

Kitty took a sidelong glance at Tony's slicked-back hair and Mafioso suit. "As the hotel's owner, Tony, what with your extremely high profile and important connections in the entertainment industry, I believe it's best to keep you behind the scenes."

"Absolutely," Tony said. "I only thought—"

"I have someone else in mind." Kitty looked at me, her tongue darting out to moisten her red lipstick. "The cameras will *adore* that handsome face of yours, Trevor."

"Me?"

"Yes, you, sweet thang. You're the perfect individual to play the role of dedicated, distraught hotel manager. With a few calls, I can get you on every talk show in this country. They'll *love* you."

"Really? Wow. I—I don't know what to say."

"We'll have to find a way to loosen you up. How are you on-camera, anyway?"

"Pretty good," I said. "I've done TV interviews before."

"Trevor, please," Shanna said. "If this morning's news is any indication, I'm sorry to say you're not the ideal candidate. More importantly, Kitty—"

Kitty held up her hand. "Shanna, if you're thinking of volunteering yourself, I've been in this business long enough to know it just won't work. We need someone, well, you know, young. And the camera adds pounds."

I could feel the heat of Shanna's glare from where I sat.

"I have no intention of volunteering, Kitty," she said, measuring her words. "But this conversation is pointless because we're not going on any talk show circuit."

"Correct," said Kitty. "Not right away, anyway. First we negotiate an exclusive with one of the big guys. We give them an all-access pass for a limited period in return for a whack of cash, then we let the floodgates open."

"I heard *Star* magazine pays big bucks," said Tony, eyes glazed.

"Spotlight Entertainment pays more than anyone," said Kitty. "They have an audience in the millions when you combine the magazine, TV show, and website. The chief entertainment correspondent, Nigel Thoroughbred, happens to be a *very* close friend." She stabbed her tongue inside her mouth in a lewd suggestion. "Trevor, I introduced you at the party, remember? Tall, thin, anemic-looking Brit with an Adam's apple the size of my tit?"

"Yes, of course," I lied, too unnerved by the image to recall him.

"How much?" Tony asked, pulling at his goatee. "It's gotta be a lot. Right? *A lot.*"

"I bet we could get a half a mil for full access," said Kitty.

"Fuckin' A!" cried Tony, jabbing his fist in the air.

"Then we're all in agreement," said Kitty. "Nigel will wanna send a camera crew right away. Trevor, when the crew gits here, you'll need to give 'em a tour of the penthouse suite and the pool deck. Tell them everything Chelsea did and said before she died. Did you keep the contents of her trash? Did she leave beauty products behind? Any meds?"

"She didn't exactly take anything with her," I said. "It's locked up, and I certainly won't be showing it to a TV crew."

"Tell them what her last meal was!" Tony shouted. "Tabloids *love* shit like that."

"Fantastic idea, Tony," said Kitty. "We can ask the chef to prepare it for the shoot."

I envisioned the on-camera interview: "Her last meal? I believe it was Jack Daniels and cocaine. Last words? 'Whenever I fucking feel like it.' Last actions? She got wasted, trashed her suite, broke the $5,500 coffee table, falsely accused an employee of creepy behavior, brushed up on some hate literature, and then leapt off the balcony."

"I don't think this is a good idea," I said.

Kitty continued, flapping her arms excitedly. "As soon as the exclusive expires, we'll launch a PR initiative to target every media outlet in the country. By that time, this li'l boutique hotel is gonna be a household name!"

"Fucking *awesome!*" cried Tony, clasping his hands together in rapture.

"This is disgraceful," Shanna said quietly.

All three of us turned to her.

"What did you say?" said Kitty, scrunching up her face.

Shanna gave her a withering look. "This is the most outrageous, unscrupulous, disgusting display of opportunism I've ever encountered. Kitty, if you think—"

Relieved to hear Shanna's opposition but fearing her confrontational approach would only compel Kitty to dig in her heels, I stood up, cutting in. "I think what Shanna's trying to say, Kitty, is we fear this might be going in the wrong direction. Wouldn't it be prudent to take a more discreet approach, to take a higher road, to …?"

Shanna stood up next to me. "I think what Trevor's trying to say, Kitty, is you're a fucking idiot."

Kitty clutched her chest. "Well, I *never!*"

"Trevor and I are hoteliers, not hyenas," Shanna continued. "Our commitment is to the comfort and well-being of our guests. Chelsea Fricks was one of those guests—our guest of *honor*, in fact. It doesn't matter how or why she died, it only matters that she died while under our care. We share some of the responsibility here, and we're not about to twist the story to make ourselves look like heroes."

"Shanna, Shanna, *Shanna*," Kitty said, also rising. "Evidently, you don't know the first thing about PR in this town. Hotels leak information about celebrity guests all the time. Celebrities encourage it. You think all those photos of stars leaving hotels and restaurants looking perfect are candid? They're staged, all of 'em."

Tony leapt to his feet. "Yeah! Chelsea agreed to let us publicize her appearance! She signed a contract!"

"A contract to exploit her *live* appearance," Shanna said, "not her tragic death. Tony, there will be no spokesperson, no publicity campaign, no tours showing close-ups of the toilet seat Chelsea sat on. We will issue a brief statement expressing our profound regret over her death and extending our thoughts and prayers to her loved ones. Then we will turn our backs on this feeding frenzy and focus on the business of running a hotel."

"Why, that's insane!" cried Kitty. "You'll be missing out on a once-in-a-lifetime opportunity." She turned to me. "Trevor, I know *you* understand the risks involved."

"I'm sorry, Kitty. I agree with Shanna."

Kitty let out a huff. "Well, then, you people don't need me. It's my job to put the spotlight on your business, not to take it off. Do you hear this nonsense, Tony?"

Tony's eyes darted from Kitty to Shanna to me. He opened his mouth and closed it. He licked his lips. "We can't say anything?" he asked Shanna. "Not even a little piece on *Spotlight Tonight*?"

"*Nothing*," she replied firmly.

"What about *Larry King*?" he said. "What if I go on just to set the record straight? Kitty said he might be—"

"For God's sake, Tony, where's your sense of decency?"

"I warn you," said Kitty, "not cooperating with the media in this town is dangerous. I learned a long time ago that if I don't feed 'em tidbits about my celebrity clients and stage photo ops for them, they do the research themselves, and that's plum dangerous. That's how pictures of stars stumbling out of a nightclub at four AM high on ecstasy show up in *Spotlight* magazine. If you don't go on the offensive, the media is gonna eat y'all alive. And I can't promise I'll be around to pick up the pieces."

A look of alarm came over Tony's face. "What do you mean, eat us alive?"

"They won't, Tony," Shanna assured him. "In a matter of days this will all blow over. We'll be remembered for our dignity and compassion. Wouldn't your friend Chelsea want it that way?"

"*Chelsea*?" Kitty cried, letting out a cackle. "She'd be the first person to exploit her own death!"

"Shut up, Kitty," said Shanna. "Well, Tony? It's your hotel."

Tony leaned back in his chair and stroked his goatee. I was certain he would side with Kitty. He was too much of an opportunist. But he surprised me.

"Maybe you're right," he said. There was great pain in his expression. "*However,*" he added, jabbing his finger at Shanna and me, "if this blows up in our face and my business suffers, it'll cost you your jobs. Understand?"

Shanna nodded without hesitation. "Of course." She turned to me.

"It won't, Tony," I said, masking my alarm. "I promise."

8

Not the Ritz-Fucking-Carlton

"We're live at the posh Hotel Cinema in Hollywood, California," Ashlee White, co-host of *Spotlight Tonight*, shouted into the camera. "Here, less than twenty-four hours ago, Chelsea Fricks, the toast of Tinseltown, took a fatal leap from the balcony of her lavish fifth-floor penthouse suite. It was a bizarre incident that some are saying was suicide, while others believe it was a publicity stunt gone terribly wrong. The Los Angeles Police Department remains tight-lipped on the investigation, leaving Chelsea's shattered fans struggling for answers to this senseless death. Meanwhile, it's business as usual at Hollywood's newest star-studded hotel, where hundreds of hopefuls are lined down the street hoping to rub shoulders with the megawatt celebrities now partying it up in the hotel's exclusive restaurant and lounge."

Watching from the hotel entrance, I cringed. So this was what Kitty meant by a dangerous game. I felt the urge to march over and set the record straight, to tell Ashlee we had, in fact, contemplated shutting down Action and Scene to honor Chelsea's memory. But Shanna and I lost that battle, overruled by Tony Cavalli, who was unwilling to sacrifice the revenues. I had hoped it would be a quiet night, that club-goers would be deterred, but the opposite seemed to be taking place. Sydney Cheevers had secured an impressive list of the rich and famous.

After the PR meeting, Kitty Caine drafted a statement, which Shanna and I rewrote before giving her the green light. The moment she sent it out, our phones lit up. We agreed to stick to the verbiage in the media release and refrain from further comment. So instead of interrupting Ashlee White, I remained where I was.

Earlier, Artie Truman had summoned me. "We're getting mobbed out here," he shouted. "I'm going to head down to the street to do some crowd control and make sure no hotel guests get lost in the mayhem. Can you take my place?"

From where I stood, I could see media tents, tarps, antennae, and camera equipment on the sidewalk. The nighttime was lit up by camera lights, candles, lighters, and the constant flash of cameras. Media and fans now jostled with aspiring lounge patrons. The doormen had organized them into two lines, one snaking down the left side of the semicircular driveway, the other snaking down the right side. The left line was designated the VIP line. It was the line on the right that Artie had asked me to man.

The crowd's attention was drawn to two thin, haughty-looking women making their way up the driveway in platform heels.

The paparazzi went mad.

"Give us a smile!"

"You look fabulous!"

"Soldiering on without Chelsea tonight?"

The women clipped past the line of hopefuls and were whisked into the lobby by a doorman.

It hadn't taken long for paparazzi to realize that the important people were in the line on the left. I regarded the line before me with apprehension. Dozens of expectant faces stared back. Recognizing me as the person who could get them into this magical place, they flashed obsequious grins and seductive smiles. A few rows down, a man stamped his foot impatiently and flared his nostrils like a bull about to stampede. I tried to smile reassuringly, avoiding direct eye contact. These desperate people had little hope of getting in. Tonight it was "List-only."

The concept of The List was a sham. There was no list, save for the names of two dozen friends and relatives Tony had scribbled onto a piece of hotel stationery and handed to Curtis, the head doorman. It was used to screen out what Sydney Cheevers referred to as "losers, wannabes, nobodies, groups of men, stags, crackheads, drunks, the underdressed, the badly dressed, teetotalers, the old, the unattractive, and the uncool." Anyone who fell into one of these categories was firmly and politely turned away. Only the stars, the beautiful, the rich, the famous, and the people who bought Cristal by the caseload were guaranteed passage.

To the other hopefuls in line, the doormen were apostles at the gates of heaven. Curtis had worked the LA nightclub scene for two decades. He knew the players, the troublemakers, the drug dealers, the hookers, the pimps, and the messy drunks. He shrewdly assessed each person who approached him, deciding in an instant whether he or she was worthy of getting in. Earlier, Sydney Cheevers had held court out here, red hair piled high like Marie Antoinette as she rejected undesirables with the callousness of the French queen. Appalled by her behavior, I had taken her aside to ask her to be more polite.

"Fucking relax, Trevor," she snapped. "This is a nightclub, not a food bank. If we let the losers in, the winners won't come. All the clubs do it. Like Tony said, this is a casting call for a first-rate production, not *Animal House.*"

Now, I looked down at two nerdy guys in scuffed sneakers standing before me. "Sorry, guys," I said as gently as possible, seeing myself as a teenager in the taller one. "There's a dress code in effect." The dress code was another means of screening out undesirables, although exceptions were made for the right people. I had turned away a half-dozen young men in T-shirts and baseball hats, yet inside Mark Wahlberg and Jared Leto were wearing just that. The nerds nodded eagerly, grateful even to be rejected by such a worthy establishment, and trotted down the driveway. I felt sorry for them, but I also felt a surge of power.

Next in line was a middle-aged, corpulent couple. The woman, wearing a white leisure suit with a gold lamé pattern stitched across the front, looked vaguely like Elvis. The man wore a Hawaiian shirt and khaki pants.

"I'm sorry, folks," I said. "It's List-only tonight."

"*What?*" cried the man. "We've been waiting for two hours!"

"I wish I could help, but we're at capacity."

"What about that line?" said the man, thrusting his arm in the direction of the VIP line. "How come they're getting in?"

"They're on The List," I said.

"We tried to book a room here, but you were sold out. We're at the Chateau Marmont. Our friends the Greenfields are staying here. We're supposed to meet them inside. We were on the same cruise."

I glanced over at Curtis. They didn't look the part, but they were friends of hotel guests and seemed harmless enough. Curtis gave a faint shake of the head. My heart sank. If I wanted to, I could pull rank and let them in. But I knew if Tony saw them mixing with the stylish, young crowd inside, he would have my head.

"I'm terrible sorry," I said. "I can't let you in. It's wall-to-wall in there."

The man gaped at me, disbelieving. He looked like a big executive who was used to getting what he wanted. He became defiant. I held my ground. His defiance turned to anger. At last he tried bargaining, pressing a twenty-dollar bill into my hand, which I handed back. The poor fellow was going through the five stages of grief.

Finally, acceptance. "I guess we're too old," he muttered to his wife, flashing me a soul-destroying scowl and pulling his wife down the driveway.

Watching them leave, I was filled with self-loathing. The line moved forward, and hundreds of eyes burned into me. A petite young lady with long, wavy dark hair marched up the driveway, bypassing the line, and straight up to me. She was wearing a sparkly silver dress that revealed delicate brown shoulders. A tiny silver bow was tied in her hair.

"Hiya, cutie!" she said, touching my forearm. "Mind if I squeeze in? I'm meeting friends. I'm, like, totally late!" She fluttered her eyes and smiled, displaying perfect teeth.

I decided an exception was in order. I reached down to unhook the rope.

Curtis was over in a flash. "Sorry, ma'am. List-only tonight."

She flashed him a haughty look and turned to me. "Please?" she pleaded.

I looked at Curtis. "Can't we make an exception? She's—I mean …"

He crossed his arms. "Good night, ma'am."

With a huff, she spun around and clipped away in her heels. I watched her go. Her long, dark hair swung back and forth across her open-backed dress.

Nancy.

My heart jolted. I turned to Curtis angrily. "Was that necessary? She was perfect."

He whispered in my ear. "She's a prostitute. She preys on men, makes them fall in love with her, then takes their money and disappears."

"You're kidding."

He shook his head.

"I don't want to play Steve Rubell anymore. Can you take over?"

"Sure."

As I turned to go inside, a deep female voice called my name. Surprised that anyone would know me in the crowd, I turned around. A pale-faced woman with gnarly black hair was pushing her way toward me, thrusting a large red leather purse into the air. The other arm pressed a cell phone against her ear. For a brief, eerie moment, I thought it was Chelsea Fricks—a haggard, disheveled Chelsea with dyed black hair. When she stepped into the light, I realized it was Moira Schwartz. She looked up from the phone as she reached me. A crude smear of red lipstick covered her lips.

Curtis hurried over to head her off, but I stopped him.

"It's okay," I told him. "I'll handle this. You know who she is, don't you?"

"Who doesn't? She's a royal pain in the ass. But we don't need to put up with her B.S. anymore. Without Chelsea, she's a nobody. I don't want her in here."

"Don't worry. I don't either." I walked over and blocked Moira's path.

She stopped inches from me. "Yeah, anyway, whatever, like I even care," she said into her cell phone and hung up. She looked up. "Trevor, how *are* you? You're looking well."

"Hello, Miss Schwartz."

"Please, call me Moira." She parted her lips into what I gathered was a smile—an expression that clearly did not come easy. "This place is sure busy," she said. "You must be pleased."

"Is there something I can help you with?" I asked.

She held up a finger and put the phone to her ear again. "Hi. Yeah, I'm here now. No, wait for me, I'll be right in. Ashton and Demi are meeting me here later." She hung up. When she saw that I was still blocking her path, a flicker of annoyance passed over her face. "Would you mind stepping aside? I'm in a hurry."

"I'm surprised to see you out tonight," I said, not moving.

She sighed. "I'm meeting some people who want me to rep them. They're *big*, if you know what I mean." Her phone must have rung again because she rolled her eyes and flipped it open. "Moira Schwartz Media Group, this is Moira … Huh? … I just got here. I'm talking to the manager … I know, there's a huge line. Tell Leo to come to the front and ask for Trevor Lambert. He'll let him in … Okay, see you soon." She closed the phone again. "Leo DiCaprio is here. *Apparently* he wants to me to represent him. Um, do you mind?" She waved her hand at me as if to swat a fly.

"Are you on The List, Moira?"

"Are you kidding me?"

"We're full," I said. "I'm sorry. I can't let you in."

"Don't be ridiculous. You know who I am."

"Yes, I do." Moira had been a nightmare from the first time Tony asked me to call her about Chelsea's fee. If I let her in, she would only create havoc.

"You're telling me after all the publicity I'm getting you, you're not going to let me in?"

"Publicity?"

"*Everyone* is talking about this hotel. I'm the one who convinced Chelsea to make an appearance."

"And throw herself off the balcony?"

Her eyes snapped as though I had slapped her.

I felt instantly remorseful. Regardless of her rude manner, she had just experienced a traumatizing incident. "I guess I'm just surprised to see you out tonight."

She lowered her eyes. "Do you know how hard it is to sit home by yourself, haunted by images of someone you love dying, feeling like it's your fault?"

In fact, I did. "I'm sorry for your grief, Moira. But I can't let you in."

"Actually, I need to talk to you," she said. She glanced over both shoulders and leaned toward me. "It's about last night. There's something you should know."

"Oh?"

"We can't talk here. Inside."

I searched her eyes, trying to determine if she was telling the truth. "Fine," I said, stepping aside. "Wait for me inside the door. I'll be there in a second."

I started to follow her when I heard someone else call my name. Cleopatra from KCAL was back, waving a microphone in the air.

Pretending I didn't see her, I slipped into the hotel.

★ ★ ★ ★ ★

Moira wasn't waiting. I had a cursory look around for her and then decided to find my mother. Earlier in the evening I had stopped by her table in Scene and promised to join her and Bruce for a drink later. It was now after eleven PM, and I doubted she was still around. Dinner service in Scene was over, and the restaurant, lounge, and lobby had morphed into one large nightclub. The music was deafening.

It was shocking to observe Hotel Cinema's transformation from quiet daytime hotel to raucous nightclub, but I wasn't entirely unprepared. Tony had shared his vision on my first day, and on his advice I checked out several local hotels with a similar concept: the Mondrian, the W, the Roosevelt, the Standard, the Viceroy. I was seduced by the young, fashionable crowds, the moody chill music, and the sexy ambience. But it was one thing to be a patron, another to be a guest—and yet another to be an employee. As I passed the front desk, I saw Simka hunched over, the telephone plastered to her ear. Next to her, David was politely asking two women to remove their cocktails from the desk. The music was unacceptably loud, I decided, and veered toward the deejay booth, located near the entrance to Action.

"Huh?" shouted the deejay over the din, removing his earphones.

"Can you please turn it down?" I repeated, jabbing my thumb down.

He looked perplexed, as though unable to fathom why anyone would want the volume reduced. Yet he knew who I was and did not argue. I watched him reach for the volume dial and move it the width of a hair. I jabbed my thumb down again. He complied—another hair. He put his headphones back on and resumed his work.

"Trevor, darling, over here!"

Mom was standing at a tall cocktail table near the center of the lounge. I waved and fought my way over.

She threw out both arms for a hug. "Darling, how wonderful to see you!"

"How was dinner?" I asked, nodding to Bruce.

"Fabulous!" Her nasal voice suggested she'd had more than one of the lime-colored martinis she was clutching. She looked youthful and elegant in a simple yellow dress, a thick white belt fastened around her tiny waist. Her thin white-blond hair was straight but stylishly cut. "Did I tell you Bruce took me on a tour of Paramount Studios? They've built entire neighborhoods on the lot! All the buildings are façades, though. They look so authentic on the outside, but there's nothing on the inside."

"Kind of like this crowd," Bruce said with a wry smile. "This is quite a scene, Trevor. You've done well."

"I can't take any credit," I said. "It's all the work of publicists and promoters."

"And Chelsea Fricks," he said. "I heard you hired Sydney Cheevers. Be careful. She knows how to deliver the stars, but she'll stomp all over everyone else in the process."

"Thanks for the heads-up," I said.

Bruce introduced two men, whom I remembered from last night: Brad, in his early forties and meticulously groomed, with thick silver jewelry on his fingers and wrists; and Joey, a bit older, with aviator glasses and a sculptured, hairless chest displayed through his open shirt.

"Brad and Joey couldn't get in," Mom said, pulling me aside. She took a generous swig of her drink. "I had to sneak them in through the back gate."

"You *what*?"

"Don't worry, they're cool."

"Mom, I can't have you breaking the rules here," I said, half-jesting. "If a bouncer throws you out, you're on your own."

"Don't worry, I can take care of myself." Her drink sloshed precariously as she pulled me aside. "Did you get a chance to look at that book?"

Mom read self-help books voraciously and was always trying to convert me to whichever faith she was following at the moment. Her missionary work had begun the moment she climbed into my car at LAX. "I brought you something," she said with a knowing nod, sliding a package over the console of the BMW convertible.

"Porn?" I asked, glancing down at the brown paper bag. "Aw Mom, you're the best."

"It's a book. A very good book."

"Another book to help me get through postmenopausal depression?"

"This one's different. It's a small book, and deceptively simple, but it contains a message so powerful it may change your life. It changed mine."

I paid the parking attendant and drove out of the lot. "Not another edition of *Who Moved My Cheese*? I told you I'm not interested in learning lessons from rats."

"They were mice, Trevor. This book is far more sophisticated."

"If it's *The Secret*, I'm going to toss it onto the freeway right now."

"You should have more faith in me." She pulled a hardcover book from the bag and handed it to me. "It's about our need to deal with unresolved issues in our past."

"Like how I was neglected by my mother as a child?"

"We often have issues we think we've dealt with, but we haven't. They prevent us from moving forward. Before we can live life to the fullest, we must take a step back and resolve our issues. When we do, we are free to progress at a pace previously unimaginable."

"*Two Steps Forward*," I said, glancing down at the cover as I stopped for a red light. I flipped it over and regarded the fiftyish woman on the back cover. Resting her chin on her knuckle, she wore a confident, self-satisfied smile. "Apparently, for Sonia Druthers, taking a step backward in time means getting a facelift," I said, tossing it down. "Can't wait."

"It's helped me immensely in dealing with the loss of your father."

"Only twenty-five years later? It's a miracle."

"It would have happened a lot sooner if this book was around." She was quiet for a moment. "Maybe it will help you recover from Nancy."

I swerved onto the 405 North. Behind us, a car honked. "I've recovered from Nancy."

"You don't still think of her all the time?"

Rain splattered on the windshield. I pressed a button to close the roof. "No."

"Have you been dating anyone?"

"Off and on." Another lie.

"So it's just work, then? Work, work, work?"

"Well, there's also work."

She didn't crack a smile. For the rest of the trip she said nothing.

Now, she was waiting for my answer. Syrupy green liquid dribbled onto her hand. I reached for her drink and took a sip, quickly handing it back. "My God, that's vile."

"It's quite lovely, I think," she said. "So? Did you start the book?"

"You gave it to me yesterday, Mom. I've been a little busy."

"Make time for it," she said, giving my arm a squeeze, as though passing on a very important secret that concerned the fate of the universe.

"I'll do my best."

Turning back to Bruce and his friends, she announced, "Gentlemen, I'll have you know my son is a hero. He jumped in the pool last night to save Chelsea Fricks."

"*Mom.*"

"Don't be so modest, dear. Shanna told me everything about your valiant attempt."

"I'm not being modest. We can't talk about this here."

"Why? Everyone else is."

"Joey and I saw the whole thing," said Brad. "We were on the pool deck when it happened. It looked like someone was chasing her."

I opened my mouth to quash that theory but reconsidered, realizing it would sound like I was covering something up.

"Bruce and I missed all the excitement," Mom said. "We were in the fitness room getting a workout."

"Too much information, Mom."

Behind me, I felt a tug on my arm.

It was Reginald Clinton, the hotel's director of food and beverage. "Tony Cavalli needs to speak with you urgently," he said.

Promising I'd be back, I made my way toward Scene. The music was even louder now. I had to resist covering my ears. A woman handed me her empty glass. Another tried to order a drink. A man asked if I could get his friend in. My role as hotel manager had devolved into nightclub attendant.

Tony was sitting with an entourage that included girlfriend Liz, twins Enzo and Lorenzo, Lorenzo's fiancée Rosario, and a few others I didn't recognize. None of the actors whose company he craved were present, which might have explained his foul mood.

"You tell the deejay to turn the music down?" he yelled, lifting his bloated body from his seat and slamming his hand on the table.

"The front desk staff couldn't hear anything."

"What the hell is wrong with you? Don't you get it? The music is *supposed* to be loud."

"Our hotel guests are paying upward of $500 a night for rooms," I countered, gesturing in the direction of the rooms overlooking the pool deck. "How are they supposed to sleep?"

"This isn't the Ritz-Fucking-Carlton, Trevor! They're not here to sleep! You think they rent a cabana room to stay in and watch *Animal Planet*? They're here for the *party*."

"Not everyone is. We've had several noise complaints already. Have you any idea how thin the walls are in this building? Did you know"—I leaned toward him—"the Fratelli brothers didn't replace some of the original fire-damaged beams? This place is built on a rotten foundation. It's a fire trap."

Tony's face turned scarlet. "Don't you *ever* say that again! This building is solid! If people complain about noise, they don't belong here. Guests reserve rooms to get priority access to the bar. We don't want them in their rooms reading the Bible, we want them down here drinking and spending money."

Beside him, Liz nodded, eyes fixed on the table. I wondered if she rarely looked me in the eye because she was ashamed of the hotel's poor construction.

"Fine," I said. "But don't blame me if guests demand a refund."

"There will be no refunds, Trevor. *No refunds!* If they don't like it, tell them to go to the Beverly Wilshire. Go tell Curtis I want another hundred people in here now. This place isn't nearly crowded enough. While you're at it, Kanye West is at the back of Action in the VIP section. I sent over a bottle of Cristal. Go tell him it's from me, the hotel owner, and bring him to my table. Liz wants to meet him."

"Me? Why can't you do it yourself?"

"That's not the way it's done around here. People send their people. While you're at it, stop by Kate Moss's table and bring her over too."

"Tony, I'm not going to disturb celebrities on your behalf. This is supposed to be a refuge from that kind of attention. If you want to meet them, do it yourself."

"You're chicken, aren't you? Where's Shanna? She'll do it. She's got *cojones*."

Apparently he didn't know about Shanna's affliction. "She was having dinner with a group of meeting planners earlier, but I think she left." In fact, she had hightailed it the moment the bar crowd started arriving.

A pimped-out man with a shaved head came up behind Tony and grabbed him by the shoulders. "Well, if it ain't Conrad Fucking Hilton!"

Tony spun around. "Arnon, you fucking homo!"

I took the opportunity to slip away. As I made my way out of Scene, doorman Curtis intercepted me.

"Someone is demanding to see you at the front door," he growled.

My eyes lit up. Had the girl with the silver bow in her hair come back to rescue me from this nightmare? Did I really care if she was a hooker?

He handed me a business card.

I looked down and back up at Curtis. "At midnight?"

"He says it's urgent."

★ ★ ★ ★ ★

When I arrived at the front lobby, Detective Stavros Christakos was grinning ear to ear. Three people stood behind him, gazing around in awe: a red-haired man even shorter and stockier than the detective, a tall and lanky man in a fedora, and a stout, dark-haired young woman who looked like Stavros in a curly wig.

"Trevor, my man!" Stavros called out. "How the heck are ya?" He slapped my arm and pumped my hand like we were old friends. He was stylishly dressed in a crisp white shirt with a scorpion stitched over the left chest. Around his neck hung another vintage police medallion. He looked taller tonight. I glanced at his shiny black boots and saw a thick heel.

"How can I help you, Detective?" I asked. I remembered I was angry over the way he had interrogated my staff.

"Meet my friends, Gustavo and Robbie, and my little sister, Star. Trevor's the big cheese around here, guys, so no funny business. And don't give him no attitude." He let out a chuckle and looked around. "Look at this place! Didn't I tell you guys it was going to be hot?"

The stench of booze wafted to my nostrils. Something told me this wasn't a business call.

Star stared wide-eyed into the crowd. "Oh. My. God. The cast of *The OC* is here."

"No way," said Gustavo, standing on his toes to follow her gaze.

"Over there!" Robbie pointed into the crowd. "Let's go see if we can meet them!"

"Detective?" I said. "You said it was urgent?"

Stavros tore his eyes away. "Yeah, right. We need to talk. Come with me." He placed his hand on my back and steered me not to a quiet place but directly into the crowd. "First let's get a drink. I'm dyin' a thirst." He veered toward the *OC* cast and stopped to scratch his ear.

Star bumped into me from behind.

I grabbed the detective by the arm and pulled him along to the bar.

The queue was a dozen people thick. "You must have pull around here," said Stavros, bypassing the line and pulling me to the side, where he climbed onto the leg of a stool and waved down a bartender.

"Evening, Trevor," said Carl. "You calling it a night?"

"Not quite," I said. "This is Detective Christakos. He's on official business, apparently, and he and his friends would like a drink."

"Sure thing. What can I get you, Detective?"

Stavros hopped onto the bar, balancing on his elbows, legs dangling in the air. "Two double Tanqueray 10 on the rocks, a Grey Goose Red Bull, and a peach daiquiri." He turned to me. "What you having, boss?"

"Nothing, thanks."

"What? Come on, it's Saturday night!"

"I'm working."

While Carl went to make the drinks, Stavros frowned at me like a concerned father. "You ever take time off?"

"As long as I'm here, I'm working. What about you, aren't you on duty?"

"I'm always on duty. In fact, I can't help but note this place is over its occupancy limit. Not my department, but one call and I could have this place shut down." He eyed two young ladies a few seats away. "And I could bust those two underage hotties drinking hornytinis over there." He lifted his hand to wave at them, but they adeptly ignored him. He turned to me and broke into a grin, teeth glowing violet in the gelled lighting.

The bartender set the drinks down before us, and Stavros relayed them to his companions, keeping the peach daiquiri for himself. He lifted his drink to toast me. "Keep these coming, and I'll try to overlook these violations," he said with a wink. He took a gulp and let out a gasp, pressing his thumb and forefinger into his eye sockets as though having slammed back a shot of tequila. "I needed that."

Star burst through the crowd and grabbed his arm. "Nick Lachey is here! Let's see if we can meet him! Can we do the badge routine again?"

"Gimme a sec, sweetie. I'll come find you."

"I'll be over there, hopefully necking with him."

"So who else is here?" Stavros asked me, surveying the crowd.

"As in…?"

"Stars, celebrities, centerfolds, twin hotties—you know. Are Kate and Ashley here? How about Angelina? I bet she's here. She ask for me? Come on, I know she was asking for me."

He found himself far more entertaining than I did.

"Is that Moira Schwartz?" he said, pointing into the crowd.

Moira was weaving her way through the crowd, cell phone permanently fixed against her ear. She appeared to be searching for someone. Wondering if it might be me, I made eye contact. She quickly turned away, disappearing into the crowd.

"She been here long?" the detective asked.

"An hour or so. Why?"

"Just curious." He turned back to the bar and cupped his hands around his mouth. "Yo, bartender! Another round!"

"Easy on the peach daiquiris," I said.

"So I like sweet drinks," he said. "That don't make me any less of a man."

"Detective," I said, "do you want to talk or is this a social call?"

He reached up for my shoulder and led me to a quieter part of the lounge. "Okay, here's the deal. I need your help. First, I need you to put me on some sort of permanent guest list. I don't want to have to justify myself to that meathead bouncer again. Strictly for investigative purposes, of course. I have a feeling I'm going to be here a lot."

"You are? Why?" I asked, alarmed. "Do you need to broaden your investigation?"

"No, I need to broaden my network of film contacts." He squinted at me and then exploded with laughter. "Loosen up! In fact, I do need to talk to a couple of your employees."

"Haven't you harassed them enough?"

"I don't *harass*, Trevor. I merely ask questions. If my questions make them feel uncomfortable, then maybe they've got something to hide." Something caught his attention in the crowd. He lifted his hand. "Bryce! Over here!"

Bryce? I turned around and saw Bryce Davies at the center of the lounge, holding court among a group of admirers, including the two "underage hotties." He spotted the detective, scrunched his eyes, and broke into a grin.

"You're friends with Bryce Davies?" I asked, incredulous.

"I only met him this morning, but we hit it off. He's going to see about getting me a part in *Modern Loving*."

"But isn't he a suspect?"

He frowned. "A suspect?"

"With all due respect, are you here to conduct a murder investigation or to audition for parts? Because I have a hotel to run, and it's not easy surrounded by media and rabid fans. The sooner you bring this investigation to a close, the sooner I can resume doing my job."

His eyes flashed and then relaxed. "Trust me, my friend. On the surface it may look like I'm having a ball, but I'm always working." He turned back to observe Bryce.

"I see," I said, suddenly understanding. "So Bryce *is* a suspect."

"I never said that."

From where I stood, I could see Bryce's flushed cheeks, toothy grin, the glint of violet in his curly blond hair. "I can't believe he's here. His girlfriend died last night. You'd think he'd be under the bed sobbing."

"Why? That what you did?"

"Me? No, but Chelsea Fricks wasn't my girlfriend."

"I mean when your girlfriend went down on Flight 0022."

"What? How did you…?"

"I'm not as bad a detective as you think." He pointed at Bryce. "He's here because he's a nobody at home. Here he's a celebrity. LA nightlife is his stage. I have no doubt he's devastated. But he craves attention, can't live without it. This is his way of coping. Some of us thrive under the spotlight, others don't."

Not far from Bryce, Moira was skulking through the crowd. "Moira doesn't strike me as the type who thrives in the spotlight. Why is she here?"

"She's trawling for clients. She's unemployed. She even hit me up." He reached up to touch his carefully mussed hair. "She thinks I have potential."

"You bought that?"

He looked genuinely affronted. "Do I look like a fool, Trevor?"

I looked around to ensure no one was within earshot. "You still think foul play was involved?"

"Maybe."

"Then explain why you're harassing my staff when these lowlifes are running free. Aren't Bryce and Moira the most obvious suspects?"

His eyes narrowed. "Not necessarily."

Suddenly I was concerned. "Which employees do you need to talk to?"

"Ezmerelda Lopez, for one."

"Ezmerelda? Can't you leave her alone? You had her in tears today. She was convinced you think she killed Chelsea."

"Who says I don't?"

"You're not serious."

Stavros looked into the crowd. Bryce was beckoning him over. He held up his index finger and turned back to me. "I tell you, Trevor, this Lopez woman is one tough cookie. I tried to talk to her, but she clammed right up. Seems she forgot how to speak English."

"You think she witnessed something and is afraid to say?"

He shrugged. "Ever heard of the National Immigrant Solidarity Front?"

I nodded slowly.

"I did a background check on your sweet 'n innocent head house-keeper. Seems she and her husband are members."

"Ez and Felix? No. You must be mistaken."

"Remember that book in Chelsea's room? *Bleaching America*? Written by Dwight Reed?" He paused. "Ever hear rumors about Chelsea being a racist?"

"What wasn't said about her?"

"The NISF isn't too tolerant of racists. In fact, they killed Dwight Reed. Imagine the attention they could draw to their cause if they took out a big name like Chelsea Fricks. Maybe they recruited Ezmerelda to do their dirty work."

"You're not serious." I burst into laughter. "You think Ezmerelda chased Chelsea off the balcony with a butcher knife? Before or after she snorted coke on the coffee table?"

The detective reached for his drink and swallowed the contents, slamming the glass down on the table so hard it cracked. "Thanks for the drinks, Trevor. I'll be by tomorrow. Make sure she's available."

I watched him push his way into the crowd and grab Bryce Davies from behind, pulling his arms back and pretending to handcuff him. Bryce threw his head back in laughter and hugged the detective, mussing his hair.

With a sigh, I signaled Carl to bring the bill.

★ ★ ★ ★ ★

After doing my rounds, I went to find my mother to say good night but did an about-face when I saw the tall, handsome man she was chatting with: Bryce Davies. Instead, I headed toward the parking elevator.

"Trevor."

Moira Schwartz was sitting at an empty table near the entrance to Scene. She gestured me over.

"How are you," she said in her monotone voice. She tried to force a smile and flicked her hair back in a coquettish mannerism that reminded me of Chelsea but had none of the same effect.

I glanced at her clothes and hair and decided Kitty was right: if she was trying to emulate Chelsea, she had a long way to go. I took a seat across from her.

"I saw you talking to that detective," she said. "What was that all about?"

"It was purely social. Why?"

She blinked but didn't answer. "You think Kitty's a good publicist?"

"Sure."

"I'd be careful if I were you."

"If you're worried we're going to exploit Chelsea's death, don't be. We intend to remain silent on the issue."

She looked puzzled. "That's what Kitty advised you to do?"

"That's what we told her to do."

"I don't know, Trevor. That might not be the smartest strategy. Things might get ugly in the next few days." She dug into her purse and retrieved a business card, pressing it into my hand. "Kitty works hard, but she's not the smartest cow in the pasture. If you're thinking of making a change, give me a call. I'm now accepting new clients. This hotel has tons of potential. Don't blow it. I can help you make it a success."

"I think we're doing just fine," I said, nodding to the packed room.

"Tonight, maybe, but this crowd is fickle. As soon as another hot hotel or lounge opens, they'll move on. You've got to make sure the right people keep coming back."

"That's what we hired Sydney Cheevers for."

She rolled her eyes. "That hysterical control freak will self-destruct in a matter of time. Stars are only magnets for the clientele you really want. You need a base of cool, affluent, attractive people who spend lots of money."

"Tell that to Tony Cavalli," I said. "Is this what you wanted to talk to me about? A job?"

"I'm not your typical publicist, Trevor. I don't lie like everybody else. I'm not an actor, and I don't want to be an actor. I work hard. I don't drink. I don't do drugs. I don't suck off reporters for stories. I'm like a good little Jewish girl from New York, except I'm not Jewish and I'm not from New York, I'm from Portland. Maybe I rub some people the wrong way, but it's because I don't sugarcoat like a certain candy cane we both know. I know all the media, and I get results. I dedicated my entire life to Chelsea. I planned every birthday party for the past three years, huge parties with loads of media coverage, and I dedicated every ounce of my energy to ensuring everything was perfect. Try getting that kind of loyalty from Kitty Caine."

"I'm impressed, Moira, but—." I got up to leave.

"Hire me, and I'll make this hotel famous. I'll make *you* famous."

"I don't want to be famous."

"Maybe I should talk to your owner, what's his name, Tony?"

"*No*, don't talk to him," I said quickly. She was talking Tony's language. "Now if you'll excuse me…"

"Wait. That detective is a bit of a dolt, don't you think?"

"Who?"

"Detective Panagopoulos. He came to see me this afternoon. I think he thinks somebody murdered Chelsea or something. Isn't that ridiculous?"

I shrugged. "What do you think happened?"

"I don't think, I know. She committed suicide."

"What makes you so sure?" I said, sitting down again.

"I was her best friend. I think I'd know. Why, what did he say?"

"If she killed herself, how do you explain the blood in her suite?"

Her mouth fell open. "There was blood in her suite?" Her eyes looked troubled, but she remained composed. "She must have tried to stab herself. She was crazy, Trevor. I loved her, but she was crazy."

The image was disturbing. It had never occurred to me. I lifted Moira's purse from the chair beside her and set it on the table, moving next to her. "She would use a knife on herself?"

Moira swallowed. "I was keeping a close eye on her. Her behavior was so volatile lately. I checked on her around ten fifteen and she was having one of her meltdowns. She wanted to be left alone, so I returned to my room. About an hour later, I was talking to my mother on the phone when I heard a commotion on the pool deck. I went to the balcony and saw her in the pool. I ran across the hall to get Bryce.

By the time we got back to my room, she was lying on the deck with a crowd of people around her." She lowered her head. "I tried to stop her, I really did. It's all my fault."

I placed a tentative hand on her shoulder, sensing she didn't like people invading her personal space. "It's not your fault, Moira."

She began to sob. "It *is* my fault."

I began rubbing her back. "Bad things happen to good people. I know it's hard to accept, but—"

She suddenly sat up, pushing me away. "How the hell would you know? Did *your* best friend just die?"

"Of course not. I just thought…"

"Don't pretend you know what I'm going through, because you don't. Nobody does. I have to suffer through this on my own. I'm tired of being surrounded by pretenders in this town."

"I'm not pretending, Moira. I *do* know. My girl—my *fiancée*…" My words drifted off.

She looked up and blinked. "What?"

"She died in a plane crash last year." Had I ever uttered these words out loud before?

Moira regarded me in silence. Lipstick gone, her lips were as pale as the skin of her face. "I heard her screaming," she said.

"Who?"

"Chelsea. I looked out my peephole and saw someone use the eye scanner to enter the suite. A few minutes later, I heard a scream. I tried to get in through the connecting door, but it was locked. I heard a splash."

"Who? Who entered the room?"

"Your maid. I think she was stalking Chelsea."

9

Panic Room

"It's wonderful to spend time with you again," Mom said, reaching around my waist to give me a squeeze.

After an early dinner at Michael's in Santa Monica, she had insisted we leave the car on Second Avenue and go for a stroll along the boardwalk. Along the way we stopped for ice cream. The sun was beginning its descent on the horizon. I shielded my eyes as we walked, wishing I had brought my sunglasses. A warm breeze was blowing, sweeping clouds of powdered sand over the paved sidewalk. Joggers, rollerbladers, and bikers whizzed past.

"We all miss you so much in Vancouver," she said, adjusting her chic oversized sunglasses, a proud new purchase she would never be caught dead wearing back home. "You must miss it too."

"I don't miss the rain." My heart was aching for Vancouver, but I didn't want her to know. For her, everything in my life was simple and obvious. "Then move back," she would say. She would never understand why I *couldn't* go back. The city was a watery graveyard for my failures: family, school, work, relationships ... Nancy.

"Now why would *you* care about the weather? You never leave the confines of that hotel. *I'm* the sun worshipper." She turned to admire the setting sun as though to prove her claim. "Glorious, glorious sunshine. It illuminates the mind. All my epiphanies occur when the sun is on my face."

"I crave sunshine too," I said. "It's part of why I love LA. But it's intense here, more dangerous."

She turned to me, her face darkening. "Don't tell me you actually like it here?"

"Sure I do. You haven't exactly been miserable yourself."

"I'm on vacation. This is a romp. I'm simply having fun." She stopped to watch two children splashing each other in the waves. "Do you ever swim in this ocean?"

"I think I've developed a fear of water."

She turned to me with a look of surprise. Deciding I was joking, she gave a hearty laugh.

I crossed the boardwalk to a garbage receptacle. She clung to my arm, obliging me to pull her along. I disposed of my unfinished cone and wiped my hands on my jeans. I felt guilty for being so edgy and taciturn, but her visit felt staged. I knew the real reason she was here, but neither of us had broached the subject. During dinner she had buzzed around it like a wasp trying to get in the window, but I kept the window tightly closed, knowing if I let her in she might sting. Her presence was comforting, and I wanted to leave it at that.

"What do you think of the hotel?" I asked.

She was silent for a moment. "It's quite a trendy little hotspot."

"You don't like it." When I told her in December I was going back to work, she was ecstatic. When I told her I was taking a job as a hotel manager, she reacted as though I were getting back together with a girlfriend she never liked. When I told her the new job was in Los Angeles, she was inconsolable.

"I'm too old, I guess," she said. "I was sunbathing on the pool deck this afternoon, and I felt like I was on the set of a *Girls Gone Wild* video." She made a face. "I hope it's not always like that."

I grinned. "Our promoter had a gaggle of models from Ford bussed in with the promise of a barbecue, free drinks, and a deejay. It's all part of building our brand." All afternoon I had come up with various excuses for going out to the pool deck. It had required all my self-control not to gawk as models sunned themselves in string bikinis, played water volleyball, staged water fights, and rubbed suntan lotion on one another. In the late afternoon, Kitty arrived with a photographer to take shots for the hotel's publicity kit.

"I met an elderly couple at the pool, Harvey and Stella Greenfield from Key West. Stella and I were lamenting the loss of modesty in young women these days. Then Harvey took off his shirt, and I don't know what was more offensive: the girls' fake breasts or his fleshy ones."

I laughed. "The Greenfields are here all week. Tony Cavalli is furious they got a reservation. He wants us to figure out a way to screen out unattractive people. Is it the fitness room you don't like? I can see about moving you."

"Oh no, I wouldn't think of it. It's the best room in the house! I'm getting fabulous workouts. There's nothing like waking up to an exercise ball in your face to motivate you." She was silent for a moment, contemplative. "There's something unsettling about that hotel that I can't quite put my finger on."

"A woman died there two nights ago."

"Perhaps that's it. To me it feels sad."

"Sad?"

"It used to be an old motel, didn't it?"

"Years ago, yes. The Tropi-Cal Hollywood Motor Inn. It caught fire."

"It reminds me of one of those pathetic women on *Extreme Makeover*. She's looked like a train wreck all her life and then she gets stretched and tucked and all tarted up to look like Cinderella. She has a reveal party and declares that her life has changed forever. But she hasn't changed on the inside. Soon nature reasserts its dominance, and she reverts to her former self, inside and out."

"That's quite a pessimistic assessment," I said, feeling hurt, as though she had just insulted my girlfriend. My mother had a way of fishing out my greatest fears and probing them as they flopped around and gasped for air.

"I guess I'm just more of a Four Seasons gal."

"Have you ever even stayed at a Four Seasons, Mom?"

"Of course I have. When you and the girls were young, your father surprised me with a trip to Toronto for our tenth anniversary. We left you with your Aunt Germaine. He reserved a room at the Four Seasons Inn on the Park and arranged for champagne to be waiting on our arrival. I was over the moon. The ice in the bucket had melted, but the champagne was still cold, and we drank the whole bottle. Then we went downtown for dinner at Diana Sweets and a show at the Elgin Theatre. What a night we had! I went back to Toronto last fall—remember? Just before I went back to work. Everything is gone now: the Inn on the Park, Diana Sweets, the Elgin Theatre."

"I didn't know Dad was the romantic type."

"He wasn't. I always lamented that he had all the irritating qualities of a Frenchman—arrogance, superiority, disdain for anything not French—but none of the redeeming qualities, like romanticism and a taste for the finer things in life. Occasionally he surprised me. But that happened less and less."

I didn't know what to say. For years after Dad's death, Mom refused to talk about him. He dropped dead of a ruptured aorta at home one morning when I was twelve years old. After an initial mourning period she clammed up, falling into a walking coma, going through the motions but not really being there. It was only a few years ago that she emerged. By then, my sisters and I were so accustomed to not talking about him that it was awkward and difficult to indulge her.

An elderly couple walked by arm in arm and smiled at us, but Mom didn't notice. She was looking out to the ocean with a melancholy smile. In a few minutes, the sun would make contact with the horizon. A quarter century had passed, and she hadn't replaced him. I put my arm around her, averting my eyes from the burning sun.

"Did they determine what happened to Chelsea Fricks?" she asked.

"I don't believe so."

"Is it true, what they're saying on the news? It was some sort of publicity stunt?"

"I don't think so."

"Maybe she was on angel dust or something."

"Angel dust? Have you been watching *Starsky & Hutch* reruns again?"

"Whatever they call it now—ecstasy, heroin, crack. I'm a nurse. I'm fully aware of the drugs people are taking nowadays. There's all sorts of gossip flying around the hotel. Drugs, booze, tantrums, suicide, foul play. Mrs. Greenfield told me she watched the whole drama play out from her room like an episode of *CSI*. She swears she saw stab wounds on her body. A gal at the front desk said your head of housekeeping may have been involved."

"One of my employees said that? Who?"

"I think her nametag said Jane. She sounds like she's from New York."

"Janie Spanozzini was *gossiping* with you?"

"Relax, Trevor. She knows I'm your mother. What do *you* think happened?"

I thought about my conversations with Detective Christakos and Moira Schwartz last night. Ezmerelda a member of a terrorist organization … Ezmerelda pretending not to speak English … Ezmerelda stalking Chelsea Fricks. I tried to conjure up an image of her chasing Chelsea around with a butcher knife. The prospect was laughable, but disturbing nonetheless, particularly if employees were spreading rumors. I had seen her several times today, and she was back to her smiling self. Fearing I would upset her, I opted not to ask any questions. The detective hadn't come by. I hoped the investigation had taken a different turn.

"A lot of people think it was suicide," I said.

"It doesn't quite add up, though, does it? What a strange way to kill oneself. If it was foul play and I was the investigator, I know who I'd go after."

"Who?"

"The boyfriend. It's always the boyfriend. I met Bryce Davies last night. Bruce introduced us. They worked together on that dreadful *Three's Company* remake. I can't imagine what possessed him to be out in a bar so soon after losing his girlfriend. Everyone knows how poorly he treated her. If it turns out she killed herself, I bet he drove her to it. I'm not fooled by his cover-boy looks. Men are all the same; they're insensitive to women's needs. It's all about ego, work, and sex. Women need affection and conversation."

I was about to remind her she was talking to a man when I realized her comments were directed at me. I chose to disregard them. "I don't care what happened," I said. "This is my first GM position, and I want to prove myself, but it's hard when the hotel is overrun with star-struck cops and two-faced actors and prying media and unscrupulous publicists. I want them all to go away."

She turned to regard me, waiting for me to meet her gaze, but I resisted. "Would you like some advice, Trevor?"

"Not particularly."

She sighed. We walked in silence for a few minutes. I knew she was hurt, but I was afraid that whatever advice she had would anger me and I'd be compelled to say something hurtful. Mom loved to dispense advice. If she couldn't get her message across indirectly through her self-help books, then she took a more direct approach. Her meddling had caused trouble between Nancy and me on more than one occasion. An incident I had still not forgiven her for came to mind. Nancy and I were staying at Mom's house while Mom was undergoing chemo treatments. We had bought a condo in Yaletown but had not told Mom, preferring to stay with her during the therapy. Mom and Nancy went shopping for a wig while I went to a job interview at the Fairmont Waterfront. When I got back, Nancy seemed off. She suggested we drive to Yaletown and go for a walk along the False Creek seawalk.

A few minutes into our stroll, Nancy said, "Your mom gave me some advice."

"Oh? I warned you she's an authority on everything."

"She told me about 'the other woman.'"

I covered my head in mock panic. "She told you about my girl-friend?"

Nancy nodded, playing along, a bemused smile creeping over her lips. But her gait seemed stiff. "She said she's glamorous and has expensive tastes and is highly demanding of your time. She told me I can't compete so don't bother trying. She feeds you and cleans for you and even does your laundry."

"I'd like to meet this woman."

"Of course, she was talking about the hotel business. She says that it's your first love, that it will always come first, and that I should be prepared for that."

My jaw clenched. "She told you that?"

"Don't be mad. She didn't tell me anything I don't already know."

"That's all changed, Nancy," I said, stopping to take her hands. "You changed me. Wherever I work, a job will be just a job. You're my number-one priority. I want us to have a family."

Her eyes flickered.

"You don't want kids?" I said.

Her eyes grew watery. "Maybe someday…" She forced a smile. "A boy."

"And a girl?"

"Just a boy."

We continued walking, exchanging a few bad jokes about the "other woman" before the conversation moved to more mundane topics: the stillness of the water, how black it looked in the afternoon sun, the bright colors we would paint our new condo. Later I admonished my mother. Was she trying to scare Nancy away? "To the contrary," she said. "I hope you'll marry her someday. But a woman needs to know everything about a man before she makes that commitment. Nancy needs to understand how important your career is to you." Little did Mother realize she had fed into one of Nancy's greatest fears. My life had been admittedly one-dimensional when we first met, but she had helped me find balance. I quit my job, and we took several months off, traveled, spent time with my family and friends, went to the theatre, played tennis, went rollerblading on the seawall. She would have been content never to go back to work, but I grew antsy. She worried I would become a workaholic again. I was determined to prove otherwise. I never got the chance.

Last night, talking with Moira, I had called Nancy my fiancée. "Girlfriend" didn't adequately describe our bond. I had wanted to call Nancy my wife. *Let's wait and see,* she had said. In time, I would have convinced her. Did I dare tell Mother? Why? It would only upset her and lead to a barrage of questions I couldn't answer.

"You know what day today is," my mother said.

"Yes."

"One whole year. Can you believe it? That poor, sweet, lovely girl."

"Mom, please … don't."

"There was a spread in the *New York Times* today about the anniversary. Did you see it?"

"You know I stopped reading that stuff long ago."

She stopped walking and turned toward the ocean as the base of the sun touched the horizon. Her hand reached for mine. "Darling, I have something I need to tell you. A man from the flight commission called. They found the fuselage. It's been dredged from the bottom of the sea."

A half-mile out, I could see the silhouette of a kayaker fighting the current. How many hours had I sat on that log in English Bay facing this same direction, eyes searching the ocean as though Nancy might appear on a life raft, somehow having drifted from Atlantic to Pacific? I thought of the ring. Where was it now? Was it still in its box, or had it somehow broken free?

I tried to pull my hand away, but her grip tightened. "They found remains of passengers still strapped in their seats. They're performing autopsies."

"Oh God. Please stop."

"No, Trevor, I won't. If they find her … it will bring you closure."

"I *have* closure, Mom."

She turned to me. "Closure isn't caging your emotions like wild animals. Closure is coming to terms with them, taming them, and moving on."

"Can we head back now?" I turned toward the car, but she remained where she was, watching the sun through her dark glasses.

"I think about her every day," she said. "She was perfect for you, Trevor: a free spirit, adventurous, a tough little cookie. She sat with me through every one of my chemo treatments. I think she was horrified by my illness, couldn't bear to see my suffering, but she never let it show. Every time she entered the room, it was like someone pulled open the drapes and let the sunshine in. Yet when I tried to nurse her through that dreadful chest cold, she wouldn't let me, couldn't stand me watching her suffer, wouldn't even let me drive her to her appointment with Dr. Rutherford. What an indomitable spirit."

Whereas I had been incapacitated by fear in the face of my mother's illness, Nancy had known intuitively what to say and do. Shortly after Mom had her breast removed, Nancy and I moved to Vancouver and into her house. Nancy took charge at once, stocking the kitchen with nourishing foods, shuttling Mom to and from her chemotherapy appointments, monitoring her medication. To ensure my mother reserved all her strength for her recovery, Nancy worked herself into mental and physical exhaustion.

One day, after I expressed my gratitude once again, Nancy had given me some rare insight into her past.

"When I was sixteen, my mother died of lung disease," she said. "It was an insidious, slow-moving disease. Over time, her lungs became so clogged they collapsed. It was heartbreaking to see her suffer, but it was equally painful to see how it destroyed my father. I would have done anything to spare him that pain."

Seven months after Nancy's mother passed away, her father died, only thirty-six years of age. "My grandmother said it was a heart attack," she told me, "but I knew he died of a broken heart. I felt so helpless back then. With your mother, there is hope. I can make a difference."

Only when the chemo treatments were finished and Mom had regained her strength did Nancy agree to move into our new condo. But first we decided to go to Europe, where Nancy could recover and I could enjoy a final break before starting my new job.

"I'm sorry, Trevor," Mom said. "I know it's hard to hear. I guess I still can't believe she's gone. I was getting used to having her around."

She wanted me to come to her, but I remained where I was, my back to the sun, hands thrust in my pockets. "Maybe it's you who needs closure."

"I wanted to be with you today," she said. "I didn't want you to be alone."

"It's good to have you here," I conceded. I had been dreading this day for weeks, but the tsunami of grief I had expected had yet to arrive. Now, the day was almost over. In a few minutes, the sun would disappear. A full year would have passed.

"Why are you so reticent? It helps to talk."

"Like you talked about Dad all the time?"

"I know I waited a long time, but it's never too late." She came to me and clasped my hands. "I've been there, Trevor. I lost your father. I know what it's like. Don't retreat into your panic room. It might feel safe and warm, but you're all alone and it's not healthy. You need to come out. You need to start living again."

After the crash, in a moment of weakness I told her about my panic room, a place inside my head I had invented as a child after my father died, where I could observe the world from a distance as though through video monitors, safe from sorrow, rejection, and heartbreak. Nancy had coaxed me out, only to break my heart. Now my mother was trying to get in. But I would never venture out again.

"I *am* living, Mom. I'm living in LA. I have a great new job. It's been a long time since I felt this good. Please don't open up old wounds."

"I watch you at work," she said, her voice faltering. "I see how much people respect you and admire you. It makes me so proud. You're the consummate host. You make weary travelers from all over the world feel safe and comfortable. Yet you never seem at home yourself. You're restless and detached. You seem so… *sad*. It breaks my heart."

"Don't worry, Mom. I'm okay. Really." I took her hand and gazed directly into the sun, willing it to blind me.

"Do you ever get the feeling she's still alive?"

"No. Never."

"I don't mean physically alive. I sometimes feel like her spirit is still with us. Or her ghost is haunting us. It's all so bizarre, isn't it? Why did her grandmother refuse to come out for the service? Nancy was supposed to be on a different flight, and—"

"Mom, can we please not go through this again?"

"—In the *New York Times* article, they interviewed that Worldwide Airways gate attendant who went on stress leave, Lydia Meadows. She's back at work now—working out of LAX, of all places. I thought we might visit her."

"Why, Mom? Why would I ever put myself through that?"

"She was the last person to see Nancy. Maybe she remembers her. It might be therapeutic."

"For you or for me? Go ahead, play Miss Marple, but don't expect me to come along. It's you who refuses to accept that she's dead, not me."

"Of course I've accepted she's dead, Trevor. What I can't accept is that *you* died with her. You were so happy when she was alive. I'm not willing to let you bury that part of you. I don't want to resurrect Nancy. I want to resurrect you."

She reached up to touch my face.

I turned to her. Her blue eyes were shining. "You don't get it, do you, Mom?"

"Get what?"

"The guilt. I can't bear it."

"Oh sweetheart, don't. It's not your fault."

"Yes, it is."

"It isn't, dear. She was in the wrong place at the wrong—"

I grabbed her shoulders and pulled her toward me. "She wasn't supposed to be on that flight, Mom. I convinced her to come home early, to go on standby."

Her face fell. "But why?"

"I—I felt bad for abandoning her on our vacation…I missed her."

"Oh, Trevor."

The sun disappeared at last. The temperature dropped instantly, sending a gust of wind over the ocean toward us. Sunspots lingered in my eyes. All at once, the grief washed over me, sending me staggering backward. I turned and ran toward the car, desperate to escape the tsunami.

10

The Truth Is In the Eyes

Monday morning, I entered my office to find a copy of the *Daily Spotlight* sitting on my desk and Shanna Virani seated across from it. Arms crossed, she observed me as I rounded the desk and sat down. She was wearing black leather boots that came up to her knees, a lavender skirt, and a crisp white blouse with winged collars. Wordlessly, she directed me to the glossy magazine with her eyes.

With a sigh, I reached for it. A photograph of Chelsea Fricks filled the cover. She was standing on her toes on the edge of a diving board in a stop-sign red one-piece bathing suit. Arms outstretched and perfectly symmetrical, she was preparing to dive. Her eyes were open but unseeing. It was a still from *Blind Ambition*. In light of how she had met her demise, it was a jarring image—and not unintentional, I realized. The headline screamed CHELSEA SUICIDE SHOCKER!

"It's official," Shanna blurted out, unable to contain herself. "She killed herself."

"I wouldn't call anything the *Daily Spotlight* reports official," I said. "I don't know why you read this magazine. They constantly distort the truth."

"Not always," she said defensively. "When they're not sure about something, they put a question mark after the headline rather than an exclamation mark." She leaned forward and pointed to the cover. "See? No question mark."

"Then it must be true," I said with a roll of my eyes. I stared down at the photograph. "Look at her eyes. Those clouded contacts make her look like a zombie. They were normally such an arresting emerald green."

"You think that green was natural? Little about that girl was natural, Trevor. The real color of her eyes was a very common, very unarresting brown."

"That's right. I forgot about the incident at check-in." I opened the magazine to page three, where a headline ran across the top of the page: TRAGEDY AT HOTEL CINEMA! In total, twelve pages were dedicated to Chelsea's death, scattered with photos, articles, and short blurbs. There were stills from Chelsea's movies, a paparazzi-style shot of her and Bryce stepping out of a limousine at the entrance to the hotel, a photograph of the façade of the hotel with the marquis-style signage above the entrance, and a photo of the marble sign out front that mourners had turned into a gravestone. Page twelve featured a ghoulish photograph of Chelsea's body being slid into the back of the ambulance, her red-painted toenails poking out from under the sheet.

I flung the magazine into the wastepaper basket in disgust. "You know how I feel about gossip rags, Shanna. Where's the *Los Angeles Times*? What do they have to say?"

"*Spotlight* isn't a gossip rag, it's an entertainment magazine. The newspapers are boring. They're playing it safe. They don't have the option of placing a question mark after a headline. *Spotlight* always gets the scoop, and they love to break news—even when it's a fabrication. They have an entire database of people willing to sell them inside information."

She reached down and plucked the magazine out of the trash can. "Allow me to paraphrase the story for you. It'll spare you the pain of reading Nigel Thoroughbred's appalling writing." She opened it to page three. "Here we are: Nigel reports that Chelsea was suffering from acute depression. She was on medication, but it wasn't helping. According to a reliable source, she had a huge falling-out with her parents last year, and they hadn't spoken since. Close friends say she just couldn't take it anymore."

"Did Chelsea *have* any close friends?"

"Didn't Kitty say Moira was like a sister to her?"

"I'm dubious." I contemplated telling Shanna about my conversation with Moira but decided against it. It bothered me that employees were gossiping about Ezmerelda, and I wasn't about to make things worse. "Shanna, I'm not interested in hearing this."

She looked crestfallen. "Don't you care what happened?"

"No, I don't. I want it all to go away."

"It won't go away just because you want it to, young man. This story is going to get bigger before it passes. I had a dozen messages from clients this morning. They all want to know what happened. It's one thing to shut out the media, it's quite another to shut out the people who are sending us business."

"We have no obligation to say anything. This is a mur—a criminal investigation."

"Did you almost say *murder*?" She leaned over the desk as though her tiny form would intimidate me. Her nails were painted the exact shade of her skirt.

"No."

She studied my face for a moment. "You better not be keeping things from me, Trevor. Tonight is our travel industry reception.

RSVPs went mad over the weekend. These people are our clients. We can't freeze them out. We need to agree on a standard response."

"How about 'none of your fucking business'?"

"Why, Trevor, I'm shocked—and deeply impressed. I'd pay money to hear you tell them that."

Chelsea's similar comment echoed in my ears: *Whenever I fucking feel like it.* Was this how she felt? All this scrutiny, this expectation? No wonder she lost it.

"Can we talk about this later?" I said. "Tony's going to call for the forecast any minute. How's occupancy looking tonight? Better?"

"Marginally. We had four cancellations yesterday and two early departures—a couple of guests with BMG couldn't bear the pandemonium outside any longer. But it's not enough. Al and Ezmerelda worked through the night to get more rooms done. They were still here when I came in an hour ago. I sent them home."

"You sent Ezmerelda home?"

"She was barely able to stand. Are we running some kind of sweatshop here? "

"No, of course not. It's just that…" I trailed off. I had a hunch Detective Christakos would come looking for Ez today. "Is there anything else, Shanna? Or can I get to work?"

She glanced down at the *Spotlight*. Her voice softened. "Actually, yes. There's an article I thought you should see. It's about Flight 0022."

I closed my eyes. "I know about the fuselage."

"I know. Your mother told me she told you. But there's more today." She rounded the desk and placed a hand on my shoulder. "They identified the remains."

My body tensed. "They found Nancy?"

"No. I'm sorry, Trevor. There's no mention of Nancy."

I felt not disappointment but relief. The thought of her strapped in her seat all this time, trapped in the carnage at the bottom of the sea, was too much to bear.

"They did make a strange discovery, however." I caught a whiff of Chanel as she flipped through the *Spotlight*. "Here," she said, pointing to an image of the tip of the wing of the 737 jutting from the roiling waves like the fin of a great white whale. I had seen the iconic image a hundred times. The tabloids had gone into a frenzy after the crash, publishing shots of wreckage floating in the sea, photos of some of the 133 doomed passengers posing with family members, and personal belongings washed to shore—an infant's blue crocheted bootie, a waterlogged iPod nano, a dog-eared paperback with a barrel-chested man on the cover. I had declined all requests for interviews, too distraught to speak with my mother and sisters let alone a reporter, but the media hounded me for weeks. During that time, I read the newspapers and magazines obsessively, poring over photos and scanning articles for any mention of Nancy. The reporting was relentless and sensationalistic, and soon I couldn't stand to look at another photo, to read another word.

"Remember that young Irish woman they thought missed the flight?" Shanna said, pointing to a photograph on the next page. "The one who disappeared?"

For a fleeting moment, I thought I was looking at Nancy. Then I recognized the pale woman with a broad mouth and dark, shoulder-length hair.

"Suzan Myers," I said.

"Turns out she *did* get on the flight. They found her body in the wreckage! Isn't that awful? All this time, her poor family thought she was alive, thought she missed her flight and went into shock when she found out it crashed, wandered off to God knows where without collecting her bags. A year later, they find out there never was any hope. Your mother thinks it's a strange coincidence."

"When did you talk to my mother?"

"I ran into her in the lobby this morning. We had a quick coffee." Shanna studied the photograph of Suzan Myers. "She has an uncanny resemblance to Nancy, don't you think? They could be sisters—even twins."

"I don't see a resemblance."

Shanna moved her chair next to mine and turned to face me. "Why didn't you tell me you convinced her to change her flight? I might have been able to help you get over the guilt. When Willard died, I spent countless hours blaming myself. Over time, I learned to accept that I can't control everything in life, but I can control how I react, how I interpret things. No matter what you did or said, Trevor, it's not your fault. It's been a year. You have to let go."

"I have let go." Feeling trapped, I stood up and squeezed around her to the other side of the desk. "There's no reason to worry about me, Shanna. My mother desperately wants me to have psychological problems so she can claim her self-help books cured me, but I'm perfectly fine." I opened the door and gestured for her to leave. "Now if you don't mind."

She didn't move. "I'm sure Chelsea's death isn't helping."

"Pardon me? You can hardly equate the two."

"That's not what I meant. I'm sorry. I just thought … I thought I might be able to offer you comfort, having …"

"Having what? Having lost the love of your life in a plane crash?"

"Of course not. But Willard *was* killed in a hit and run. I lost him as instantly and unexpectedly as you lost Nancy. I was crazy about him. I know it's not the same, but it's—"

"Close? *Really?* Did Willard die because you cut your vacation short to go back to *work?* Because you convinced him to catch an earlier flight home? A flight that crashed into the fucking Atlantic Ocean?"

She looked horrified. "Of course not. I don't mean to diminish your loss. I—I thought we could talk. I wish we could relate to one another on a deeper level. It's always work with you and me, and there's so much more to life. I have no relatives here besides my children. I was so happy when you decided to move to Los Angeles. I consider you like a brother. Your mother told me about your panic room, and—"

"She *what?* Oh Christ."

"It's okay. I can relate. I have my own—"

"I prefer to keep things on a professional level, Shanna."

I gestured for her to leave, closing my eyes, loathing her scrutiny. I felt a gust of perfumed air sweep past me. When I opened my eyes, she was gone. The tabloid was on the desk. I snatched it up and tore it into strips, feeding it into the shredder.

★ ★ ★ ★ ★

"Trevor?"

Valerie Smitts was standing in the doorway, a stricken expression on her face.

I rose from my chair. "What is it, Valerie?"

"I need to show you something. Can you come with me?"

I followed her down the hallway to the back stairwell. She walked briskly, eyes fixed ahead, not saying a word. On B2, she waited for me to catch up and hurried down the corridor to the general storeroom.

Olga Slovenka was standing at the window. "Come!" she shouted, as though expecting us. She opened the door and gestured for me to

153

follow with an arthritic claw. I stepped inside, and Valerie and Olga followed, pulling the door closed.

I looked around. The storeroom looked as tidy as ever. I glanced warily at the door to the mini-bar room. Was Ezmerelda locked inside again? But Valerie and Olga were staring at one of the three housekeeping carts. It had been pulled from its parking space to the center of the room.

"What is it?" I said, baffled.

"Have a look," Valerie said, lifting the linen curtain on the cart. She averted her eyes and let out a small whimper.

"See!" Olga shouted, pointing to the bottom shelf.

I squatted down. There, nestled in a bed of bloody facecloths, was a gleaming butcher knife.

★ ★ ★ ★ ★

Detective Stavros Christakos let out a whistle. "Well, well, well. Come have a look, Georgie."

Officer Gertz squatted down beside him. "Bingo," he said.

"I'm gonna take a wild guess and say this knife matches the set in the penthouse suite," Stavros said, turning to look up at me.

I looked over at Olga, who was in charge of inventory.

"Same!" she shouted.

Officer Gertz opened a duffel bag and withdrew a plastic bag and pair of tongs. He pulled on a pair of latex gloves and used the tongs to lift the knife off the shelf, holding it up to the light. The knife glinted, looking like it belonged in a Middle Earth treasure chest. Stavros circled around, inspecting it from all angles. He nodded to George, who dropped it into the plastic bag. Next, George retrieved the bloodied facecloths and dropped them into a separate bag. He placed both bags in the duffel bag.

"Are you going to swipe the knife for fingerprints?" I asked.

"Sure, but we won't find any," the detective said. "Looks like the killer used the facecloths to wipe the knife clean."

Olga made a choking sound at the word "killer." I had made her and Valerie swear not to say anything to the other staff about the knife, and now she was privy to even more explosive information.

"Olga," I said. "I think you'd better leave us alone."

"No," said Stavros. "She stays." He stood up and circled the cart, inspecting it carefully. "How long has this cart been here?" he asked Olga.

She let out a grunt and walked to the wall to retrieve a clipboard. "Friday. Last time use," she said, smacking the coversheet with her hand.

The detective took the clipboard and studied the sign-out sheet. I held my breath. Having already gone through this process, I knew Ezmerelda Lopez was the last person to sign the cart out, at 6:03 PM on Friday evening. She signed it in six hours later, at 12:09 AM.

"EL stands for Ezmerelda Lopez?" the detective asked.

"Yez," Olga replied.

He turned to give me a knowing look, but I avoided eye contact. He let out a snort of self-satisfaction and handed the clipboard to Officer Gertz, who placed the sign-out sheet in his bag and then took out a camera and began snapping photos of the cart.

"Is Mrs. Lopez on-property?" asked the detective.

I shook my head. "We sent her home a few hours ago."

"You sent her home?"

His tone ribbed me. "She worked all night, Detective."

He eyed me for a moment with an expression of disappointment and then turned to Olga. "This cart has not been used since Friday night?"

She shook her head adamantly. "No use. Ezmerelda only."

"Has anyone been near it?"

"No! I here always. If go, lock door."

"We have one cart per floor and two spare ones," I explained. "They work on rotation. Olga says she pulled this one out to stock it and send it up to a floor this morning. That's when she found the knife."

The detective turned to her for confirmation.

"Fill! Facecloth! Go!" she paraphrased.

The detective caught his reflection in a mirror on the wall and touched his hair. "Well," he said, turning to me, head bobbing.

"Well, what?" I said, unable to mask my irritation. "The knife was probably placed there while Ez was in the penthouse suite. She brought the cart down without knowing."

Stavros turned to Olga. "Is that what *you* think happened, Mrs. Slovenka?"

"Ezmerelda veddy veddy angry!" Olga shouted.

I turned to her in shock. "What?"

"Miss Fricks yell. Tell her get out. Ez veddy angry!"

I now understood what compelled Tony Cavalli's four-year-old daughter to fire Olga. "What on earth are you talking about?" I said.

Stavros took a step closer to Olga. "Did they have a fight?"

"I can explain," I said. "Olga's English isn't very good. She's trying to say that Miss Fricks encountered Ez cleaning her room and—"

"If you don't mind, Trevor," Stavros interrupted, holding his hand up to silence me. "I'd like to hear it in her own words."

"Fine. Be my guest."

"*Alone.*" He nodded toward the exit.

I was floored. "You want me to leave? But—but I can help translate."

"You speak Polish?"

"No, but…"

"Then scram. Mrs. Slovenka's English is more than adequate."

"Very well," I said, backing toward the exit.

Olga cast me a withering look as I passed.

"I'll come up and find you later," said Stavros. "Maybe we can grab some lunch."

★ ★ ★ ★ ★

"Thing is," Detective Christakos said over lunch in Scene, a sizable bite of Emmenthal Foie Gras Burger bulging in his cheek, "she may look like a half-brained Mexican fishwife, but don't let her fool you. I learned long ago never to trust appearances in this city. It's infested with actors."

"Ezmerelda Lopez is not an actor," I said testily. "She's a highly respected housekeeping director." I looked over my shoulder for the server to bring an extra napkin. Ketchup was smeared over the detective's right cheek, and I couldn't bear to look at it any longer. Flavia Cavalli, Tony's sister, was the only server on duty until eleven thirty AM, and she was nowhere to be seen. Fortunately, the restaurant was empty save for a young couple sipping matcha tea a few seats over, both reading the *Daily Spotlight*.

"I know you're Canadian, Trevor, which means by nature you're naive and idealistic. Don't get me wrong—I'm not being racist, I'm just telling you a truism about your culture based on experience. I dated a Canadian girl for three months, chick from Saskatchewan, fucking *hot*. I swear she had never stepped outside her igloo before she came to LA to get 'discovered.' Believe me, *everyone* in this town is either an actor or an aspiring actor. If they're not actively pursuing an acting career, they still secretly hope Quentin Tarantino will spot them buying Dentyne at Walgreens and will cast them in his next movie. The business gets into everybody's blood. Why wouldn't it? Stars are idolized. They're treated like gods. Not like cops. We save lives, yet we're treated like dirt."

"Well, I for one don't want to be a star."

"Oh yes, you do." The detective swallowed and flashed a knowing grin, displaying a chunk of foie gras trapped between his teeth. "You're telling me if Steven Soderberg asked you to star in his next movie with, say, Gwyneth Paltrow, you'd refuse?"

"Of course I'd refuse. I don't even know who Steven Soderberg is."

"Bullshit! You're a bad actor, Trevor Lambert. If this is your best performance, don't hold your breath for Steven!"

"If you think I'm lying, then you're a bad detective. No wonder this investigation is going nowhere." I brushed my cheek with my hand, hoping he'd follow suit.

He didn't. "Who says it's going nowhere?"

"Then it's going in the wrong direction." I pushed away my shrimp Caesar salad, barely touched. I couldn't get the image of the knife out of my mind … the white terrycloth facecloth soiled with blood … the sharp metal blade sliding into Chelsea's soft skin. I felt nauseous, and the smear of ketchup on Stavros's face wasn't helping.

"My point is," he persisted, "this city is crawling with people who dream of making a living out of lying, which is essentially what acting is—pretending you're someone you aren't. Even when actors aren't acting, they're pretending to be somebody they're not: dressing up, putting on makeup, playing nice, pretending they're smart and interesting, that they care about anybody or anything but themselves. It's all a façade."

"That's a pretty bleak perspective for someone who aspires to be an actor himself."

"Not all actors are like that, of course. Some of us are real."

"But don't all jobs involve pretending? You think hotel staff are this friendly and accommodating off duty?"

He shrugged. "I know Ez Lopez isn't."

"Will you please get off Ez Lopez?"

He stuffed another quarter of burger into his mouth. "See, as a detective, it's my job to strip away the lies and pretense, to get to the core of people. I'm like the anti-director. You know where I find the truth? I don't listen to their bullshit. Everyone lies. I look into their *eyes*." He leaned toward me and pointed two fingers at his big black eyes. "The truth is in the eyes, Trevor. Remember that. The eyes don't lie because they can't. Sometimes it's frightening when you see what's really going on in there."

"You're trying to tell me you can read people's thoughts through their eyes?"

"Not thoughts, *emotions*. When the emotion in their eyes matches the words in their mouth, I know they're telling the truth. It's that simple."

"That's quite a talent," I said. "So when you look beyond Ezmerelda's feather duster and apron and into her eyes, you see a highly trained assassin."

"I see someone who is very afraid. Someone who is *hiding* something." A chunk of ground beef flew out of his mouth and over my shoulder. We both pretended it didn't happen. "Is it murder? I don't know yet. What I do know is she's not so sweet and innocent as you like to think. This 'me no speak English, me work hard take care family' persona is crap. People like that don't join the NISF."

"I think you're wrong about her being a member of the NISF."

"I don't care what you think. I just need you to *cooperate*."

"I *am* cooperating." The red smear was still there, as though someone had slashed his face. I looked around the restaurant. Flavia had dropped off our meals twenty minutes ago and never returned. Since when had Scene become a self-serve restaurant? Where the hell was Reginald Clinton? I got up and retrieved a napkin from another table. "What did Olga tell you?" I asked, handing it to Stavros.

He took the napkin and set it on the table. "She told me that late Friday night, Mrs. Lopez stormed into the housekeeping office in a rage because Chelsea had kicked her out of the suite, had sworn at her, insulted her, made racist remarks, and threatened to have her deported."

"*What?*"

"Olga says Ezmerelda ranted and raved about Miss Fricks, cursing in Mexican, and then a while later she stormed back up to the suite." The detective shoved the last of his burger in his mouth. "A half-hour later, she came down in a completely different frame of mind: frightened and subdued. Olga asked her what was wrong and she didn't say a thing. She went to the changing room and Olga didn't see her again."

"You got all this from a woman who speaks in imperatives?"

"She got her message across just fine. Unlike Ez Lopez."

"Ez was subdued because she just found out Miss Fricks jumped off the balcony. What did Olga expect? I wouldn't put too much weight on her comments. Our room attendants are divided into two camps: the Eastern European block and the Mexican cartel. The Mexicans think the Eastern Europeans are cold and impersonal, and the Eastern Europeans think the Mexicans are sloppy and obsequious. Olga thinks the Mexican cartel is out to get her. Ez told me what happened that night. She knocked on the door and no one answered, so she let herself in. Chelsea surprised her while she was dusting—"

"Snooping."

"*Dusting.* She knocked over the Bourgie lamp. Miss Fricks told her to leave and to come back later. If Miss Fricks had threatened or insulted her, Ez would have told me."

"Maybe she was afraid."

"Of what, Chelsea's threat to deport her? Ez is legal, Detective. She's lived in this country for twelve years. I've seen her papers. I arranged for her family to move here from New York. Chelsea Fricks is the guilty one here. You saw the racist literature."

"And so did Ezmerelda."

The innards of the burger were all over Stavros's hands and face. He looked like a two-year-old. Swallowing his mouthful, he picked up the serviette at last. His beady eyes scanned the restaurant as he wiped himself off. I turned to see Flavia emerge from the kitchen, straightening her skirt. I lifted my hand and waved her over, eager to end lunch.

"You okay, Sparky?" asked the detective. "You seem nervous."

"I'm not nervous, Detective, I'm deeply irritated. I find it unfathomable that you're focusing all your efforts on the most unlikely of suspects."

He made a sucking sound as he cleaned his teeth. "Who said I'm focusing all my efforts on Ezmerelda? That reminds me, I need to see her personnel file." He rose in his seat suddenly. "Jesus, is that Sharon Stone?"

I planted my elbows on the table, refusing to look. "I'll get you the file."

"Holy shit, it is! She's coming in for lunch!"

"Is anyone there to seat her?" I asked.

"Some black guy in a suit."

Good. Reginald had appeared just in time.

"Look at her, she's still hot. Remember her in *Basic Instinct*? That movie made me decide to become a detective. That and *LA Confidential*. Kim Basinger ever come here?"

Flavia finally made her way to our table. "Get you guys anything else?" she asked, resting her knuckles on the table as though exhausted from work.

I looked up at her. "Flavia, is your back sore?"

"No, why?"

I shook my head, not wanting to correct her posture in front of the detective.

But she got the message. She straightened up and saluted me, pushing her breasts out. "That better?"

"Much better," said the detective, grinning.

I noticed her skirt was hemmed several inches shorter than it should be. Leaning closer, I saw she must have done it herself with messy glue.

"Trevor, please," she said, pulling her skirt down.

"I wasn't—I …"

"Thanks for a fabulous lunch, Rico," Stavros said, reading her nametag.

Flavia's face reddened. "I lost mine, so I borrowed Rico's." She had the same long, untamed black hair as her cousin Janie and a look as vacant as the unfinished rooms on the fourth floor.

"Ask HR to get another nametag made today, okay, Flavia?" I said, willing myself to remain calm. An employee this poorly trained, this inappropriately dressed, should not have been permitted on the floor. Across the restaurant, I saw Reginald chatting with the table he had just seated. The lunch rush was beginning, and a half-dozen guests were waiting at the entrance. So many things needed my attention, and my time was being dominated by this aggravating detective, this bizarre case.

"Sure thing, Trevor." Flavia cleared our plates, balancing them on one arm.

"What did I tell you?" said Stavros, watching her go. "Everyone in this town is trying to be someone they're not." He turned in his seat to get a better look at the table in the corner.

"Detective," I said, "tell me the truth. Do you really think Ez Lopez had anything to do with Chelsea's death?"

He crossed his hairy arms, biceps bulging. "I haven't formed an opinion yet, my friend. I can't even say for sure if she was murdered. I'll know this afternoon when the autopsy's done. I'm still gathering evidence. I'm like Hansel, I follow breadcrumbs. Some lead me to a dead end, others to a clue, others will lead me straight to the culprit. At this point, a lot of the breadcrumbs are leading to Ez Lopez." He reached for the breadbasket on the table and withdrew a slice of olive walnut bread. "She was the last person recorded entering Chelsea's suite," he said, pulling off a hunk and placing it on the tablecloth.

"That report is not conclusive. There are unidentified entries and exits."

"Moira Schwartz saw her through the peephole letting herself in and a heated argument breaks out between her and Chelsea minutes later." Another hunk.

"Moira is not the most credible witness."

He pulled off another hunk. "Olga Slovenka—a very reliable witness, in my opinion—confirms Mrs. Lopez had an argument with Chelsea and Chelsea threatened her. We can assume immigrant rights are something Mrs. Lopez strongly believes in, considering her NISF membership, and Chelsea had racist books in her room." He placed another hunk of bread on the pile. "A bloodied knife is found hidden on the cart assigned to her." He gestured to the pile of breadcrumbs. "A lot of crumbs lead to your chambermaid, Trevor."

"Hardly enough to convict her."

"Oh, I neglected one little morsel." Stavros placed an entire slice of bread on top of the pile. "Olga told me when Ezmerelda came down the second time, there was blood on her hands."

"*Blood*?"

The detective nodded. "Blood."

"The broken lamp?"

"It was cracked, not in pieces, and it's plastic. Couldn't have cut her."

"The glass on the floor? There could be any number of reasons."

He raised his eyebrows in a shrug.

I looked down at the pile of bread next to the detective's soiled napkin with a sense of despair. Could Ezmerelda be responsible for this mess? I pictured her in the mini-bar room, tears spilling down her cheeks, brown eyes staring at me in fright.

Impossible.

"I thought detectives used fingerprints to solve cases, not breadcrumbs," I said.

"Fingerprints aren't telling me anything in this case. They were all over the suite, but nowhere conclusive. If nothing else, your executive housekeeper is guilty of sweeping a few details under the carpet. Tonight I'm going to pay her a visit at her house in Temple City."

"Fine," I said, standing up from the table, "but go easy on her, okay? In time, you'll realize you're on the wrong track. In the meantime, I can't afford to have her go on stress leave."

"Mind if I stick around and have dessert?" His eyes searched the restaurant again, darting from table to table and resting on the blond actress in the far corner.

"Be my guest," I said. I reached down and swept the pile of crumbs into my hand, squeezing them into a ball.

"Oh, Trevor?" he called after me. "One more thing. Your maintenance guy, Al Combs? He around?"

I hurried back to the table. "Able Al? I thought you already questioned him."

"I have more questions."

"He's off today. Don't tell me he's a suspect too?"

"Breadcrumbs, my friend. Just following breadcrumbs."

★ ★ ★ ★ ★

As anticipated, that night's travel industry reception was extremely well attended. Shanna was magnificent. Stepping onto the makeshift podium at the edge of the lounge, she captured everyone's attention with a brilliant performance, giving a quick, inspiring overview of Hotel Cinema and why it was *the* place to stay in Hollywood. She alluded to the Fricks incident with the expert evasiveness of a seasoned politician, expressing compassion and concern, and then delicately extricating the hotel from any association. Under the spotlight the technician had set up over the stage, her white suit glowed like an apparition. Her entire being radiated sophistication.

When she introduced me, I stepped onto the podium and felt instant panic. Unlike Shanna, I didn't thrive on attention; I preferred to manage from behind the scenes. Fortunately, she saved me from losing the crowd by hopping back onto the podium a few minutes later and announcing, "It's time to give away prizes! Prizes, prizes, prizes!"

After the reception, I took Mom for dinner at the Grafton Hotel on Sunset Boulevard, and got home to bed shortly after midnight.

An hour later, I was just drifting off when the buzz of my cell phone woke me. Who would be calling at this hour? It had to be a wrong number. Or a hangup. I rolled over, covering my head with a pillow. It stopped buzzing after a while, and then started again.

I reached for the phone. "Trevor Lambert here."

"Hello there, Trevor Lambert here!"

He sounded like a game-show host. I almost hung up. In the background I heard voices, loud music, laughter—a nightclub? I thought of my high-school friends. When I was in New York, they used to call at all hours from bars or clubs, unwitting or uncaring of the three-hour time difference. They passed the phone around the table and I spoke to each of them, listening to their slurred voices as they dredged up "the good ole times" and made the memories sound far more appealing than they actually were. One night Nancy was sleeping beside me when I received a call at four AM. I chatted with Phil, then Steve, then Marco, and finally with Derrick, my best friend from high school. "What's Nancy doing?" he asked. "Staring at me," I replied. When I got off the phone, I snuggled up against her warm body. "Sorry. They do this every few months." "Why don't you just hang up?" she asked. "It's so inconsiderate." But I could never do that. Unlike me, Nancy had swiftly, almost callously broke off contact with school friends when she was sixteen, after her parents died, when she chose to live alone in their house in Cleveland rather than move to England to live with her grandmother. I liked hearing from my old friends, even in the middle of the night.

Now, I found myself wishing this was one of these calls. "Who is this?" I said.

"You don't recognize me? It's Stav!"

I sat up in alarm. Why would he call at this hour? "What's up, Detective?"

"Where the heck are you, my friend? I came by the hotel for a drink, but you're not here. I thought you lived here!"

"I'm in bed," I said. "It's one AM."

"Huh? I can't hear you."

"I'm *sleeping*, Stavros."

"Hold on, I'm heading out to the pool deck … Jeez, it's crazy here too! Can you hear me now?"

Why was the music so loud? I could already hear the guest complaints. Who was in charge tonight? The night manager was David. The restaurant manager was Shareen. Earlier, when I walked Mom back to the hotel after dinner, the lounge had been quiet. It was Monday. I assumed it would remain that way. Clearly things had picked up. I chided myself for not staying.

"You're missin' out!" Stavros shouted, sounding like he'd had a few drinks. "I just met your owner, Tony Cavalli. Great guy!"

That explained the volume. "Did you need me for something, Detective?"

"You forgot to put me on the VIP list! Those thugs at the door almost didn't let me in. I don't want to go through that again, Trevor. You promised to get me on the permanent list."

"I didn't promise anything. There's no 'permanent' list anyway. It's reinvented every night."

"They made me stand in line. I had to watch thirty people parade past me before they decided I was worthy. It's a sad statement when a reality-show contestant gets priority over a cop. I warn you, if I have to line up again, it's going to impede my investigation."

"Fine, I'll talk to the doormen. Is that what you're doing now—investigating?"

"I told you, I never stop working. You got a tab here I can use?"

In the background, I heard a loud splash followed by shouts and laughter. "Stavros, did someone just …?"

"Holy crap, Tony's cousins just threw some chick in the pool! You should see her! Her dress is sopping wet, and it's clinging to every curve. Uh-oh, she's not happy. Look out, Lorenzo, behind you! Or maybe that's Enzo. I can't tell them apart. Jesus, I think it's Denise Richards!"

There was another splash, followed by more laughter.

I fell back on the bed. Tony was turning the hotel into his private frat party, and neither David nor Shareen would have the courage to rein him in. Should I get dressed and go in to shut down the party? There was little hope of getting back to sleep now.

"Serves you right, Lorenzo!" Stavros shouted. "Watch out, Enzo, you're next! She's got your number! Trevor, these guys are crazy!"

"Stavros, I'd like to try to go back to sleep now."

"Hold on a sec, 'kay?" I heard him talking to someone in the background. "I'll be just a minute, doll. Why don't you go get us some drinks? No, he's not here. Tell him to put it on Tony's tab. I'm on official business." He came back on the phone. "I wanted to let you know I went out to Ez Lopez's house in Temple City."

"And?"

"Whole *colony* of Mexicans there. Bunch of tight-lipped, mean bastards. They eyed Georgie and me like we walked off a spaceship. We had a look around, but Ez and Felix weren't there. No one admitted to speaking English despite a shelf teeming with English books. They denied even knowing Ez and Felix until I found a framed photograph of them on the dresser in one of the bedrooms. I managed to intimidate one of the kids into speaking, but all he said was, 'No see them, no see long time, maybe week, maybe never, no even sure who they be.' Georgie and I paid a visit to the old lady across the street. She

168

said they all speak English. The younger ones don't even speak Spanish. We waited outside a couple hours, but I knew they weren't coming back. They're on the lam."

"On the lam?" I tried to picture dutiful Ez and affable Felix screeching away in a getaway car. The detective's impression of the Lopez household contrasted sharply with my own. I had been there twice, once for a housewarming party and another time, a few weeks ago, for daughter Bella's fourth birthday party. The family couldn't have been more hospitable. And the neighbor was right: they all spoke English. "Are you sure you were at the right place?"

"I'm a detective, for Christ's sake. Of course I was at the right place." His voice grew distant. "Thanks, doll. No? Okay, fine, take some money." I heard him slurp his drink. "Yowsah!"

Another peach daiquiri? I was seated on the edge of my bed now, fully awake. I ran my hands through my hair. "What does this mean, Stavros?"

"I wanted to give you the heads-up. We got preliminary results from Chelsea's autopsy today. I held a press conference tonight. It's going to be all over the news tomorrow."

My pulse quickened. "What is?"

"Chelsea was alive when she hit the water."

"So she drowned?" My thoughts went back to the night of the party. I remembered staring into the blue water, waiting for her to surface. I had hesitated before jumping in, afraid to embarrass myself. Meanwhile, she was drowning before my eyes.

"Nope, she didn't drown. She cracked her skull on the bottom of the pool and broke her neck. There were three knife wounds to her body, one in the lower left abdomen, another in her lower back just below the kidney—those two were fairly superficial—and a third, deeper one in her upper back. It pierced her aorta. That's what killed her."

"So she *was*…?"

"Murdered? Yep. We matched the blood on the knife with Chelsea's blood, so we have the weapon. The angle of the stab wounds indicates the killer was right-handed, but that doesn't narrow things down. All my suspects are right-handed. No fingerprints on the knife either. Whoever killed her must be skilled at cleaning things. You know what else I found out? Ezmerelda Lopez is a member of the Chelsea Fricks Fan Club."

"So? What does that have to do with anything?"

"We might have a stalker on our hands. Maybe she was infatuated. Maybe she had always dreamed of meeting her, and things went terribly wrong. Chelsea didn't live up to her image. She was a slob, she read racist literature, she was verbally abusive and threatened to have her deported. Mrs. Lopez must have snapped. Most fans never get this close to their idol. It's lucky they don't, because this might happen more often."

My mind raced. Moira had also suggested Ezmerelda was stalking Chelsea. I recalled Ez's insistence on personally overseeing the upkeep of the penthouse suite. At the time, it had seemed like another example of her dedication. Could she have had a more sinister motive? She was in the suite when the police arrived. Had she stuck around to cover her tracks—to sweep things under the carpet? For the first time, I found myself questioning Ezmerelda's innocence.

"What's next, then, Detective Christakos?" My throat felt dry.

"Is she scheduled to work tomorrow?"

"Yes."

"If she shows up, don't let her go anywhere. I'll be by in the morning to take her in."

11

Swept Under the Carpet

"You need to see this, Trevor," Shanna cried, tossing a copy of the *Daily Spotlight* on my desk. "You're going to die."

I wasn't surprised to see a photo of Chelsea on the cover. It was a paparazzi shot, capturing her as she climbed out of her limousine at the entrance to Hotel Cinema. She was dressed in pink and powder blue yoga wear, dark glasses, and a camouflage engineer's hat. She was scowling at the camera. The hotel's name figured prominently marquee-style over the canopy above her. To the right of the photograph ran the headline CHELSEA MURDERED! DID THE MAID DO IT?

"I was afraid of this," I said, lunging for the magazine.

Shanna snatched it from my hands. "Listen to this. 'The Los Angeles Police Department ended its silence last night with the shocking revelation that foul play is suspected in the death of film star Chelsea Fricks. "Miss Fricks was attacked by a knife-wielding intruder," disclosed Detective Stavros Christakos, the dashing young detective in charge of the case…' blah blah blah… Here: 'The autopsy report indicates Miss Fricks was *stabbed three times with a butcher knife.*'" Shanna looked up, her face filled with horror. "She was stabbed, Trevor. Practically under our noses."

I lowered myself into my chair. "I should probably tell you—"

"Wait, it gets worse. 'Police confirmed that a bloodied butcher knife was recovered from one of the hotel's maid carts on Monday morning.'" Shanna squeezed her throat and made a choking sound. "'Furthermore, a source close to the investigation confirms that *a heated argument broke out between Chelsea and the hotel's head maid, Ezmerelda Lopez, in the suite only moments before her death*.'" She looked up again. "Have you ever heard anything more preposterous? Imagine, our darling treasure Ezmerelda a cold-blooded killer! If it wasn't so hurtful I might find it comical."

"Are all the newspapers reporting this, or only *Spotlight*?" I asked.

"All the news outlets are reporting it was murder," she said, thumbing the magazine. "Police held a press conference last night. That insufferable little Greek fellow was grandstanding on all the stations this morning. *Good Morning America* speculated the culprit is an obsessive fan. FOXNews thinks Moira is guilty. The *LA Times* fingered Bryce. On my drive in, the announcers on KIIS-FM were taking a call-in poll, and everyone from Moira to Bryce to Tara Reid was on the ballot—was Tara Reid even at the party? KCAL raised the possibility that a hotel employee might have been involved, but so far only *Spotlight* has been audacious enough to name Ezmerelda."

"So far."

"That's what I'm afraid of. This bastard writer, this Nigel Thoroughbred"—she pronounced his name with a pompous British accent—"doesn't go as far as to outright accuse her—there aren't enough question marks in the world to protect him—but the damage is done. It's going to be mad today, Trevor. The crowd outside has already doubled in size. They've surrounded the castle gates like angry serfs. They're going to want to burn Ezmerelda at the stake."

I reached for the phone. "We better warn her."

"I tried her cell phone, but she didn't answer. I left an urgent message." She looked back down at the magazine. "Who is feeding this information to *Spotlight*? Do you think it's one of our employees?"

"It must be Moira Schwartz," I said. "She's the only one who knows about the argument, aside from Christakos." It occurred to me that Olga knew about the argument too, yet I couldn't imagine her calling up the *Daily Spotlight* and tipping them off. Despite her abrasive nature and resentment of the Mexican cartel, she had always been honest and forthright, never devious. Could she be stirring up trouble in order to exact revenge on the Cavallis for allowing their four-year-old daughter to fire her? It was possible, but a stretch.

Shanna's hands squeezed her throat. "So there *was* an argument between Ezmerelda and Chelsea? About what? And what's this nonsense about a butcher knife?" She studied my face. "You knew about this, didn't you? Why do you keep withholding information from me?"

"I'm sorry, but I wasn't at liberty to divulge such confidential information."

"Perhaps now that this 'confidential information' is all over the news, you might do me the favor of filling me in. I'm the second-in-command of this hotel, Trevor. I need to know these things."

"Fine," I said. Taking a deep breath, I sat back and related everything I knew.

When I was finished, Shanna closed her eyes to process the information. After a moment, she opened them. "There was blood on Ezmerelda's hands yesterday morning too," she said. "She was hiding them from me. Her poor little hands were calloused and torn like a worker in a labor camp! But the wounds weren't slices—nothing a knife would make—they were from working her fingers to the bone: flipping mattresses, changing linens, scrubbing floors, reaching under beds, washing glasses. Regardless, I can't imagine *anyone* could fathom a worthy woman like her—"

"Shanna, the detective is coming to arrest her."

"*Arrest her?*" Her words came out as a shriek. She covered her mouth and glanced toward the window. The hallway was empty. "He's convinced it's her?"

"It appears that way."

Her eyes moistened in a rare display of emotion. I felt my own eyes sting. We had watched Ezmerelda evolve from room attendant to supervisor to assistant manager in the housekeeping department at the Universe. Now she was head of the department at Hotel Cinema and doing an outstanding job. We needed her desperately. What would happen to her family if she were arrested? By the look on Shanna's face, I could tell she was thinking the same thing: whether Ez was guilty or innocent, we were partly responsible for her predicament. We had convinced her to relocate from New York. We had allowed her to work herself into exhaustion. If she had snapped, we shared the blame.

"Do you think she did it?" Shanna asked, reaching for a tissue to dab her eyes.

I was silent for a moment. "I was starting to wonder, but I know in my heart she didn't."

Her face brightened. "Me too."

★ ★ ★ ★ ★

At eight AM precisely, Ezmerelda strolled into the Pre-Production Suite on the second floor for the operations meeting. She was all smiles as she made her way around the table and settled into a chair.

Opening her notebook, she withdrew a pen from the pocket of her pale blue shirt and waited for the meeting to begin.

The room, which had been buzzing prior to her arrival, fell silent. All eyes turned to her.

There were nine of us present, the heads of each department. Across the table, human resources manager Dennis Claiborne discreetly tucked away the copy of the *Daily Spotlight* he had been holding up like a Wanted poster. He had put forward the suggestion that Ezmerelda be fired in order to distance the hotel from the controversy, prompting a chorus of protests and a heated debate, silenced only by her arrival.

So much for Detective Christakos's theory she went on the lam, I thought smugly, flashing a reassuring smile at Ezmerelda. By her sunny disposition, I surmised she had no clue about the *Spotlight* cover story. Shanna's frantic calls had not been returned. We had devised a plan to take her aside before the meeting and warn her. I had suggested hiding her in a guestroom. "Brilliant," Shanna replied. "A dirty guestroom! We can put her to work. When she's done that room, we'll move her to another. Who cares if her hands are bleeding?" In the end, we resolved not to hide her since she had nothing to hide. There was an explanation for the argument with Chelsea, the knife in the cart, the blood on her hands. We would hear her side of the story and communicate it to the detective, thereby averting the trauma of an arrest. But she had arrived too late for us to forewarn her.

Before commencing the meeting, I took a quick look around the table. To my left, front office manager Valerie Smitts was regarding me with a faint, beguiling smile. Her lovely dark hair cascaded over her shoulders to the stack of reports on the table before her. Next to her, Al Combs leaned back in his chair, arms folded over his massive chest, head lowered. To Al's left, controller Ahmed Lammi pretended to study the forecast while sneaking furtive glances at Ezmerelda. Next to him, Reginald Clinton stared unabashedly at Ezmerelda, one eye half-closed, the other eyebrow raised as though trying to determine her guilt. Shanna sat perched in the throne chair opposite me, eyes fluttering with impatience. To her left, Dennis stared fixedly at Ezmerelda with pursed lips. On Dennis's left, revenue manager Rheanna Adams reached out to rub Ezmerelda's back. Ezmerelda's smile faltered, confused by the attention. I tried to catch a glimpse of her hands, but her right hand was curled into a fist around her pen and her left hand was buried under the table.

"Welcome, everyone," I said, clearing my throat. "Rheanna, would you like to start off by reporting in?"

"Certainly, Trevor. We had eighty-three rooms occupied last night, two no-shows, six comps, thirty-nine out of order, and an average rate of $347.01." She went on to report the next week's occupancy statistics—oversold every night—and reviewed the long list of incoming VIPs, many of which were household names, along with special-care guests, extended stays, and group arrivals. After Rheanna finished, each department head reported in, beginning with Dennis Claiborne. He raised the issue of the poor performance of Tony's forced hires, namely his sister Flavia and nieces Janie and Bernadina. A chorus of complaints ensued.

"Yesterday I had to send Flavia home early," said Reginald. "The bartender caught her sneaking sips before she brought drinks to tables. By six PM, she was hammered."

"I got an irate call from Mrs. Greenfield in 507," Valerie chimed in. "She asked Bernadina at the concierge desk to make a reservation at Spago and book a limousine. She sent them to Spaghettios."

I assured them I would address the issues with Mr. Cavalli. "In the meantime, it's our responsibility to give all employees as much training as necessary. These young ladies have enormous potential, and—"

Dennis made a gagging sound, igniting a few giggles.

"—and they're not going anywhere," I said. I stopped short of informing them that Janie, Bernadina, and Flavia were heirs apparent to the future Cavalli Hotels & Resorts International. "Is that understood?"

Heads nodded all around.

"Thank you. Reginald, can you report in next, please."

"Not to harp on the Cavallis," said Reginald, glancing around uneasily, "but I have concerns about Saturday's wedding reception for Lorenzo Cavalli and his bride, Rosario. Mr. Cavalli says there are five hundred RSVPs for dinner. There's no way I can staff for that number."

"He's instructed me to give Bernadina, Janie, and Flavia the night off to attend," added Valerie.

"That should help," said Dennis, prompting more snickers.

"He wants to transform the restaurant into an ancient Italian villa using kitsch from Cavalli Fine Imports," Reginald continued, unable to mask his distaste.

"Oh, and he has a big block of comp rooms," Rheanna chimed in. "He says Sydney Cheevers is arranging for a bunch of celebrities to fly in for the wedding. And he wants me to move Lenny Kravitz—who will *not* be attending, his booker has emphasized—out of Penthouse 2 so he and Liz can stay there."

"What about Penthouse 1?" I asked.

"It's reserved for the bride and groom."

"I'll talk to Mr. Cavalli," I said. "Do your best to juggle things. Shanna, you may have to call Mr. Kravitz's office to say there's been an unfortunate double-booking." I saw fear in her eyes as she imagined

Mr. Kravitz himself answering the phone. I turned to Al. "Anything to report?"

Al read off an exhaustive list of maintenance issues, most related to the work of Fratelli Construction. When he raised the issue of the support beams I cut him short, seeing the alarm in the faces around the table.

"Let's review your list offline," I said.

A quick recalculation from Rheanna informed us we would be relocating eleven guests tonight. Valerie Smitts would be heading up this unpleasant task, and I would be summoned to deal with any irate guests. I dreaded telling Tony about the relocates.

Last to report in was Ez Lopez. Everyone turned to her with an encouraging smile as they tried to envision her chasing Chelsea Fricks off the balcony with a butcher knife.

"Very busy in housekeeping," Ez reported, pushing a wisp of black hair out of her eyes. "But everything okay. Everybody work hard, no problem." She nodded her head several times and smiled.

"That's it?" I said.

"That's it!" She looked down at her notebook and made a check mark, as though having written this down as a formal item to raise. I caught a flash of red on her palm.

All eyes lingered on her.

"Then I guess we're finished," I said, breaking the silence.

They stood up all at once and rushed for the door.

I called after Ezmerelda. "Would you mind sticking around for a minute?"

Shanna also stayed behind.

I closed the door. "Ez, did you happen to see the *Daily Spotlight* today?"

"I see," she replied.

Shanna and I exchanged a look of surprise. "Did you read it?" I said. "Do you know what it says about you?"

She lowered her eyes. "What I can say? Is not true."

"Of course it isn't true," I said, breathing a sigh of relief. "It's outrageous. Shanna and I want you to know that, whatever happens, we support you fully."

Her chin trembled. "I really appreciate."

I wanted to rush over and give her a hug. By the expression on Shanna's face, she felt the same way.

"Ez, there's something you should know," I said. "Detective Christakos is—"

At that moment there was a loud knock on the door. The door was flung open, and Olga Slovenka appeared, pointing an accusing finger at Ezmerelda. "There! See! Go!"

Detective Christakos and Officer Gertz rushed into the room.

Stavros, in uniform, marched up to Ezmerelda. "MRS. LOPEZ, I NEED TO TAKE YOU IN FOR QUESTIONING," he yelled.

Ez turned to regard him squarely. "I under arrest?"

"NO MA'AM, YOU ARE NOT UNDER ARREST. I AM SIMPLY REQUESTING—"

"For God's sake, she's not deaf," I said, placing a protective arm around Ezmerelda.

Shanna moved to her other side.

Detective Christakos lowered his voice. "Mrs. Lopez, you are not under arrest at this time. I would like to ask you more questions regarding the Chelsea Fricks case. If it is all right with you, I'd like to do that at the station. If you don't want to go, you don't have to. If you wish to consult an attorney, it is your right."

Ez shook her head. "I don't need attorney."

"It might be a good idea," said Shanna. "Just in case."

But Ez was adamant. "I no hiding nothing."

"Fine," said Stavros. "Will you come with me? I have a car waiting out front."

"Wait a minute, Detective," I said. "Ez, show us your hands."

She had them behind her back. Looking up to meet my gaze, she pulled them out and slowly uncurled them.

We gathered around. Her hands were hideously calloused, bruised, and raw.

"Do these look like cuts from a butcher knife to you?" I asked Stavros.

"Mr. Lambert," said the detective, eyes flashing, "would you be so kind as to step aside and allow me to do my job?"

"But—"

"*Step aside. Now.*"

Officer Gertz grabbed me by the shoulders and held me back as the detective hustled Ezmerelda to the door.

"Ez, are you going to be okay?" I called after her.

She turned to me and nodded. "Of course."

I struggled free of Officer Gertz's hold and caught up with Stavros in the hallway. "Do you mind if I escort her, Detective? This is her place of employment, after all."

"Fine," he said, stepping aside.

The instant Ezmerelda and I appeared at the top of the staircase, all activity in the lobby ceased, and everyone turned to stare. Ez placed her hand on the banister, holding her head high, and descended the stairs at my side. I admired her poise, her lady-of-the-manor comportment, as though she were not under police escort but arriving at a ball in a long, flowing gown. Behind me, Shanna gave a reassuring nod. Next to her, the detective was watching Ezmerelda like a hawk.

At the foot of the stairs, Ezmerelda halted. Her eyes scanned the lobby, head nodding as though greeting her subjects. At the front desk, Beth Flaubert was weeping openly. Bellman Gustavo was standing at attention at the door, fighting off tears as though watching his beloved queen walk to the gallows. At the concierge desk, Bernadina was eyeing Detective Christakos with a lascivious expression.

I turned to him. "You're not going to make her face that crowd? Can we take the back exit?"

He shook his head adamantly. "The car's out front."

Officer Gertz stepped in front of us. Ezmerelda detached herself from my hold and followed him unaccompanied, gliding gracefully across the marble floor. Gustavo opened the door and saluted her.

As we stepped outside, we were hit with an orchestra of shouts and jeers. A dozen police officers struggled to control the crowd as it surged toward us.

"Murderer!" someone cried.

"Tell us why you did it!"

"You killed our Chelsea girl! I hope you rot in hell!"

Detective Christakos took Ez by the arm and pulled her toward the waiting police car. My heart melted as I watched her go. She remained stoic as she made her way to the car. Halfway there, she swayed on her feet and clutched Stavros's arm to steady herself. The notebook she had brought to the meeting was still tucked under her arm.

I hurried after them. "Detective, can I come?"

He shook his head, waving me back with his hand.

I returned to the curb and stood next to Shanna. We watched helplessly as the detective pushed Ez into the cruiser. The crowd went mad. Officer Gertz went around to the passenger door and climbed in while Stavros lingered, enjoying the attention. He looked like an actor on set, aware of the cameras but not looking into them. He knew his marks, his best angles, his "money shot." Keeping his head up, eyes visible to the cameras, he moved slowly and deliberately to the driver's side, stopping to pose every few steps. He checked for his gun, adjusted his club, pivoted his body left, then right, moved a few more steps, and stopped in front of the vehicle. There he surveyed the area, eyes squinting as though in search of perps, placed his hands on his hips and squared his shoulders. At the driver's door, he stopped again to speak into his radio, tilting his head back, allowing the cameras maximum eye exposure. The paparazzi lapped it up, snapping photo after photo.

At last, he climbed into the police car. He rolled down the window and leaned out, adjusted the side-view mirror, checked the rear-view mirror, and smoothed his chiseled jaw. The cruiser rolled into motion. As it made its way down the driveway, the crowd descended on it, thumping on the hood, banging on the windows, crying out for Ezmerelda's blood.

I lifted my hand to wave goodbye, but Ez wasn't looking back. She was staring straight ahead, neck rigid, having retreated into her panic room.

★ ★ ★ ★ ★

"What a glorious day!" Mom cried, lifting her hands toward the sun. "I'm having a marvelous time."

"I'm glad someone is," I said.

Mom was determined to enjoy her vacation regardless of the chaos around her. Shanna had joined us at a table on the pool deck for a late lunch. There was no breeze, and the sun was mercilessly beating down on us. I loosened my tie and unfastened a button on my shirt, sliding my chair under the small circle of shade the umbrella provided. Mom basked in the heat, throwing her head back and lifting her freckled brown chest to greet the sun. Across the table, Shanna sat with her back to the sun, wearing Gucci sunglasses, a silk scarf tied around her head like a movie star from the sixties.

A few tables away, a young couple sat sipping iced tea and fanning themselves. Every lounge chair and cabana around the pool was occupied; the beautiful people were back. A gaggle of bikini-clad women were splashing in the pool and giggling. The pool at the Playboy Mansion was under repair, and the ever-opportunistic Sydney Cheevers had invited them here, sending a fleet of limousines to retrieve them. A businessman lay sprawled on a chaise longue in a suit and loosened tie, talking on a cell phone and eyeing the Playmates.

With the fate of Ezmerelda weighing heavily on my mind, it was impossible to share my mother's joie de vivre. Five hours had passed since she was taken away, and no one had heard anything. I tried to reach Detective Christakos several times, with no success. At the Lopez household, no one was picking up. My work was piling up, yet, unable to focus, I had agreed to join these two women, one on vacation, the other acting like she was on vacation, for lunch.

"I'm famished," Mom announced, sitting up to open the menu.

I stared down at my own menu. Across the table, Shanna regarded the menu with apathy, her mouth set in a grim expression. Our usual light-hearted banter was gone. It was calm on the pool deck, but we knew a much different scene was being played out front. No longer was Hotel Cinema merely the scene of the crime, it was now an accomplice, the harborer of the culprit. I could feel the heat of the public's contempt. Things would calm down once she was exonerated, I assured myself. But the more time that passed, the less likely that seemed.

Reginald Clinton came out to greet us. "Hot enough for everybody?" he asked, fanning himself. An affable, elegant black man from

Louisiana, he had run some of the city's most popular restaurants, including the Ivy and Koi.

"I love the heat," Mom said. "The hotter, the better."

After we ordered, Mom watched Reginald walk off. "My, my," she exclaimed, pressing a hand against her heaving bosom. "So many beautiful people in this city, I don't know which way to look."

"Mom, would you mind not flirting with my staff? It's embarrassing."

"I was not flirting, Trevor. I was simply enjoying the company of an attractive young man. Everyone is *so* nice in this city. It's nothing like I expected."

"Don't be fooled by the smiles, Evelyn," Shanna said. "People are just as miserable here as everywhere else, even more so—they just look better. Beautiful people flock to Los Angeles to be discovered, but most are forced to take other jobs, so there is an unusually high percentage of beautiful—and disappointed—people in this town. When their looks start to fade, they become miserable. They get injections and implants and surgery to slow things down, but it brings only temporary relief, and soon they're even more miserable. Most of us have never been beautiful, so we don't know what we're missing. But when beautiful people see their beauty fading, year by year, month by month … well, that's why there are more miserable people in Los Angeles than anywhere on earth. At least, that's my theory. Not that I've given it a lot of thought."

"Clearly not," I said.

Mom turned to me, a glint of hope in her eyes. "You must hate it here, then, darling. I know how you like being around happy people. Maybe it's best that you come back to Vancouver."

"Shanna's being cynical," I said. "I think people *are* happier here. This city is full of optimists. It's like the sun has seeped into their souls."

"Trevor will never go back to Vancouver," Shanna said. "He's becoming *so* LA. Look at that tan suit, that sassy unbuttoned shirt, those aviator sunglasses. Now if we could only get him a tan."

Mom looked crestfallen.

"Never say never," I said, partly to assure Mom and partly to end the conversation. I buttoned my shirt back up and tightened my tie. They were thinking about themselves, not me. Mom wanted me in Vancouver, where she could conduct experiments on me with her armchair psychology. Shanna wanted me in Los Angeles to share the burden of Tony Cavalli. They were acting like jealous girlfriends.

Reginald arrived with our drinks. I sipped mine, facing Shanna but sneaking glances over her shoulder through my reflective glasses at the Playmates. They were chasing each other around the pool with water balloons. Desire stirred within me. Just steps away, an empty cabana suite. Unthinkable, of course, but I allowed my mind to wander in that direction for a moment. When was the last time I got laid? *Nancy.*

"I hope you're enjoying this vulgar display," said Mom.

"I hadn't noticed."

"This place is crawling with frisky women," Mom said. "I don't know how you restrain yourself. I was watching you in the lounge on Saturday night, and girls in little more than negligees were throwing themselves at you, yet you acted like a perfect gentleman."

"Trevor *is* a perfect gentleman," said Shanna.

"I'm not about to prey on guests like a lounge lizard."

"Why?" Mom said, lifting her sunglasses. "I've dated the odd patient from the hospital—*odd* being the operative word. Life is too short. Where else are you going to meet someone? You spend all your time here. You're the general manager. Take advantage of your position to meet women. It's been a year. Just do it. Use it or lose it."

"Good advice, Mom. I'll keep it in mind."

Our meals arrived. Shanna glanced at the enormous club salad before her and made a face. She picked up a scrap of radicchio and nibbled on it, then set it down. I stared at my prawn cocktail with similar aversion and pushed it away. The sun had moved the circle of shade, and I was now exposed to its full intensity. Circles of sweat were forming under my armpits.

Where was Ezmerelda? Why hadn't the detective called?

Mom dove into her chicken-and-brie focaccia sandwich. "Delicious!" she exclaimed, offering her fries to Shanna.

Shanna held her hand up. "God, no."

Mom's eyes moved to Penthouse 1. "I keep thinking about that poor girl," she said, "but I'm having a hard time taking it seriously. The whole situation feels contrived, scripted, like a bad made-for-TV movie. Oh look, here come the Greenfields." She lifted her hand to wave at a family of four wearing Disneyland T-shirts and toting various inflatable devices. "They must be looking after their grandchildren."

Mrs. Greenfield, a large woman with thighs like rolls of dough, waved back. All the deck chairs were taken, so they settled on a corner of the pool. The husband pulled his shirt off, his white belly bouncing. The grandson headed straight for the pool, leaping into a cannonball, sending a gale of water in our direction.

Shanna shrieked and sprang from her chair. She pulled off her sunglasses and turned to stare daggers at the kid, who was splashing toward the shallow end. "Who let that little urchin in here?" she cried. "I thought I banned children from this place."

"How civilized," my mother said, shaking water from her shirt.

"Don't let Wendy and Janet hear you," I said, sponging droplets of water from my pants with my napkin. I turned to Shanna. "Mom has six grandkids."

"Shhhh!" Mom said. "Bruce is coming by this afternoon, and I don't want him to know. He saw their photos in my wallet, and I told him they were my nieces and nephews."

"Bravo, Evelyn," said Shanna. "You look far too young for grandkids anyway."

The pool attendant hurried over with an armload of towels to dry us off.

Shanna thanked him and sat down, crossing her legs and resuming her elegant posture. "I pray my children never procreate. You're lucky Trevor hasn't, Evelyn." She must have seen me flinch. "Yet," she added.

"I would *love* Trevor to have children. How are your children, Shanna?" Mom asked. "Do you see them often now that you're living here?"

"My children?" Shanna placed her sunglasses back on. "Oh yes, I see them frequently, quite frequently." She gave a nervous laugh. "Of course, they're busy."

"I know how you feel." Mom glanced at me.

"I have to go," I said, rising from my seat.

"But you've barely touched your meal," said Mom.

"I'm not hungry."

Reginald was back, clearing our plates. "Another round?" he asked.

"No," I said, glancing at my watch. "We'll take the bill."

"That would be lovely!" Mom interjected. "Shanna, will you join me?"

"I believe I will." Shanna handed her empty glass to Reginald. "Trevor, darling, why don't you have a margarita with us? Our afternoon will be much easier to face behind the haze of good tequila. We could all go swimming with the bunnies."

"Trevor is afraid of water," said my mother.

"Shanna, it's three o'clock on Tuesday afternoon. We have work to do."

Mom's cell phone rang. She dug into her purse and flipped it open. "Hellooo? Evelyn Lambert speaking."

"Why are you such a spoil sport?" Shanna said to me. "We work like dogs every day. Can't we take a little break in the middle of the afternoon?"

I turned to survey the deck. Everyone but the businessman had taken refuge in the pool. I wanted to join them, to tear off my clothes and dive into the pool, to splash around with the bunnies and drink margaritas. How did anyone get work done in this city with so many distractions? It was like a never-ending spring break. Yet as I watched the rippling surface of the pool, I wondered if I would ever be able to swim again without being haunted by the image of Chelsea's body, blood seeping from her lacerations, mixing with chlorine and blue dye to form a purple haze, or by the thought of Nancy striking the surface of the ocean and plunging into its icy depths.

Beside me, Shanna let out a small gasp as four muscular men in Speedos trotted onto the pool deck. "Good heavens," she said, fanning herself. "Now I'm definitely not going back to work."

"That settles it," I said. "I'm heading back to the office." I waved to my mother, who was hunched over the phone a few feet away.

"I see ..." she was saying, a note of angst in her voice. "So there's no way the boarding passes could have been switched? They were both on standby. That gate attendant is in her sixties, isn't she? Mistakes happen—they just don't usually have such grave consequences ..."

Boarding passes? Standby? She was talking about Flight 0022.

"...of course I understand, Mr. Lee...I just find it a strange coincidence. That *poor* family, after all this time...Did you reach her grandmother? ... Is she okay? ... All right, well, thank you again."

Mother came back to the table, visibly distraught.

"What was that was all about?" Shanna asked.

Mom removed her sunglasses and wiped her eyes. She turned to me, lifting a hand to shield her eyes from the sun. "That was Dexter Lee from the WWA-0022 Commission. Trevor, when you told me Nancy took an earlier flight, and then I read about that Irish woman being found in the wreckage, I had to know more. I called him yesterday. He just called back with some unsettling news."

"Don't tell me it *was* a terrorist attack," Shanna cried, pressing her hand against her chest.

"No, no, they're still certain it was a mechanical failure." Mom came to me and placed her hands on my shoulder. I smelled citrus and tequila on her breath. "Darling, the seat assigned to Nancy was occupied."

Shanna let out a small gasp.

Bile rushed to my throat. "They found Nancy?"

"No. That's what's so disturbing. It *wasn't* Nancy." Mom searched my face until our eyes locked. She spoke calmly, assuming her nurse's bedside manner. "It was Suzan Myers."

"The Irish woman?" Shanna cried. "Why was she in Nancy's seat?"

Mom looked away. "I don't know."

"Then who was sitting in Suzan's seat?" Shanna asked.

"Nobody. It was empty. Nancy's body wasn't found on the plane."

★ ★ ★ ★ ★

For weeks after the crash, I had fantasized that Nancy was alive, that by some miracle she had survived the crash and would be found on a deserted island, turn up on a Russian ocean liner, or drift to the coast of Scotland on a life raft. Maybe she had never boarded the flight and her strange, elusive grandmother was holding her captive. Maybe she had amnesia. I scoured the news obsessively, searching for clues to her survival. The tabloids in particular fed into my fantasies, reporting sightings of other passengers—most often Suzan Myers, but sometimes others—in Edinburgh, in Iceland, in London, on the Canary Islands. I had envied Suzan's family for having hope. I knew my obsession wasn't healthy, but it was better than accepting she was dead.

Two months after the crash, an official with the commission called. Nancy's suitcase had washed to shore and was found by a Scottish fisherwoman. He asked if I wanted it back. Fearing I would open the waterlogged suitcase and be hit by a gale of grief so powerful I would drown, I told him to give it to her grandmother. "She doesn't want it either," the man said. "Then burn it," I told him. My mother was horrified. "How could you be so unsentimental?" She called the commission back, but the suitcase had been incinerated. Its discovery extinguished all hope for me. I stopped reading tabloids and newspapers, stopped watching the news, and stopped deluding myself that Nancy might walk through the door one day.

Yet all this time a tiny pilot light of hope had persevered within me, and now it flared back to life. Suzan Myers was sitting in Nancy's seat. Suzan's seat was empty. What did it mean? Shanna and Mom talked it through on the pool deck while I listened in stunned silence. Dexter Lee had said there was a simple explanation: they switched seats. They were assigned seats in the same row near the back of the aircraft. Nancy was assigned seat 68K, a window seat, and Suzan 68H, an aisle seat. The seat in between them was unoccupied. "Didn't you say Nancy wasn't feeling well?" Mom said. "Maybe Suzan offered her the aisle seat." More likely, I thought, Suzan told Nancy it was her first trip to Canada and Nancy offered her the window seat.

"Then why was Suzan's seat empty?" Shanna asked.

Mom spoke slowly, carefully selecting her words, her eyes darting to me every so often to make sure I was okay. "Dexter said the impact would have sent people flying out of their seats if they weren't wearing seatbelts—and in some cases even if they were. He said that passengers likely lost consciousness during the initial plummet, but some regained consciousness before the plane struck the ocean. Several were found clutching rosaries, photographs, and cell phones. Two male passengers, strangers when they boarded, were found gripping each other's hands. Nancy might have been in the bathroom when the engine failed. It all happened very fast. She wouldn't have been able to return to her seat. Hers wasn't the only body missing from the fuselage."

Shanna pressed her with the questions I wanted to ask but couldn't bring myself to. I was rendered speechless, clutching my chair like I was experiencing those last harrowing minutes myself. "Then who was the woman who missed the flight?" she asked.

"According to Mr. Lee," Mom replied, "the gate attendant, Lydia Meadows, insists she was holding Suzan Myers' boarding pass. Suzan was on standby too. When she didn't materialize, her bags were pulled—aviation policy. Moments after the plane pulled away, a woman came running to the gate. Lydia insisted it was Suzan. She handed Suzan's boarding pass to her and told her to retrieve her luggage and go to ticketing to be booked on the next flight. No one ever saw Suzan again."

"Could they have accidentally switched boarding passes?" Shanna asked. "Could it have been Nancy who missed the flight?"

Mom shook her head. "That's what I wanted to know. Dexter says there is no doubt Nancy was on that flight. Only part of the fuselage was found, and almost a third of the bodies have not been recovered. The inquiry will release its final report in a few weeks. We should expect no surprises. When I heard they found the fuselage, I hoped we could put this ordeal to rest once and for all. But it's not meant to be. We need to accept that our lovely Nancy drifted into the ocean and will never be found."

There were more questions from Shanna, but I had heard enough. The searing heat of the sun was more than I could bear. I retreated to the air-conditioned lobby, where I was temporarily blinded by darkness, and went to my office, shutting the door and closing the blinds.

There, I ignored the persistent ring of the telephone, the knocks on my door, the incessant ding of my computer each time a new email message arrived. I allowed my thoughts to drift back to Nancy ... that flicker in her eyes when I proposed. I thought of Stavros's claim to be able to read people's eyes and to find the truth by comparing emotion to words. There was hesitation in her voice, fear and heartache in her eyes. *Let's wait and see.* Wait for what? See what? The fear ... of commitment? The heartache ... because she couldn't marry me? Why would an independent spirit like her marry a work-addicted, one-dimensional man like me? Had she wanted to wait and see if I would resume my work-obsessed lifestyle after the trip? Had I failed the test by cutting our vacation short?

I thought of Chelsea Fricks' desperate leap off the balcony. Did she feel a sense of relief to be bailing from her miserable life? Did Nancy feel the same way as the plane jolted and dipped, skipping in the air like a whitewater raft? The fantasy that Nancy was somehow alive always led to the same wretched questions. Where was she? Why hadn't she called? Why hadn't she come back to me? These doubts surfaced once again, as though the discovery of the fuselage, the anniversary, my mother's visit, and Chelsea's death had conspired to summon Nancy back from the dead.

I had to stop tormenting myself. They switched seats, that's all. Nancy was languishing somewhere in the ocean depths, perhaps the long-forgotten meal of a deep-sea predator. Any other theory was as implausible as a tabloid headline: WOMAN THOUGHT TO BE ON DOOMED FLIGHT WALKS INTO MCDONALD'S AND ORDERS A SHAKE! People believed such outrageous stories because they wanted to. I refused to fall back into that trap. Had I been given the chance to prove myself, Nancy would have agreed to marry me. End of story.

Enough.

★ ★ ★ ★ ★

Later that evening, when I tried Ezmerelda's home number again, to my surprise someone picked up.

"Hello? Felix here."

"Felix, it's Trevor at Hotel Cinema. How are you doing?"

"Okay." He spoke with the same Mexican accent as Ezmerelda, but his English was much better.

"Ezmerelda ... how is she?"

"She's okay."

"Is she ... where is she?"

"Lying down."

I felt a rush of relief. "That's wonderful. How did everything go at the station?"

"Okay, I guess."

His reticence was frustrating. I couldn't ask outright if his wife had been charged with murder. She was at home. It was a safe bet she hadn't. "Ezmerelda is okay, then?"

"She's okay."

"I'm glad, Felix. We were worried about her."

"She feels bad about missing work. She'll be back tomorrow for sure."

"Tell her to take all the time she needs," I said. "But we do miss her. Is there anything I can help with?"

"No, everything is fine, thank you."

I wanted to ask about the knife, about their involvement in the NISF, about Ezmerelda's membership in the Chelsea Fricks Fan Club, but such questions were an invasion of privacy, none of my business. "Well, then, I suppose I should be going. Please give her my best."

"Um, Trevor?"

"Yes?"

Felix lowered his voice to a whisper. "She's not in trouble, is she?"

"In trouble? No. Why do you ask?"

"Please hold on, okay?" I heard him put the phone down. A moment later he was back. "She's still resting," he whispered. "She doesn't want to say anything. I tried to convince her, but she's so stubborn, so loyal."

I pressed the phone to my ear. His voice was so faint I could barely hear it. "Convince her of what, Felix? Loyal to whom?"

There was a long pause. "When she was leaving the suite, someone was waiting. She held open the door. It doesn't show on the security report."

"Who?"

"I have to go. She's up now."

"No, wait! Felix? Tell me quickly—who?"

But he had already hung up.

★ ★ ★ ★ ★

"There he is!" Detective Christakos shouted, springing from his table in Scene and pumping my fist. "There's my man! How's it goin', Trev?"

"Good evening, Detective," I said, pulling away from his sweaty hand.

I had finally reached him earlier, but he sounded busy and didn't want to talk. I asked if we could meet. "Not tonight. I got a date!" Only when I offered to comp his dinner in Scene did his interest perk up. "A really good table?" he asked. "In the center of the dining room, in the middle of the action? For surveillance purposes, of course."

"Of course."

As soon as I hung up, I went to Reginald to beg him to find a table.

Now it was nine PM, and the restaurant was jammed. Over thirty people were in the lounge, waiting for reserved tables. Soft chill music was playing at a tolerable, even pleasant level. As the night progressed, it would increase in volume and pace, transforming the restaurant, lounge, and lobby into what staff now called Club Cinema. The pool deck was closed for a private function, which meant even more people were crammed into Scene and Action. There was no sign of Tony Cavalli or his clan—yet.

"I want you to meet a very special lady," Stavros said, gesturing to a young lady sitting at his table. "Trevor, meet Cappuccino."

The name was impossible to forget: the girl from the house party. Like a good detective, he had tracked her down. She stood up and thrust her hand out, not to shake mine but to allow me to kiss hers.

Her long black eyelashes fluttered. She was stunning. And young. Could she even be old enough to drink? Her black hair was long and straight, bones as thin as a foal's, skin the color of—yes, cappuccino.

"Please to metchu," she said in an unusual accent.

"Cappy's from French Guyana," Stavros explained. "Ain't she gorgeous?"

I nodded, forcing a smile, unnerved by her beauty—and consternated by her age. A martini glass full of gin or vodka sat on the table in front of her. Would a cop bring a minor here and feed her alcohol? I certainly hoped not. Observing her affected manner as she sat down, prim and poised, and folded one arm over the other, I recalled that Stavros said she was an actress. A model too, no doubt—likely an actress-model-screenwriter-producer-choreographer-waitress like so many others in this town.

"What a lovely name you have," I said, wondering if her real name was Patty or Sue and if she was from Denver. Yet her features were undeniably exotic, her eyes enormous, dark brown, and mesmerizing. I felt a stir of lust, followed by guilt. A glance at Stavros's glassy-eyed gaze told me he was smitten.

"Tunk u," mouthed Cappuccino, flashing a row of perfect teeth.

A strange accent indeed.

Stavros sat down in his chair, arms folded, legs spread wide. "You eaten, Trev? Why don't you join us?"

"Sorry, I can't. But I was hoping we could talk."

"Of course we can talk. Have a seat, my friend! We have much to celebrate."

"Oh?" I said, pulling up a chair.

He leaned toward me, covering his mouth with his hand. He was freshly shaven and coiffed. His skin glowed. "Ez Lopez is off the hook."

"That's great news. Not that I ever doubted her innocence."

"Neither did I, really."

"You *arrested* her, Stavros."

"I didn't *arrest* her. I took her in for questioning. I knew she was hiding something, I just didn't know what. Now I know." He turned to Cappuccino. "Sorry, babe, official business."

"Okie dokie!" she replied, lifting her glass to cheer us. She gulped at it and gazed dreamily into the dining room.

Stavros leaned toward me and lowered his voice. "Miraculously, Mrs. Lopez remembered how to speak English at the station today. I sat her down in an interview room, and she opened her mouth and started singing. I don't pay much attention to words. I watched her eyes. The truth is always in the eyes, Trevor." He pointed two fingers toward his own eyes. "Remember that."

"So you told me," I said quietly.

My eyes moved to Cappuccino. Her black hair fell to her breasts, camouflaging the black fabric of her form-fitting dress. I moved my gaze up her delicate neck to her full lips and long lashes. What was she thinking? Were *any* thoughts running through her mind? Nancy's eyes were the same dark, impenetrable brown. *Let's wait and see.* Was it fear of commitment in Nancy's eyes or fear of something else?

"When the words match the emotion, I know they're telling the truth," said Stavros, taking a wedge of bread from the basket and ripping into it with his teeth.

Was this what had been nagging at me all this time? Was there no match between the emotion in Nancy's eyes and the words she told me? Was she lying to me? I put the notion to rest. I had vowed to stop torturing myself with questions I could never answer.

Stavros chewed with his mouth open. "The eyes are the windows to the soul. Right, Cappy? The eyes are the windows to the soul?"

"*Absolument!*"

"See, right now I can tell exactly what you're thinking."

"What I am tinking, den?"

"You're thinking you want to jump my bones."

She let out a mock gasp. "No, I am not!"

"Yes, you are! You want me bad!"

She giggled and swallowed the rest of her martini. "You crazy, Stagrosh."

"No, *you* crazy! Crazy for me!"

"Detective, do you mind?"

He turned back to me, his face growing serious. "So, like I was saying, this time I see a match between what Mrs. Lopez's words are telling me and what her eyes are telling me. First time I met her, I saw fear, hostility, and guilt in those eyes. Today, after we talk awhile, the hostility and fear dissipate. She starts to trust me. I knew she was telling the truth. Her story checked out."

"So what was her story?" I asked.

"Felix is illegal. They got married in Pueblo twelve years ago and decided to move to the States. They've got family in New York and here in LA. Mrs. Lopez came first, stayed at his brother's place in New York, and got a job in a hotel. She got landed immigrant status no problem, but the government refused to let Felix in because he was charged with shoplifting in Mexico City when he was nineteen. In America's eyes, he's a criminal, and there's no way they're letting him in. So she mails him his brother's passport and he gets in that way. Now he can't apply for immigration or he'll be thrown out. They moved to LA a few months ago so Mrs. Lopez could take this job. He works under the table as a carpenter. They keep their heads down, work hard, obey the law, do everything to avoid attention.

"Chelsea flipped when she caught her in the suite. Mrs. Lopez insists she wasn't snooping, and I believe her, but Chelsea didn't. She called her a spic, threatened to have her deported—I guess she assumed anybody with an accent was illegal—and told her to get the fuck out, which she did. Next day, Mrs. Lopez finds herself at the center of a highly publicized murder investigation. I come knocking, and she's terrified I'm going to find out her husband's illegal and have him deported. So she says, 'I no see nothing make bed go home eberybuddy happy okay no problem' and clams up. Today, when I told her I know about Felix and wasn't going to do anything about it, she started to relax. She explained everything. I promised to put her in touch with an immigration judge who owes me a favor. Things will work out for her and Felix."

"That means a lot, Stavros. But what about the NISF membership?"

"A friend invited them to a meeting a couple of years ago in Queens. He told them it was about immigrant rights. When they arrived, they signed their names on a list and became instant members. When they realized what the meeting was really about—using violence as a tool for advancing their rights—they got up and left. End of story."

"And the Chelsea Fricks Fan Club?"

"She joined to qualify for advance tickets to Chelsea's fall concert. She planned to surprise her niece."

I was starting to feel a great sense of relief. "The knife in the maid cart?"

Across the table, Cappuccino let out a loud yawn. Stavros glanced uneasily at her. "Someone planted it there."

"Moira or Bryce?"

"I'm done talking. Let's get some drinks! Cappy, you ready for another drink?"

"*Absolument!*"

"So much for your breadcrumbs," I grumbled.

"Hey!" he said, eyes flashing. "My breadcrumbs are serving me just fine, thank you. They led me to Mrs. Lopez, who pointed me down another path, which I am now following."

"So she told you someone entered the suite as she was leaving?"

He glowered. Either she hadn't told him or he was angry I knew. His black eyes flickered and went blank. There was a story in those eyes, but he wasn't about to tell it.

He lifted his hand to wave the server over. "Excuse me! Miss!"

I struggled to regain his attention. "Detective, come on. You owe it to me. Who did Ez let into the suite?"

"Let's have some champagne! Cappy loves champagne, don't you, baby?"

"Chompoine!" she cried, clapping her hands.

Stavros beamed at her. Was he so clueless that he couldn't tell her accent was phony? Couldn't he see the truth in *her* eyes? She was a small-town American girl pretending to be an exotic princess. If he couldn't see that, I had grave doubts about his ability to solve the case. His eyes gleamed at the treasure across the table, blinded by her beauty.

He turned and clamped his hand on my shoulder. "Whaddya say, Trev? Shall we order some champagne?"

I stood up. "Not for me, thanks."

He pulled me back down. "Don't you ever let loose? Ever have *fun*?"

"Not if I can help it," I muttered.

"Join us for a drink."

My first impulse was to politely refuse and excuse myself, but for what? To work late or to go home and wallow? I felt a sudden urge to be part of this party that raged around me. Mom was out for dinner with Bruce. The hotel was under control. Ezmerelda was off the hook. The hysteria outside would die down. And this might be the last time I had to deal with Stavros Christakos. Perhaps a little champagne was in order. I sat down.

Stavros and Cappuccino cheered.

When the server, Suzanne, came bustling over, I ordered a bottle of Veuve Clicquot.

"What?" shouted Stavros. "Cristal!"

I turned to him. "Are you paying?" It was $650 a bottle.

"On my salary? You kidding? I could arrest you for the prices you charge!"

I turned back to Suzanne. "Veuve, please."

She smiled and sailed off.

The detective glared at me but quickly recovered. He turned and surveyed the room. "So. Who's here?"

"As in suspects?"

"As in stars."

"This is what you mean by surveillance?"

"Don't get all testy, Trevor. You're the one who convinced me to come here tonight. I promised Cappy we'd see stars, but I don't recognize anyone. Don't tell me the A-list has already moved on? I don't do B-list, Trevor, I don't do B-list!" He roared with laughter. "Cappy, I wasn't lying. This place is normally packed with famous people. They're all here to see me, of course."

Cappuccino giggled.

Suzanne arrived and poured the champagne.

Stavros reached for his glass and held it up. "To Ezmerelda Lopez!" he said.

"Zelda Lopess!" Cappuccino echoed, with no idea who she was toasting.

We clinked glasses. The champagne tasted wonderful. I leaned toward the detective. "Have you released a statement to say Ez is no longer a suspect?"

"Don't worry your pretty little head. A statement went out." He held up his champagne glass. "To Trevor Lambert, hotel manager extraordinaire, my new friend, for whom, although he's an uptight, guarded little prick at times, I have a great deal of respect."

"To Tray-vorrrr!" Cappuccino purred.

I lifted my glass. "Thank you, Detective," I said. "I think."

"No, thank *you*," he replied, "for so graciously hosting us tonight. And for ensuring I never have to line up to get in here or pay for a thing." He winked.

The champagne had a quick effect on me, and soon I was feeling more relaxed than I'd felt in weeks. The conversation moved from Cappuccino's impoverished childhood in French Guyana to Stavros's audition class to the various movers and shakers who began to populate the room. The detective pointed celebrities out like a boy in a toy store discovering his favorite action figures. Cappuccino was amused but aloof, making it clear she considered herself the biggest star in the room. Like a big shot, I ordered a second bottle of champagne.

"What the hell?" I said. "A bottle of Cristal!" As Cappy squealed and Stavros cheered, I wondered how I would explain the promo bill to Tony.

Later, sufficiently sauced, I got up the nerve to work the room a bit, introducing myself to various VIPs but steering clear of the superstars out of respect for their privacy. When I returned to the table, Cappuccino had crawled onto Stavros's lap and was practically giving him a lap dance. Over the course of the evening, her accent had morphed from faintly Caribbean to Southern Italian to Russian, occasionally slipping into Midwestern. Now she was so drunk she was mostly incoherent. I wondered if the world's oldest profession might also belong on her list of careers. But Stavros seemed happy, and because I was drunk I was happy that he was happy. Despite his irritating tactics, I had grown quite fond of this unconventional detective, this strange man Shanna called "the insufferable little Greek."

"Cheers," I said, lifting my glass.

"To what?" asked Stavros.

"To your brilliant detective work!"

"Bravo!" cried Cappuccino, and we all drank again.

★ ★ ★ ★ ★

Several glasses of champagne, a glass of port, and two Irish coffees later, I said good night to Stavros and Cappy, signed the $1357 bill to my promo account, and stumbled around the hotel for a last walk-around before going home. The crowd seemed more subdued than on previous nights. Tony Cavalli had never showed up, and the music was loud but not obnoxious. Wishing Reginald a good night, I listed toward the front door.

As I passed the front desk, I saw Valerie Smitts standing alone, filing registration cards. She looked up and saw me, breaking into a magnificent smile. Nancy used to smile at me like this as I passed the front desk at the Universe. I lumbered over, concentrating hard on walking straight.

"How was your night?" I asked, carefully enunciating my words.

"*Busy*," she replied. "I did six relocates myself. One gentleman got really nasty." She swept her hand across her forehead, pulling a clump of luscious brown hair out of her eyes. "I'm dying for a drink."

I blinked. Had Valerie just opened a window? For some time now I had suspected she harbored a secret crush on me, yet I chose to disregard it. She was an employee. As hotel manager, I had rules to uphold. And how could I ever be unfaithful to Nancy? Moreover, I had vowed never to make myself vulnerable to heartbreak again. Yet, in the back of my mind, I heard a medley of clichés from my mother, the queen of pop psychology: *Life's too short. Just do it. Use it or lose it.* I regarded Valerie, feeling my body sway slightly. That wonderful, dark, lustrous hair … I wanted to reach out and touch it. Suddenly it made perfect sense that Valerie and I should be together. Tonight.

"Thirsty, are you?" I said, stupidly.

"Totally." She smiled again and resumed filing.

I felt an impulse to flee. But look at her, she was gorgeous! I glanced at the freckles on her brown chest, the swell of her breasts under the pale pink shirt. Could she really like me—an uptight workaholic? Remembering the detective's advice, I peered into her eyes. Was that desire I saw?

"You okay, Trevor?" she asked, her face scrunching up.

I blurted it out. "Can I buy you a drink?" *Caibuyadinkch?*

"Sorry?" She leaned closer to me, covering her ears to drown out the clamor around us.

"A drink. Can. I. Buyadrinkch?"

"Oh, a *drink*." She gave a short, high-pitched, soul-destroying laugh. "Sorry, I can't. I, um, have plans."

"Okay."

"We're going to Whiskey Blue at the W. You can join us if you want."

"Who?"

"Me and ..." She stopped, eyes bulging slightly. "Maybe you should go home, Trevor."

"Home?" I felt my body listing to the left and gripped the surface of the desk.

"Want me to call you a cab?"

"No. I'm fine. I'll walk."

I lurched toward the exit, making a full-scale retreat into my panic room.

12

Hangups

Wednesday morning, I arrived at work groggy and feeling foolish about my behavior the previous night. My mood didn't improve when I found Shanna encamped in my office once again.

"You moved in," I said as I brushed passed her. "I missed the memo."

"Things are going from bad to worse, Trevor." She held up a copy of *Spotlight*. The words CHELSEA MURDERED BY MAINTENANCE MAN? were emblazoned on the cover.

"What the hell?" I said, snatching the magazine from her hands.

Two side-by-side photographs occupied the cover: a shot of Chelsea walking blithely on the beach in a white bikini and a shot of Al Combs clipping the hedges at the front of the hotel. Al was holding his hand up and squinting in the sun, which made him look angry and a bit sinister. A caption on the bottom right announced: MAID COMES CLEAN!

Glancing at Shanna, who was biting her thumb and staring wide-eyed into space, I opened the magazine and found an article entitled, DID THE CHIEF ENGINEER FIX MORE THAN A LEAKY FAUCET? A photo of the exterior of the hotel and the tent city that occupied the front accompanied the article. Below it was a photo of

Ezmerelda Lopez ducking into the police cruiser under the watchful eye of Detective Christakos.

"Our intrepid reporter Nigel Thoroughbullshit got the scoop once again," Shanna said wryly.

"Scoop? You mean fabrication. Don't tell me you believe this?"

"Of course not. I'm quite sure *Spotlight* doesn't either; note the question mark in the headline. It's a shameless attempt to boost sales. Unfortunately, it doesn't matter if it's true or false. People will believe what they want to believe, and this story is going to ignite another feeding frenzy. Able Al will be eaten alive. I was so relieved when I saw the news last night and learned Ezmerelda was exonerated. Now this."

"I'd better warn him," I said, reaching for the phone. "He'll be mobbed."

As Al's cell phone rang, I watched Shanna thumb through the magazine. This time she had purchased a second copy for herself. A sensationalistic headline ran across each page: FRICKS FAMILY PLANS CLOSED FUNERAL, HOLLYWOOD SNUBBED; HEART-THROB BRYCE SHUNS MEDIA. She stopped to peruse a photo spread entitled CELEBS CAUGHT WITH BOOGERS! VOTE FOR THE GROSSEST!

"He's not answering," I said, placing the phone down. I sat back in my chair, mind spinning. "That headline is going to destroy him. He's so shy and sensitive. What possible grounds do they have to point the finger at him?"

Shanna flipped back a few pages. "'In confirming that Mrs. Lopez is no longer a person of interest in the case,'" she read, "'the Los Angeles Police Department announced that activity reports generated by the hotel's electronic security system indicate that Allan Robert Combs, head of the hotel's maintenance department, visited Chelsea's suite in the hours before her death. According to a trusted inside source, Mr. Combs was summoned to the suite to repair a leaky faucet. Although police questioned Mr. Combs the following morning, no arrest was made. *Spotlight* was unable to reach Mr. Combs at his West Hollywood apartment. A tall, imposing figure at six foot four, he is thirty-two years old and has never been married. Our source divulges that this is not the first time Mr. Combs encountered Chelsea, having worked at the chic Hotel Mondrian on Sunset Boulevard, where Chelsea was a regular guest. According to the Mondrian's general manager, Alyson Parker, Chelsea was asked to leave the hotel for 'lewd behavior' and was not welcomed back.'"

"Alyson never told me Chelsea was kicked out," I said, surprised.

"Shush. Listen. 'Did Mr. Combs do something more sinister in Chelsea's suite than repair a leaky faucet? Determining the answer will be up to Stavros Christakos, the hotshot detective in charge of the case. Mr. Christakos has an illustrious history with the LAPD, having solved some of Hollywood's most notorious crimes during his five short years in the homicide division. In an interview with *Spotlight* early last evening, he elaborated on his legendary investigative tactics. "The truth is in the eyes," he said—'"

"God, please stop," I said, the effects of last night's revelry stirring within me. "I heard enough last night. I can't believe they're trying to connect Al to her murder when he left the suite *hours* before she jumped. And for God's sake, who is this source? If it's Moira, I'm going to kill her."

Shanna inspected the cover photo of Al. "Do you think they darkened his eyes to make him look evil? He normally looks so wholesome. He looks downright creepy here."

Creepy. The same word Chelsea had used to describe him. Should I tell Shanna about the complaint? I noticed a tray on the bookshelf behind her containing two paper cups and a white bag stamped with a Hollywood Café logo.

"What's that?" I asked.

"Oh, I forgot," said Shanna, reaching for the tray and sliding it toward me. "I brought us some breakfast. I felt like something fattening."

I opened the bag. "Donuts? We have a kitchen full of gourmet pastries." I pulled out an apple fritter and handed the bag to her. "Don't tell me you're converting my office into a precinct?"

"I'm on a strict new diet: fatty foods only." She plucked a jelly donut from the bag and regarded it thoughtfully. "I've had no appetite since Friday, and I've lost six pounds. A woman's dream, right? Not mine. My face has aged twenty years. When I'm fat, it fills in my wrinkles like collagen. I've decided I'd rather be fat than old." She took a sizable bite and resumed flipping through *Spotlight*. "There's a nice plug for the hotel here." She adopted a Robin Leach-like British accent. "'The ultra-swank Hotel Cinema boasts a state-of-the-art security system that uses iris-scan technology in place of traditional room keys.'" She looked up. "Tony and Kitty will be ecstatic."

"Speaking of Kitty, where has she been? I haven't heard a peep from her in days."

"I know. It's been marvelous."

"So *Spotlight* fingers Al as the chief suspect simply because he was in the suite the same night she died—even though it was hours before? Can journalism get any more despicable?"

"Mr. Thoroughbred speculates that Al was stalking Chelsea. He interviewed a former Mondrian housekeeper who claims Al used to break things in her suite just so he could spend time around her. She says she thinks he was infatuated."

"Infatuated with Chelsea?" I laughed. "He's gay."

She looked startled. "Gay? Who told you that?"

"*You* did."

"I certainly did not."

"A few months ago, when we were debating whether to hire him, you said, 'He's single, in his early thirties, buff, and lives in West Hollywood—you do the math.'"

"It was an offhand remark, mere speculation. He's not gay, Trevor, believe me. Besides, even if he were gay he could still be infatuated. A lot of gay men were obsessed with Chelsea."

I was stunned. "He's straight? Are you positive?"

"Why do you care?"

"Because I happen to have lent a great deal of credibility to your 'offhand remark.' Tell me, I need to know: is he gay or straight?"

"Most certainly straight."

My jaw dropped. "Don't tell me you ...?"

"Of course not, silly. Although I'm sure he lusts after me, like all other men." She stood up and went to the mirror. "Or so they used to. My God, I think I've aged five years since breakfast!" She turned to me. "Besides, I would never fraternize with a colleague. It's against company policy."

I was about to remind her about Willard Godfrey, but her arched eyebrows made me reconsider. Did she know I'd asked Valerie out in a drunken stupor? I winced, recalling her rejection. I would have to face her every day. Maybe I should fire her, I thought, feeling wicked and vindictive. She was off today. The awkwardness could be postponed. When I did see her, I would be cordial and professional, as though nothing had happened. And then I would fire her.

"How do you know he's straight?" I persisted.

"Word is he's been seeing someone—a female."

"Who?"

She opened the Hollywood Café bag, fishing out a chocolate sprinkle. "I really must get to work," she said, heading for the door. "So much to do."

"Don't even think about leaving."

She stopped and turned. "I thought you weren't interested in gossip." She was acting coy, but I detected a flicker of apprehension in her eyes. "Are you sure you want to know?"

"Oh God. It's not my *mother*?"

She rolled her eyes. "Please. It's … well, it's … Valerie."

"Valerie Smitts?" I coughed and pounded my fist with my chest. "How do you know?"

Shanna nodded toward the window. Dennis Claiborne was peering into the window, lips pursed, a copy of *Spotlight* tucked under his arm.

"Dennis told you?" I said.

"I didn't upset you?"

"Why should I care if Valerie and Al are dating?"

"I thought … I got the impression you liked Valerie."

I glanced out the window again. Rheanna was standing at the photocopier. Dennis leaned toward her and whispered something in her ear. She threw her head back and screeched with laughter, and then looked over her shoulder into my office. They were laughing at me. Valerie told them. I marched to the window and closed the blinds. "Shanna, I'm not interested in Valerie. End of discussion."

"Fine. But what's all this fuss about Al's sexual orientation?"

I went to my desk and sat down. "I'm going to tell you something, but you can't tell anyone else, okay?" I gave her a recap of Chelsea's complaint and my meeting with Al.

As the story unfolded, her expression grew increasingly alarmed. "Does the detective know this?" she asked when I finished.

I shook my head. "I didn't think it was relevant."

"*Not relevant*?"

"It isn't relevant, Shanna. Al was in the suite long before Chelsea jumped. There's no record of him going back. I gave the detective all the information I felt pertinent to the investigation. As hoteliers, it's our job to protect the privacy of our guests and our employees."

"Yes, but we're not doctors or psychiatrists. We have no legal or moral obligation to maintain confidentiality. This is a *murder* investigation, for God's sake. You've withheld information that might be critical to the case. Whose privacy are you protecting, anyway?"

It was a good question. "I was so distraught by what happened that night," I said, trying to piece things together. "The detective was irritating me. He seemed more interested in which stars were staying here, in what Chelsea looked like in a bikini, than in solving the case. In the penthouse suite, I saw the remnants of drugs and booze, clothes strewn everywhere, makeup and beauty products lining the counter, her party dress laid out on the bed. The glass coffee table was cracked in the middle like a broken heart. And the blood… It was like Chelsea's tragic life story was laid out in that suite. Why didn't I inform the detective of Chelsea's complaint then? Al's visit, hours before her death, was irrelevant then and it's irrelevant now. Christakos is a loose cannon who will trammel anyone to 'solve' his case. I'm not about to put innocent employees in his sights.

"When the detective raised the possibility of foul play, I knew the media would go hysterical. I felt protective of the hotel, of our staff, of Chelsea. It didn't matter that she was a spoiled party girl. She was a human being. The state of the suite, the state of her life, was nobody's business. So I said as little as possible."

Shanna was frowning. "But you didn't even know her. Why would you—?"

"Shanna, I wanted to treat her death with dignity."

"An actress you never met?"

"Don't you understand? There are parallels: Nancy, Chelsea. Both fell from the sky like angels, plunging into water, causing a tidal wave of heartbreak and leaving unanswered questions. Remember how the tabloids sensationalized the crash? I was helpless to stop it. This time, I wanted to exercise what little control I had."

Her expression softened. She lifted herself from her chair and came to me, placing a tentative hand on my shoulder. "I think I understand. But you can't protect these people anymore. It's time to give full disclosure."

"I know."

Shanna went to the window and pulled up the blinds, turning to me with a bright smile as though opening them to a sunny day. Dennis, Rheanna, and Ahmed were standing with ears pressed against the glass. They scattered in all directions.

"You need to call a meeting and talk to your staff," said Shanna.

I shook my head. "I refuse to dignify this sensationalism by discussing it. We're taking the high road, remember? We agreed not to feed the fire."

Shanna came to my desk and leaned over it, sending a cloud of perfume in my direction. "Darling, we agreed to not feed the *media* fire, not to ignore our staff. You can't hide in this office any longer. You're the general manager of this hotel. It's time for leadership. You need to step outside and talk to your employees. They're feeling lost and overwhelmed. Some are terrified. *I'm* terrified. A murder occurred here a few days ago, and the murderer is still out there. It could be one of our guests, one of our employees. We're lucky they're even showing up for work. You need to reassure them that they're safe, inspire them, tell them we stand behind Ez and Al."

I licked my lips. "Fine. I'll call a staff meeting. Now can you please leave me alone? I need to catch up on my work."

She didn't move. She locked eyes with me, engaging me in a stare-down.

I glared back, trying to push her out the door with my eyes. After a moment, my lower lip quivered. I broke eye contact.

"Wimp," she said.

"Battle-axe."

"I'll spread the word that there will be a general staff meeting at ten AM," she said. "Oh, and *Daily Spotlight* is coming in to do an interview and photo shoot with Natalie Portman this afternoon. The timing's not great, but Tony wants celebrities here, so I approved it. Our intrepid reporter Nigel Thoroughbred is doing the interview. Moira Schwartz set it up. She's going to accompany him."

"Moira has found a new client, has she?"

Shanna shook her head. "It sounds more like Moira is tagging along with Nigel, hoping to sign on Miss Portman. She was a bit vague about the details."

"Fine," I said. "I'd rather not see Moira. Will you do the meet-and-greet?"

"*Me?*" Her hand flew to her chest. "I'm terrified of Natalie Portman."

"Are you serious?"

"She's so young and beautiful and talented."

"Perhaps a little exposure would help desensitize you. Why don't you drop by and say hello?"

She let out a gasp and cowered back. "I could *never*. Reginald agreed to oversee it. I'll be hiding in my office until she's gone."

"Fine, then. Kindly close the door on your way out." As she left the office, I glanced down at the magazine she left behind. I called her back.

She leaned in the doorway. "Yes?"

"Do you think he did it?"

"Absolutely not."

"Me neither." I hesitated. "Are we blindly loyal to our staff? Too loyal?"

"Never."

★ ★ ★ ★ ★

The instant Shanna was gone, Janie Spanozzini appeared in the doorway.

"Tony's tryin' to reach ya, Treva." A wad of pink gum tumbling in her mouth, she pointed at the ringing phone behind me. "You betta pick up. He's really mad."

"Thank you, Janie." As I went to close the door, I caught a glimpse of Ezmerelda in the hallway waiting for me, a troubled expression on her face. I smiled and waved, happy to see her back at work, and signaled I'd be just a minute.

I picked up the phone. "Trevor Lambert speaking. How may I help you?"

"Is this part of your brilliant PR strategy—getting hammered in the press?" Tony barked. "Every time I pick up *Vanity Fair*, I read an interview with some big-name actor at Chateau Marmont like it's the coolest fucking hotel in the world. It looks like an old lady's knitting room! Meanwhile, a few blocks away *is* the coolest hotel in the world, yet every time I pick up *Spotlight* I read that one of its employees killed Chelsea Fricks."

"Then maybe you should stop reading *Spotlight*, Tony."

"Don't get smart, Trevor. Is it true? Did Al Creep-o Combs kill her? He try and rape her or something?"

"How could you say such a thing? Of course not."

"I never liked that guy. Acting all sanctimonious around the Fratellis like he could do better. How many rooms are still out of service—*twenty-five*?"

"Thirty-three, actually. He expects to get more completed today."

"That's going to be pretty difficult from jail, don't you think? What's your contingency plan? You going to fix the rooms yourself? These delays are costing me a fortune, Trevor. Meanwhile, 'Able Al' Fuckwad is wasting time harassing VIP guests. I assume you fired him?"

"No, I named him employee of the month."

"I'm warning you!"

"Al had nothing to do with Chelsea's death, Tony. I'd wager my job on it."

"Then who did? That fucking terrorist maid? Or maybe it was the butler in the library with a candlestick? My hotel is the laughingstock of Los Angeles, Trevor. It's humiliating. Janie tells me all the staff are freaking out, no one knows what happened, no one knows what to think or say, and meanwhile you're hiding in your office eating donuts and drinking coffee with Shanna."

"Janie told you that?"

"She's the only one holding that place together. Have you given any more thought to promoting her to assistant director?"

"Assistant director …"

"Whatever you call it—assistant front office manager, duty manager, director of operations. She's a key employee, and I need her to learn as much as possible. I'm looking at a property in South Beach, and I may need her to run it."

I found myself caught between the delightful prospect of transferring Janie and the horrifying prospect of having to tell my managers that Janie was now one of them. "I don't think Janie's quite ready for a management position, Tony. Maybe once she stops taking two-hour smoke breaks. In fact, there are a number of issues I need to discuss with you."

"I don't want to hear it! Janie's the only person I can trust to tell me what's *really* going on around there. She says Al Combs is always staring at her tits."

Who isn't when she's got them on display like that? I thought to myself. "Al Combs is one of the most decent human beings I've ever worked with. I assure you, no hotel employee had anything to do with Chelsea's death. It was Moira Schwartz or Bryce Davies or an intruder. The detective is close to making an arrest. For now, I'm focusing on running your asset."

"Yeah, into the ground! I tell you, I regret the day I let Shanna brainwash me into hiring you sight unseen."

And I regret the day she brainwashed me into thinking you were smart. "I'm trying, Tony, but I'm under a lot of pressure here. What I need is your advice and support."

"I'll give you some advice: stop fucking up!"

"Thanks. That really helps."

"I demand respect! R-E-S-E-P-C-T!"

I didn't dare tell him he had misspelled it.

"I'll give you until Saturday to pull us out of this media clusterfuck!" he shouted. "My entire family will be there for Lorenzo and Rosario's wedding, and everything needs to be flawless. My mother thinks the hotel is cursed. My father is threatening to pull the plug.

You know what that means? You and I will both be out of jobs. And believe me, you'll be the first to go."

"The reception will be flawless, I promise."

"It better be!" He slammed the phone down.

★ ★ ★ ★ ★

The instant I put the phone down, it rang again. Impulsively, I picked it up. "Yes?"

There was no response.

Thinking I had frightened the caller, I assumed a more cordial tone. "Good morning, Trevor Lambert speaking, how may I help you?"

Still no response.

A hangup? I was in no mood. I was about to put the phone down when I detected the sound of breathing—that familiar labored breathing, as though someone were smothering his or her mouth with the receiver.

"May I help you?" I said.

The breathing stopped.

"Who is this?" I said, exasperated. "Why aren't you speaking?"

The breathing resumed, crackling like Velcro.

I wanted to slam the phone down, but it seemed magnetically bonded to my ear. I listened intently, as though if I listened hard enough I would hear the secret to these mysterious calls.

"*Please* stop calling me," I said. "Identify yourself, or I'll call the police."

The caller hung up.

I set the phone down. Then I snatched it up and dialed *69, knowing it was futile. I had done this before, and the operator always said the phone number was unavailable.

An electronic voice announced, "The number is 4-4-1-7-2-2…"

I lunged for a pen and scribbled down the number. I listened a second time to ensure I got the numbers right. I stared down at them. 44 was England. 1722 was the city code for Salisbury, in Wiltshire.

Edna Swinton, Nancy's grandmother.

I dialed the number. As I waited for her to pick up, I thought about the peculiar old woman. Nancy had often talked about her father's mother, how spry and independent she was, how she had hoped to live as long and age as well. She predicted the two of us would get along famously. Yet after the crash, the woman had taken no interest in keeping in touch. She declined my invitation to come to the memorial service, even though I offered to pay. I assumed her health was an issue. She was in her mid-eighties, after all. After the service, I called to offer to visit her in Salisbury, thinking Nancy would have wanted that. But she declined. After a few more attempts to establish a relationship, I had given up.

Now she was calling me.

The phone rang ten times, twelve, fifteen. I didn't hang up, imagining her hobbling toward the phone along a frayed old carpet, navigating a room full of dusty antiques and cats. After twenty rings, I was about to hang up when the phone clicked.

"Hello? Who is this?" I recognized her tiny voice and British accent.

"Mrs. Swinton, it's Trevor Lambert."

"Who?"

"Trevor Lambert. Nancy's boyfriend? You just called me."

"I did?"

"Yes. At my office in Los Angeles. How are you?"

She let out a sigh. "Good as could be, I suppose. Memory's fading fast."

"I was going to call you the other day, on the anniversary. I assume that's why you called? One year, isn't it hard to believe?"

"What?"

I raised my voice. "It's been a year since Nancy died."

"Oh, yes, of course…" There was a prolonged silence.

"Are you there, Mrs. Swinton?"

"Yes, yes. I'm here. Still here. After all these years." She chuckled softly.

"I understand the flight commission called you?"

"Who? Oh, no."

"They didn't call you?"

"Oh, I suppose they did. I can't really recall. It was so long ago."

"They found the fuselage. They raised it, but Nancy wasn't there."

"Of course she wasn't, now, was she?"

She sounded more senile than ever. "I moved to Los Angeles," I said to make conversation. "I work at a new hotel in Hollywood. But I guess you know that. You called me here."

"Yes, of course."

"How did you find me? Did you read about Chelsea Fricks in the newspapers?"

"Oh no, I don't read newspapers, never have. Full of bad news, aren't they?"

"Then how did you—?"

The line went dead.

I redialed several times, but the line was busy. I grew concerned. What if the old woman fell and couldn't get up? I wanted to call someone to check on her, but who? Nancy had been her only living relative. I tried the number several more times. On the last attempt it rang, but no one picked up. Deciding she was well enough to place the phone on the hook, I gave up.

★ ★ ★ ★ ★

Ezmerelda was no longer waiting in the hallway.

I made my way down the corridor, ducking into offices along the way to ask if anyone had seen her, but no one was around. I went down the back stairs. On B2 I checked the housekeeping office, the cafeteria, and the locker rooms, but no one was around.

Olga Slovenka was standing in the window of the storeroom.

"Where is everyone?" I asked.

"Meet!" she cried, pointing upward.

Meet? I looked at my watch: 10:20 AM. I was late for the general staff meeting.

Almost one hundred employees were crowded inside the Screening Room. It was set up theatre-style, with every seat occupied and a dozen employees standing at the back. Conversation halted as soon as I entered, and heads began to turn in my direction. I forced a smile as I made my way up the aisle, anxious about arriving unprepared and rattled by the morning's events. Every department in the hotel was represented: kitchen, front desk, sales and catering, accounting, restaurant, lounge, housekeeping, reservations, and human resources. I quickly scanned the room for Al's towering figure but couldn't see him. Ezmerelda was seated in the back row, near the exit. I tried to make eye contact with her, but she was staring down at her hands.

A large screen for private screenings filled the front wall. I stood in front of it and turned to face the audience.

Shanna was perched on the edge of her seat in the front row to my right, smiling in encouragement. She knew I was shy about addressing groups—particularly a large group of people who depended on me for their livelihood—and was prepared to come to my rescue if I started to babble. I took a deep breath and tried to slow my palpitating heart, determined to make a solo performance.

"Good morning, everyone," I began. "Thank you all for volunteering to come to this mandatory meeting." It was meant as a joke but elicited not a snicker or a smile. "Shanna and I felt it important to gather you all to discuss recent events and what they mean to us as employees of this hotel. I know it's been a challenging week, and I want to thank each of you for your positive attitude and professionalism."

Gathering my thoughts, I paced back and forth, sensing my shadow following me on the screen. I stopped in front of Shanna, and my shadow disappeared.

"I know that you, like me, are deeply distraught over Friday night's tragic incident. Opening night was challenging enough without the added stress of a death on-property. Add to that the ensuing media frenzy, the throng of fans outside, and all sorts of rumors and intrigue, and it's all a bit overwhelming, isn't it?"

There were assenting nods around the room.

Such an attractive bunch, young and fresh faced, well groomed and capable. Even the Spanozzini sisters looked the part today, seated side-by-side in the middle row, wild hair tamed into ponytails. Shanna was right: these people simply needed a bit of reassurance and leadership, someone to tell them their jobs were safe, they had nothing to fear, and things would return to normal soon.

I resumed pacing, accompanied by my shadow. "This hotel is fully committed to the safety and security of its employees and guests. Police are still investigating the incident that took place Friday night, but I can tell you with full confidence that there is no danger to you. All the same, we are taking extra precautions. Your head of security,

Artie Truman, is a former LAPD officer, an accredited first-aid professional, and one of the most paranoid guys I know."

There were chuckles in the crowd.

"In addition to doubling door coverage this week, Artie has tripled the number of security officers on duty. During daytime, no one is permitted on-property except registered guests, patrons with reservations, and accredited employees. At nighttime, the bar and restaurant crowd is tightly controlled. If you see or hear anything unusual, you must report it to Artie or me at once. If you are feeling stressed or anxious, tell your department head and we will accommodate you however necessary, even if that means giving you time off."

I paused. "As for this hysteria in the media, the public was obsessed with Chelsea Fricks when she was alive and is even more so in her death. The media is sensationalizing every aspect of this case. I urge you to be patient and understanding. There is danger in believing one's own press, and I assure you there are many lies and untruths flying about. Be careful what you read and what you believe. Things will settle down soon, I assure you, and the people outside will move on. In the meantime, it feels like the world is watching Hotel Cinema, doesn't it?"

Heads nodded.

"This is our opportunity to shine. Let's show the world that, despite the circus around us, the employees of Hotel Cinema are consummate hoteliers. We are dedicated, professional, compassionate, and discreet. We have nothing to hide, and we stand fully behind our employees. We will *not* dignify the outrageous rumors and speculation in the media. Understood?"

The group broke into a cheer.

Someone shouted in the back, "Where's Able Al?"

Dennis Claiborne shot up in his seat. Resting knuckles on his hips, he announced in an insinuating tone, "Al called in *sick*." Overnight, Dennis had switched his disloyalty from Ezmerelda to Al. I flashed a warning look at him, urging him to sit down. As manager of human resources, he should know better.

"Did he kill Chelsea?" Janie Spanozzini called out.

"Able Al is innocent!" cried Manny the houseman.

"We love Al!" Valerie chimed in, rising to punch her fist in the air. She looked around, face turning red, and quickly sat back down.

"Al the best!" said one of the stewards.

There were cheers and claps of support for Al.

"Ezzy innocent too!" one of the room attendants shouted out.

"We love Ezmerelda!" cried Melanie from sales, leaping up like a cheerleader. "Hurray for Ez!"

Everyone rose in a standing ovation, clapping and cheering, stamping their feet and thumping chairs. A few room attendants got up to put their arms around her. She sat quietly, head down.

"Indeed, we love Ezmerelda," I said, clapping along. "We're so glad to have her back."

Rather than stand and bow to her subjects like a queen, Ez folded over, covering her face with her hands, and rocked back and forth with sobs. Then she sprang from her chair and dashed out of the room.

Valerie got up and ran after her.

The room fell silent.

"What happen?" asked one of the line cooks.

I turned to Shanna, who looked equally puzzled.

"It's been a stressful time for her," I said. "We need to give her time to recover." I paused and resumed my speech. "I remind you of the values that guide our conduct as employees of Hotel Cinema. One, discretion. We respect the privacy of our guests and do not release any information whatsoever. Two, professionalism. We are role models who always act in the best interests of the hotel and its guests. And three, dedication. We are dedicated to providing the highest quality of product and service."

Realizing I was losing them, I quickly wrapped up. "Thank you all for upholding these values these past few days. In the coming weeks, I urge you to pull together and support one another, to remain focused on your work, and to maintain your integrity regardless of what the people around us are doing and saying. If we adhere to these principles, we will have a bright future ahead. Can I count on everyone?"

There were shouts of "Yes!" and "Absolutely!" Everyone rose to their feet, clapping, whistling, and cheering. Clearly, the death of Chelsea Fricks was not about to deter this fine group of hospitality professionals.

I called the meeting to an end and stood at the door with Shanna, thanking them as they filed out. When the last of the attendees was gone, Shanna and I turned to one another and let out sighs of relief.

"Congratulations, Trevor. You were marvelous."

"I did okay?"

"You could be press secretary for the president."

"Only press secretary? How about president?"

"Don't push it. But what came over Ezmerelda? Yesterday, while being escorted off-property by police under a cloud of suspicion, she was a vision of strength. Today, free of suspicion and applauded by colleagues, she falls apart."

"I don't know," I said, "but I'm going to go find out."

★ ★ ★ ★ ★

I found Ezmerelda on the third floor, making the bed in Room 307. Rico had put the finishing touches on the room that morning, and it was almost ready for final inspection. She looked up as I entered and quickly resumed her work, movements jerky.

"Ezmerelda, I'm sorry I missed you before the meeting."

"Is okay."

Over the years, the room attendants' job had become increasingly physical and complex; gone were the days of two flat pillows and a floral bedspread. Hotel Cinema's bed linens included three layers of crisp white sheets, a pillow-top mattress, six pillows—four feather and two foam—a bolster, throw, and goose-down duvet.

Ez flipped the top sheet into the air, and it floated down softly.

I reached out for the other side and tucked it under the mattress. Ezmerelda's eyes were lowered. Her face was gaunt and pallid; there was no sign of her sunny disposition.

"I hope I didn't say anything to offend you?"

She shook her head. She lifted the duvet and threw it into the air.

I reached for my end and together we arranged it into place. "I thought you'd be relieved now that police aren't chasing you around like a bank robber anymore," I said.

She didn't smile. She stared down at the bed, blinking, and burst into tears.

I rushed to her side. "What is it, Ez? What's wrong?"

She shook me off. "The bed," she said, fussing around. "Is not proper. Very messy!" She pointed to the side I had made. In contrast to her smooth side, mine was rumpled and amateur.

"Oops," I said, "my fault." I tried to smooth out the fold.

"No!" she cried, pushing me out of the way. She lifted the duvet cover and pointed to the top sheet. "Look!" I had done a sloppy job of straightening the top sheet. "Must make every layer perfect," she said. "No can hide flaws."

"Of course," I said, feeling foolish. I stepped back and allowed her to work her magic. For such a stickler for detail, I mused, she had certainly overlooked her share of details regarding her encounter with Chelsea Fricks. I wanted to know the whole story this time: who had slipped into the suite as she was leaving? Who was this person she was so loyal to?

Ez smoothed the duvet back into place. The surface of the bed was now immaculate. "See? Much better."

I nodded my approval. Her face looked sad and fearful. "Are you worried about your family?" I asked.

She gave a shake of her head. "The detectib say he's going to help us. He knows an immigration judge." Tears began flowing down her cheeks.

I went to the bathroom to grab a few tissues from the dispenser and handed them to her. "Then why are you so upset?"

She pressed them against her cheek. "I feel so bad. I promise to no say anything. I don't want to make trouble. Is not my business."

"Make trouble for who?"

She returned to the bed and began fluffing pillows and arranging them.

"Ez?"

As she fetched the bolster from the armchair, a red smear on one of the pillows caught my eye. I went for a closer look. Blood. There was another smear on the duvet. Spinning around, I caught Ez by the wrists and turned her hands over. "Open your hands, Ez."

She shook her head and looked away.

"Ezmerelda, open your hands."

Slowly, she unfurled them. They were bound with gauze, but the gauze was soaked with blood.

"Ezmerelda," I said softly. "Go home. You've been working too hard."

She shook her head. "I can't. Too busy."

"I'm not giving you an option. I'm grateful for your work, but it's time to rest. I don't want you back until your hands are fully healed, okay? We'll manage without you. And don't worry, you're not in trouble, and I'll ensure you're paid for your time off."

She dropped her head and sobbed, her entire body convulsing.

I put my arms around her and held her.

"He make me to promise no say nothing," she sobbed onto my shoulder.

"Who?"

She pulled away and dabbed her eyes. "When I leave suite, about 11:15, he is standing outside door. I go, he comes in. Next day he makes me promise don't say anything. I say no problem, is not my business anyway. I don't think he did anything bad. Now I not so sure."

"*Who*?" I said again.

Anguish filled her eyes. She opened her mouth and closed it, lower lip trembling. "Able Al," she said at last.

She collapsed on the bed and burst into sobs, pulling the sheets and pillows over her, destroying the order she had just created.

★ ★ ★ ★ ★

Back in my office, I tried Al's cell phone again, with no success. I was angry with him now. I had been too quick to assume his innocence. First I find out he's straight, now I find out he returned to Chelsea's suite that night even after I forbade him. Rico and Stephen were on duty at the time; if Miss Fricks needed something fixed, they should have handled it. And why didn't Al tell me he went back? More importantly, *why* did he go back? I decided to reserve judgment until I heard his side of the story. But he was making this difficult by avoiding me.

I looked down at the phone. The message light was flashing like a distress signal. Maybe he had left a message. I dialed into my voice mail. Twenty-three messages were waiting: Chelsea fans, journalists, two hangups, and several guest inquiries and complaints. Too distracted to deal with the guest requests, I forwarded them to Valerie. Next came a message from Detective Christakos. "I'm coming down to see you," he hollered over the sound of traffic. "If Al Combs shows up, don't let him leave." Moira Schwartz had also left a message: "Call me. It's important." I deleted it. Next came my mother. "Where are you now, dear? This may be too much to ask, but I'd like to spend some time with my son while I'm here." I scribbled down a reminder to call her.

There was no message from Al. When I placed the phone on the hook, it rang instantly. Hoping it was Al, I picked it up.

"Hiya, Trevor! It's Alyson from Hotel Mondrian. How's it going?"

Why did I pick up? "Things have been better, Alyson. How can I help you?"

"I have to tell you, we're a little disappointed over here. When we heard your executive housekeeper might have killed Chelsea, she was our hero. My room attendants were parading around, singing 'Ding, dong, the witch is dead' and collecting donations for her defense. We all decided it was justifiable homicide."

"Hilarious, Alyson."

Beth Flaubert appeared in the doorway and tiptoed into the room, sliding a note toward me. "Detective Christakos is here," it said. I nodded, feeling my pulse quicken, and held up a finger to indicate I'd be out in a minute.

"...really don't get the controversy surrounding the funeral," Alyson was saying. "If you ask me, they should burn her body at the stake and be done with it. While they're at it, they should set Moira Schwartz on fire too. If Chelsea was the Wicked Witch of the West, Moira's got the Eastern Hemisphere covered. I don't know how Bryce put up with those two. He was such a great guy, always so courteous and respectful with staff. I could never understand what he saw in Chelsea. She treated him like..."

"I have to go, Alyson. Someone is here to see me. But while I have you on the phone, why didn't you tell me you banned Chelsea from your hotel?"

She hesitated. "Sorry. It was related to a confidential personnel issue. But now that it's out in the open, what's your take on today's *Spotlight* story?"

"About Al Combs? It's ludicrous. I'm sure you agree."

"A detective was just here to see me. Short, stocky Greek guy with major attitude."

"Detective Christakos came to see you? What did he want?"

She hesitated. "Did Al ever tell you about the incident?"

"What incident?"

"The ... indiscretion ... with Chelsea Fricks."

Suddenly I was filled with dread. "No, he did not."

"Oh, boy ... well. I don't want to stir things up, but since I told the detective, I thought you should know."

"What, Alyson? What incident?"

"Al and Chelsea ... you know ..."

I stood up. "No, I *don't* know. *What*?"

"How do I put this politely? ... Last year, a maid walked in on Al banging Chelsea in her suite."

★ ★ ★ ★ ★

My mind was spinning when I went out to greet Detective Christakos.

He rushed at me, his hand diving for mine in a bizarre street-
punk handshake that left my thumb feeling broken. "Hey, I want you
to meet a very special lady in my life." He gestured toward a heavyset, plain-looking girl standing in the shadows. She stepped into the
light, revealing long ringlets of black hair and a faint moustache on
her upper lip.

I knew Stavros liked them young, judging by Mocha or Espresso
or whatever her name was, but this girl was no older than fifteen, possibly as young as twelve.

I turned to him in shock. "*Detective . . .*"

"What?"

I pulled him aside. "How *old* is she?"

"Twelve, why?" His eyes grew dark. "She's my *niece*, Trevor. Perv!
Meet Athena Persephone Christakos. My brother and sister-in-law
moved here from Sacramento last week. She's a natural actress and a
fabulous singer, and they're trying to get her into the biz."

"Hello there, Athena," I said, smiling down at her.

"Hi," she said. She folded her arms limply in front of her, looking bored and slightly hostile, like a young Moira Schwartz. "Is Hilary
Duff here?"

"Not today, I'm afraid," I replied.

"JT?"

"Who?"

"Justin Timberlake?"

"No, he's not here, either."

She turned to stare daggers at her uncle.

"Hold on a sec, okay, sweetie?" Stavros said, flashing a big grin. "Uncle Stav needs to talk to Trevor for a few minutes. Why don't you go have a seat over there? Keep your eyes peeled. You never know who you'll see. But don't touch anything, okay?" He steered me toward the lounge. "I promised her she'd see a celebrity. Anybody around? We got about ten minutes before she sets this place on fire."

"Stavros, will you please stop bringing friends and family here to gawk? This isn't Universal Studios." I spotted the *Spotlight* crew in the lounge setting up for the Natalie Portman shoot and veered in the opposite direction.

"You've got the wrong idea," he said defensively. "I'm here on official business. As you may recall, I'm investigating a murder."

"It's Bring Your Niece to Work Day at the station?"

The detective cocked his head. "You miss your coffee this morning?"

"I'm busy, Detective. Very, very busy. And stressed."

"I take it you don't have kids."

"Kids?" How did the detective manage to get through with these little jabs? "No, no kids." I stopped at the front desk and turned to him. "Now why is it you came here?"

He flashed a toothy grin at Beth and then turned to me, his expression growing serious. "Where's Al Combs?"

"He's not here today. He called in sick."

"Why am I not surprised?" He turned around. "Where'd she go? She was there a minute ago. Oh God, I hope she's not in the kitchen. She can't be near matches or open flame." He raced across the lobby.

Athena was standing at the entrance to Action, hands pressed against her cheeks, mouth open in a silent scream as she regarded Natalie Portman. A makeup artist and a hair stylist were working on her, and a photographer was setting up his equipment.

"Athena, get over here!" Stavros hollered. He turned to me, eyes bulging. "Is that …?"

"No," I said, "it's not. Athena, listen to your uncle." When she didn't move, I made my way over and took her by the hand. "I'm terribly sorry for the disturbance," I said to Miss Portman.

"It's okay," she said, smiling down at Athena. "You want to watch for a while?"

Athena looked panic-stricken—a budding Shanna Virani.

"Why don't you have a seat over here?" Miss Portman said, gesturing to an ottoman a few feet away.

The detective sauntered up to her. "Hello there, *Na-ta-lie*," he said, plugging his thumbs into his pockets and bobbing his head foolishly.

"Um, hi."

"Stavros, please don't." I marched over and jostled him out of the way. "Miss Portman, I'm Trevor Lambert, the hotel's general manager. It's a pleasure to have you here." I nodded to the others. "How did the interview with *Spotlight* go?"

"Great," said Miss Portman.

"Except this really annoying publicist was lurking around and kept hitting Natalie up," said the makeup person. "We had to ask her to leave."

Stavros pushed me aside and flashed his badge. "Detective Stavros Christakos of the Los Angeles Police Department."

Miss Portman looked him up and down. "Am I in trouble?" she quipped.

"I'm afraid so," he replied, tucking his badge away. "You're under arrest for aggravated assault. I'm aggravated because you're assaulting my sense of decency by looking so damned hot."

I groaned. "*Detective.*"

The makeup artist laughed. "Wait 'til I'm finished. You'll have to lock her up for life."

"That can be arranged," said Stavros. "You mind if Athena, my *niece*, watches for a while?"

"Of course not," replied Miss Portman, turning to smile at Athena again.

"You be good, Athena!" he said sternly. "Don't hurt anyone!" He called out to the hair stylist, "Keep her away from the scissors."

As we walked off, he grinned ear-to-ear. "We couldn't have staged that better! Athena *loves* Natalie Portman. She's watched *Star Wars*, like, four hundred times." He looked over his shoulder. "I can't believe you get to meet stars like this all the time. I only meet washed-up has-beens like Phil Spector. It must be hard not to follow them around."

"I wouldn't think of it. This hotel is supposed to be a refuge for stars, Detective."

"It wasn't for Chelsea."

Choosing to ignore that remark, I ushered him through the doorway and into my office. To my relief, Shanna wasn't loitering there.

The detective glanced around. "Pretty plain Jane in here," he remarked. "Not like outside." He studied the photographs on the shelf. "That your late wife?" he asked.

"That's my *mother*."

"Nice-looking lady."

"You said it was urgent?"

He sat down and lifted his backside, pulling his tight pants away from his crotch. "You see me on *ET* last night?"

"*ET*?"

"*Entertainment Tonight*. It was only a twelve-second spot, but I've TiVo'd it and watched it fifty times at least. God I'm a handsome devil." He flashed his teeth. "I was also on *CNN Showbiz Tonight*, *FOXNews*,

Star TV, and *Spotlight Tonight.* I pitched *Spotlight* on becoming a regular—you know, like a law-enforcement correspondent—and they said they'd think about it. My agent says I need to build a portfolio."

I rested my elbows on the desk and massaged my eyeballs. The detective was exhausting. "Is this what you came to tell me?"

"No." His face grew dark. "Your chief engineer, 'Able Al'—he's in a lot of trouble. We've got his apartment staked out, his gym, his sister's house, everywhere, but he's disappeared. You think Ez Lopez tipped him off?"

"What would Ezmerelda tip him off about?" I asked, feigning ignorance.

"Mrs. Lopez informed me yesterday that Mr. Combs entered Chelsea's suite as she was leaving. This occurred at 23:14, twenty minutes before Chelsea jumped—which makes Able Al the last visitor to the suite before she jumped. A few minutes later, Bryce Davies heard a commotion in the hallway. He opened his door and saw a man hurrying down the hallway to the stairwell exit. This morning, Bryce identified that man as Al Combs." Catching his reflection in the mirror, the detective fluffed his hair.

"Al didn't tell you this when you interviewed him?"

"No, he did not. I guess he forgot." His words were heavy with sarcasm. "Did you know about this?"

"Of course not."

"You're lying."

There was no point in trying to protect Al any more. "Ez just told me today. I'm as surprised as you are. I instructed Al to not go back after Miss Fricks registered the complaint."

The detective's eyes closed to two narrow slits. "Complaint?"

Taking a deep breath, I told the detective about Chelsea's complaint and then sat back in my chair, bracing myself for his wrath.

The detective squinted at me, furrowing his eyebrows so hard they looked like a long black caterpillar. Throwing his arms in the air, he slammed his fists on the desk.

"*Why* didn't you tell me this before?"

"I didn't think it was relevant."

"A woman complains about creepy behavior two hours before she's murdered, and *you* don't think it's *relevant*?"

I shrunk in my seat. "I should have told you. I apologize."

He placed his elbows on the desk and leaned toward me. "I thought we had an understanding. I thought we *trusted* each other. What is it with you hotel people? All this time, you've been preaching about how honest and forthright you are, yet you've been lying all along."

"I wasn't *lying*. I chose not to tell you information I felt was irrelevant."

"You *lied* to me, Trevor. I bet you think you're pretty clever. Fooled the detective, didn't you? Think you're a pretty damned good actor, hey? Going to reconsider that acting career?"

"Hoteliers are trained to be discreet. Sometimes we're obliged to withhold information to protect our guests."

"This is a *murder* investigation, Trevor, not an interview with *Celebrity Bad Girls* magazine." He let out a huff. "Why are you so loyal to this creep? There a shortage of maintenance people in this town or something?"

"Why would he attack her? Because she complained? That seems a bit extreme."

"I want you to set aside this blind loyalty for a sec and see things objectively. Imagine you're a simple maintenance guy from the Midwest who comes to Hollywood and discovers he can have direct access to some of the most beautiful girls in the world. How many fucking guys have fantasized about seeing Chelsea Fricks in her panties? I'm not talking about some blurry crotch shot on the Internet. I'm talking live, in the flesh, within grabbing distance. Al is in the bathroom, and she's in a robe and nothing else. Would you look?"

"Of course not."

"Liar!"

"I wouldn't. I've been in similar situations. Female guests drop towels regularly in front of hotel staff. I've never looked. Nor would Al. We're at work, not at a peep show."

"Al sees Chelsea in her panties, maybe catches a glimpse of her snatch, goes fucking insane with desire. Leaves, can't stop thinking about her. Later he slips back into her room to seduce her. She's not a willful participant. He grabs a knife. She's quick. He chases her around the apartment and stabs her. He corners her in the living room. She's bleeding. He's finally got her. Then she runs onto the balcony and leaps off. He panics, wipes the fingerprints off the knife with a face-cloth, hides it in the maid cart in the hallway. Goes home. Next day he shows up to work, acting all shocked that she's dead. He begs Ez Lopez not to say anything, maybe threatens her with *her* life."

I shifted in my seat, disturbed by the scenario. "I still can't imagine Al hurting anyone."

"You are *so naive*. I'm going to tell you something, but only to get it through your thick skull that people aren't always what they seem." He pulled a piece of paper from his pocket and slid it toward me. "Have a look."

I looked down. It was the activity report he had shown me that first morning, now soiled with coffee stains and marked with unintelligible scribbles. I lifted my head. "I've seen this. So what?"

"You know the great thing about technology? It won't lie to you. Not like people. I paid a visit to your counterpart at Hotel Mondrian this afternoon. Alyson—a lovely, charming woman. She said the same things about 'Able Al' as you: gentle giant, dependable, wouldn't harm a fly. But when I pressed her, she happened to recall a little incident between him and Miss Fricks early this year. Al was caught screwing Chelsea in her suite."

"*What?* You're kidding."

He narrowed his eyes. "Don't play dumb, Trevor."

"I just found out myself a few minutes ago. I—Alyson called me, and…"

"Still think he's innocent?"

I threw my hands in the air. "I don't know what to think anymore."

He stabbed at the report with his finger. "Look at the two system bypasses at 23:12. Know what that means?"

"I told you. Access from the adjoining rooms was canceled. We've already established that Miss Fricks requested it."

"Why would she lock out her boyfriend and publicist? They're supposed to be going to the party together."

"Maybe she was afraid of them."

"Guess who made the request, claiming it was on behalf of Miss Fricks?"

I didn't respond. I didn't want to know.

The detective answered his own question. "Al Combs, that's who."

★ ★ ★ ★ ★

"Uncle Stav!" Athena squealed, waving a cocktail napkin in the air. Her hair was teased into an enormous afro. "They gave me a makeover! She gave me her autograph!"

Stavros squatted down to inspect her heavily made-up face. "Jesus, Athie, you look like Jodie Foster in *Taxi Driver*." He ran his thumb over her upper lip. "What the …? They shaved you?" He shot an angry look in the direction of the set. "Her mother's gonna kill me."

"Her mother *wants* her to have a moustache?" I said.

"She's afraid if it's shaved it'll only grow back thicker."

Athena danced around the lobby, leaping into the air like a clumsy ballerina. "I'm pretty!" she shrieked. "I'm an actress! I'm just like Natalie Portman!"

"Ever heard of laser treatment?" I ventured.

"You think I don't know about laser treatment?" He reached for the back of his neck and pulled at a thatch of black hair. "Athena, get over here!"

She stopped dancing and came over, shoulders slumped.

"I want you to wash that muck off your face immediately."

"No!" she shrieked. She backed away, eyes flashing demonically, and turned to race back to the set, where the crew was packing up. Miss Portman was gone.

"Damn her!" muttered Stavros, chasing after her. He carried her back, kicking and screaming. "I'm going to drop this little menace off at my sister's. Then I'm heading over to you-know-who's apartment in West Hollywood. If he shows up here, don't say a thing about our conversation. Call me right away. And don't let him go anywhere. You understand?"

"I understand."

"I warn you, Trevor, if you try to protect him, I'll arrest you for obstructing a criminal investigation."

★ ★ ★ ★ ★

That evening, I went to the fitness room to pick up Mom for dinner. She was in full workout attire—lululemon stretch pants, tank top, and purple headband—and was doing jumping jacks before the mirrored wall. In the center of the room, a rollaway bed faced a television suspended from the ceiling like in a hospital.

"Did I just walk into an Olivia Newton-John video?" I asked.

She reached for a towel. "Just trying to work off all that rich food Bruce keeps feeding me. I thought Angelenos only ate leafy greens, but he's a meat-and-potatoes guy. Can we go for a salad tonight?"

"I thought we'd stay in and order room service. There's a great crab and avocado salad on the menu."

She looked around and sniffed. "In this sweaty fitness room?"

"It's only your sweat. No one else has been working out in here."

"Bruce left a bit of sweat behind too."

I covered my ears.

"Bruce isn't the only one. Janie at the front desk keeps forgetting the fitness room isn't open and programming access for guests. When I got back yesterday, Mrs. Greenfield was doing leg raises on my cot. This morning, a young man walked in while I was spread-eagled over an exercise ball in a bra and panties."

"Please tell me you're joking."

"I wish I was." Dropping the towel, she walked over to the weight rack and lifted two barbells. She carried them to the mirror and started doing curls, grunting like a professional weightlifter. "The poor man is probably scarred for life."

I couldn't help but notice the drooping fabric in her white tank top where her left breast should be. I quickly looked away. "I'm going to kill Janie."

"She was very apologetic when I called down. In fact, I think she called me Mrs. Lambert twelve times in our two-minute conversation. She used to call me Evelyn, which I thought was a tad over-familiar. She's a bit of an odd girl, isn't she?"

"She's Tony Cavalli's niece."

"That explains it."

I tried to quell the frustration inside me. I had promised myself to set aside work tonight and enjoy my time with Mom. "You're in terrific shape," I said. "You'll probably fuel that man's fantasies for weeks."

"Oh, please." She dropped the weights on the floor with a thud, making me wince; there were guestrooms directly below. "Can't we go out?" she said, flexing her tiny biceps in the mirror. "I stay in enough in Vancouver. We're in Los Angeles. It's all so exciting. I saw Natalie Portman in the lounge today! I also met Moira Schwartz, Chelsea Fricks' former publicist. We had quite a long chat. I was surprised you told her about Nancy."

"I told her the night after Chelsea died in an attempt to console her. I didn't think she was listening."

"She says she was addicted to stories about the WWA crash. She couldn't believe your girlfriend was a passenger. She asked me all about it."

"I hope you didn't tell her anything. That woman makes a living out of selling stories to tabloids."

"Well, nothing she couldn't read in the papers. Where shall we go for dinner, then? I asked your concierge Bernadina about recommendations, and she said she always goes to this great place called Mel's Diner."

"We won't be going with any of Bernadina's recommendations. She's another of Tony's nieces."

"Those girls certainly do stand out from the others, though I must say their down-to-earth approach is refreshing. I find your other staff a bit obsequious. When people are that nice to me I find it unnerving."

"Unlike at the Four Seasons, where staff are rude and condescending," I said sarcastically.

"Somehow staff at the Four Seasons make it seem more natural." She began doing weightlifter poses. "Check out these pipes! From now on, I'm going to insist on staying in the fitness room at every hotel." She mopped her brow with the towel. "I need to have a quick shower and change."

"I'll do a walk-around. I'll see you in the lobby in twenty minutes?"

"Perfect."

Downstairs, the lounge was gearing up for another busy night. Tony Cavalli was dining in Scene, hosting a table of a dozen friends and relatives. I was glad to be taking the night off.

Mom came down twenty minutes later, looking tanned and toned in an sleeveless pink dress. I sneaked a peek at her bosom, which was back to perfectly symmetrical. I couldn't even remember which breast was fake.

"Left one," she said, catching my eye. "It's firmer."

"Do you still wear a wig, Mom?"

"Oh no, I got rid of that thing long ago." She pulled at her wispy white-blond hair. "This mess is the real thing." She waved a map in the air. "I thought we'd go for a drive after dinner. I bought a star map today."

"Great." I didn't tell her it was the last thing I felt like doing. After six months in LA, only five days since the hotel opened, I'd already had enough of stars. But tonight it was time to be a dutiful son. I would set aside my apocalyptic thoughts about the future of the hotel and focus my attention on the woman who had brought me onto this earth.

We took the elevator to the parkade and drove out, taking Schrader south to Sunset Boulevard, carefully bypassing Hollywood Boulevard.

Since Mom was eager to star-watch, I decided to take her to the Ivy. As we were escorted to a quiet table in a dimly lit corner of the restaurant, my eyes searched the room, hoping to spot a few faces to discreetly point out, but the crowd appeared to be comprised of tourists on the same mission.

Over dinner, Mom quizzed me on the latest in the Chelsea Fricks case, and I told her in confidence about Al.

"That lovely tall man who delivered the treadmill to my room?" she cried. "*He* did it?"

"Shhh!" I said, glancing over each shoulder. "That's only the detective's theory. But it's going to be tough for Al to prove his innocence. The circumstances are pretty incriminating."

"He was such a pleasant man. And so handsome! I couldn't imagine."

I remembered Detective Christakos warning me that LA was full of actors who dreamed of making a living essentially through lying, through pretending they're someone they aren't. Had Al arrived in Hollywood with similar aspirations?

Over dessert, Mom buzzed around the topic of Nancy, but, again, I refused to let her in. I considered telling her about the strange call from her grandmother but opted not to, knowing she would concoct some maddening connection that didn't exist.

Tired of waiting for me to open a window, Mom found her own way in. "I don't know why you're so eager to solve the mystery of Chelsea's death, yet you don't seem the least bit interested in the mystery of Nancy's death. Don't you want to know what happened?"

"There's no mystery, Mom. There's no conspiracy, no miracle, no shocking revelation. Cut it out with the tabloid mentality. Nancy was a real person, and she's dead."

"And Chelsea wasn't?"

I turned away and surveyed the restaurant. For all her talk about wanting to see stars, Mom hadn't glanced around the room once. Her attention was fixed on me.

"I've been thinking," she said, lifting her knife to cut into her steak. "Did you say Nancy was ill in Europe? Was it that persistent chest cold or something else?"

"She was still recovering from the cold. But no, it was something else."

"Like what?"

I shrugged. "I don't know."

"What were her symptoms?"

"She was tired a lot. She had headaches and felt feverish at times. Why does it matter?"

"I'm a nurse. Maybe I could determine what was wrong. Did she get those test results from Dr. Rutherford before she left?"

"No. She was going to see a doctor in Salisbury. She planned to ask him to contact Dr. Rutherford to have the results forwarded."

"So you were concerned about her health too?"

"No."

"Trevor, you're not making sense. Why would you—?"

I threw my fork and knife down. "Fine. You won't give up until you know the whole story, will you? You won't leave me alone until you've squeezed every painful detail out of me, until you've reduced me to a sobbing, guilt-ridden mess?"

"What on *earth*? That's not fair. I was simply—"

"I asked her to marry me, Mom."

"What? When?"

"In Paris."

I could see pain in her eyes. "Why didn't you tell me?"

"I couldn't."

"She said yes?"

"She said, 'Let's wait and see.'"

"Let's wait and see? Wait for what?"

I hesitated. Could I reveal this notion that had been my greatest hope while Nancy was alive and became my greatest fear when she died, this notion that explained so much but was so painful to contemplate?

"I think she was pregnant, Mom."

13

Mr. Fix-It Man

"Well, we did it," Shanna announced, dumping a load of newspapers and magazines on my desk. "Hotel Cinema is the most talked-about hotel in the country. Unfortunately, you and I can't take credit, nor can our publicist. It's all thanks to our maintenance department." She picked up one publication after another and tossed them toward me. Al's photo adorned the front page of the *Daily News*, the *Los Angeles Times*, *Daily Spotlight*, the *New York Times*, and *USA Today*, among others.

I looked up at her in dismay. "What are they saying?"

"Al is the prime suspect and a wanted man. Have you heard from him?"

"No."

Her eyes narrowed. "Your confidence in his innocence is faltering, isn't it?"

"Yes." I quickly briefed her on my conversation with the detective.

Shanna almost fell off my desk. "Al and Chelsea had an affair?"

"Apparently."

"I'm in shock. I must say, my confidence started to waver last night after my fourth consecutive hour of news. I couldn't tear myself away, even though all the stations were running the same dull footage of Al watering the hedges, looking more like, well, a *gardener* than a cold-blooded killer. No one close to Chelsea will talk to the media. Chelsea's family has shut them out. Moira won't give an interview. Bryce won't talk. And we won't talk. Last night, the stations resorted to interviewing a former limousine driver, a next-door neighbor who clearly had never met her, and her newspaper deliverer. People who happened to see her once at the A & P are now experts."

She went to the mirror and gasped. "My God, I look like Moira Schwartz!" Grabbing her purse, she pulled out a hairbrush, a can of hairspray, and a tube of lipstick. "I barely had time to get dressed this morning. I was up at five watching the same mindless drivel. A swarm of media tracked down Al's poor mother in Louisville and chased her into the local church. They held an all-night vigil outside the doors, but she refuses to come out. They're treating it like a hostage situation." She leaned toward the mirror to apply bright red lipstick.

"Al must be sick about this," I said.

"Then where the hell is he?"

"Maybe he'll show up to work today. If he doesn't, we're screwed—in more ways than one." I leafed half-heartedly through the publications on my desk. On the cover of *In Touch* was an aerial view of Chelsea's sprawling Bel-Air estate. "Mom made me drive past Chelsea's house about a hundred times last night," I said. "I thought all her fans were here, but there are three times as many outside the gates." On the cover of the *Daily Spotlight* was a still of Al watering the hedges, beside the headline BEHIND CLOSED DOORS: THE PRIVATE WORLD OF THE MYSTERIOUS MAINTENANCE MAN. A sub-article on the front page of the *LA Daily News* announced HOTEL MANAGEMENT STONEWALLS MEDIA.

"Do you think it's time to reconsider our approach?" I said, holding it up for her to see.

She stood back from the mirror and scowled at her reflection. "I was wrestling with the same question yesterday. Against all better judgment, I called Kandy Caine—I mean Floss—I mean Kitty Caine—whatever the hell her name is. She almost had an orgasm when I told her I was wrestling over whether it might be time to come forward and defend the hotel. But after listening to her pant and moan for twenty minutes, I pulled out. We have to be strong, Trevor. If we speak out now, we'll only open ourselves to greater scrutiny, harsher criticism, and ridicule."

I looked down at the cover of *Us* magazine. Another photo of Al trimming the hedges, under the headline WHY HE DID IT. Inset was a photo of an hostile-looking red-haired woman, over the caption FORMER MONDRIAN HOUSEKEEPER TELLS LURID STORY OF CHELSEA'S ROMP WITH MAINTENANCE MAN.

I groaned. "It's frustrating to stand by and do nothing."

"At least we're not alone in splendid isolation," Shanna said, brushing her hair. "I find it interesting that Bryce Davies won't give an interview. He's never shied from publicity before. Is he afraid he'll say something incriminating?"

"You think Bryce did it, then?"

"I'd rather think he did it than Able Al."

"Maybe he found out about Chelsea's fling."

"Who knows." She sprayed hairspray all over her hair, filling the air with a sweet aerosol scent.

"Shanna, do you mind?"

She looked over her shoulder. "I'm sorry. How thoughtless of me." Stuffing the hairspray can into her purse, she turned to me. "Al's going to have a hard time explaining why he bypassed access to Chelsea's suite and then slipped in after Ezmerelda without telling anyone.

Now that I know this, I'm even more adamant that we need to remain silent."

"I don't know that I can afford to wait and find out," I said, plucking a long black hair from my sleeve. "Tony gave me an ultimatum yesterday. If I don't turn the bad publicity around by Saturday, I lose my job."

She turned to me. "He did not!"

"He did. Remember, I convinced him to take the high road and stay silent. I promised it wouldn't blow up in our face. And that's exactly what's happened."

"We both made that promise, Trevor. If you go, I go."

"At this point, being fired doesn't seem like such a bad thing."

"*What*?"

"Maybe I made a mistake in taking this job."

Shanna reached over the desk and slapped me across the face. "Don't ever say that again!"

Stunned, I touched my face and checked my hand for blood. "Shanna, for Christ's sake."

She was instantly remorseful. "I'm sorry. I don't know what came over me. It's just so upsetting to hear. We need you here. *I* need you here. Have you noticed the change in morale since yesterday's meeting? There's renewed optimism in the air. We're under more scrutiny than ever, yet employees are conducting themselves with such professionalism, such poise—I'm truly impressed. You're a great leader, Trevor. You were born to manage hotels."

"I had a little pep talk with Janie Spanozzini the other day. As a result, she stopped calling my mother by her first name—"

"You see? You're even getting through to her."

"—and called her Mrs. Lambert twelve times in two minutes."

"These things take time."

"Don't worry, Shanna. I'm not going anywhere. But I do think we need to take a more proactive approach. I need Tony off my case. Kitty is no help; she's as good as vanished. Maybe we should call up that *Spotlight* reporter and invite him to dinner, get him loaded, and convince him to write a positive story."

Shanna looked skeptical. "Let's see if Al turns up first."

A knock on the window interrupted us. Valerie Smitts was standing in the hallway looking in, an anxious expression on her face. It was the first time I had seen her since my drunken overture. I lowered my head, embarrassed.

She flung open the door. "The police are here to arrest Al!"

"Al? But he's not here," said Shanna.

"We just drove in together. He's downstairs changing."

I stood up. "You were with him?"

Valerie nodded, biting her lip. "He called me in a panic yesterday when he saw the *Spotlight* story. A crowd of reporters had gathered outside his apartment building. I let him hide out at my place."

"You harbored a wanted man?" Shanna said, ushering her into the office and quickly closing the door. "Not the wisest thing to do, Valerie."

Valerie turned to me. "Al wants to speak to you, Trevor. He needs to explain what happened."

"Does he ever," said Shanna.

Valerie turned to Shanna angrily. "Al is innocent! He would never harm anyone!"

"Valerie," I said quietly, trying to calm her, "we want to believe he's innocent too, but—." I stopped. "Did you say the police are here?"

She nodded. "They're in the lobby."

"Trevor," Shanna said, "why don't you go out there and talk some sense into the detective? We don't need him grandstanding in front of the media again. If he needs to talk to Al, he can use one of our meeting rooms."

I squeezed past Valerie without meeting her gaze.

Detective Christakos was standing in the lobby, staring into the flame of the glass fireplace. I spotted Officer Gertz nosing around Scene and two other uniformed officers at the front door and on the pool deck. They had the hotel staked out.

"Mr. Lambert," Stavros said with no trace of his usual jocularity. "We're looking for Allan Robert Combs. We know he's on-property."

"Detective, I want your assurance that—"

A loud shriek drew our attention to the concierge desk. Bernadina leapt from her seat, recoiling at the sight of Al, who had emerged from the security office behind her desk.

"There he is!" the detective cried out. "Get him!"

Officer Gertz and the two other officers rushed toward him.

Al put his hands in the air. "Am I under arrest?"

"Not yet," said the detective. "But don't try any funny stuff. I need to ask you some more questions. If it's all right by you, I'd like to take you to the station. Officer Gertz is gonna frisk you first."

Al dropped his hands, defeated.

Officer Gertz stepped forward cautiously and patted him down.

Behind the concierge desk, Bernadina crouched on all fours, peering around the corner. Her shriek had attracted a number of guests, who gathered to watch the spectacle.

"Is this necessary, Detective?" I asked. "Can we go to my office and talk this over?"

"We're done talking, Trevor," he replied. "Stand back."

Officer Gertz unlatched Al's tool belt and handed it to one of the officers, who rifled through it. "Hammer! Screwdriver! Wrench!" he called out as though they were weapons, passing them to the third officer.

"He's a maintenance man, for God's sake," I said. I watched Al, who stood passively as the officers manhandled him, hands behind his back as though already shackled. Why wasn't he putting up a fight? Why wasn't he loudly proclaiming his innocence? Why no indignation or outrage? I looked at the wrench in the officer's hand and thought of the faucet in the penthouse suite. Al had claimed he fixed it, but it was still dripping when I toured the suite the next morning. Why hadn't I probed further?

"Al, do you have an attorney?" I asked quietly.

He gave a slight shake of his head.

Shanna sidled up beside me. "How about a publicist?"

I turned to glare at her.

Her face turned red. "Well, this *is* LA. I just thought, considering all the media attention…"

"Let's move," said Detective Christakos, pushing Al toward the door.

"Detective?" I called out, chasing after them. "Can't we use the back exit this time?"

He shook his head without turning around.

In a replay of the scene with Ezmerelda only two days prior, the crowd went wild at the sight of Al. The doorman struggled to keep it at bay as Detective Christakos escorted Al to a waiting cruiser. In contrast to Ezmerelda's proud and defiant demeanor, Al walked with shoulders slumped, head down, looking resigned and guilty. Stavros shoved him inside the cruiser and proceeded to pose for the cameras.

"That detective looks like Paris Hilton at a press conference," Shanna remarked.

"He's almost as pretty."

"I think I better change our tagline," she said. "There's been far too much high drama in Hollywood for my comfort."

★ ★ ★ ★ ★

Later that afternoon, Shanna arrived at my office door holding up a bag from Baja Fresh. "Hungry?"

"No."

"Me neither. I just had lunch two hours ago. Mind if I eat in here? It's freezing in my hovel."

"Ever consider the staff cafeteria?"

"Perish the thought. You know I can't stand mixing with staff."

I stepped aside reluctantly.

She sat down in her usual chair and withdrew a burrito the size of a football. As she unwrapped it, shreds of lettuce spilled onto the carpet. The odor of hot sauce wafted toward me. Reaching into her purse, she withdrew an old issue of the *Daily Spotlight*. Chelsea and Bryce were on the cover, surrounded by African children, on a "fact-finding" mission to Malawi. ADOPTION ON THE HORIZON FOR BRYCE & CHELS? read the headline.

"Don't you have work to do?" I asked.

"Do I ever. You should see my desk." She bit into her burrito.

"Shouldn't you get on with it, then?"

"Research, darling, research."

"Uh-huh." I slumped into my chair, regarding the stack of résumés Dennis had pulled for me. I had been flipping through them, feeling increasingly dejected. I didn't want to look for a replacement for Al. My thoughts drifted to our first interview. He had seemed so sincere and earnest. I had wanted to hire him on the spot but resisted, passing his résumé to Shanna for a second interview. She had loved him too. Why hadn't I detected something diabolical in his personality? I prided myself on being able to detect red flags—of course, red flags like attitude problems or lack of focus or a spotty résumé, not murderous tendencies and sexual liaisons with guests. It occurred to me now that interviewing job candidates was not much different than how Stavros described interviewing suspects. If there was a disconnect between the story the résumé told and the story the candidate told, it was a red flag. This wasn't the only similarity between my job and the detective's job. Both positions required an eye for detail, listening skills, persistence, humility, and a strong work ethic. Had Stavros Christakos demonstrated strength in *any* of these areas? Perhaps I underestimated him. After all, he had detected a dark side of Al that I never saw. This time Stavros was right, and I was wrong.

Catching a whiff of refried beans, I lifted my head and glared at Shanna.

She looked up with a guilty expression and offered the burrito to me. It was so large she needed both hands to hold it.

I recoiled, shaking my head, still repulsed by food.

She stuffed the remains of the burrito into the Baja bag and dropped it into the trash can, ensuring the odor of refried beans and mole sauce would linger until I disposed of it. All week she had been behaving like an idle, irritating roommate: all sorts of time on her hands, hanging around, wanting to chat, interrupting me repeatedly, using my office as a lunch room and beauty parlor. I waited for her to leave, but instead she sat down. Opening her arms in a stretch, she let out a loud yawn and folded them on her chest, as though settling in for a nap. The only way to get rid of her was to leave myself. Getting up, I retrieved my suit jacket from the coat rack and opened the door. But a sidelong glance at her made me reconsider. Her expression was troubled. Her behavior today—all week, in fact—was out of character, peculiar. Something was bothering her, and it was more than the Fricks case.

I closed the door and observed her for a moment. She was leaning her head back, furtively watching her reflection in the mirror, a tinge of—sadness? Yes, sadness—in her eyes. I hung up my coat and returned to my desk. As her manager, I knew I should order her back to work, but I sensed she needed to talk. The truth was I liked her company, even if she smelled like refried beans.

"Want to give me a hand?" I asked, pushing a stack of résumés toward her. "There's got to be another Al out there, preferably one who isn't homicidal. If we don't find one soon, you and I will be strapping on tool belts."

"Now *that* would be fun." She began sifting through the résumés. "I've been meaning to ask you, Trevor, does murdering a guest result in automatic dismissal?"

"I'm not sure we cover that topic in the employee manual. Why do you ask?"

"I'm thinking about offing the Greenfields. I made the mistake of striking up a conversation with Mr. Greenfield in the lobby—you know how I loathe talking to guests. It wasn't so much a conversation as me telling him to put his shirt on. Now he and Mrs. Greenfied are using me as their personal concierge. They haven't forgiven Bernadina for sending them to Spaghettios. This morning, Mrs. Greenfield asked me to arrange for a baby elephant at her granddaughter's birthday party on Sunday. She says it needs to be pink—her favorite color."

"Sounds reasonable enough. What did you tell her?"

"I told her I might be able to get a pig. I considered suggesting we paint her husband. Her granddaughter probably wouldn't notice the difference."

I howled with laughter.

"Here's one," she said, plucking out a résumé. "Manjit Sidhu. He's never picked up a hammer before, but he owns a donut shop and has a 'passionate desire to fix things.'"

"Hired."

"If only for his donut-making expertise." She slid the résumés back toward me. "These candidates are pathetically underqualified. If Al's arrested, could the hotel post bail and ask him to pick up a few shifts while awaiting trial?"

"I don't see why not."

"Do you think you'll ever answer your phone?"

It had been ringing incessantly, but I had learned to tune it out. "I told my assistant to hold all my calls."

"She's not doing a terribly efficient job. Perhaps *she* could strap on a tool belt."

I sighed and reached for the phone. "Trevor Lambert speaking."

"It's Moira. How are you." Her voice sounded as listless as ever.

"Busy, Moira. How may I help you?"

"I need to book a function at your hotel. The Peninsula desperately wants me to hold it there, but I thought I'd give you the business."

"What kind of function is it?" I said.

"It's for my new client, Ripley Van Vleet."

"Never heard of him."

"*She* is huge. Or at least she's going to be. She just finished a big-budget action-romance-comedy for Universal with Jamie Foxx. I need to introduce her to the entertainment media as the latest client of Moira Schwartz Media Group. The exposure for your hotel will be extremely valuable. I'll expect you to comp it."

"You'd like us to pay for your reception?" I said, exchanging a bemused look with Shanna. "I'm sorry, but I think our function space is booked for the next few weeks." I pressed the speakerphone so Shanna could hear.

"I don't want your function space," said Moira. "I want the lounge. Monday night. Early, like five to seven PM."

"I'm terribly sorry, but—"

Shanna held up her hand. "It's a quiet time," she mouthed. "Tony wants stars here."

"We might be able to squeeze you in," I said. "I can have someone from catering contact you."

"Fine. I also need a block of rooms for out-of-town guests of Chelsea's memorial service. The Roosevelt offered this big sponsorship deal, but I told them I want to give you first dibs. This is only a small taste of the business I can send your way. Chelsea's parents are being total assholes. They haven't invited any of her friends or colleagues from Hollywood to her funeral in Portland. Everyone's having a fit. They want a proper service in Hollywood. Guess who it falls to? I hired an event-planning company to help, but I'm handling sponsorships."

"You're recruiting sponsors for a funeral?" I said, glancing at Shanna, who looked equally appalled.

"*Memorial* service. How else are we going to pay for it? It will all be tastefully done. I can see about getting you and that bossy Indian woman on the guest list. *Everyone* is clamoring for an invite."

Shanna's hand flew to her chest. She opened her mouth to retort, but I held a finger to my lips. "We won't be able to come on board as a sponsor," I said. "The hotel is booked."

"The service will be down the street at Kodak Theatre, so I thought it made sense."

"You're having the service at the home of the Academy Awards?"

"Chelsea would have been there in March to collect an Oscar for Best Actress for *Blind Ambition*. Instead she gets a memorial service. Ironic, no? I might be able to get you into the gift bags, if you're interested. I'll need a thousand gift certificates."

"I think we'll pass. But thank you."

"Has your maintenance guy turned himself in yet? I heard he went AWOL. I remember him at the Mondrian. He used to harass Chelsea. If I had known he worked at your hotel now, I would have warned her. Well, at least we know what happened now."

"We don't know that for sure," I said, bristling. A few days ago, she was pointing the finger at Ezmerelda.

"Why, have they found some other evidence or something?"

"Why don't you ask your friend Nigel Thoroughbred? He seems to know everything."

"Are you finally ready to admit you need me?"

"Things are under control, Moira."

"Are you kidding me? You're mired in the biggest public-relations disaster in the history of hotels. What's Kitty doing for you? Nothing."

"We've instructed her to do nothing."

"She's doing worse than nothing. She's disassociated herself from your hotel because her other clients are upset that she represents you. Someone needs to start defending your hotel. Bryce Davies is breaking his silence tonight on *Larry King Live*. That's not good news for you."

I shot Shanna a look of alarm. "I'm sure we can handle it," I said. "Why aren't you going on with him?"

"That's not my thing. I work behind the scenes. Plus, I would never associate myself with that lying weasel. Like it or not, Trevor, you need my help. Kitty's too dumb to figure out the obvious way to turn your hotel from pariah to hero."

"No one thinks of Hotel Cinema as a pariah."

"Not yet."

Her words were foreboding. "So what's your big idea?"

"Show me the money."

I looked up at Shanna, who was cutting great swaths through the air. "I'll be honest, Moira. There's no way I'm ever going to hire you. You're just not the right fit."

"Maybe I should call Tony Cavalli."

"No!" I shouted, watching Shanna almost leap out of her skin. "He . . . he has no interest in that side of the business."

"I was thinking about dropping by tonight with—"

The audacity! She wanted on The List! "We're very busy tonight, Moira. I'll have catering call you about that reception. Have a great afternoon." I disconnected.

"How dare she call me bossy!" Shanna huffed. She fell back into her seat and emitted a long-suffering sigh. "This is all so distressing, isn't it? I know you want me to go back to my hovel and get some work done, but I can't concentrate."

"I find work therapeutic," I volunteered.

"Work is not therapeutic, Trevor. It's merely distracting—and only temporarily so."

"Have you been talking to my mother again?"

She smiled. "She gave me a book yesterday, something about a great leap forward. Is your mother turning into a communist?"

"*Two Steps Forward.* More of her misguided pop psychology."

"You've read it?"

"I saw the author's photo on the jacket cover—that was enough. She's more Suzanne Somers than Mao. Seriously, Shanna, my job is on the line. I need your help."

She picked up a fragment of taco chip from the desk and bit on it. "The hotel is sold out for weeks. We have waitlists for rooms, meeting rooms, functions, Scene, and Action; it's a sad statement, but Chelsea's tragic swan dive has made Hotel Cinema more popular than we could ever imagine. Our problem is the opposite of other hotels—we have too many reservations and not enough rooms. With Ezmerelda on leave and no chief engineer, there's no point in generating more business. I've doubled our rates, and it still isn't deterring people. My sales staff can field calls on their own just fine."

"Might as well call it a day, then," I said sarcastically. "Spend more time with your kids."

"My kids." Her tone changed. "Brilliant, Trevor. I'll just call them up. They'll be delighted to hear from me. We'll spend the night together, the weekend. We'll—"

She got up and turned around suddenly, as though something in the hallway caught her attention.

All I could see was Rheanna's large behind at the photocopier. I waited for Shanna to continue, but she remained silent. "Is something bothering you, Shanna?"

"No." She didn't turn around.

Rheanna left. Shanna was gazing at nothing now. I got up and went around the desk. "Shanna, what's wrong?"

I saw a tear roll down her cheek. She turned her head away, waving me off.

"Is there anything I can do?" I said, feeling helpless.

After a moment, she composed herself. "They have no time for me."

"I thought you were seeing lots of them."

"I was lying. I've only seen Eliza twice since I moved here; Bantu once."

"In nine months?"

She nodded and reached for a tissue from my desk, dabbing her eyes. "They're so busy with school."

"It's summer, Shanna."

"How should I know why they won't see me? They never tell me anything. They're not interested in having a relationship with me. Their diabolical father and that adolescent Iranian trollop have turned them against me. They think I abandoned them."

"Why don't you tell them the truth?"

"It *is* the truth." She turned to me. Her face was wet with tears.

"You abandoned your kids?"

"I was broken-hearted when Ramin left me for that child prostitute. The kids wanted to live with him, and over time he brainwashed them into hating me. I couldn't bear to be in the same country, so I left. I traveled the world, worked at hotels on every continent, immersed myself in my career. I wrote to my children regularly, but they never replied. Remember when they visited me in New York last year? We had a breakthrough, a joyous reconciliation. I thought all was forgiven. I moved here and took this job, thinking a small hotel would allow plenty of time to spend with my kids. But this job's been a nightmare, and my kids want nothing to do with me."

"I'm sorry, Shanna."

"Remember when you and I had dinner in New York a couple of years ago, and I warned you to get out of this business? I told you I sacrificed everything for my career—my family, my interests, my mental and physical health. When Willard died and I sold the hotel, I was left with a small sum of money. I considered early retirement. But after a few weeks I went insane with boredom. Now I'm mired in this job. For what? For the glory of Tony Cavalli and his family?"

"I don't mind the work," I said. "It's a lot better than what I was doing at home."

"I'm sorry, I don't mean to diminish your work. I'm feeling hormonal. I love working with you; I adore you; you're doing a wonderful job. I'm happy that you're happy. This has nothing to do with you."

"What is it, then? Your kids?"

"Yes, my kids. Well, mostly."

"There's more?"

"The truth is I can't bear to be around all the young, slim, gorgeous people that frequent this place. I see my haggard reflection in their faces. I used to be like them. Ramin and I would get dressed up and go dancing every weekend, out for dinner almost every night. We were so happy. How was I supposed to know that happiness was transitory? This hotel is a constant reminder that it's over. I'm old and ugly and tired. And now I'm fat too, and the wrinkles aren't fading." She stood before the mirror and pressed her hands against her face.

I came up behind her. "Shanna, you're beautiful."

She spun around. "Can I have three weeks off?"

I blinked. "No. What for?"

"I'm going to get a facelift. It's the only way I can stand working here. Everywhere I look in this town, I see women in their fifties stretched and pulled and tucked to look thirty again. I want that too."

"Why? Gravity will prevail soon enough, and you'll be miserable. Didn't you say that yourself the other day?"

"It's easy for you to say," she said quietly. "You're still young."

Of all the disheartening things I had witnessed this week, nothing made me sadder than seeing Shanna in this state. "I'm not giving you time off to get a facelift, Shanna. You don't need a plastic surgeon, you need a counselor. *That* I'll give you time off for."

A knock at the door interrupted us.

Shanna went to the door and opened it.

A tall, hulking figure stood in the doorway. "I didn't want to go back up to her suite!" Al Combs cried. "She insisted!"

★ ★ ★ ★ ★

Al Combs and I were seated on folding chairs in Room 330, surrounded by paint cans and walls spotted with plaster. A drywall panel had been removed, exposing another support beam ravaged by fire. It was one of the rooms he was supposed to be working on.

"So," I said. "Miss Fricks insisted you return to her suite?"

He nodded, blue eyes wide. "Know how she complained I was acting inappropriate? Truth is, *she* was acting inappropriate. When Beth radioed me to fix the faucet, I told her I was busy and Rico could do it, but she said Miss Fricks had asked for me personally. Ask Beth, she'll tell you."

"Why didn't you want to go?"

He hesitated, wringing his giant hands. "When I worked at the Mondrian, Miss Fricks stayed with us for about six weeks while she was filming *Blind Ambition*, and they shot a few scenes on the pool deck. She kind of took a shining to me. She liked to tease me whenever I was around, ask embarrassing stuff about my tools. She was playing that blind swimmer, and sometimes she wore contact lenses that made her eyes look cloudy. She would chase me around the pool, holding her hands out like a zombie and howling, in nothing but a bathing suit. The crew and my coworkers would watch and laugh. It was real embarrassing.

"I saw her fairly regularly, mostly because things kept breaking down in her suite. Air-conditioning, mini-bar, oven—you name it. Sometimes she watched while I worked. She was super friendly most of the time, but sometimes she seemed down. She told me she hated her parents because they lied to her about who she was. She tried to tell me she was shy like me, but I only laughed." Al broke into a smile. "She always asked if I thought she was pretty, and of course I said yes. Once she told me if it weren't for all her cosmetic surgery she'd be 'a total dog face like Moira.' I told her I didn't believe she could ever be ugly. She was the prettiest girl I'd ever seen. It seemed to cheer her up."

"Go on," I said, fascinated.

"One day I was reviewing the maintenance log book, and it occurred to me that her calls only came in during my shifts. I assumed it was because of her shoot schedule, but when I flipped back to all my notes, I started to wonder."

"About what?"

"I thought maybe she was playing games. I wondered if she had that psychological disorder—you know, when girls hurt themselves for attention?"

"Munchausen syndrome?"

"Yeah, except instead of hurting herself, she was breaking things in her suite. It bothered me a lot, but I didn't say anything to anyone. About a week before she was supposed to check out, she summoned me to her suite. I found the plasma TV smashed on the floor. She said it fell from the wall, but I had anchored it there myself, and I didn't believe her. Somehow that tiny thing pulled it down. But what really made me uncomfortable was what she was wearing."

I leaned forward. "What?"

"Nothing but a white lace bra and a thong." He ran a hand over his bald head. "I circled around the TV, trying to concentrate, and then muttered something about having to get it replaced and left. I sent two bellmen to retrieve the TV." Al stopped and swallowed. "The next day, I got another call. When I got there, she told me a priceless diamond ring had fallen underneath her headboard. She was wearing a bathrobe, so I thought I was safe. I was businesslike and professional, as usual. I climbed onto the bed and peered under the headboard. I could see the ring, but my arm was too big to fit through the space. When I turned to ask her for help, she was naked."

"*Naked?*" I coughed and composed myself. "She had nothing on *at all?*"

"Nothing." He gave me a long, meaningful stare. "I rammed my arm into that opening so hard I took a layer of skin off."

"You *what?*"

He lifted his right arm and ran his fingers through a mat of blond hair, revealing a large scar. "But I got that ring. I handed it to her and headed for the door, eyes on the floor. She shouted for me to stop. 'I'm sorry, Miss Fricks,' I said, without turning around, 'but I gotta go.' 'Al!' she said in a kinda singsong voice. 'Look!' I turned around and saw her march over to the bed and throw the ring back under the headboard. 'Oops, I did it again,' she said."

A smile crept across my face. Why, the little vixen. I fought it off, seeing Al's tormented expression.

"She was standing there, stark naked, a goddess. She started saying stuff." He stopped, his face reddening.

"What kind of stuff?"

"You know, sex stuff. Role-playing stuff." He broke into a sultry, breathy impression. "'Come on, Mr. Fix-It Man, I'm all broke up. Use that big screwdriver on me. I got an itch only your tool can scratch.'"

Unable to help myself, I burst into laughter.

Al glowered.

"Sorry," I said, clearing my throat. "So … what did you do?"

"What would *you* do? *Chelsea Fricks* was stark naked, begging me to have my way with her. Have you any idea how many times I—?"

He stopped, realizing his words weren't helping to convince me of his innocence. "Me, a lowly maintenance guy! I'd never stand a chance of getting a woman like that in real life. She must have had some kind of sick role-playing fantasy. She pushed me down on the bed and climbed on top of me. I struggled to get free, but she was really strong!"

"Uh-huh," I said. "A 115-pound woman?"

"She had me under a spell. I was powerless to resist. Before I knew it, she had my shirt unbuttoned. She untied my tool belt and put it on the bed, then started unzipping my fly. I pushed her off and stood up, backing away, telling her I couldn't, it was wrong. She got really upset then. That confused me. I mean, all these years I've been conditioned to never say no to guests, to do whatever it takes to make them happy, and here I was upsetting the hotel's most important guest. Where was I supposed to draw the line?"

"Al," I said, "I think you found that line."

"Okay, I admit, I didn't want to go. But I didn't want to lose my job either. So I backed away, muttering apologies, and went for the door. But she ran up to me and ripped my shirt open and whipped my pants down. She pushed me back to the bed. I surrendered. She grabbed my tool belt and started buckling it back on me. I let her do it. Then she jumped on top of me and …" He stopped, licking his lips. "She started howling and riding me like a cowgirl."

"Then what?" My voice was an octave higher than normal.

"I heard a knock at the door, and someone called out 'Housekeeping!' We froze. Before either of us could do a thing, a room attendant walked in. I got up, pulled my clothes on, and ran out. The housekeeper told Miss Parker, and an hour later she hauled me into her office. I told her I was attacked, seduced, practically raped!"

"She believed you?"

He frowned. "Why wouldn't she? It was true. She always liked me, said I was the best chief engineer ever, that I was irreplaceable. She was not a fan of Chelsea Fricks. She confronted her for harassing me and told her to leave, told her she wasn't welcome back. I think she was looking for an excuse. Miss Fricks was a nightmare guest. I got suspended for a week, but the incident stayed off my file. Miss Parker kept it a secret, but I know that housekeeper told people. I felt like I was working under a cloud of shame. So when I heard about this job, I applied. I didn't see Miss Fricks again until she checked in here."

"Okay, then, fast-forward to Friday night."

"I was hoping to avoid her. I was on the pool deck, putting fuel in the fire basins, when she surprised everyone by coming down for a swim. I left before she saw me—or so I thought. A couple hours later, I got that call from Switchboard. I went up at 8:10, hoping she wouldn't be there. I told you what happened. I rang the doorbell, and nobody answered. What I didn't tell you was when I bumped into her in the bedroom, she was wearing a hotel bathrobe and nothing else. It was open. She had a glass of whiskey in her hand. 'Well, if it ain't Mr. Fix-It Man,' she said. 'Maybe we can finish what we started.'"

Al stopped, his face coloring.

"Go on," I croaked.

He reached up to massage his neck. "She launched into her routine." He resumed his seductive female imitation, which was unnervingly similar to Chelsea. "'What do you say I take your big fat tool and—'"

I held up my hand. "I get the picture, Al. What happened next?"

"You have to believe me, Trevor, I wasn't going to go down that path again. I wasn't even attracted to her anymore. She was psycho. I said, 'Listen, ma'am, if you want me to fix your faucet, you're going to have to cover yourself up and wait in the living room.' Then she got all ugly. 'Are you a homo or something?' she said. She told me to get the F out, so I left. A little while later, you called to tell me she complained."

"That explains why the faucet wasn't fixed," I said. "What about the second time? I told you not to go near her again, to go home for the night."

"I planned to, but I wanted to get at least one more room finished. We were so far behind. When you told me she complained, I wanted to tell you the truth, but then I'd have to explain what happened at the Mondrian, and I didn't want anyone to know.

"Around eleven PM, I was getting ready to leave when Miss Fricks called me in my office. She said she was hiding in the bathroom. She was bawling—I could barely understand her. She told me to cancel access to her suite from the adjoining rooms. 'I don't feel safe,' she said, and then muttered something about a fight. I said sure, no problem, I'll call Security. But then she said she needed me to come up to her room. I said no way. She started begging. She kept repeating, 'I don't feel safe!' I was going to hang up and call Security, but then she started screaming that she could hear someone in the living room. It freaked me out. I called Security, told them she wanted access canceled, and then raced up the back stairs to her room."

"Why didn't you ask Security for backup?" I asked.

"I was afraid she was up to her old tricks. I didn't want them to burst in and find me there with her naked. I planned to make sure she was okay, and then get the hell out. When I got to the door, I could hear her shouting. The door opened, and Ezmerelda came rushing out. Miss Fricks was yelling, 'Get the F out, you snooping spic!' Poor Ez looked like she was going to cry. She took off down the hall. I stepped inside. Miss Fricks was all red-faced and fuming, clutching a bottle of Jack Daniels and a glass. She poured some into the glass and slugged it back. She was in nothing but a black bra and panties."

"Was anyone else in the suite?"

"Not that I could see. It must have been Ezmerelda she heard in the living room. She just looked at me and said, 'What the F do *you* want?' I said, 'You told me to come up! You said you didn't feel safe!' She swallowed the contents of the glass and threw it on the kitchen floor, smashing it. 'I didn't say I felt unsafe, you moron,' she said. 'I said come and *fix* my safe. It's broken.'

"I felt duped. I told her I'd send someone else up, but she blocked my exit. 'Open the f'ing safe!' she screamed. So I went to the closet and squatted down in front of the safe. It wasn't broken, she forgot the code. I could hear the phone ringing. She screamed out, 'F off, Bryce!' She was standing right behind me. I used my master key to reset it, and the door popped open. She pulled me away and told me to get the F out."

"And then what happened?" My nose was inches from his face.

He shrugged. "I left."

I sat back, almost disappointed. "That's it?"

"Well, there is one other thing," he said. "I caught a glimpse of what she was so eager to get at in the safe. There was a bag of white powder in there."

"Cocaine?"

"I guess."

"Did you see anything else unusual?" I asked.

"I saw Ez's cart parked in the hall, but that's about it. I was so angry, I went directly home."

"And you told all this to the detective? Every detail?"

He nodded. "I didn't hold anything back this time."

"Why didn't you tell him the whole story in the first place? It would have saved you—all of us—a lot of trouble."

"When I came into work the next morning and saw all the reporters and paparazzi, it scared the heck out of me. Everyone was saying Miss Fricks killed herself. I didn't want our encounter to get into the tabloids—I would die if I had to endure all that attention—so I kept it to myself. I asked Ez not to say anything. But it backfired. People started saying she was murdered, and suddenly everyone was pointing a finger at me."

"Detective Christakos must have believed your story if he released you."

"Of course he did," said Al. "What, did *you* think I had something to do with it?"

I felt my face redden. "Your behavior was bizarre, Al. You didn't return my messages. This morning when they took you away, you *looked* guilty."

"I *felt* guilty. Being taken away by police, getting heckled by those nasty people, it made me feel like a criminal. I'm not a good actor, Trevor. I wear my heart on my sleeve."

"What convinced the detective of your innocence?"

Al reached into his pocket and pulled out several crumpled sheets of paper. "When I came in this morning, I printed these off in the security office."

I looked down at the first sheet. "The parkade activity report?"

He pointed halfway down the page. "It records my departure at 23:28. According to the police report, Miss Fricks jumped five minutes later, at 23:33. And look at this." The next sheet was the activity report for the penthouse suite. "See the exit at 23:14? That's Ez leaving and me arriving. The next exit at 23:18 is me leaving. But look at this. At 23:20, it says Chelsea came *in*. But she was inside when I left."

"What does that mean?"

"I don't know. The only explanation I can think of is she somehow slipped out behind me before the door closed. She must have stayed in the hallway or knocked on Mr. Davies' or Miss Schwartz's door. She couldn't have gone far, because two minutes later she used the eye scanner to reenter."

I was baffled. "What are you getting at, Al?"

"No one else was in her suite when I was there, I'm positive. Which means someone came in with her at 23:20. Either that person was in the hallway—and I didn't see anybody—or in a nearby room."

I thought of the incident at check-in with Chelsea's colored contact lenses. "Al, do you remember what color her eyes were?"

He nodded confidently. "Green. I noticed, because the first time I went up they were brown, her natural color. She was getting ready for the party, so she must have put her contacts in. Why?"

"Just curious."

He unfolded a third sheet of paper. "This is the activity report for Bryce Davies' room," he said. "The same time I left the suite, he left his room, at 23:18. See?"

"He told the detective he looked out when he heard a commotion. He saw you retreating down the hall."

"What if he stayed in the hall and entered the suite two minutes later, at 23:20, with Miss Fricks?"

My cell phone vibrated, making me jump. I flipped it open. "Yes, Shanna?"

"Trevor, you must turn the television on at once."

"Why? There's no TV in this room."

"There are over 150 televisions in that hotel, for God's sake. Find one and turn it to CNN. Quick! Bryce Davies is on *Larry King*. He's blaming the hotel for Chelsea's death!"

14

High Drama in Hollywood

When I reached the screening room and found the remote control and *Larry King Live*, a close-up of Bryce Davies filled the screen. I backed away, regarding in awe the giant image of the handsome, rosy-cheeked, square-jawed actor, his tight blond curls glowing like a halo under the studio lights. On the bottom of the screen appeared the caption CNN EXCLUSIVE: CHELSEA'S BOYFRIEND SPEAKS OUT.

"I'd do anything to bring her back," Bryce was saying. "She was everything to me."

"Did you talk about marriage?" Larry asked.

"Sure, we talked about marriage. But we were so busy. Life was a whirlwind with Chelsea."

"And kids?" Larry asked. The camera cut to a wide shot of the two men facing one another across a table, a world map made of dots of colored lights behind them. "Did you talk about kids?"

Bryce smoothed his jaw. "Yeah, Larry, we talked about kids. But we weren't ready."

"What about the adoption rumors?"

His eyes flickered. "You mean Malawi? Rumors, only rumors. We went on a fact-finding mission. Everyone else was going to Africa, so Chelsea decided she wanted to go too. We talked about building an orphanage, but the idea never got off the ground. Chelsea fell in love with the locals, but she wasn't ready to have her own children. She and Britney used to talk, and—"

"Britney Spears."

"Right. Chelsea saw how she struggled with her career, her lifestyle, her role as a mother. She didn't want that. *I* didn't want that."

I sat down in the third row from the front, admiring how perfectly at ease Bryce appeared. How could he sit before millions of people and discuss this personal tragedy only a week after it happened? Was he heartless or just very strong? My mind wandered to the key report Al had shown me. Bryce had left his room around the same time Al left the suite. Had he seen Al leaving Chelsea's suite and killed her in a jealous rage? I observed his face closely as he spoke. His grim expression, watery eyes, flaring nostrils—he seemed sincere and distraught. He was either a brilliant actor or a complete sociopath.

"What do *you* think happened that night?" Larry asked him.

"I know it wasn't an accident. It wasn't suicide, and it wasn't a foolish prank. Someone chased her off that balcony with a butcher knife. The police have confirmed that."

"Why would someone want to kill her?"

"The public was obsessed with her. There are some crazy people out there."

"Who do you think did it?"

He held up his hands. "I'm not about to point fingers. Regardless of who did the deed, I believe a number of people share the responsibility for her death. It could have been prevented."

"Such as?"

"Such as me. I was in the room next to her. She needed her space, but she always wanted me close by. I should have protected her. I'm going to have to live with that."

Larry hunched forward. "Who else is responsible?"

"There were some serious security breaches at the hotel," Bryce said, placing his hands on the table and sitting back, muscles flexing. "It was the hotel's first day of operation. We were scheduled to leave for Lima the next day, so we decided to spend the night. We arrived around five thirty PM, and a female manager escorted us to our rooms. Chelsea looked around her suite, seemed to like it, and sent her bodyguards home. I was worried about her. She'd been going nonstop since Rome. I tried to convince her to take the night off, but she'd promised the owner of the hotel she would come to the party, and she never reneged on a favor."

"*Favor*?" I shouted at the screen. "You call $150,000 a *favor*?"

"Moira called the owner—"

"Moira Schwartz," Larry interjected. "Chelsea's publicist?"

"Right. She told him Chelsea was suffering from acute exhaustion and asked if she could bow out. She promised to make it up to him. The response was a resounding no. We decided to make the most of it. I told Chelsea to relax for a while, maybe go for a swim, take a bath, have a glass of wine—"

"Jack Daniels," I corrected.

"—and I'd knock on her door around ten thirty to pick her up for the party. I went to my room, had a nap, watched some TV. A movie I starred in a couple years ago was playing, *Ulterior Motives*. It's about this guy who—"

"Was that the last time you saw her?" Larry interrupted.

Bryce blinked. "No. I went to see her around ten forty-five. Moira had just left. Chelsea wasn't ready, and she was in one of her moods. She had been online and came across a nasty article on Slate.com. The writer had resurrected the rumor about her being adopted. That story always got to her. She was estranged from her folks, but she still loved them, and she hated to read anything that hurt them. She had just had a big argument with Moira over it. She expected Moira to control everything that was said about her, but of course that was impossible. She ranted about the Slate article, about Moira, about the hotel. She wanted to check out. Housekeeping staff hadn't bothered to provide nighttime service. They didn't seem that on the ball, to be honest. They missed my room too."

"You had privacy signs on your door!" I cried.

"She'd gone down to the pool for a swim, and staff members had gawked," Bryce continued. "She had eyes in the back of her head for these things. The maintenance guy was leering at her. She recognized him from Hotel Mondrian, where he used to work. He used to leer at her there too. She stopped staying there because of him."

"This is Allan Robert Combs?" Larry said, glancing down at his notes. "Hotel Cinema's chief engineer?"

Bryce nodded.

A clip of Al being led out of the hotel by the puffed-out Detective Christakos filled the screen. His downcast eyes and twisted mouth made him look like a child molester. I let out a groan of sympathy. Al was upstairs, working in Room 330. I was glad there was no television there.

The screen returned to Bryce and Larry. "After her swim she decided to have a bath," Bryce continued, "but the faucet was broken. She called down to have it fixed. They sent up the same creepy maintenance guy. She said he made her feel uncomfortable. She called the manager to complain, but he acted like he didn't believe her. He didn't seem to care."

"*What?*" I cried, leaping from my seat. "I apologized profusely. She hung up on me!"

"Then she started freaking out because the safe in her room was broken, and the jewelry she wanted to wear was locked inside."

"Jewelry?" I howled. "Drugs!"

"She was afraid if she called down they would send up the same creepy maintenance guy. I told her I would take care of it, but she said she just wanted to be left alone for a while. I gave her a hug and a kiss, told her I loved her, and went back to my room. That was the last time I saw her alive."

Bryce lowered his head into his hands. The camera lingered on him. He let out a sob and lifted his head. "Ten minutes later, I heard a commotion outside my door. I opened it. Chelsea's door was closed. There was a maid's cart parked in the hallway. I looked down the hall and caught a glimpse of a man walking into the stairwell exit. I didn't think much of it at the time. Only later did I realize it was that maintenance guy. I closed my door and continued watching *Ulterior Motives*. Fifteen minutes later, Moira banged on my door, hysterical, saying Chelsea fell off the balcony. I followed her into her room and looked over her balcony. There she was, lying on the pool deck with a crowd gathered around her." A close-up lingered on Bryce's watery blue eyes.

Larry turned to look into the camera. "There's more to come as boyfriend Bryce Davies speaks out for the first time on the tragic death of beloved actress Chelsea Fricks. And we'll be taking your calls. Don't go away."

A mélange of clips of Chelsea's film and television roles followed: rebellious daughter of a Republican senator in *Modern Loving*, Mary Ann in a remake of *Gilligan's Island*, a meth-addicted Cleveland prostitute in *Rehab*, and an Olympic diving champion in *Blind Ambition*.

I got up and paced the aisle, my mind swimming. Bryce's testimony, full of lies and half-truths, was devastating. Poor Al. This was exactly the kind of attention he had hoped to avoid. My cell phone vibrated in my pocket. I peered into the display window: Tony Cavalli. I switched it off and placed it on the table. The show was back on. I would deal with Tony later.

"Was Chelsea suicidal?" Larry asked Bryce.

Bryce tilted his head, contemplating the question. "She had a lot of sadness in her, but no, she wasn't self-destructive. Recently, the scrutiny got to her. It was so invasive. She couldn't get a moment of peace. Everywhere she went, people snapped photos, took secret videos, and used cell phones to secretly film her."

Larry nodded. "Did she do drugs?"

"Absolutely not. Chelsea was against drugs."

I rolled my eyes along with the rest of the country. I thought back to the drug residue on the coffee table. What happened to the bag of cocaine in the safe? Moira said she didn't do drugs. Bryce was a known user. The detective said he had been too coked out that night to be a reliable witness. Had the detective done a proper search of his room, his body?

A video clip showed Chelsea stumbling out of a nightclub in daylight, eyes dazed, hair disheveled, mascara smudged. She muttered something incoherent and fingered the camera.

"No drugs," Larry said.

"No way," said Bryce. "She had a few drinks on occasion, but she didn't care much for booze either. Publicity was her addiction. She craved attention, yet she despised it. She was both intensely private and flagrantly self-exploitative. That was her paradox. She loved to see beautiful photos of herself in magazines, went wild over gushing stories, but didn't have the stomach for lies and mean-spiritedness. The more famous she became, the nastier the media got, and the public ate it up."

"But she played the game. Both of you did."

"Of course we played the game. But it got out of hand for her. She couldn't stop posing for cameras and talking to reporters."

"Was she a narcissist?" Larry asked, shifting his glasses.

"A narcissist?" Bryce tilted his head back and chuckled. "Larry, we're all narcissists in this business. Was she worse than the rest of us?" He paused. "I don't believe so."

"She was on the show a few months ago. A charming young lady." Muted footage of Chelsea filled the screen. She was perched on a chair in the studio, clad in a simple burgundy dress and string of white pearls. Her green eyes shone as she chatted with Larry. She looked graceful and elegant, like a modern-day Audrey Hepburn, her caramel hair swept around her head.

Larry reappeared, shaking his head. "We have a caller from Chester, Tennessee. Chester, you're on the line."

"Hi, Larry," said a woman with a Southern twang, "I *love* your show. I have a question for Bryce. I read that a hotel maid was involved. Is that true, and if so, is it possible that she conspired with the maintenance man?"

From where I was sitting, I choked.

Bryce shrugged. "Anything's possible. I know Chelsea had words with the maid that night."

"You're referring to Ezmerelda Lopez, Hotel Cinema's executive housekeeper," Larry said.

A photo of Ezmerelda filled the screen. It was Christmastime, and she was sitting by a tree in a red silk dress, smiling brightly, a gift wrapped in gold foil in her hands. Her eyes, red from the flash, looked demonic.

"When the hotel finally sent up a maid, she barged in without knocking," Bryce said. "Chels caught her snooping through her personal belongings. She would have lost it."

"Chicago, Illinois, your question?"

"Hi, Larry. Hi, Bryce. Bryce, how accountable is the hotel for what happened? It sounds like security was pretty lax that night."

"The hotel is largely accountable, in my opinion," Bryce replied firmly. "They were careless and dismissive about Chelsea's safety that night. Since it happened, they haven't even apologized. I find it unforgivable. I can only assume they're afraid of self-incrimination."

"What the *fuck*?" I cried, leaping from my seat and charging at the screen. "What do you mean, self-incrimination?"

The telephone began to ring. My cell phone buzzed.

"We're going to take a break," said Larry. "We'll be back with one of Chelsea's closest acquaintances, a young lady who was at the party the night of her tragic death." He turned to Bryce. "What would Chelsea want us to learn from her death?"

He was silent for a moment, stroking his square jaw, blue eyes intense. "I think Chelsea would want us to recognize the dangers of America's obsession with celebrities. Such intense scrutiny is not healthy, not for consumers and certainly not for the subjects. I hold the media partly to blame for her death. They pursued her relentlessly. And I hold Hotel Cinema to blame. In the entertainment business, we rely on hotels to provide a safe haven. Outside our homes, hotels are the last bastion of privacy. If we can't trust hotel staff to protect our privacy and safety, who can we trust? Because of their negligence, the love of my life—the woman I was to marry, the future mother of my children—is dead."

"When we come back, Tara Reid joins us in the studio," Larry said softly into the camera. "Don't go away."

I grappled for the remote control and switched off the television, breaking into a salvo of profanities. What a complete and utter disaster. Could things possibly be worse? The telephone was ringing again. My cell phone was vibrating its way to the edge of the table. I lunged for it. My mother's cell number appeared in the display window.

I glanced at my watch: 6:43. I was late for dinner.

★ ★ ★ ★ ★

By the time I reached the lobby, I was fuming. It was jammed with guests—stupid, partying, star-gawking loiterers. It took all my self-control not to shove them aside as I hurried toward the restaurant. I was tired of this crowd, tired of being polite, tired of being dumped on by liars, bullies, and despicable people.

As I reached the entrance to Scene, I heard someone call my name from behind. I turned, for once not trying to erase the scowl from my face. Moira Schwartz was near the front desk, next to a tall, chicken-necked man with a large Adam's apple. She was waving me over. I turned and kept going.

"Trevor, wait," she called after me. "Come here for a sec."

Reluctantly, I marched over. "What is it, Moira?"

"How are you." She was all smiley and charming again—phony. "What's wrong. You look upset."

"Did you see *Larry King*?"

"I TiVo'd it." Reading my expression, she winced. "Was Bryce that bad?"

"If you call blaming this hotel for Chelsea's death bad, then yes, I would say he was that bad."

Her eyes widened. "What did he...?" She glanced at the man beside her.

"He accused the hotel of negligence, of apathy, of lax security," I said, feeling compelled to vent on this odious woman who was one of the major causes of my problems. "He blamed Al Combs, Ezmerelda Lopez, me—everyone but himself."

"I'm sorry," said Moira, "but I'm not surprised. Hey, I want you to meet—"

"I can't believe that miscreant had the audacity to accuse the hotel of negligence when he was in his room watching TV while his philandering girlfriend was next door trying to seduce my chief engineer."

Over Moira's shoulder, Valerie let out gasp at the front desk. Janie was standing beside her, regarding me in shock. I didn't care. I couldn't stop. I was tired of being polite and courteous while ignorant, self-serving assholes like Bryce and Stavros and Moira walked all over me. "When Al rejected her advances, your 'best friend' Chelsea had the nerve to call me to complain about *his* behavior. Later—"

"Trevor," Moira said, gripping my forearm. "This isn't the time or the place."

I wrenched my arm away. "Later, Chelsea summoned Al back to her suite, claiming to fear for her life. She was drunk and abusive. She demanded he open her safe. Why? So she could get at the bag of cocaine she had locked there. She was too wasted to remember the code."

"Shut *up*, Trevor!" Moira cried. "That is so not true! Chelsea didn't do drugs! She would never seduce anyone, she—"

She shot a frantic look at her companion, who was holding up what appeared to be a large cell phone.

"Would you excuse us for a moment?" Moira said to him.

"I prefer to stay," he said in a British accent. He touched the side of his large, aristocratic nose and turned to me, enthralled. I stared at his Adam's apple. He looked vaguely familiar.

"Trevor, let's *go!*" Moira shouted, tugging at my arm.

My feet remained planted where they were. "Listen, Moira," I hissed. "I'm tired of all these lies. You need to know the truth."

"No, Trevor!" she said through her teeth. "Not here!"

She refused to let go of my arm. A number of people had gathered to watch. At the concierge desk, Bernadina was eyeing me in alarm. I knew I was being inappropriate, but fury was roiling inside me. I had to set the record straight, and I wanted witnesses.

"Bryce was going on about what a saint Chelsea was," I said. "She was a monster! She trashed her suite, guzzled the Jack Daniels we sent up by her request, and snorted cocaine on the coffee table before she broke it. You know what her reading material was? *Bleaching America. Ignorant Immigrants.* But I suppose I don't have to tell *you* she was a racist. Meanwhile, Bryce is shifting the blame to Al Combs when it's clear *he's* the one who killed Chelsea. You're horrible, all of you. Chelsea Fricks was the worst of the lot. A liar, a cheater, a psychopath, a guest from hell. I don't blame Bryce for killing her. Someone had to put her out of our misery." She released my arm. "And if you don't leave my hotel now, I'll do the same to you."

Moira was speechless. She looked back at her companion.

The relief I felt was quickly dissipating as remorse set in. A large crowd had surrounded us. There was a flash of a camera. I looked down and saw my nametag. I swallowed hard. My eyes moved to the chicken-necked man's face. I had met him before...where? At the opening party...and I'd seen him outside in the mosh pit.

A sense of dread washed over me.

"Trevor," Moira snapped, "I'd like to introduce you to Nigel Thoroughbred, chief entertainment correspondent for the *Daily Spotlight.*"

"*Very* pleased to meet you," said Nigel, breaking into a catlike grin.

★ ★ ★ ★ ★

"Well, look on the bright side," Mom said. "When the story hits, you'll be famous."

"*In*famous." We were sitting in a booth in the far corner of Scene, far away from the boisterous crowd.

"Does it matter *why* people are famous these days?" she countered. "It seems to matter only that they're famous. You might as well enjoy your fifteen minutes."

"I never wanted fifteen minutes."

"Then why did you move to Los Angeles to run a hotel that panders to people desperate for fame? As long as you work here, you'll be in the spotlight, dear. Why not enjoy it?"

"Don't you understand the severity of what I've done? I'm a hotel manager, and I trashed a beloved, dead celebrity to one of the biggest entertainment journalists in the country." I slumped into my chair. "My career is over."

"I think you're being a bit dramatic." She reached for her glass of wine and tipped the last drops into her mouth. "Mmm, delicious!" She set down the glass and eyed mine. "Maybe he won't publish your comments. It all seems a bit unsavory to me."

"Have you read *Spotlight*? It's *all* unsavory." I pushed my glass toward her.

"Why don't you just call the reporter up and apologize, admit you were wrong?"

"Because I wasn't wrong. I was telling the truth."

"Then stop fretting."

Our waitress, Suzanne, swept by our table. "Ready to order now?" she shouted over the din, beaming like she was having the time of her life. Another actress. How would she react to tomorrow's story? Shock, outrage, shame. Like everyone else, she probably adored Chelsea, dreamed of attaining that height of fame someday. Only yesterday, I had lectured staff on the importance of discretion, a principle I treasured, an essential value in my profession. Such hypocrisy! In the dim lighting of the dining room, Suzanne's teeth glowed eerily, as though suspended in air. Was there derision in that smile?

"I'm ravenous," Mom said, lifting the menu and putting her reading glasses on. "Let me see … I think I'll start with the grilled polenta, and then … hmm … why not? The Moroccan lamb chops with couscous. Oh, and another glass of the pinot, please. It's lovely." She returned Suzanne's smile with a smile of her own. Had she had her teeth whitened? Was I crazy, or was Mom going Hollywood? The big sunglasses, the tan, the bleached teeth, the casually dropped phrases like "He's in the biz." Her skin looked smooth and taut. Was it the lighting, or had she had work done? Or, more likely, was I going insane?

"And you, Trevor?" Suzanne said, her teeth turning in my direction.

"I'll have the pan-seared scallops and the grilled sea bass," I said. "And make it a bottle of the pinot."

"Certainly." Suzanne's teeth floated off. I reached for my wine, took a gulp, and slid it back to my mother.

"A bit of controversy will be good for you, dear," she said. "You have an unnatural aversion to unpleasantness. You've avoided it all your life. It goes back to when your father died. You built your little panic room and withdrew. There must be a medical term for your condition, fear of unpleasantness. I'm sure it's why you pursued a career in an industry dedicated to the avoidance of unpleasantness.

Remember your attempt at a career in film production? You were horrified by the physical work, the long days in the freezing rain, the blunt, abrupt way the crew communicated."

"Yes, well, nobody liked me. They were suspicious of my cheerfulness."

"You'd probably fit in better now. You've been such a grouch this week." She sipped her water and crunched on an ice cube. "You didn't care much for university either. Why was that again?"

"I failed all my classes."

"Only because you didn't try. All that thinking and studying and stress—just more unpleasantness. I guess you found your calling here. How lucky they are to find someone willing to work day and night, to sacrifice everything. But let me warn you: don't confuse your work identity with your personal identity. This environment is artificial and superficial. It's a job and nothing more. It's all smiles and 'my pleasure,' everything is polished and sparkling. You have a hundred employees paid to treat you with respect and deference. However—"

"I beg your pardon? My staff respect me because I've earned their respect."

"Of course they do, but do you really think they'd try so hard to please you if you didn't sign their checks? It's all so contrived." She swept her hand around the crowded, noisy room. "This isn't reality, Trevor. It's no more real than a movie set filled with actors."

"Well, it's my life, and I happen to like it."

"Uh-uh. No way. This isn't life; this is a *job*. Life is what happens outside these walls, the place you fear to tread. You call this a place of refuge—for whom, Trevor, your guests or you?" She reached for a wedge of flatbread and broke it in half. "*Life* is messy and unpredictable, rife with wretched people, the desperately poor, the depressed, the sick, and the dying. It's full of unmade beds, soiled carpets, bland food, and nasty surprises. I've been watching you, darling. I can see the toll this chaos is taking. You can't control everything, and it's driving you mad. Don't fight it, embrace it. Life is chaotic. You'll never be able to control it, even in the pleasant environs of a hotel you manage."

Suzanne arrived with a bottle of wine and displayed the label for my approval. As she uncorked it, I glowered at Mom in the candlelight. All I wanted was a sympathetic ear. It felt like the whole world was at war with me. Tomorrow's siege might be fatal. Tonight I had hoped to convalesce in a no-fire zone and build my strength. What better refuge than the company of one's mother? Yet instead of dressing my wounds, she was acting like a terrorist who had sneaked into camp. Suzanne poured a taster. I nodded, and she filled Mom's glass and topped up mine.

Mom chomped on her bread, crumbs falling onto the tablecloth as she plotted her next assault. "What you *can* control," she said, "is how you perceive things."

Instead of provoking her by arguing or firing back, I employed a tried-and-true tactic for defusing hostile guests: I surrendered. "You're right, Mom. Your advice is excellent. I'll certainly take it into consideration."

She gave me a puzzled look. "Well … good." But she wasn't ready for a truce. "Have you started *Two Steps Forward* yet?"

"I've been a little busy."

"Dr. Druthers says at the root of our troubles are unresolved issues in the past. It's not a revolutionary idea, of course, but she explains it with such clever poignancy. She's helped me understand that my cancer was a form of poison created by negative emotions related to your father's death. The book has helped me come to terms with my guilt."

"You mean the guilt you inflicted on your children?"

"*My* guilt. I was such a bitch. When he died, he had been unemployed for four months. I was terrified we were going to lose the house, yet he was so nonchalant. He had that French arrogance. I needled him constantly. The morning he died, he was sitting at the kitchen table reading the newspaper, and I remember feeling especially resentful. As I fussed around, getting you kids ready for school, I asked him if he knew that jobs were listed in the classified section, not the sports section. Did he think he might find time in his busy schedule to shovel the sidewalk? Was he going to call that bricklayer friend about odd jobs? Meanwhile, the heartburn he had been complaining about, which I chose to ignore, was his aorta bubbling inside him like a balloon. After Mrs. Graham picked you and the girls up, I stormed out, slamming the door. Moments later, he fell to the floor. I feared that all my needling caused the bubble to burst. I went into shock. It took twenty years to recover."

"It wasn't your fault, Mom."

"I wished desperately I could go back in time and change things. But I've learned to accept that I can't change the past. I revisited his death, and I don't blame myself anymore. I did the best I could at the time. Now I live guilt-free, and it's liberating. I've taken great strides forward in my life, Trevor. Ironically, cancer *saved* my life. It forced me to resolve my issues, and I've never been happier. *One step back, two steps forward.*" She reached for her wine, arching her eyebrows to indicate it was my turn. We had been through similar discussions before. Every self-help book taught her a similar lesson using a different metaphor. Had she ever considered that her needling might cause *my* aorta to burst?

"I'm happy for you, Mom. Problem is, when I take a step back, I see myself calling Chelsea a psychopath."

"You need to accept that you had good reason. You did your best given the situation."

"Calling her a guest from hell was my best?"

"So you said a few things you shouldn't have. Who cares? Nobody with an ounce of self-respect reads that trashy magazine. Accept it, and you can start moving forward."

"Okay, fine. Except when I take two steps forward, I see Tony Cavalli firing me."

Her eyes flickered with irritation. "He won't fire you. Where's he going to find someone as dedicated as you? This will all blow over soon. Just wait out the storm."

I sat back and surveyed the room sullenly. In the center of the dining room, Tony Cavalli was holding court at a large round table. I slid out of his line of vision. After *Larry King,* he had left a series of threatening messages on my voice mail. Wait until he saw the *Spotlight* tomorrow. There were nine others at his table, but none were the stars whose company he thirsted for. Had he been shunned by Hollywood because of Chelsea's death or because of his obnoxious personality? Most likely the latter, but undoubtedly he would attribute it to the former—and blame me.

"Look at this place!" Mom exclaimed. "It's hopping! This hotel is a smashing success. You should be proud. Of course, you still have a few minor service issues to work out."

At that moment, Flavia Cavalli, hair askew, cheeks flushed, wiggled up to our table, holding two plates. "Who ordered the scallops?" she asked, hip leaning to one side. When I raised my hand, she slid the plate in my direction, contents sliding precariously toward my lap. "The placenta?" she said, setting the other plate down.

"*Pardon me?*" Mom said.

"You didn't order the placenta?" Flavia's voice was loud enough that the couple next to us turned to stare.

"I think you meant *polenta*," Mother said. She lifted her fork and stabbed at the grilled cornmeal as though afraid it would wriggle. It was accompanied by a chunky green salsa and asparagus tips.

Flavia covered her mouth with her hand. "Oh my Gawd! *Sorry!*" She fled.

I looked at Mom. "*Minor* service issues?"

"Perhaps an understatement. Is that girl related to the girl at the front desk?"

"They're cousins."

"It's all making sense to me now." She lifted a granule of polenta and tasted it, making a face. She set her fork down. "I don't think I can eat this." I offered her a scallop, but she declined. Her eyes surveyed the dining room, darting from one table to another. "I don't imagine you'll find someone like Nancy here," she said wistfully. "I can't stop thinking about her now that I know she wasn't meant to be on that flight, that she was *pregnant*. Life works in such mysterious ways."

That was the trigger, the grenade she pulled in the no-fire zone. I clenched my teeth. "Why don't we get this on the table right now?"

She was taken aback. "Get what on the table?"

"I'm tired of your pop psychology, Mom. Stop giving me your stupid self-help books and using clichéd metaphors to oversimplify my life. How can you tell me to stop blaming myself for Nancy's death when *you* blame me?"

"That is so untrue! I don't blame you."

"You do. Admit it!"

"I will do no such thing. I'm sorry she's dead. I wish I could change things, but I can't."

"You think Nancy was my only hope of being happy, and I ruined it."

"*I* do? Or *you* do? I don't blame anyone, Trevor. It was just bad luck—the wrong place at the wrong time. That's life. This is what I'm trying to get through your thick skull. You're blaming yourself, and you've got to stop. Until you forgive yourself, you'll continue to carry the torch for her. You love her like she's alive. You need to let go. Do you understand?"

I wanted to vomit my feelings onto the table. I fell back in my seat. "Why did I ask her to come home early, Mom? Why didn't I let her stay?"

She slid around the banquette and placed her arms around me. "You didn't know what would happen. Nobody knew. You missed her, and you wanted her home. Who can blame you for that?"

"She was pregnant. I shouldn't have convinced her to travel."

"How do you know she was pregnant? You never asked her. I've been thinking, Trevor. Those symptoms you described—the persistent cough, the fever—it doesn't sound like a pregnant woman to me. I'm a nurse. Even before you went away, she was sickly. She didn't have that horrible lung disease that killed her mother, did she? Pulmonary fibrosis can be genetic, you know. Didn't her maternal grandmother die young too?"

"She was pregnant, Mom. I know in my heart she was."

"How could you know?"

"I could see it in her eyes. When I asked her to marry me, I expected her to be ecstatic. We were so in love. We were in Paris, by the Louvre, sipping wine in a venerable old hotel. It was so romantic. But her eyes flickered, and she said, 'Let's wait and see.' She wanted to see if she was pregnant. She was hoping she wasn't. Nancy was a free spirit.

She thought I was a hopeless workaholic. When I cut our vacation short to go to work, her fears were validated."

"Nancy wanted to marry you, Trevor. She told me before you left for Europe, when I was helping her pack."

I turned to her, surprised. "Then why didn't she say yes?"

"A girl needs to think these things through."

"That's what I thought. I decided it was good I was going home early. She would have time to think. When she got to Salisbury, she went to see a doctor. That night we talked. She was crying. She wouldn't tell me what he said, but I knew she was pregnant. She was going back to him the next day. I knew what she was planning to do. I begged her to come home, hoping I could talk her out of it."

"Talk her out of what?"

"Out of getting an abortion."

15

Two Steps Back

In my career, I have mistaken the daughter of a prominent hotel guest for a prostitute, confused the head of an international pediatricians association for a vagrant, and given an entertainment industry mogul's room key to a jilted girlfriend I mistook for his wife. Yet never have I committed a blunder that threatened such grave consequences as my rant in the presence of Nigel Thoroughbred—a man I had met six days prior and should have recognized.

Yet on Friday morning, I woke up feeling refreshed and ready to face the day. Yesterday had been a day of catharsis. After years enduring rudeness and condescension from guests for the sake of preserving the peace, I had reached my limit. To vent on the despicable Moira, to say what I really felt instead of what I thought people wanted to hear—before an audience!—was thrilling. No wonder some hotel managers publicly chastised employees as a matter of routine. It made them feel powerful...in control...dangerous. It provided an outlet for the pressure: pressure from ownership, guests, staff, and from within; pressure to be friendly, charming, accommodating, impeccable, and uncompromising at all times. Without the occasional rant, such expectations might lead to self-destructive behavior: drinking problems, anger issues, abuse—perhaps even the urge to jump off a bridge. Or a balcony. My outburst might have saved me from the same fate as Chelsea Fricks.

As I got ready for work, I spotted the copy of *Two Steps Forward* on the nightstand. I felt guilty for offloading on my mother, for so cavalierly rejecting her attempt to help me find happiness. Painful as it was to admit, there was an element of truth in her words. I couldn't change the past, but I could accept it. I could change my attitude. I could take control of my future. I left my apartment vowing to stop the madness, to regain control of Hotel Cinema.

It was a beautiful morning, and I decided to walk. As I made my way down Whitley Avenue, I looked up to an early morning sun tempered by pink haze—the ironically beautiful effect of air pollution. At Hollywood Boulevard I veered left, passing gaps in storefronts that revealed the HOLLYWOOD sign in the distant hills. How many aspiring actors had been lured here by this sign, only to meet rejection and disappointment? I passed a tattoo parlor, a trio of homeless men sifting through an overflowing garbage bin, and a tall, hunched-over man in a Darth Vader costume. I too had arrived in Los Angeles with great expectations, only to discover I was to run a tarted-up motel with a rotten foundation. Before arriving, I had read up on the transformation of Old Hollywood and the plans to reestablish it as the "It" neighborhood. On my first visit, as I walked along the Walk of Fame, carefully stepping around the names out of deference and respect, I grew increasingly excited as I drew closer to one of the most famous intersections in the world: Hollywood and Vine. Yet when I reached it, I felt only disappointment. The area was drab and depressing. Signs promised a new W Hotel and new stores, office buildings, and condominiums, but they seemed a long way off. Would Hotel Cinema survive long enough to see it? Each night, with the help of good lighting, expert makeup, and competent staff, the hotel magically transformed into a beautiful young woman. But it was all smoke and mirrors; like Chelsea herself, the hotel was rotten on the inside. Over time, would it age well and preserve its appeal or fall to pieces and disappear into obscurity?

I thought of Vancouver and its backdrop of snow-capped mountains, rustic beaches, its endless seawall and fresh, salty air. For years I had shunned my hometown, preferring to leave my troubles there and move on. Yet all at once it held a powerful draw. After five years in New York, I hadn't felt at home. Would it be the same in Los Angeles? Was Mom right—was I destined to be a restless and lonely traveler, the consummate host who never found his own home? Or was it time to stop blaming the city for my failures? Was this the step back my mother meant—a step back to my only true home? *No.* I wasn't about to abandon the hotel and my colleagues. I had a job to do, staff to nurture and protect, an owner to manage, a detective to rein in, media to appease, disaster to avert. I would prove to Mom that I wasn't afraid of unpleasantness. It was time to come out of my panic room.

As I passed a newsstand on the corner, I caught a glimpse of the *Daily Spotlight* on display. I backed up and stooped down to pick it up. I had prepared myself for the worst, yet it was shocking to see my photograph on the cover, under the headline HOTEL MANAGER TELLS ALL! CHELSEA'S BIZARRE BEHAVIOR, DRUG USE, AND SEXUAL ADVANCES ON FATEFUL NIGHT! I felt the vein in my temple throb as I studied the photograph of me on the curb at the hotel's entrance in a black Ralph Lauren suit, a haughty, superior expression on my face. I was watching Detective Christakos escort Ezmerelda toward the waiting police car. Tearing open the magazine, I located the story on page three.

Hotel Manager Calls Chelsea "Guest from Hell"

In the latest episode in the melodrama surrounding the death of beloved actress Chelsea Fricks, Hotel Cinema took center stage last night when suave manager Trevor Lambert delivered a blistering rebuke of the star in the hotel lobby before a stunned audience of hotel guests and restaurant patrons.

The normally reserved Mr. Lambert broke the hotel's stoic silence by calling Chelsea "a liar, a cheater, a psychopath, a guest from hell." Lambert accused the late actress of attempting to seduce the hotel's chief engineer, Allan Robert Combs, in her lavish penthouse suite on the night of her death. Yesterday Combs was released after questioning by the Los Angeles Police Department. Claiming that Chelsea was "guzzling Jack Daniels" and snorting cocaine in her suite, Lambert called her "a monster" and "a racist," disclosing that books promoting racism were found in her suite.

Lambert saved his harshest words for Bryce Davies, whom he called Chelsea's "miscreant" boyfriend. He was reacting to Davies' appearance on *Larry King Live,* in which he accused hotel management of negligence in Chelsea's death. Accusing Davies of murdering Chelsea, Lambert said, "I don't blame Bryce for killing her. Someone had to put her out of our misery." Lambert then threatened to kill Moira Schwartz, the late actress's loyal publicist and friend.

Schwartz later said she "refused to dignify" Lambert's remarks by responding to them, but wanted to clarify that "Chelsea was not a racist and never did drugs. The books were research for an upcoming movie in which she was to play the daughter of Dwight Reed [the notorious white supremacist]. Chelsea welcomed people of all cultures and colors into her home. Practically all her domestic staff were Mexican."

Unable to read more, I closed the magazine and inspected the cover. My expression in the photograph was foul. My comments were incendiary and reprehensible. Yet I experienced a tiny thrill. I was on the cover of a magazine. A trashy magazine, to be sure, but circulation was enormous. On closer inspection, the photo wasn't *that* bad. I looked tall and distinguished and, well, managerial. My face was turned to the left, half in light, half in shadow, my jaw thrust out just so. I looked almost ... well, I might as well admit it ... aristocratic. My expression wasn't so much foul as defiant—even a tad heroic. They were carting off my employee, an innocent woman. A smile tugged at the corner of my lips. Me, Trevor Lambert, on the cover of a gossip magazine—no, an *entertainment* magazine. Like a celebrity. I occupied the same exalted space as Brad Pitt, Bryce Davies, Tom Cruise. Did my remarks really matter? What did Mom say last night—it didn't matter why people were famous, it only mattered that they were famous.

Someone was watching me. I looked up to see the newsstand vendor, an elderly, stunted woman with a missing front tooth, pointing at the cover.

"*Usted?*"

"Why, yes," I replied. "It is me." I fought off a self-satisfied grin and assumed a casual, somewhat bored, faintly irritated expression, as though cover stories were a regular occurrence. I bought three more copies, left a large tip, and wished her a pleasant day, and then hurried off, not to escape her scrutiny but to admire the photo further.

As I made my way down the Walk of Fame I found myself stepping not around the stars but on them. Perhaps one day my name would be here. It was a silly thought, but I might as well enjoy this moment, this tingling, titillating, intoxicating feeling of notoriety. I looked up and saw the HOLLYWOOD sign gleaming in the morning sun.

My cell phone rang, jolting me from my elated state. Anticipating the first in a flood of congratulatory calls, I answered immediately.

"You fucking moron!"

And with that, the moment was gone. I yanked the phone from my ear and stared into the display window: Tony Cavalli. Who else? I should have screened the call. "Tony, good morning," I said. "I take it you saw *Spotlight.*"

"*Spotlight. FOXNews. Good Morning America. The Today Show.* They're *all* talking about your rant."

"Really?" There it was again, that tremor of excitement. Across the street, a middle-aged couple was staring in my direction. The woman pointed at me. Was I the subject of a star-spotting? The couple charged across the street in my direction. Did they want an autograph? I didn't even have a pen. I was totally unprepared for this moment. They reached my side of the street and walked into the Starbucks behind me.

"How could you be so stupid?" Tony barked. "It was bad enough watching Bryce Davies screw us over on *Larry King*—now I read *Spotlight* and you're trashing Chelsea Fricks?"

I glanced down at the stack of magazines in my hands. In the sunlight I could see the image more clearly. I was a sour-faced, shameful little rat, a hotel manager spilling dirty secrets, violating the industry's sacred principles. After fighting to protect Chelsea's reputation, in one fell swoop I had taken her down.

Still, I felt compelled to defend myself. "At least *I* told the truth. Unlike Bryce. He—"

"Nobody wants to hear the fucking truth! Chelsea Fricks is a saint. You committed blasphemy. Her fans are confused, angry, desperate for someone to blame, and you delivered yourself on a platter. It should be Bryce they're loathing, but because you arrogantly refused to launch a media offensive, you gave him time to rally his troops. Now he's the hero and we're the villain. This is how you break your silence? Delivering an obnoxious rant against a beloved murder victim? You fucking hypocrite!"

"Tony, I'm sorry," I said, slowing my pace. "I screwed up. When I saw Bryce on *Larry King,* I lost it. I ran into Moira in the lobby and vented. I was defending the hotel's honor. I had no idea she was with a reporter from *Spotlight.*"

"Brilliant, Trevor, just brilliant! I built this hotel to welcome Hollywood's elite, and they won't even look me in the eye. I've been ostracized. I can't even get an invite to her memorial service. It's your fault! I gave you three days to turn things around, and *this* is your solution?"

"I have one more day. I'll fix this. I'll talk to Kitty and—"

"Kitty? That useless Texan twat is fired."

"You fired her?"

"Not yet, but I'm going to. She's been badmouthing the hotel to media. I hired Moira Schwartz to replace her."

"*Moira*? Tell me you're joking."

"I can't stand the broad either, but she knows her stuff. She says she can get us out of this mess. She's going to make Hotel Cinema a star, just like it was meant to be."

"Tony, I have serious doubts about Moira's integrity. She—"

"I don't give a fuck what you think anymore, Trevor. I'm tired of your bullshit. I'm taking charge of the hotel like I should have done in the first place. I will not let you stand in the way of the future of Cavalli Hotels & Resorts International!"

"But—"

"You're fired, Trevor. Fired!"

★ ★ ★ ★ ★

I stumbled to the entrance of a vacant store and lowered myself to the grungy pavement.

Fired.

The sun was rising over the buildings to the east. The first rays hit my feet and moved up my body, making me recoil like a vampire. Shielding my eyes, I rested my chin on my knees. After finally getting a backbone, for lashing out against contemptible people in defense of the hotel and its staff, I had been fired. No wonder I was always so agreeable, why I worked hard to avoid confrontation. To lose this job was my greatest fear, like losing my father or failing a class or being rejected by the woman I love. This job had summoned me back from the dead. Without it, I had nothing—an estranged family in another city, no friends, no Nancy. I had whittled life down to a job. Without the role of hotel manager to anchor my persona, who was I? Nobody. Nothing. Where would I go? Not back to Vancouver, graveyard of my failures. Another hotel in Los Angeles? My name would be dirt in this town. Another city, another country? My work permit was sponsored by Hotel Cinema. The paperwork could take months. Given my conduct, I might never find a hotel that would hire me. Derailed, I would fall into the miserable state I was in before I took this job: reclusive, oppressed by fear, incapacitated by grief.

I thought of my staff at Hotel Cinema. With me gone, they would be subjected to Tony's wrath and delusions of grandeur. Where would that leave them? Shanna would have no one to confide in, no office to hide out in. Ezmerelda, Al, Valerie, Reginald—who would take care of their needs, make sure they were appreciated? I thought of Rheanna and Dennis and Olga and Ahmed and Simka. Even the Cavalli sisters and cousin Bernadina didn't deserve to suffer Tony's ineptitude. Or maybe . . . maybe they would be happy to see me go. I had violated the very policies I preached. I had broken their trust and confidence. I had lost their respect.

It was better for all that I was leaving.

I lifted myself to my feet and tossed all four copies of *Spotlight* into the trash receptacle. Taking a deep breath, I set forward, toward the hotel. I would pack my things, call my mother to say goodbye, and retreat to my apartment until I could figure out where to go from here.

$\bigstar\ \bigstar\ \bigstar\ \bigstar\ \bigstar$

As I neared the hotel, I saw two LAPD cruisers blocking the street, lights flashing. A large crowd occupied the front of the hotel. A group of middle-aged women were holding up a banner that said HOTEL SHAME! STOP PLAYING THE BLAME GAME! Behind them, the crowd was chanting angrily and waving placards. A tall, slender black man jabbed a poster in the air that said REVENGE FOR CHELSEA! BURN HOTEL CINEMA! Across the street, two young girls held up a sign in red crayon: WHO KILLED CHELSEA? HOTEL CINEMA! Another sign proclaimed HOTEL ENEMA SPEWS CRAP!

I halted in my tracks.

One of the middle-aged ladies spotted me. "Hey, it's him! The manager! The guy who called her a psychopath!" Protesters turned in my direction. The phalanx of middle-aged ladies charged toward me.

I ducked down a side street, racing up the back alley, toward the employee entrance on the east side of the hotel. There, three men and a woman, two carrying cameras, were staked out at the entrance. I recognized the choppy-haired woman as Cleopatra from KCAL.

"Stop!" cried the middle-aged ladies in hot pursuit.

This caught the attention of the group outside the entrance.

"It's Trevor Lambert!" shouted Cleopatra, whistling for her crew. "Get over here quick, guys!" A member of the crew hoisted a television camera over his shoulder and jogged toward me.

Lowering my head, I made a beeline for the door. Two of the paparazzi jumped into my path, snapping photos. I covered my face and charged forward. People were rushing toward me from all directions. I bulldozed through the gauntlet, sending the paparazzi stumbling back. They chased after me, cursing, shutters clicking like gunfire. Reaching the door, I stood in front of the eye scanner and waited for the beep.

Nothing happened.

I glanced over my shoulder. A dozen angry-looking people surrounded me.

"Why did you call Chelsea a psycho and racist?" shouted Cleopatra.

"Chelsea was like a daughter to me!" cried one of the middle-aged ladies.

"How do you respond to allegations of negligence?" asked another reporter, jabbing me with his microphone.

I turned back to the scanner. Why wasn't the door opening? There was no beep, no green light. I positioned my eye before the panel again. Nothing. I took a step back, blinking to clear my eyes, and stepped forward. Had Tony cut off my access? Or did the scanner no longer recognize the person I'd become?

"How are you coping with the guilt of being responsible for Chelsea's death?" someone shouted.

I spun around. It was Cleopatra. My eyes flashed with rage. "Pardon me?" I roared.

She didn't flinch. "How do you feel about compromising the last bastion of privacy for stars?"

"As if you're one to talk. You people are parasites!"

There was a collective gasp. Glancing at the cameras around me, I told myself to shut up, to get the hell out of there. They fired more questions. I turned to give the scanner one last try. If I couldn't get in this way, I would have to navigate the unruly crowd out front. There was no beep, yet suddenly the door was flung open. An arm reached out and grabbed me, pulling me inside. Al Combs was standing there with Ezmerelda Lopez. They pushed the door closed with all their might. I heard the thud of a reporter's head.

"Animals!" Ezmerelda exclaimed.

"No respect," said Al.

I turned to them, overwhelmed with gratitude. "Thank you. I thought they were going to lynch me."

"The scanner is broken," said Al. "I was just resetting it."

"You okay? You don' look so good," said Ezmerelda.

They took me by the arms and led me to the staff cafeteria.

"Let's get you some water," said Al.

"Janie tell us Mr. Cavalli fire you," said Ezmerelda. "If you don't work here, we don't want work here."

"Our loyalty is to you," Al said. "If you go, we go."

★ ★ ★ ★ ★

Shanna was waiting in my office. This time, there was no tabloid on my desk. She was daintily perched on the chair, legs crossed. From the somber expression on her face, I knew she had spoken to Tony.

"Moving day," I said wryly. I closed the door behind me and shut the blinds. Looking around for a box to put my things in, I settled on the trash can. I began opening drawers, placing contents into the can.

"What are you doing?" Shanna asked.

I was surprised to see a smirk on her face. "Didn't Tony call you?"

"He did," she said. "We had the most delightful conversation. He told me he fired you. He offered me the position of general manager."

"Well. I guess congratulations are in order."

"I told him to stick it up his ass."

"So you're out of a job too, then." The trash can was full now. I tried to fit my mother's photo in, but it fell out, almost breaking.

Shanna got up and took the photo from me, placing it back on the shelf. "I told him if he fired you, I would quit on the spot. Janie's been going around telling everyone her uncle fired you. Already, six managers and a dozen employees have come to me to say if you go, they go. Including Reginald Clinton, who's responsible for leading the service team at tomorrow's wedding reception."

"I'm grateful for the support, Shanna, truly I am. But I'd rather go quietly."

"Tony just called back. He's reconsidered. You can expect a call from him shortly."

"You're serious? That's terrific. I guess."

"Frankly, I'm a bit disappointed too. I was looking forward to walking off the job."

"That isn't your style, anyway." I pushed aside the garbage can and sat on the edge of my desk, studying Shanna. "Something else is bothering you. What is it?"

A look of shame passed over her eyes. "I've made a deal with the devil."

"You did the right thing, Shanna. Tony can't—"

She looked up at me with a pained expression. "I don't mean Tony. I mean Moira Schwartz."

★ ★ ★ ★ ★

Shanna and I were sitting at a banquette in a quiet corner of Scene.

"She's not going to show," I said, my eyes darting to the front lobby.

"Oh, she'll show all right."

"I still can't get my head around this. Tony hired Chelsea's former publicist to defend the hotel against accusations of negligence in Chelsea's death? It's crazy."

She splayed her nails and admired them. "It's LA, Trevor."

I squirmed in my seat, feeling increasingly anxious. "What do you think her big idea is?"

"I told you, I don't know. What did Tony tell you?"

"That if I don't cooperate with her, I'm toast."

"Charming. I'm sorry for misleading you into thinking he's anything but a complete and utter swine."

"You should be."

Flavia Cavalli appeared at our table and dumped off a coffee tray and plate of large cookies. She tilted her head in sympathy, lower lip protruding. "Sorry to hear about your job, Trevor." I detected a trace of vindication in her tone.

"Trevor's not going anywhere," Shanna hissed. "Now scram."

Flavia's mouth dropped open. She pressed a hand against her chest and spun around, muttering, "Just wait 'til my brother hears this!" as she marched off.

"There goes the future of Cavalli Hotels & Resorts International," I said. "Remind me why we're fighting so hard to keep our jobs?"

"Because we made a commitment, Trevor. Because our employees are depending on us. And because I spent my entire life savings on shoes last night."

I checked the lobby again. "What if she wants me to go on a talk show circuit or something?"

"We're not *that* desperate."

"I'm not *that* bad on camera."

"Mmm-hmm."

"She's going to want us to do something that compromises our integrity, I know it. Moira and Tony have less than a quarter-ounce of integrity between them. If she wants me to go public with—"

"Trevor, if you don't stop fidgeting and fretting, I'll slap you again. As loath as I am to admit it, Tony and Kitty might have been right all along. This week, while we passively stood by, the hotel's reputation has been sullied by the head of housekeeping, damaged beyond repair by the head of maintenance, defamed by the publicist, and misman-aged by management. Our strategy has blown up in our faces."

"It might have worked had I not ranted at Moira."

"Even before then, we were getting savaged."

Just then, Moira arrived at our table, escorted by bellman Gustavo. Shanna and I rose to greet her.

"My, you're looking well," said Shanna in a flagrant attempt to flat-ter. Moira looked anything but well. She was even paler than normal. Her dyed black hair was stuck together in clumps, and there were half-circles like bruises under her eyes. Her lumpy black pantsuit looked like it had been rummaged from the bottom of a thrift-store barrel.

"I haven't slept all week," Moira said in her monotone voice, sling-ing her red purse onto the banquette with a huff and sliding in after it. She looked as thrilled about the meeting as we were. She gave me a withering look.

"I imagine it's been a difficult week," said Shanna, pouring her a cup of coffee.

"You're not kidding," Moira said. "Ever tried planning a memorial service for a thousand people with only a few days' notice?"

"I can't say I have," said Shanna. She offered Moira a cookie, but she declined. She bit into one herself. She was being unusually cordial. "Shall we get down to business?"

Moira gulped her coffee down black. She turned to me, eyelids drooping. "Did Tony tell you my conditions?"

I nodded. "He told me he agreed to comp up to $5,000 in food and beverage charges at Monday night's reception."

"And $15,000 cash up front."

"He didn't tell me that part." She sounded like a contract killer.

"I don't pick up the phone for anything less." Reaching into her purse, she withdrew two copies of a thick contract and slid them toward me. "I need you to sign on the bottom. If you decide to keep me on permanently, I'll draw up a new one. Tony offered to combine my fee with the amount you still owe for Chelsea's appearance, but that's her estate."

"Amount we still owe?" I said, puzzled. "But she didn't make it to the party."

"Oh yes, she did. She made her appearance. You got your publicity photos. This hotel got more coverage than you could dream of."

Shanna's nostrils quivered as though a foul odor had permeated the room. "Moira," she said, struggling to be gracious, "you're telling us that Chelsea fulfilled her contractual obligation to appear at the party by throwing herself to her death before horrified guests?"

Moira's tone was decidedly less cordial. "Chelsea was murdered by your maintenance man, Shania."

"*Shanna.*"

"That's not true," I said. "Al Combs has been exonerated."

Moira fixed her big brown eyes on me. "What? When?"

"Yesterday."

She nodded slowly. "Then who's Detective Constantinopolous after now?"

Shanna flashed me a look of caution, but I knew enough not to say anything Moira could sell to *Spotlight*. "I have no idea," I said, and I was being truthful. I hadn't heard from the detective since he dragged Al away. I slid the contract back to her. "I have no idea what you and Tony discussed. You'll have to ask him to sign."

"Fine," Moira said, stuffing it back into her purse. "Before I divulge my plan, I need to know everything you know about the case. Now that I'm representing you, you can't hold anything back."

"You know as much as we do," I said.

Moira squinted at me through half-closed eyes. "You mean about Bryce?"

Shanna and I leaned toward her. "What about Bryce?" Shanna said.

"It's obvious, isn't it?" said Moira, swallowing the rest of her coffee. "Bryce killed her."

"A week ago, you were accusing Ezmerelda Lopez," I said. "Then you decided Al Combs was guilty. Now it's Bryce? What took you so long to get around to him? You were next door when it happened."

"I never thought it was those other two," Moira snarled. "I simply reported what I saw and heard. I've always known it was Bryce. He was jealous."

"Jealous of whom?" asked Shanna. "Al Combs?"

"Jealous of Chelsea's success, of her fame, of my close relationship with her."

"So he killed her?" I said.

Moira pushed a clump of hair away from her eyes. "I went to her suite to see her that night, just before Bryce came by. She told me what she was going to do. That's why he killed her."

"What?" Shanna and I asked simultaneously.

"Chelsea dumped Bryce that night."

16

Publicity Stunt

I saw Mom off in the privacy of the parkade, where, in order to avoid the circus out front, I had arranged for the hotel car to pick her up.

"You didn't steal anything, I hope?" I said as I loaded her bags in the trunk.

"Only the bath amenities," she said. "I would have taken the whole fitness room if I could fit it in my bags."

"No towels, bathrobes, silverware? Do I need to inspect your bags? Is there anything left in the mini-bar?"

"There's no mini-bar in the fitness room, you'll recall."

"What about Bruce Leonard? Are you taking *him* home?" I slammed the trunk and opened the back door, placing her carry-on on the seat.

"Certainly not. He was just a fling."

"Does he know that?"

"He'll accept it in time." She opened her arms to hug me. "I'm going to miss you so much!"

"Me too, Mom."

"I've had such a wonderful time! Sunshine, celebrities, and murder. I feel like I've been at a summer drive-in movie. It's been entertaining, but I'm glad it's over. I'm looking forward to going back to work at the hospital." She padded her purse. "I bought a half-dozen copies of the *Spotlight* for your sisters and friends."

"Be sure to defend my honor."

"Now why would I have to defend your honor? Everyone knows what an upstanding young man you are. You're an innocent victim of the tabloid culture that's poisoning our society. Besides, no one will read the article. It's enough that you're on the cover—and you look so handsome!" She regarded me fondly. "I'm sorry I've been so hard on you, dear. You know it's because I love you. I understand you so much more now."

"I'm glad. No more talk about Nancy, promise? That chapter of my life is over."

She nodded faintly and gave a half-smile. "If things don't work out here, there's always the Four Seasons in Vancouver. I hear they're looking for a general manager."

"I'll keep that in mind."

"Oh, I almost forgot." She reached into her purse and handed me a bag from Book City. "I started reading the *Truth* one last night, and it's fantastic."

"Thanks," I said, casting a nervous glance inside the bag. I closed the door and waited as she figured out how to roll down the window.

She stuck her head out for a kiss. "I love you, darling."

"Love you too, Mom."

"We'll watch for you on TV tonight!"

"Don't feel obligated."

As the car rolled up the ramp I waved after it, feeling a tugging at my heart, as though she had stuck a suction cup on my chest and was clinging to the string. I opened the bag and pulled out two books. One was entitled *Managing Hotels the Four Seasons Way*, the other *The*

Truth Shall Set You Free (But Boy Can It Hurt!). I smiled, tucking them under my arm, and headed back upstairs.

One step forward, two steps back.

★ ★ ★ ★ ★

Ashlee White, one of the perky on-air personalities at *Spotlight To-night*, arrived with her crew at three PM sharp. I had seen her out front this week and on TV many times, and I had always lunged for the channel-changing button. She was much smaller in person than I had imagined, in her mid-twenties, and physically perfect, except that everything about her—hair, makeup, skin, breasts, personality— seemed fabricated. She reminded me of an android.

"Nice to meet you," she said icily, making it apparent she saved her perkiness for the camera. Her hand felt limp and cold as I shook it. She scanned the lobby, unimpressed. Minutes earlier, an army of housekeeping staff, led by Ezmerelda, had swept in to do a total overhaul, leaving everything polished, orderly, and sparkling. Briskly introducing me to her crew, who were friendlier, she wandered off to stare at the fireplace.

"Nice place you got here," said Barbs, the producer, a boyish-look-ing woman with spiky silver hair and narrow glasses. She attached a microphone to my lapel and handed me a small electronic box. "Here, sweets, shove this in your inside pocket."

The crew went to work immediately, setting up for the first shot in the lobby. Hector the makeup artist dusted my cheeks while Samir the lighting technician switched on a bright light, shining it on me from various angles. Cameraman Bradley lifted his camera and panned the lobby.

Meanwhile, Android Girl stood quietly a few feet away, unresponsive to my nervous attempts at conversation. When the crew was ready, she took her place beside me and let them fuss over her.

"*Spotlight Tonight* airs all over the world," Barbs told me, brushing lint off my jacket. "By tomorrow morning, you'll have been seen by at least ten million viewers worldwide. The Queen of England herself likes to watch it."

"No pressure there," I said.

"You'll be great. We've got less than an hour to get to the studio for editing, so we need to move fast. Remember to look at Ashlee, not the camera. She'll do an intro, and after that she won't be on-camera most of the time. She'll prompt you with questions. Try to repeat the question in your answer, and keep your answers short. Cool?"

"Cool," I said, blinking in the glare of the light. I looked at Ashlee, hoping for a reassuring smile. Android Girl was staring blankly into space as though Barbs had powered her down. My eyes glanced at the camera and quickly looked away. Ten million viewers—they would scrutinize every word, every stammer, every inflection, every pore on my face.

When I had expressed concern to Moira earlier, she was flippant. "This isn't *Dateline*, Trevor. It's a fluff piece. They promised not to refer to your rant or to ask any inappropriate details about Chelsea's death. They owe me. I'm giving them the exclusive at the memorial service. Give them a tour of the hotel and answer their questions. It's for the 'In the Spotlight' segment, so don't hold back on the personal stuff. You want to show viewers a more compassionate side of Hotel Cinema."

Moira had promised to get their list of questions in advance and to role-play them with me, but then she had left two hours ago to deal with organizational issues concerning the memorial service and never came back. Shanna and I took a few minutes to review my core messages: 1) Hotel Cinema is committed to the safety, security, and privacy of our guests; and 2) Hotel Cinema has become the premier destination for celebrities, locals, and international travelers. "Say our brand name as frequently as possible," Shanna coached. "And loosen up. Have a good, stiff drink beforehand—but only one."

"I don't want to do this," I had told her in one last attempt to weasel out. "This isn't me."

"You have no choice," she said. "Our livelihood is at stake. Suck it up."

Now, Shanna was nowhere to be found, having left the property for fear of running into Ashlee White. It was fine by me. I was struggling with my conscience, and having her around would only add to my anxiety. Glancing at the huge camera resting on Bradley's shoulder, I found myself wishing I had taken Shanna's advice to down a stiff drink. My eyes moved to the rows of shiny bottles at the bar. I could dash over and—

"Rolling!" Bradley announced.

Ashlee sprang to life, straightening her posture, pushing out her breasts, and breaking into a capped-tooth smile. "I'm here at Hotel Cinema," she enthused, assuming the perky host persona I remembered, "the *stunning* new Hollywood hotel with the clever movie theme that *everyone* is talking about. Only one week ago, Hotel Cinema held its opening party—an extravagant, star-studded affair that had all the ingredients of a Hollywood premiere. Yet tragedy struck minutes before midnight when guest of honor Chelsea Fricks, acclaimed actress and celebrity bad-girl, leapt to her death from the balcony of her luxurious fifth-floor penthouse suite. Since then, the hotel has refused to participate in the storm of speculation and intrigue swirling around the mysterious death that police are now calling murder.

Management has taken a great deal of heat for its stoic silence and has been accused of heartlessness and indifference. Recently, Chelsea's bereaved boyfriend, heartthrob actor Bryce Davies, accused the hotel of negligence and complicity in her death. Tonight, *Spotlight Tonight* has been granted an exclusive first look at the stylish and über-hip interiors of Hotel Cinema. We get up close and personal with dashing hotel manager Trevor Lambert—only on *Spotlight Tonight!*"

Ashlee stared into the camera, smile unfading as though she could stand all day that way, until Barbs called "Cut" and Bradley lowered the camera. Barbs turned to me. "This is the special part of the show where our 'In the Spotlight' guest introduces himself." Repositioning me in front of the fireplace, she instructed me on what to say and do. A crowd of employees, guests, and patrons began to gather. I clenched my fists, unclenched them, and licked my lips, wishing I had a glass of water—or vodka. Hector fussed around me, dusting my face with powder, moving strands of hair into place, adjusting my lapels, and smoothing his hands over my chest—ostensibly to smooth out creases.

Android Girl maintained her aura of cool detachment.

"Ready to roll!" Barbs called out.

Feeling exceptionally foolish, I mustered a smile for the camera and announced, "Hi, everybody! I'm Trevor Lambert, general manager of Hotel Cinema! And I'm in the spotlight tonight!"

Over the next eight takes, Barbs called out words of encouragement like a hopeful stage mom: "Smile, Trevor, smile! You're having a ball! Let's see some zest! Some zeal! Some zippity-doo!" At last, they decided they had a good-enough take—or perhaps they gave up.

We moved to Action's entrance and stood before a backdrop of white leather furniture, pearl shimmer screens, and soft violet lighting.

Ashlee snapped back into perky mode. "Trevor, tell us about who stays at Hotel Cinema."

I tried to smile like her. "Well, Ashlee, here at Hotel Cinema, we get a mix of corporate and leisure guests. It's a bit early to say for sure—we just opened a week ago, after all—but we estimate about half our guests will be tourists—Americans, Canadians, Europeans, Japanese—and half will be corporate."

"What about stars? I bet a lot of stars stay here."

"Indeed, Hotel Cinema is very popular with stars." I sensed I was being stiff. "But we also get a lot of corporate travelers! Executives in industries like pharmaceuticals, finance, the automotive industry! International business travelers! Incentive groups!" Now I sounded like a game-show host.

"Tell us about some of the big celebrities who have stayed here."

"Hotel Cinema has quickly established itself as *the* celebrity hot-spot!" Big grin.

Ashlee's smile was frozen on her face. "Like who?"

Hadn't Moira briefed her on our privacy policy? "At Hotel Cinema, the privacy of our guests is paramount," I said. "We don't divulge names or details about our guests."

Ashley lowered her microphone and let out a huff. "Um, Barbs? Can you please explain to this guy who we are?"

Barbs hurried over. "Listen, um, Trevor? Our audience wants to hear about celebrities, not Japanese businessmen, okay? It's actually all they care about. We need names. You cool with that?"

"Well, of course I want to cooperate, but it's hotel policy not to—"

"Oh, please," Ashlee snapped, storming off the set.

"'Cuz if you're not willing to give names?" Barbs said cheerfully. "I'm sorry, but we're wasting each other's time."

Was she threatening to call it off? Blowing this interview would bring my employment to an abrupt end. "Could I give a few names off-camera?" I asked Barbs. "I trust you understand my reluctance, given last week's incident. We're trying to rebuild the public's confidence."

"You okay with that, Ash?" Barbs called out.

"Fine. Whatever."

"Fantastic! Why don't we do some shots on the move," said Barbs. "We'll reenact Chelsea's arrival at the front door, go to the front desk to check in, and then into the elevator and up to the suite. Cool with you, Trevor?"

"Cool," I said, nodding eagerly to be a good sport. But I was becoming increasingly uncomfortable about agreeing to open the hotel's doors to *Spotlight Tonight* and exploiting Chelsea's death like a macabre Robin Leach. For the next fifteen minutes, I stood by passively as the crew shot footage on the main floor. At the front entrance, the filming prompted an outcry in the encampment from *Spotlight's* jealous rivals. We moved to the front desk, where I demonstrated the iris scanner, and Valerie, as comfortable in front of the camera as a seasoned actress, staged a phantom check-in. We piled into the elevator next and went to the penthouse suite, which was reserved for a late arrival. Along the way, Bradley filmed everything: carpet, ceiling, doors, gold stars, Opti-Scan panels.

As the crew set up at the entrance to the penthouse suite, I rehearsed lines in my head while Android Girl wandered off and powered down. When the camera started rolling, I borrowed a technique from Ashlee and lit up like a Christmas tree. "Hotel Cinema is fully committed to the safety, security, and privacy of our guests!" I said brightly, trying to steady my hands as I gave a demonstration. "Our state-of-the-art Private-Eye Opti-Scan security system works on digital iris technology. Since no two irises are alike, the safety of our guests is 100% guaranteed! If your eye isn't an exact match to the digital snapshot stored in our database, the door won't open!" For the next ten minutes, I explained the system in detail, using every opportunity to emphasize the hotel's commitment to safety and security while Bradley shot from various angles. I began feeling much more comfortable in my role.

"I think we get the idea," Barbs said, cutting me short. "Can we go inside now?"

As we entered the suite, Hector said, "Oh my God, I can't believe this is where it all happened."

The crew gazed around in silent awe.

Barbs said, "Let's move. We're falling behind."

I guided the crew from room to room, providing commentary and pointing out the designer furnishings and contemporary artwork.

Ashlee's questions were mostly innocuous until we stopped in the kitchen. "What was Chelsea's last meal?"

I was prepared for this one. "Chelsea's last meal was a clubhouse sandwich and a Diet Coke from room service," I lied.

"Really?" said Ashlee. "I thought she was vegan."

Why hadn't Moira told me? "It was a *meatless* clubhouse," I said quickly, sneaking a glance at the camera. I tried to recall what vegans ate. "With no cheese," I added. Did vegans eat wheat products? "Or bread."

Ashlee scrunched up her face. "A clubhouse with no meat, cheese, or bread? That sounds yummy. Can we have a look in the bathroom now?"

They filmed the bathtub, shower, counters, tiles, walls, toilet, fixtures, and bath products. I kept out of the way, fighting off the distaste that kept creeping over my face. Next we toured the bedroom.

"Pajamas or birthday suit?" asked Ashlee as the camera zoomed in on me in front of the king-sized bed.

"Pardon me?"

"Don't you ever watch our show? We always ask people if they sleep in the raw or in pajamas. Viewers want to know."

"I see ... well, normally I wear boxers, but—"

She let out a derisive laugh. "I meant Chelsea."

I was beginning to loathe Ashlee White. What an unsavory question. "I really can't say," I replied testily. "Miss Fricks never actually slept here."

"Can we shoot the balcony?" asked Barbs.

I led them into the living room and pulled open the sliding-glass door. The crew piled outside and gazed over the railing, pointing down at the pool excitedly. They came back into the living room.

"Take a run at it like you're Chelsea," Barbs said to Bradley.

Camera resting on his shoulder, Bradley backed up a few steps, waited for the lighting to be put in place, and raced across the carpet, onto the balcony, and up over the railing, lunging so far I feared he would topple over. He backed up and repeated the action three more times.

I felt sick to my stomach as I watched them reenact Chelsea's last moments. Why was the public so fascinated with these morbid details? My cell phone buzzed. Happy for the distraction, I wandered into the dining room.

"Trevor, it's Valerie. You need to get out of the penthouse suite right away. Our VIP guest arrived early. He's on his way up."

I hung up and hurried over to Barbs. "We've got to go now," I said. "Our guest has arrived."

"No prob," said Barbs. "We can do our final shots on the pool deck."

As the crew filed out, I hurried around the suite to tidy up. Normally, a room should be immaculate upon arrival, not a smudge or scratch or fingerprint or speck of dirt or any sign that another human being had occupied it. Room attendants were required to vacuum their way out of a room to ensure no footprints were left behind. Unfortunately, there was no time for housekeeping to give the suite a final once-over. By the time I ushered the group down the hall, our VIP guest, a thin, straggly haired fellow wearing dark glasses and a fedora, was heading toward us.

"Good afternoon, sir," I greeted as I passed.

The man grunted a reply, noticed the crew behind me, and lowered his head.

"Holy crap, was that Johnny Depp?" Hector whispered at the elevator.

"Who? I don't believe so."

Barbs flashed a knowing smile. Behind us, Ashlee stopped to chat with the guest.

★ ★ ★ ★ ★

The pool deck was quiet. About a dozen occupants lounged in the late afternoon sun. Bradley panned the deck with the camera, lingering on the pool and zooming in on the hotel logo etched on the bottom. He lifted the camera to the balcony of the penthouse suite, moving it down to the pool and back up again, following the arc of Chelsea's dive.

The crew set up for the next segment at the edge of the pool. The penthouse balcony loomed in the backdrop.

When the camera rolled, Ashlee perked up again. "By now, everyone knows that Chelsea Fricks dove into this pool to escape a knife-wielding assailant," she said into the camera. "What people *don't* know

318

is that a heroic attempt was made to save her life on that fateful night. Of hundreds of people at the party, only one person had the courage to dive into the pool to rescue her: Trevor Lambert, Hotel Cinema's general manager. Trevor, tell us about your heroic attempt to save Chelsea's life."

The question caught me off-guard. *Hero?* So this was Moira's "big idea." With the camera rolling I felt obliged to respond, but I was deeply embarrassed.

A few probing questions later, and I found myself rising to the occasion. Under the glare of the afternoon sun, before a television crew and a live audience, I told my story, reenacted the scene, recounted dramatically my thoughts and actions. Part of me detested myself for pandering to *Spotlight*, and yet a growing part relished the attention. Today *Daily Spotlight*, tonight *Spotlight Tonight*! No wonder actors sacrificed everything for this time in the limelight. It was intoxicating. A remark Shanna made last November came back to me: "In LA, hotel managers are celebrities in their own right." Perhaps she was right. I had always avoided attention, loathed scrutiny, cowered from the spotlight. Now I was thriving in it. Moira set this up. She was brilliant. As soon as filming was over, I would give her the green light to launch a full campaign, to contact all the talk shows, newspapers, magazines, and radio stations and set up more interviews. I was good at this, and I wanted more.

"Trevor?" Ashlee was saying. "He-lo-o?"

I snapped to attention. Bradley had lowered his camera. "It's not over, is it?" I said, spirits sinking.

"We thought we'd do our last setup in that cabana," Barbs said. "This is the 'In the Spotlight' part of the show, our up-close-and-personal celebrity interview."

Minutes later, Ashlee and I were sitting side-by-side in a cabana at the north end of the pool, our knees almost touching. Over fifty people had gathered to watch, lining the periphery of the pool, leaning over the balconies, faces pressed against the windows of the lobby and bar. I felt like I was onstage in an outdoor theater. The afternoon sun had disappeared, and the set was lit by floodlights, TV lights, and fire basins. Ashlee flashed her lovely smile at me. I decided I was wrong about her. She was sweet and very pretty—she wasn't a robot. Her knee sent jolts of electricity raging through my body. As Hector powdered our faces and Barbs arranged my microphone, I felt a profound connection to Ashlee. It hadn't escaped me that Barbs called this a "celebrity" interview. Remembering my mother's suggestion to take advantage of my position to meet women, I wondered if I should ask her to dinner after the shoot.

The camera rolled. Ashlee stuck out her lower lip, eyes softening in an expression of deep sorrow. "Tell us what it was like to watch your guest of honor die in your arms," she said tenderly.

This wasn't exactly how it happened, but by now I was a slave to the camera, willing to do or say anything, no matter how personal or sensationalistic, to extend my time in the spotlight.

"It was heartbreaking," I told her, assuming a somber tone. "I wish I could have saved her, but she was already gone."

"Is there anything you'd like to tell Chelsea's fans?"

I turned to face the camera. "I'm sorry I couldn't save her. I tried. My heart goes out to you in this time of sadness."

Ashlee nodded, seemingly pleased. "I'm sure it will mean a lot to them. Now, I understand that tragedy is no stranger to you. Tell us about the death of your fiancée, Nancy Swinton."

I blinked, thinking I had misheard. "Pardon me?"

"Your fiancée, Nancy Swinton," Ashlee repeated, "who perished in the Worldwide Airways crash last year. Were there parallels between her death and the death of Chelsea Fricks?"

I was thunderstruck. How did she know about Nancy? *Moira.* She had set me up.

"Trevor?" Ashlee said, shifting in her seat.

I stared into her pale blue, watery eyes. My mood plummeted like a plane falling from the sky. I felt my eyes turn to stone. "Nancy Swinton was not my fiancée," I said. "She never accepted my proposal. We never even got a chance to say goodbye." I turned away from Ashlee, my eyes moving past the glaring lights and over the sea of observers.

"If Nancy were still alive," said Ashlee, "what would you say to her?"

I turned back to her. "I would say I'm sorry. I would tell her I've changed. I would say goodbye." Out of the corner of my eye, I caught my shadow on the surface of the pool, distorted and flickering in the light of the fire basin.

Nancy. My sweet, lovely Nancy. How could I allow her death to be sensationalized like this?

Ashlee moved closer and said softly, "If Chelsea were still alive, what—"

"Enough." I stood up and pulled the microphone from my lapel. "This interview is over."

I walked off-set, leaving the crew, audience, and Android Girl staring after me in shock.

★ ★ ★ ★ ★

I couldn't bring myself to watch the show. I sat at my desk, door closed, and ordered room service, half-heartedly scrolling through email. The photo of my mother sat on the bookshelf where Shanna had replaced it, facing me as though observing me work with a trace of disapproval. Next to it sat the copy of *Two Steps Forward*. I got up and opened the bag from Book City, pulling out the two books and setting them on the shelf. I glanced at the spine of the one closest to me: *The Truth Shall Set You Free (But Boy Can It Hurt!)* by Erma Glottstein. Every self-help book she gave me was written by a female, as though men had nothing to teach me. I wondered what message my mother was trying to convey through this book, which personality disorder she had diagnosed this time. I had received her message loud and clear from *Two Steps Forward* and had grudgingly committed to reading the book and at least listening to its message. But what about this: *The Truth Shall Set You Free*? Nancy, without a doubt.

My cell phone vibrated in my pocket.

"Did you watch it?" Shanna asked.

"I couldn't. How bad was it?"

"It was fantastic! Absolutely fantastic!"

I wanted to believe her, but I knew better. "That bad?"

"You looked like a movie star."

"I did?" That thrill again. "How did the interview go?"

"It was very quick, less than three minutes."

"Only *three* minutes? We shot for over an hour."

"That's show biz. They called you the Heroic Hotel Manager."

"Me? You're kidding."

"'I'm Trevor Lambert, and I'm in the spotlight tonight!'" she mimicked, breaking into wicked laughter.

My face burned. "You're the one who put me up to this, Shanna."

"Tony did, I didn't. Don't fret, you did a great job. You somehow managed to be perky and robotic at the same time, but I suppose that was nerves. The hotel looked fabulous, although I was disappointed you said nothing about security and privacy. Wasn't that the whole point?"

"*What?* That's practically all I talked about."

Shanna sighed. "Well, they edited it out. They showed a collage of actors spotted at the hotel, half of whom have never set foot on-property, and footage of the penthouse suite, the balcony, the pool, and then your 'In the Spotlight!' interview with Ashlee. I was surprised you agreed to talk about Nancy."

"She ambushed me. What did they show?"

"Well, they talked about the WWA crash and how your fiancée died in it. Then they showed a close-up of you saying you regretted that you never had a chance to say goodbye to her. The camera lingered on your earnest little face. Then it was over."

"I could kill Moira. I knew I couldn't trust her."

"It was quite touching, really. As much as I'm loath to admit it, Moira was right. It showed a human side to the hotel."

"Have you talked to Tony?"

"Hold on, that's him on the other line." A moment later Shanna was back. "Well, it worked. Tony *loved* it! You get to keep your job. Well done, Trevor!"

"That's a relief. Why don't you come down for a drink to celebrate?"

"I'm in my pajamas. Besides, Naomi Watts is booked to come in for dinner. I would faint if I had to sit in the same room as that gorgeous little waif. Careful, darling, if you get any more famous, I might have to start hiding from you too."

★ ★ ★ ★ ★

At ten PM, I decided to do one last walk-around before calling it a night.

As I passed the front desk, Simka, who had just reported in for her night shift, called out to me. "I saw you on *Spotlight*! You were incredible. You are very famous person now!"

"Whatever it takes to defend the hotel's reputation," I said, blushing nonetheless. I glanced at Valerie beside her, who smiled demurely.

Action was packed. Adrenaline from the day's events was still racing through me, and I decided to calm down over a drink at the bar. Ordering a Grey Goose on the rocks, I turned to observe the crowd. For the first time I felt at ease in this environment—a part of the cast rather than one of the crew. Was it my imagination or were people stealing furtive glances at me, whispering, gesturing in my direction? Had I been recognized as the Heroic Hotel Manager? I stood tall to make myself more visible and squared my shoulders. A very pretty, petite young lady with shampoo-commercial hair was eyeing me from the other side of the lounge. Pretending not to notice, I assumed the air of bored detachment mastered by Ashlee White.

In an instant she was at my side. "Are you Trevor Lambert, the manager of this hotel?" she asked, eyes hopeful. She was clutching a glass of white wine.

"And who would like to know?" I asked coyly, lifting my glass to my lips and giving her a thin smile.

"I'm Jennifer. I recognize you from the *Daily Spotlight*. My friends and I were just talking about you!"

"Were they now?" I asked, trying to sound disinterested. I looked over and lifted my glass to cheer them.

"They were too shy to come over, so they sent me."

What pretty brown eyes she had. What pert little breasts. I bent over to whisper in her ear and breathed in eucalyptus and lavender. "Their loss, I guess."

"Yeah, so we want you to know we think you're the biggest asshole who ever walked on this earth."

I almost dropped my glass. "Pardon me?"

"Chelsea Fricks was our hero. She was a saint. You told outrageous lies about her to get your name in the tabloids. You're despicable." She threw her drink in my face and marched off.

I stood there stunned, unable to move. Wine was dripping off my chin onto my suit.

A nudge on my arm made me turn. Detective Christakos was holding out a napkin. "I think you've got something on your face," he said.

I took the napkin and dried my face, humiliated. "Thank you, Stavros."

"Don't mention it. Next time you try and pick up a chick, you might want to run lines with me first." He looked over his shoulder to the bar. "Sure am thirsty."

"The usual?"

"Make it a double."

"What brings you here?" I asked after I ordered, glancing down at his black mesh shirt, black jeans, and silver-studded belt.

"Oh, you know..." His eyes darted around the crowd.

"How's...?" My mind filtered through various coffee varieties. "Cappuccino?"

"That relationship went down the drain quick. I did a background check. Her real name is Debbie Smith from Lawrence, Kansas."

"Shocking. I'm sorry."

He stared at the napkin in my hands, and then up at my face. "You wearing makeup?"

I looked down at flesh-colored smears on the napkin. "I shot a segment on *Spotlight Tonight*." I peered closer at his own powdery complexion. "You are too."

He ran his hand over his jaw and regarded it. "So I am. I guess I forgot to clean it off. I filmed my scene for *Modern Loving* today."

His daiquiri arrived, and he made a lame attempt to pay. I waved him off. We lifted our drinks and clinked them. "How did it go?"

"This might be it for me, Trevor. I'm going big-time. I played a cop." He adopted a menacing expression and gripped my arm. "You'll have to come with me, sir," he said, his tone faintly simpering. He threw his head back and exploded with laughter.

"That was your line?"

"Yeah. I was basically playing myself, except I played him gay."

"You conveyed a gay cop with one line?"

"It wasn't easy, but I pulled it off. The script didn't call for a gay cop, I just interpreted it that way. I played this guy who's tormented because he's a closet homo trapped in the homophobic police department."

"So you played yourself."

"Not funny! It took a few takes—I'm a perfectionist—but I nailed it. It might become a recurring role."

"Congratulations."

He nodded, pleased. Leaning against the bar, he searched the crowd.

"How's the investigation going?" I asked.

"It's going."

"Did you know Chelsea broke up with Bryce that night?"

"Moira told me as much. Bryce has a different interpretation."

"You've seen the activity reports. He left his room minutes before she was attacked."

"I seen 'em."

His reticence was irking me. "Are you going to arrest him, then?"

He shrugged. "We'll see." Someone caught his eye in the crowd, and he lifted his hand to wave. "There's my man! Hey, Mr. Costar, over here! Get over here, you handsome devil!"

Bryce Davies burst through the crowd, looking smashed, and gave Stavros a bear hug.

17

One Step Forward

I pressed the phone to my ear and listened to the breathing, the eerie crackling sound. Another hangup. In the distance, I could hear muffled voices—a television? And then the unmistakable music that signaled the end of *Spotlight Tonight.* I looked at the clock on my computer screen: 11:59 AM.

7:59 PM in London.

"*Scusi,* Treva?" Janie Spanozzini was at my door, face flushed and spotty. "There's a guy here to see you."

I set the receiver on its cradle and stared down at the phone.

"Treva? You okay?"

I looked up. "You mean a *gentleman*, Janie."

She tittered. "That's debatable. It's BRYCE DAVIES."

I rose from my desk. "What does he want?"

"How should I know? Let me say right now he is SO HOT!" She pressed the back of her hand against her forehead and fell back against the doorframe. "His eyes are the *exact* color of Bernadina's sapphire earrings. I don't think I can go back out there. Tell him I'll bear his children—anything he wants."

"Compose yourself, Janie." Pulling on my suit jacket, I squeezed past her and stopped to fix my tie in the hallway mirror. In the reflection, I saw Janie pull out her cell phone. "What are you doing?"

"Sendin' a text message to cousin Sophia. She's upstairs gettin' ready for the wedding. She's gonna die."

"Put that away and get out there. You're the only one at the desk." I held the door open for her, gesturing impatiently.

She stopped to check her hair and makeup. Taking a deep breath, she pushed her boobs together, straightened her shirt, and walked out with eyelids fluttering.

Bryce Davies was pacing the lobby in dark Prada sunglasses and torn white jeans. His head was down, hands thrust into his pockets. A number of patrons had stopped to stare at him.

"How may I help you today, Mr. Davies?" I asked.

He turned around and grinned amicably, swooping his hand in sideways for a handshake. "Trevor, how you doing? Call me Bryce. Listen, can we talk for a sec?" He gestured toward the lounge.

I hesitated. Last night's encounter had been brief and awkward. I was shocked by his audacity to appear at the hotel two days after bashing it so mercilessly on *Larry King*. I hadn't been able to stomach watching Detective Christakos fawn over him when he should have been arresting him. Now he was back. Why? I wanted to throw him off-property and tell him he wasn't welcome here.

Yet my hospitable nature prevailed. "Certainly," I said. "Come with me."

As we passed Janie, Bryce flashed a smile and thanked her. She let out a gasp and swooned. We walked past the concierge desk, where he waved at Bernadina, almost toppling her from her chair. Several guests turned to stare as we walked past. We entered the soft lighting of the lounge, and his clothes and hair took on a translucent hue.

Bryce Davies radiated star power. I thought back to my flirtation with fame yesterday. How did it feel to command this kind of attention all of the time? Bryce seemed oblivious.

Near the back of the lounge, I parted a shimmer-screen curtain and led him into a circular seating area. Bryce fished through his pockets, withdrawing a set of keys, a faded leather wallet, and a cell phone, and removed his sunglasses before taking a seat on the white leather cube across from me. His eyes were stony and bloodshot. I wondered if I should feel unsafe. Could someone this pretty be a cold-blooded killer? Had Detective Christakos not arrested him because he was blinded by his looks, by his fame, by the lifestyle he lived—a lifestyle Stavros seemed to crave? Maybe he had a man-crush. I told myself not to fall into the same trap. If Bryce killed Chelsea—and I was now certain this was the case—he was the enemy.

"Mind if I order a drink?" Bryce asked.

His breath indicated it wouldn't be his first. "Be my guest," I said, lifting my arm to hail the server.

Eva bustled over. Bryce ordered a vodka Red Bull. I asked for a San Pellegrino.

"So," I said after she left, "what brings you back to Hotel Cinema?"

He crossed his legs and uncrossed them. "I saw you on *Spotlight* last night. Normally I don't watch those shows, but I couldn't sleep. I didn't know you tried to save Chelsea. I want to thank you for that." He thumped his fist over his heart. "It means a lot."

"I wish I had been successful."

"You tried, unlike those sons-of-bitches preening around the pool." He massaged his jaw with his hand. "I feel bad for being so brutal on *Larry King*. When I first met you, I thought you were, like, you know, a typical hotel manager, walking around with a pole up your ass. When I heard you lost your fiancée on that Worldwide Airways flight, I was shocked. I thought, maybe this guy isn't so bad after all. I bet he understands what I'm going through."

"I wish you had come to me before appearing on *Larry King*. I would have shown you a different side of this hotel."

"Yeah, well, I was fucking angry, okay? Everyone was saying your maintenance guy tried to rape Chelsea and killed her when she resisted. How was I supposed to feel? Yesterday Stav told me he wasn't even on-property when it happened."

"No, he wasn't."

"I'm going to be honest with you," he said, leaning forward and resting his elbows on his knees. "But first I need you to promise not to say a word of this to anyone. If it gets in the news, I'll fucking kill you, okay?" He lifted his hand in oath. "Swear?"

Too curious to decline, I held up my hand. "I swear."

"Chels wasn't exactly the most faithful girlfriend. She loved to conquer men. She had a weakness for blue-collar types, so I wasn't too surprised when I heard what really happened with that maintenance guy. She couldn't stand rejection. Chels didn't give a shit about the people who loved her; she only cared about the people who seemed indifferent. She wanted to convert them. It's like when you throw a party and everyone shows up except one person, and instead of celebrating, you spend the whole night brooding over the guy who didn't show. Chelsea would make certain that guy showed at the next party. And when he did, she'd quickly lose interest. Know what I mean?"

"Yes."

He hesitated. "So I guess I wanted to say I'm sorry."

"Apology accepted. I'll be sure to pass it on to Al. And I'm sorry for calling Chelsea a guest from hell."

He chuckled. "I can't blame you. She *was* a nightmare with hotel staff. She liked to have people fuss over her, clean up her mess, accept abuse with a smile on their face. But she wasn't always that bad. There was a stupid rumor flying around that she hated it when people looked her in the eyes. It made things awkward for hotel staff in particular, because they've got this eye-contact rule drilled into their heads. It was bullshit. She just didn't like people staring at her when she wasn't in character as the fabulous Chelsea Fricks."

"Those books in her room—was she really studying for her next role?"

He nodded. "Chelsea wasn't exactly politically correct, but she wasn't a racist."

Our drinks arrived. Bryce reached for his and gulped at it, wiping his mouth. "I feel like a jerk for discussing her death on *Larry King* like I was selling a product on the Shopping Network. At first I refused, but my publicist said I'd disappear into obscurity if I didn't step up. There was huge currency attached to being Chelsea's boyfriend. But that currency is depleting fast. People say I'm furious because she left her estate to her parents, but I didn't want her money; I wanted her fame. She couldn't leave that behind. She would have encouraged me to go on the circuit. She wasn't one to pass up an opportunity to get in front of the camera."

He gulped at his drink again. "Fuck, I miss her. When I first met her, she was down-to-earth, sweet, humble. Fame turned her into a monster. Losing her has been devastating. Shock, guilt, anger, resentment, fear, despair—it's like an endless fucking monologue class. Know what I mean?"

"I guess so." I wanted to believe him but reminded myself he was an actor, a master of disguise and a tireless self-promoter. Was I just another stop on the talk-show circuit? But there were no cameras here, no reporters. I was the only audience. Why would he care what *I* thought? Was he being genuine? My mind wandered back to Moira's assessment of Bryce: a lying weasel who murdered Chelsea out of jealousy.

Deciding I had nothing to lose, I asked, "Why did Chelsea break up with you that night?"

He sat upright. "Who told you that? Moira did, didn't she? That conniving little…" His words trailed off. He reached for his drink and stirred it with his finger. "Okay, fine, it's true. Chels did dump me that night. But she'd dumped me a hundred times before. Whenever she was feeling down, she decided all her troubles stemmed from me, and she sent me packing. Before long, she'd realize she still had the same problems, plus one more: no Bryce. So she'd beg me to come back. I always did. That night, when I came by the suite to pick her up, she was throwing things around, ranting and raving about her complicated life. Moira had just left, and they'd had a big fight. She was high as a kite. I locked the coke in the safe and refused to tell her the code. She went ballistic, told me to get the fuck out, we were finished, she was going to Peru alone. I went back to my room and waited for her to calm down. Fifteen minutes later, Moira bangs on my door, hysterical, saying Chelsea fell off the balcony."

I observed him closely. "On *Larry King,* you said Chelsea didn't touch drugs."

"You think I'm going tell the world she was an ecstasy-popping, meth-loving coke whore? Millions of girls idolized her. Even if she wasn't a role model, she had to seem like one. I went on *Larry King* to tell the fairy-tale version of her life. That's what the public craved to hear from me. What she did in the privacy of her hotel room was nobody's business."

"I totally agree," I said. I thought of telling Bryce that I had tried to protect Chelsea's privacy after her death, but knew my tirade in the *Daily Spotlight* had erased those efforts.

Something near the entrance to the lounge caught my attention. Janie and Bernadina were huddled together with a half-dozen girls of various shapes and sizes in wedding attire, ogling Bryce through the translucent shimmer screen. Careful not to alert him, I discreetly shooed them away.

"I hear you hired Moira," he said.

I coughed. "Yes … but only for a short-term project."

"She's good, but be careful. She double-dips. She made a fortune leaking stories while on Chelsea's payroll."

"Why didn't Chelsea stop her?" I asked.

"Are you kidding? Chelsea encouraged her. Whenever Chels wasn't getting the admiration and applause she yearned for, she pulled a stunt to get back into the news. She and Moira loved to stage photo ops and invent stories to leak to the press. They fabricated stories about me all the time, although they denied it, always making me out to be the bad guy: 'CHELSEA CATCHES BRYCE CHEATING! BRYCE TELLS CHELS NO KIDS, CHELS HEARTBROKEN! BLACK-EYED CHELSEA SAYS "ENOUGH"!' I tried not to let it bother me, but sometimes it hurt. I never cheated on her, never raised a hand to her. It was me who wanted kids, she didn't. She insisted we go to Malawi on that 'fact-finding mission,' holding a press conference to announce her intention to build an orphanage, but she hated it there, couldn't wait to get home. She was far too self-absorbed to have a kid."

He paused, peering across the lounge through the beaded curtain.

I turned, fearing he had spotted the groupies, but they had dispersed. He was watching a young woman bent over a baby stroller in the lobby.

"You still under oath?" he asked.

I raised my hand.

"I thought she was pregnant. She was throwing up every morning, but that could have been the stress or the booze or God knows what else. I had this hunch. I tried to get her to slow down, tried to convince her to see a doctor, but she was as wild as ever. After she died, I became obsessed with knowing the truth. Know what I mean?"

I swallowed, thinking of Nancy. "I do."

"I called her doctor, but he didn't know anything. So I called the coroner."

I leaned forward. "And?"

"She wasn't, thank God. It was hard enough to lose one person."

I breathed a sigh of relief, as though if Chelsea hadn't been pregnant, then Nancy couldn't have been either.

Bryce lifted his glass and rattled it. "Mind if I order another? I'll pay."

"Not at all." I flagged Eva down.

Bryce's eyes wandered the empty lounge. "Knowing Chels, she would have turned pregnancy into a media spectacle too. It got to the point where it didn't matter what people said, it only mattered that they were talking about her. She never went as far as those other celebrities—she didn't flash her crotch or make a sex tape or take drugs in nightclubs—but I feared she was heading in that direction. She spent so much time in Italy this year, she started to worry that North America was forgetting about her. When those shots of her sunbathing topless showed up, it solved everything."

"I heard she was furious," I said, glad that Shanna had filled me in. Listening to Bryce was like a private viewing of an *E! True Hollywood Story*. Shanna would be jealous—if she could bear being so close to someone this famous.

"Furious?" Bryce rolled his eyes. "She was ecstatic. She and Moira orchestrated the whole thing. Moira hired the photographer, gave him access to the pool, and then let him into Chelsea's suite. Chels didn't care that they published photos of her breasts, sex toys, and prescriptions, she only cared that they got worldwide attention. Chelsea was back in the headlines—woo-hoo! To cover their tracks, Moira accused a bellman and got him fired."

I was floored. "That's shameless."

He shrugged. "Chels was a junkie, Moira was her pusher. That's all they cared about. Those two were more alike than you know."

Eva arrived with the drinks, and he reached for his. "Moira can't be trusted, Trevor. She'll seduce you with the promise of fame, earn your confidence, blind you with the spotlight, and sell you out."

It was exactly what Moira had done in telling Ashlee about Nancy. "Does she do it for the money?" I asked. "Or does she aspire to be famous herself?"

"Moira? Are you kidding?" He laughed heartily. "That's the irony. She's a publicist, yet she's intensely private herself. She always lurked in the shadows when press was around. If the spotlight happened to fall on her, she melted like a vampire. She's a bizarre woman. I used to think she was a lesbian, but now I think she's asexual. I'm not even sure she has a pussy. She won't let anyone near her. Chelsea was the opposite. She'd hop into bed with anyone who showed her love, then she'd toss him or her aside. One night in Rome, Chelsea came home wasted and crawled into bed with Moira. Moira freaked out. I think she was afraid the media would find out. Chelsea wasn't above leaking a rumor she was a lesbian if it meant getting headlines. After that, things changed between them. Moira was cagey. Chelsea started questioning the volume of coverage she was generating. She feared Moira's media contacts were drying up."

A much clearer portrait of Moira was beginning to form in my head. "Have you told your friend Stavros about this?" I asked.

"Let me get this straight, Trevor: Stavros is *not* my friend. He acts like my buddy, but I'm not stupid. I know what he's up to."

"He wants you to help him with his acting career?"

He snorted. "Marrying Nicole Kidman wouldn't help his acting career. He had one line yesterday, *one line*. We didn't audition him because we thought it was a no-brainer. I mean, he's a cop playing a cop—how hard could it be? Yet he kept flubbing his line, missing his mark, staring into the camera. He was pretending to be dark and sinister *and* flamboyant. All in one line. The director was incredulous."

I burst out laughing. "He thought it was his big break."

"The guy's full of shit. He's acting like he wants to be an actor. He's undercover, Trevor, trying to get close to me. Like if he earns my confidence, I'm going to tell him I murdered my girlfriend."

"He'd go that far? Take an audition class? Appear on your show?"

"Oh, I have no doubt he aspires to be an actor. But he won't be appearing on *Modern Loving*, that's for sure." He lifted his drink and drained it. "He's an even lousier detective. I'm terrified he's going to show up on-set one day, slap cuffs on me, and throw me in jail. It won't matter that I'm innocent. He doesn't listen. I told him all about Moira, but he's decided to believe her version of events. She's been working him, telling him she can make him a star, blinding him with the promise of fame. She's brainwashed him into thinking that after your maintenance guy left Chelsea's suite, I slipped in."

"You didn't?"

"Uh-uh. I left through the connecting door around eleven and didn't go back. I tried, but Chels had access through the adjoining door canceled. I called her on the phone, banged on the wall, but she ignored me. I opened my door for a few seconds when I heard the maintenance guy in the hallway, but I didn't leave the room and I didn't open it again until Moira arrived to say Chelsea fell in the pool."

I searched Bryce's eyes. *The truth is in the eyes.* Detective Christakos made it sound easy. Bryce's steely blue eyes were impenetrable. He was an actor. How could I distinguish between truth and lies? I looked down at his hands. One was gripping his knee, the other was wrapped around his glass. Something about his story bothered me.

"What happened to the cocaine?" I asked.

His eyes lit up. "That's exactly what I'd like to know." He lowered his voice. "Moira somehow got into Chelsea's room undetected, I know it. Chelsea must have opened the door for her. Stavros won't listen. He says she's got a solid alibi and it checks out. She was on the phone with Chelsea's mom when Chelsea jumped."

"You mean Moira's mom."

"No, Chelsea's. Moira's parents were killed in a car crash ten years ago."

"Wasn't Chelsea estranged from her parents?"

"She was, but her mother, Alice, kept in touch with Moira to keep tabs on Chelsea." He scratched his jaw, thinking. "Or it might have been..." He stopped, suddenly uneasy.

"Might have been who?" I asked.

He was quiet for a moment, contemplative. "I guess it doesn't matter anymore. About a year ago, Chelsea found out she had been adopted. She was shattered. She confronted her parents, demanding to know why they had lied to her all these years. They said they were only trying to spare her the pain, didn't want her to think they loved her any less. Chels stopped talking to them. She became obsessed with finding her real mother, and Moira offered to help. Miraculously, they found her. Moira set up the first meeting, Chels was so hopeful. I think she expected someone like Sophia Loren. She had already envisioned the publicity campaign, the mother-daughter reunion reenacted for TV, the talk-show circuit, the spread in *Daily Spotlight*. But I guess it didn't go well. I think the woman was more like Charlize Theron in *Monster* than Sophia Loren. Chelsea refused to have anything to do with her. She made Moira and me promise not to say a word about it. I didn't, of course—I didn't even know her name—but I was pretty sure Moira would find a way to leak it. I'm surprised she never did. Not yet, anyway."

"So Moira was talking to Chelsea's birth mother on the phone?"

He shrugged. "Either her or Alice."

I frowned. "Why are you telling me this? What do you want from me?"

He leaned even closer. "I need your help. You have access to everything here: key reports, closed-circuit monitors, employees, witnesses. There's got to be something around here to prove I'm innocent. Find it, and Christakos might listen to you."

I nodded slowly, feeling my pulse quicken. Until now, I had stood by passively as Stavros bungled the investigation. More than a week had passed, and he seemed no closer to solving the case. He had almost arrested two innocent people. Was Bryce next?

"What makes you so sure Moira did it?" I asked.

He laughed. "Ask any PR person in this town if they've fantasized about killing a client. Moira sacrificed everything for Chelsea. When Chels broke the news that night, Moira must have gone ballistic and stabbed her. Chelsea jumped off the balcony to save her life. Moira gave herself away by committing the ultimate act of a publicist: she took the coke. She doesn't do drugs. She probably flushed it. Who else would do that?"

"What news did Chelsea break?" I asked.

"Chelsea fired Moira that night."

★ ★ ★ ★ ★

The afternoon shift arrived early to relieve Janie, Bernadina, and Flavia to attend the Cavalli family wedding. At the same time, Sydney Cheevers and an army of event planners descended on the hotel to prepare for the reception.

Reginald Clinton came to me in a panic. "Sydney just ordered a wedding party off the pool deck! The bride was promised the space until three PM, and she's having a meltdown. Now Sydney wants me to kick out a table of twelve before they've had dessert."

I found Sydney at the pool bar studying a clipboard. The wedding party was gone. "Sydney, forgive me," I said, selecting my words, hoping to avoid another confrontation. "I must have confused times. Weren't you scheduled to start tear-down at three?"

She made a few checkmarks on her clipboard, ignoring me.

"Sydney?"

She looked up. Her upper lip glistened with perspiration. "Um, forgive *me*, Trevor, perhaps *I'm* confused, but I believe I was hired to organize a wedding reception for the *owner* of this hotel?" She looked down at her list, dismissing me. The bartender, Enrico, set a glass of Perrier on the bar, and she sipped it. She let out a gasp. "Oh my God, this is *lemon!*" She grabbed her neck with both hands, making choking sounds. "I told you *lime*, you fucking idiot! I'm allergic to lemons!" She swept her arm across the bar, sending the glass flying to the floor.

"I'm so sorry, Miss Cheevers," said Enrico. "I'll get you—"

"No! Forget it! *God*, you people!"

"Are you going to be okay?" I asked Sydney, wondering if it was medically possible to be allergic to lemons and not limes. She behaved this way to draw attention to herself, to flaunt her power as Hollywood's pied piper to the stars, considering herself as important as them, if not more so.

"Why is that old couple still here?" she yelled at Enrico, glowering at Mr. and Mrs. Greenfield, who were sunning themselves on the other side of the pool. "I said I wanted this deck *cleared*!" Before I could stop her, she marched over. "Scoot!" she hissed, jabbing her finger at the exit.

I hurried over.

Mr. Greenfield removed his sunglasses and sat up. "Why us? What about those people?" He gestured to a group of men lounging near the far corner of the pool. A bottle of Cristal sat in a champagne bucket next to them. It was hard to tell from where I stood, but two of the men resembled Justin Timberlake and LL Cool J.

"Can't you see who that is?" Sydney cried in exasperation.

"I don't care who it is," said Mr. Greenfield. "I'm a guest here."

"Well, *I* am acting on behalf of the owner of this hotel, who is holding an important family wedding tonight, and I insist you leave immediately," Sydney said.

"Sydney, please," I said. "Let them stay for a while. They won't be in the way." I apologized profusely to the Greenfields and grabbed Sydney's arm, pulling her away. "How can you be so rude? The Greenfields have been staying with us all week."

"If it were up to me, I would have turned them away at the door," Sydney snapped. "Did you see those liver spots? Those people are just plain wrong for the image we're cultivating here. They have no facial validity whatsoever."

"Please don't use that hateful term. We can't choose guests based on looks."

"Why not? You don't get it, do you? This city revolves around stars and beautiful people. They're the only ones who matter."

"We can't fill this hotel every night with stars."

She sighed. "Unfortunately not. The rest is filler—the audience. The stars attract the audience. Remember that, Trevor. Without stars, no audience."

"And without an audience, no stars and no hotel," I countered. "Which means no overpaid job for Sydney. Why are you evicting people now? The Cavalli wedding guests won't be here for four hours."

"I've got four hours to transform this place into a tacky Roman villa, and I don't have time to deal with your prissy little concerns. If you've got a problem, talk to your boss."

"Shhh!" Her loud voice was attracting attention. "Kindly keep your voice down."

"Don't you shush me!"

"I'm going to call Tony." I stormed off.

I stepped into Reginald's tiny office at the back of the restaurant and dialed Tony's cell number.

"What is it?" Tony hissed. "I'm at Lorenzo's wedding, for Christ's sake."

"Sydney Cheevers is shutting us down in the middle of lunch service."

"I told you that was happening a long time ago. What's the problem?"

"You told me it was a *dinner* function. Sydney's treating our guests like trespassers." I peeked out the porthole window into the dining room. "Two of her guys are erecting a banner on the wall right next to a table of twelve!"

"Oh yeah? How's it look?"

"They spelled *congratulations* wrong."

"*What?* Fucking hell! Don't tell me they used a 't'? I told them—"

"Tony, it *is* spelled with a 't.' They used a 'd.'"

"Motherfuckers! Well, it's not like anyone's gonna notice. Half my family can't speak English, other half can't read. Heh heh."

"Can I call Sydney and her thugs off for an hour?"

"Okay, an hour, but not a second more. Tell Sydney she better have things ready by six or I'll have her head. And ask her if she was able to confirm any names. I gotta go. The bride is coming down the aisle. I'm gettin' dirty looks."

"You're in a pew on your cell phone?"

"Of course not. I'm the best man. I'm at the altar."

★ ★ ★ ★ ★

An hour later, Sydney and her crew swept back in, dismantling furniture and carrying away everything that wasn't nailed down, save for chairs and tables. The items were replaced with fake urns, plaster columns, and Styrofoam sculptures courtesy of Cavalli Fine Imports. In the restaurant, tables were cloaked with elaborate white lace and thick gold threading and set with silver chalices and gaudy floral displays. Restaurant employees were issued togas and headdresses ringed with fake olive branches. They were not amused.

I was in the dining room watching the transformation when Sydney walked past hefting an enormous Styrofoam Venus di Milo.

"Don't even start with me," she muttered. "I know it's hideous."

"Tony wants to know if you confirmed any more 'names' for tonight."

She set down the statue and let out a huff. "He's been on my fucking case to get stars to attend the reception. I can't even pay anyone

343

to come." The statue toppled over, barely making a sound. "At least a hundred people on his special 'VIP' list aren't going to show, so staff can relax—we have plenty of manpower, and I told Reservations to release the room block. The VIPs want to come *after* the reception, but he's shutting the whole place down for the party—on a Saturday night, only a week after opening! Jackass. He's afraid if the public sees a bunch of fat, balding Italian men and their bottle-blond, black-browed wives, they'll never come back. He's right. If it were up to me, I'd push the relatives out the door at ten and let in the listers. But what do I know? I've only been planning parties for twenty years."

"I know the feeling," I said.

"Don't blame him. His father calls all the shots."

"His father?"

"Gi-Gi's got Tony on the tightest string you can imagine. Papa Giancarlo doesn't understand why Tony can't run a luxury hotel on the same budget as a three-star villa in a suburb of Napoli. Gi-Gi insisted on preserving the original rotten foundation of this building and then paid off the city for the occupancy permit. Now he's got Tony under more pressure than ever to cut expenses and make money. If Tony fails, it's back to the import business for him. The guy's a heart attack waiting to happen."

"No wonder he's threatened to fire me a half-dozen times this week."

"I can't count how many times he's fired me. Don't let it get to you. His bark is much worse than his bite. He's actually very loyal. I don't think he's capable of firing anyone."

★ ★ ★ ★ ★

At 6:15 PM, guests of the Cavalli wedding arrived en masse and filed onto the pool deck for the cocktail party. An hour later, they moved into Scene, where dinner service began at eight and the excessive drinking gave way to excessive eating. Service staff scrambled to keep up with the voracious appetites, hustling course after course out of the kitchen as Sydney resumed her soccer mom persona, chasing them around, barking out orders, and chastising for the most minor of offenses. I assisted where needed, replenishing wine and water glasses, clearing dishes, expediting food, helping elderly relatives to the washroom.

I was surprised to see Kitty Caine at a table snuggling with one of Tony's brothers. She blew a kiss as I passed. Apparently all was forgiven.

Janie, Flavia, and Bernadina were seated at the next table, sporting big hairdos and shades of nail polish to match their taffeta dresses.

"Hey, Treva!" Janie called. "What did Bryce Davies want? He ask about me? He want my numba?"

The three girls burst into giggles.

"Sorry to disappoint," I said.

"I should warn you I might be late tomorra," said Bernadina. "Open bar, all the Kahlúa I want—it could get ugly. But don't blame me, blame Uncle Tony."

"Pace yaself," Janie advised her. "Lorenzo says he might have a potty in the penthouse suite tonight."

"A potty?" I said.

"A *party*!" Flavia corrected, honking with mirth.

I stopped at the head table next. Tony and Liz were sitting with daughter Emily and the twins Enzo and Lorenzo, Lorenzo's new bride, Rosario, Rosario's parents, Tony's parents, and Tony's grandmother, Maria. A dozen staff attended to their table, and Tony was keeping all of them busy. Bottle after bottle of fine wine was presented, uncorked, and poured, only to be sent away with a haughty sniff and wave of his hand. I circled the table, congratulating the newlyweds, who looked miserable, and took the hand Tony proferred.

"Good job with that *Spotlight* interview," he said, eyes manic. "Kitty set that up?"

"Kitty? Moira did. Kitty doesn't work for us anymore."

"You're kidding. What happened?"

"You fired her, Tony."

"Why would I fire her?"

"You told me she's been bad-mouthing the hotel. Don't tell me you didn't?"

"I guess I forgot." He licked his lips, eyes darting in the direction of her table. "She's practically family now."

"You have to fire her, Tony. We can't afford to pay both."

"Okay, okay. I'll do it after dinner."

At eleven PM, trays of desserts were shuttled out along with bottles of grappa for each table. The deejay cut the music, and a spotlight appeared on the podium. I stood in the shadows and watched as one speaker after another delivered a maudlin speech in various blends of English and Italian. When Tony sauntered up, he struck a lighter note, starting off by saying he was glad Lorenzo was getting married because he was starting to believe rumors he was a "homo." The crowd roared with laughter. "We thought it was a shotgun wedding," he continued. "But turns out Rosario's just getting fat." More laughter. Tony looked pleased. He threatened to present Lorenzo's parents with the dinner bill "'cause this place ain't cheap, and I gotta start gettin' a return on my investment or Papa's gonna take it away." There were spots of nervous laughter. Tony's eyes moved to Giancarlo Cavalli, who crossed his arms and harrumphed.

The final speech was delivered by Lorenzo's twin, Enzo. It was a syrupy monologue on brotherly love, interrupted by long bouts of sobbing. When he finished, the room rose to a standing ovation.

Around one AM, the party began to thin out, and I decided it was safe to go home. I was in my office shutting down my computer when night manager David hurried in.

"Mr. Cavalli's looking for you," he said. "He's freaking out."

What now? About twenty guests remained in the restaurant, the men at one table drinking grappa, the women at a separate table whispering to one another.

Tony jumped to his feet. "*Major* drama in the penthouse suite," he said, his voice slurred. "Almost as big as the opening night drama."

"What happened?"

"The twins," Tony said. "It's always the fucking twins." He led me away from the others. "Rosario gets tired, goes up to the penthouse suite to lie down. Enzo decides he's gonna play a joke on Lorenzo and sneaks up to the suite, slips inside, crawls into bed with Rosario. Before he knows it, Rosario's got his pants down and his dick out. Lorenzo walks in, freaks out. Rosario says she thought it was Lorenzo and says she's been violated. Enzo insists she knew it was him, says *she* violated *him*. Now I've got Rosario crying in my sister's room, Enzo crying in my room, and Lorenzo crying in the penthouse suite."

"How did Enzo get in?"

He pointed a finger at me, eyes fierce. "That's what *I* want to know. Enzo said he stepped in front of the scanner and the door opened like magic. What kind of fucked-up security system did I pay $200,000 for that opens at will? This is the second time in a week the system's gone wonky, Trevor. *Spotlight* was right: our security sucks. It ruined my nephew's wedding! I want an explanation, Trevor, or heads will roll!"

I nodded. "I'll see what I can find out."

18

Walking the Black Carpet

"You find out what happened last night?" Tony's voice boomed across the lobby.

I had spotted him earlier and hoped to slip by unseen. With a sigh, I made my way over. He was sitting in one of the bouquets of furniture near the lounge, a copy of the *LA Times* in his lap. Next to him, Liz sat curled in a chair like a kitten while daughter Emily played at her feet. It was eleven AM on Sunday, and they were all in nightclothes. Tony was wearing a hotel bathrobe and, judging by the matte of chest hair peeking out of the open flap, nothing else. Liz was wearing a pink satin negligee and Emily a cotton pajama dress dotted with bunnies. A silver tray containing a coffee urn, three glasses of orange juice, and several carcasses of partially eaten pastries sat on the table next to them. It was a heartwarming display of family togetherness, but it didn't belong in the middle of our busy lobby.

"Good morning!" I called out cheerily, bending down to remove the tray. "All done here?"

"No!" Tony shouted, smacking my hand. "We got bacon and eggs coming."

"Wouldn't you be more comfortable in your suite?"

Emily strummed her fingers along the beaded curtain, making the sound of a harp. She looked perfectly angelic, not the sort of four-year-old who fires a housekeeper after a lifetime of service.

"Liz doesn't like it up there," said Tony. "She says it's too stark."

My eyes moved to Liz, the *designer* of the hotel. Her head was buried in a book, *Everything Worth Knowing*.

"Says in here the investigation is closing in on Bryce," Tony said, flicking the newspaper. "'Bout time they nailed that little slime."

I felt compelled to defend Bryce but resisted. I didn't want to get into an argument in the lobby over who had killed a hotel guest.

Tony sat up to reach for his coffee cup.

I shielded my eyes. "Tony, do you mind?"

He looked up, then down, and pulled the robe over his thighs. "Who's responsible for these crappy shortie robes, anyway? They're made for midgets."

"You are," I said. "Remember that cousin who could get us Frette robes for half price? Well, he got half the robe for twice the price. And they're Frappe, not Frette."

"Why didn't you tell me? I'll kill him. He was at the wedding last night."

"I did tell you."

Tony stood up and tied the belt around his corpulent waist. "What did you find out about that malfunction?"

"To be honest, I'm not convinced it *was* a malfunction. The twins were probably horsing around. It wouldn't be the first time. You'll recall the switcheroo they pulled when Enzo interviewed for a bellman position."

Tony stroked his goatee. "True. After all these years, *I* can barely tell the little fuckers apart."

"Fuckers," echoed Emily, pulling stuffing from a split in the chair Liz had procured for $2800.

Liz reached out and swatted her, eyes not leaving the page. "Don't say *fucker*, Emily."

"Did you consider the possibility that Rosario *opened* the door for Enzo?" I said.

Tony's eyes narrowed. "You calling her a whore?"

"No, but—"

"Enzo swears the door opened on its own. You calling him a liar?"

"Why don't I look into it further," I said.

"Damn right you will. I didn't pay all that money for faulty technology! I'm holding you accountable, Trevor. You convinced me to buy that fancy-ass system when regular keys would have been fine."

"*I* convinced you," Liz said without looking up. "And regular keys would *not* be fine. A modern hotel requires state-of-the-art technology. You should have gone with the high-res version, but your tightwad father cheaped out."

"Tightwad," said Emily.

"Liz is still mad about last night's Roman theme," Tony said, grinning. "She says it 'destroyed the aesthetic' of her design. I thought the place looked awesome, didn't you?"

"If you're into that kind of thing," I said.

"Fucking right I am—it's the family business! Heh heh." He fell back into his chair, exposing himself again.

"Tony," I said, "as much as you might like to think otherwise, a view of your family jewels isn't helping business."

Liz burst out laughing.

"I'll do whatever the fuck I want," Tony yelled, jumping to his feet and opening his robe wide to gasps and cries of horror. "It's my hotel! *My* hotel!"

"Fuck," said Emily, and giggled.

Shaking my head, I crossed the lobby to the security office.

Artie Truman was seated in the cramped room surrounded by monitors. "The cameras recorded that obscene act if you want to sue for harassment."

"I couldn't put a judge through the trauma," I said. "Did you hear about last night's fiasco?"

"Yep. Raj wrote up an incident report. I tested the system, and everything seems to be working fine. I put a call in to our Opti-Scan rep just to be sure, but we won't hear back until Monday. To be honest, I don't expect him to tell us much. It's an eye scanner, not a lie detector."

"My sentiments exactly."

★ ★ ★ ★ ★

Moira called me later that morning. "I left two tickets for the service at the front desk for you."

"Moira, I really have no desire to go."

"You have to, Trevor. After the nasty things you said, it would be disrespectful to miss the service. It's all part of the new, compassionate face of Hotel Cinema. You can bring that huffy Indian lady if you want. Just don't bring Tony Cavalli. He's obnoxious."

"I'm still furious at you for telling Ashlee White about Nancy. It was an invasion of my privacy."

"Privacy? You were on a show called *Spotlight,* for God's sake. What did you expect?"

"It's a topic I prefer not to discuss."

"What*ever.* Tony gave me permission. I'll see you at the service. Don't be late."

She hung up.

I reached Shanna on her cell phone.

"Are you joking, Trevor?" she said. "I couldn't possibly. There will be hundreds of *those* people there."

"Perfect. You can recover from your phobia in one fell swoop."

"I detest funerals."

"And I don't? Listen, if I can prostitute myself on *Spotlight,* the least you can do is accompany me to the service."

Eventually, she agreed, but she wasn't happy about it.

She arrived at 12:45, looking stunning in a simple black dress and string of white pearls. Her hair was tied into a tight chignon, accentuating her striking features. I had been doing room inspections and hadn't yet changed.

"For goodness sake, hurry!" she said, eyes grazing my Sunday casual wear disapprovingly.

I hurried down to B2 and headed to the housekeeping office to retrieve my tuxedo. Olga Slovenka was lurking at her station like a troll under a bridge. I greeted her cheerfully, whistling my way down the hallway. She grunted back. To my dismay, my tuxedo pants and bow tie had come back from the dry cleaner ruined after my plunge into the pool. The shirt was fine, as was the jacket, which I had removed before diving in. My other suits were at home.

I looked down at the outfit I had on. Corduroy blazer, tan dress pants, brown loafers, pink socks, no tie. Unacceptable. The tickets for the memorial service were stamped "Black Tie Funeral Wear." I rifled through the staff dry-cleaning rack for something to borrow, but the selection was sparse. The next rack held guest dry cleaning. I pulled out a brown pin-striped suit and held it up in the light: too short and too wide. I put it back. My eye caught a bow tie next to it. It was a snap-on and appeared to be flecked with tiny purple dots, but it would complement the tuxedo shirt and hopefully distract from the pants and loafers. According to the dry cleaner's slip, the bow tie belonged to Mr. Greenfield in Room 507. Dare I borrow it? I was late. I could return it before anyone was the wiser.

I changed quickly, paying extra attention to my hair in order to compensate for the outfit.

★ ★ ★ ★ ★

Shanna's eyes widened as I rushed into the lobby. "What on earth are you wearing?"

I looked down. "Is it that bad?"

"Yes, but it'll have to do. We're late." She herded me to the door.

Outside, the campground of fans and media had been virtually abandoned. Two housemen were cleaning up, and Al Combs was replanting the garden. The afternoon sun beat down on us mercilessly as we walked. Hollywood Boulevard was closed on either side of Kodak Theatre, and a convoy of limousines and luxury cars were letting passengers off at Highland Avenue. A stream of people in black flowed toward the entrance. Black-velvet stanchions lined the street, separating spectators from invited guests. An army of paparazzi and media occupied the foot of the staircase leading to the theatre. Subdued and respectful, the crowd observed us as we filed past.

"You going to be okay?" I asked Shanna.

"No. Are you?"

"I'm not afraid of celebrities; I *am* a celebrity."

She didn't smile. "I assume this is the first memorial service you've attended since…"

"I'll be fine."

She clutched my arm as we walked, nails digging into my skin, ready to yank me in another direction if we got too close to someone famous. As we joined the back of the line, her grip tightened. "Uh-oh. Look who's here."

A few feet ahead, a mass of hair and teeth and boobs careened in our direction. "Trevor? Shanna? Is that you?"

I waved to Kitty Caine, bracing myself for a Texan tirade.

Instead, she jiggled over and hugged us both. "I was hopin' to see y'all here!" Her breath smelled like menthol cigarettes. "Tony said you needed to speak to me, Trevor."

My eyes darted to Shanna. Tony had wimped out. "It's nothing urgent," I said. "We can talk tomorrow."

Kitty fanned herself with her hand. "What a cooker!" She was one of few people in the line not wearing black, having squeezed herself into a tiny red cocktail dress lined with white fur. A shiny black belt and black patent-leather shoes were her only nod to the occasion. She surveyed my outfit. "Golly, what an unusual ensemble!"

"It's fashion-forward," I said. "It's going to be all the rage."

She flashed her teeth, displaying a smear of red lipstick. "Shall we?" she said, holding out her arm.

I winked at Shanna to assure her we would ditch her at the first opportunity and locked arms with Kitty.

"Look, they've rolled out the black carpet!" Kitty exclaimed, pointing to the river of carpet that stretched across Hollywood Boulevard to the theatre.

At the foot of the carpeted area, four large men in tuxedos asked for tickets and identification and frisked us. We passed through a metal detector, where a sign announced that cameras and recording devices were not permitted.

"Look, there's Nigel from *Spotlight*," Kitty cried. "Yoo-hoo, Nigel! Over here, doll!"

I groaned and averted my gaze as he ambled over.

Kitty gave him a big hug. "You remember Trevor Lambert, my client at Hotel Cinema?" she said, not introducing Shanna.

I nodded curtly, still hurting from his article.

Beside me, Shanna let out a low growl.

"Got any more rants for me, ol' boy?" Nigel said, slapping my shoulder. He turned to Kitty. "Isn't Moira repping Hotel Cinema now?"

"Are you kiddin' me?" Kitty laughed and jiggled. "As if!"

I sensed Shanna stiffen. Fortunately, a racket behind us caught everyone's attention.

A thin, fiftyish woman with permed, wet-looking blond hair and pockmarked skin was arguing with two security officers. "You *gotta* let me in!" she shouted in a throaty smoker's voice. "I came all the way from Canada!"

"A fellow patriot," Shanna mused, nudging me.

"I told you, ma'am," said one of the officers, "this is a *closed* service."

"But I came to say goodbye to Chelsea!"

"Please step aside."

The woman fell to her knees. "I beg of you, please let me in! Oh, please!"

The officers took her by the arms and began dragging her off.

The woman struggled to free herself. "Let me go! You don't understand! I'm her *mother!*" Her words ended in a guttural scream that sent hundreds of heads spinning in her direction.

The officers exchanged uneasy glances.

"She's not her mother," someone in the line jeered. "Take the crazy lady away."

Reassured, they resumed lugging her away.

"Don't take me from my baby!" she cried, struggling to free herself. "She's my daughter! She's my lovely, lost daughter … Oh Sharon, my dear little Sharon, rest in peace, my darling." Her voice faded off as she was carried into a white tent marked First Aid.

"*People!*" Kitty exclaimed, shaking her head. "They'll try anuthin'."

Nigel was squeezing his Adam's apple and making sniffing sounds as he watched the spectacle. Suddenly, he bolted toward the tent.

"Now what's gotten up his butt?" Kitty said, dismissing him with a shrug.

We entered a tented area, where cabanas on either side advertised luxury brands.

Shanna eyed the Tiffany's booth. "Can we go in?" she asked.

"Uh-uh," said Kitty, pushing her along. "Stars only."

As we emerged from the tent we halted, regarding in awe the chaotic scene before us. To reach the theatre, we would have to pass a wall of paparazzi, bleachers of fans, and a gauntlet of TV crews.

"I thought *Spotlight* had an exclusive on this event," I remarked.

"Moira's no fool," Kitty explained. "She sold the exclusive for *inside* the theatre. Out here, it's a free-for-all. And she charged $25,000 each for those booths we passed. Shall we?" She pushed her boobs out, fluffed her hair, and charged ahead, hips swaying like a plus-sized fashion model.

Shanna and I cowered back, huddling together like we were facing the Yellow Brick Road.

"Trevor, you go ahead," said Shanna. "I just remembered a group convener is waiting for me at the hotel."

"No way. You're coming with me." I pulled her along.

It was easier than I anticipated, mostly because we were ignored. Fans and media shouted at the more famous guests.

"We love you, Brad!"

"Wynona, who are you wearing?"

"Got a minute for your Much Music fans in Canada, Shakira?"

At the foot of the bleachers, a shrine dedicated to Chelsea had been erected; it overflowed with flowers, cards, candles, and photographs. Fans waved posters in the air: REST IN PEACE, CHELSEA GIRL! CHELSEA FOREVER! DIE, CHELSEA KILLER, DIE! A group of teenaged girls stood locked arm-in-arm singing and swaying on the top row.

As I passed the wall of paparazzi, someone cried, "Hey, it's the heroic hotel manager!" I turned and was assailed by camera clicks and flashes. I stumbled back, shielding my eyes. They recognized me! I was a star again! Elation surged through me like morphine. Remembering my foul expression in *Spotlight,* I tried to smile and pose.

"Look, there's Clooney!" someone shouted.

In an instant, I was abandoned.

I looked around for my companions. Shanna was making a dash for the stairs, clutching her purse under her arm like a charging full-back. Kitty Caine was posing for paparazzi, back arched, hand resting on her sizable rump, turning in circles. No one was paying attention.

"Trevor! Over here!"

Ashlee White from *Spotlight Tonight* was beckoning to me from the clusters of camera crews lining the path to the stairs. Thrilled to be singled out, I hurried over.

"How *are* you?" Ashlee cried, looking genuinely happy to see me. There was no trace of Friday's disinterested, detached aura; she was oozing warmth. She reached for my arm and pulled me in front of the camera. "Come talk to *Spotlight!*" she said.

I could feel her breast pressing against my arm. Beaming into the camera, I smoothed my jacket and adjusted my bow tie.

Ashlee lifted her microphone. "I'm here with Trevor Lambert, the heroic hotel manager who made a valiant attempt to rescue Chelsea Fricks on that fateful night. How *are* you, Trevor?"

"Great!" I said. Recalling the nature of the occasion, I adopted a more somber expression.

"And who are you wearing today?" She glanced down at my clothes. Her smile faded.

"Who?" I said as the camera moved down my body, pausing at my loafers. I reached down to yank my pant legs over my pink socks. "Um, well … I'm wearing a combo tuxedo-suit thingie."

"I guess I missed that issue of *GQ*," Ashlee quipped. "Tell us, how does it feel to manage the most infamous hotel in the world?"

I opened my mouth to reply but was interrupted by Kitty, who sidled up and placed her arm around me. "Hi y'all!" she cried into the camera. "Kitty Caine, CAINE PUBLIC RELATIONS, putting the spotlight on your business! My client, Trevor Lambert of HOTEL CINEMA, feels *so* fortunate to be a part of today's celebration. He wants to thank all the celebrities who have made HOTEL CINEMA the hottest li'l boutique hotel in Hollywood!"

Trying to extract myself, I rasped into her ear, "This isn't an awards show, Kitty, it's a funeral."

"It's *not* a funeral," she cried, "it's a celebration, a celebration of Chelsea's life!" She threw her arms out wide and turned to let the camera catch a side-view pose, placing her hands on her knees and throwing her head back like a Broadway dancer.

I gave Ashlee an apologetic look.

She was staring at my neck. "Is your bow tie flashing?"

I looked down. "What the—?"

Ashlee shrieked with laughter. "Get a shot of this, Bradley! He's wearing a flashing bow tie!"

Heads turned. A thin, blond woman who looked like Reese Witherspoon smiled.

Mortified, I pulled off the bow tie and shoved it in my pocket. By then, attention had been diverted elsewhere. My moment in the spotlight was gone, ruined by an exhibitionist publicist and a gag bow tie.

Ashlee was waving to someone else. "Bryce, come say hi to your fans at *Spotlight Tonight!*"

Bryce looked dashing in a classic black tuxedo. I slinked away, not wanting him to see my own outfit.

Shanna and Kitty were waiting at the foot of the staircase.

"What a hoot!" Kitty cried.

As we made our way up the stairs, someone called out my name from behind.

"Hey, Trevor Lambert! Over here!"

Recognized again! I turned and scanned the crowd, feeling hundreds of eyes on me. The voice came from the bleachers. A fan? I spotted a lanky, bearded fellow in a soiled rugby shirt waving. I grinned and waved back.

"Chelsea killer!" he screamed at the top of his lungs. "Burn in hell, motherfucker!"

Slowly, I lowered my hand. People around the man joined in, hissing and jeering.

"Fink!"

"Scab!"

"Nice outfit!"

Shanna grabbed my arm and wrenched me up the stairs. "Don't listen to them," she said. "They're crazy."

"Animals!" Kitty shouted, turning to give them the finger.

When I reached the top of the stairs, I was shaking. Such venom in the man's voice! We entered a crowded reception area.

Shanna cast a fearful look at the famous faces around us. She looked like she might faint. "Let's get a drink," she said.

I followed her to the bar, and Kitty tagged along.

A moment later, we were standing on the periphery of the circular reception area, clutching glasses of chardonnay and trying not to ogle. Three *Spotlight* camera crews roved the crowd.

"You okay?" I asked Shanna.

She took a generous gulp of her wine. "So many pretty people," she said in a raspy voice.

"Don't forget to pick up a gift bag on your way out," Kitty said, pointing to a booth near the exit. "They're loaded with goodies."

Shanna made a face. "Gift bags at a funeral? Isn't this all a tad distasteful?"

"They're Chelsea Memorial Keepsake Bags," Kitty explained. "*Spotlight* did a story on them last night. Moira got donations from the makers of Chelsea's favorite products—Gucci, Kiehl's, Swarovski, et cetera. She also included a DVD of clips from Chelsea's best work, a framed headshot, and an eight-ounce bottle of Chelsea Girl perfume. The total value of each bag is over a thousand dollars! I hope they don't run out before I get one."

I spotted Moira Schwartz pushing her way through the crowd, cell phone pressed to her ear. She looked remarkably fetching in a long, elegant black dress. Her hair was tamed and coiffed to one side. She was pulling along a pretty young lady with choppy blond hair.

"Moira!" Kitty called out, waving both hands at her. "Moira! Over here!" She turned to me and muttered under her breath, "Girl has no shame, walkin' around in that Oscar dress like she's Chelsea-Friggin'-Fricks."

Shanna and I exchanged frantic looks, anticipating fireworks.

"Gotta go," Moira said flatly into the phone as she reached us. She looked up. "Hello, everyone. How are you."

"*Fabulous* party," Kitty gushed. "Fa-bu-*lous!*"

"It's not a party," Moira snapped, eyes grazing first Kitty's outfit, then mine.

"I mean a celebration of life," Kitty said.

"Chelsea's dead," said Moira. "There's nothing to celebrate." She gestured to the young lady beside her. "This is Ripley Van Vleet, my new client. Or at least she's going to be—right, Ripley? She's the next, hottest thing. This is Trevor and Shania, managers of Hotel Cinema, where we're holding your event tomorrow."

To my relief, Kitty caught sight of someone she knew and disappeared into the crowd.

"It's *Shanna*," Shanna said, regarding Ripley with apprehension but boldly thrusting her hand forward. "A pleasure to meet you. Are you speaking at the service, Moira?"

"Me?" Moira shook her head. "No way." She reached into her bag and pulled out a program. "Alec Baldwin is emceeing, Julia Roberts is giving the eulogy, Gwyneth Paltrow is reading a poem by Walt Whitman, and the Dixie Chicks are singing a ballad. It's going to be incredible."

"No one from Chelsea's family?" I asked.

Moira rolled her eyes. "Are you kidding me? They blame Hollywood for her death."

"I thought I saw her mother outside," I said to test Moira's reaction.

Moira scrunched up her face. "Huh? Impossible."

"Don't be silly, Trevor," said Shanna, giving a shrill laugh. Ripley's presence, even though neither of us had ever heard of her, seemed to make her nervous. "That was some crazy woman trying to lie her way in."

"I thought she seemed genuine," I said.

"Fans are trying anything to get in," said Moira. "What did she look like?"

"Dirty blond, permed hair," said Shanna. "Black polyester dress. Possibly drunk."

Moira's eyes looked troubled. "Definitely not Chelsea's mother," she said. "She's a teetotaler and a high-society lady." She pulled out her phone, checked the display window, and stuffed it back into her purse. She turned to Shanna. "They didn't let her in, I hope? I'm concerned about security."

Shanna shook her head. "She couldn't even get Chelsea's name straight—she called her Sharon. Two security officers dragged her away."

A chime began to sound. Moira grabbed Ripley's arm and disappeared into the crowd.

"Shall we?" I said to Shanna.

She nodded, putting on a brave face.

We were seated on the balcony in the third row from the back of the auditorium. As we waited for the service to commence, memories of the last funeral I attended began to surface. I pushed them down, determined not to become emotional.

Sensing my tension, Shanna reached over and patted my knee.

The crowd hushed as Alec Baldwin walked onstage.

Despite a thousand people present, the service felt intimate and real. The screen flashed stills and clips from Chelsea's career throughout. At the end, when the Dixie Chicks came onstage to sing a cappella, there wasn't a dry eye in the theatre. Shanna placed her hand over mine. I turned my head and saw a tear rolling down her cheek. Squeezing her hand, I allowed my thoughts to drift back to Nancy's service. I had sat through it like a zombie, praying for its conclusion, longing to go home, to lock the door and be alone. In the days prior,

362

Mom had tried to convince me to deliver the eulogy, but I couldn't. So she did instead. She did a beautiful job, but since then I had regretted my decision. The room had been full of my acquaintances, my family, and friends of my family. Only a few present knew Nancy, and none knew her like I did. It was my duty to honor her memory, to explain why the world was a lesser place. I had shirked it, and I would never get another chance. I wondered why Bryce had opted not to speak today. Maybe he wasn't asked, given the cloud of suspicion he was under. I thought of our conversation: *After she died, I became obsessed with knowing the truth. I called her doctor.* Whereas he had become obsessed, I had pushed the notion of Nancy's pregnancy away. Was denial keeping me from moving on? Mom's remarks had shaken my conviction that Nancy was pregnant. Did I need to know for sure before I could find the closure my mother thought I so desperately needed?

Shanna pulled her hand away as a gospel choir appeared onstage, and the crowd rose to sing along.

After the service, Shanna put her arm around me as we filed into the reception hall. "You okay?"

"I hate funerals."

"I take it you're not up for the after-party at Madeo?"

"No. Let's walk back to the hotel."

As we made our way down the stairs, I kept my head down, bracing for more heckling, but a commotion near the street had captured everyone's attention.

"Look, there's Bryce," Shanna said, pointing toward the street. An army of media had encircled him as he left the service. He walked with hands thrust into his pockets, head down, trying to navigate his way around them as they threw themselves into his path. I felt a wave of empathy for him. After the agony of a two-hour farewell to the woman he loved, he now had to face this pack of hounds. Up ahead, I noticed a group of uniformed LAPD officers gathered on the curb next to two police cars. I recognized Detective Christakos among them. Suddenly the officers charged toward Bryce, pushing reporters out of the way and surrounding him.

Bryce halted. I expected him to run, but he stood passively as they wrenched his arms behind his back, pushing him toward one of the police cars. Paparazzi, reporters, and spectators swarmed after them. Bryce was flattened over the hood of a car and cuffed while Detective Christakos read him his rights. The door of the cruiser was pulled open and Bryce was shoved inside.

The detective lingered to pose for the media.

★ ★ ★ ★ ★

Back at the hotel, Shanna asked if I wanted to go for a drink.

"I think I'll catch up on some work and call it an early night," I said.

"You have plans?" she asked.

"Yes, I plan to read a book my mother gave me."

"That can wait. Come with me." She pulled me into Action. "It took me a long time to figure out that you never catch up in this business. No matter how late you work, there's always a pile of work waiting in the morning."

The lounge was empty save for a handful of patrons; everyone was outside enjoying the sun.

Shanna led me to a quiet table and pulled open the shimmer screen. "You can keep an eye on the lobby," she said. "It will give you the illusion of working." She sat me down and arranged pillows around me like a nurse comforting a patient.

Eva came over. "San Pellegrino, Trevor?"

"Absolutely not," Shanna said. "He'll have a Grey Goose martini—make that two. For him. I'll have a Tanqueray 10 martini straight up." She sat on the ottoman next to me and gazed around. "I adore this lounge when it's empty."

"You're in good spirits. I should take you to funerals more often."

"In fact, I had a good cry during the service. Not that anyone would know—I've mastered the art of crying inside while looking bored and slightly pissed off."

"Not quite. I saw a tear."

"Impossible. It must have been a drip of humidity from the ceiling. And you? You were squeezing my hand so hard I thought you'd crush it. Was the service cathartic or torturous?"

"A bit of both, I'd say."

Janie Spanozzini bustled across the lounge toward us. "Sorry to botha you guys," she said. "Treva, Mr. Greenfield is lookin' for his bow tie. He said it didn't make it back with his suit. Olga Slovenka said she saw you wearin' it."

Embarrassed, I reached into my pocket and pulled it out. It was still flashing.

Janie held her out hand, lips pursed. "He's really angry. He's late for his daughta's birthday potty."

"Did he happen to mention if the flamingos arrived?" Shanna asked.

Janie shook her head. "He didn't say nothin' about that." She hurried off.

I turned to Shanna. "Dare I ask?"

"We couldn't get an elephant. I found some flamingos. You stole that hideous tie from Mr. Greenfield?"

"I was desperate. I had no idea it was a gag tie."

"Evidently." Our drinks arrived, and Shanna raised her glass in a toast. "To Vegas."

"Vegas?"

"I was on the internet this morning. I found a website for a hotel under construction called the Millionaire Hotel & Casino. They plan to cater to millionaires only. Doesn't that sound fabulous? They're looking for a general manager and a director of sales. I say we talk them into flying us out for interviews. If we don't like it, at least we get a trip. Imagine the fun we'd have! We're both single, you're young and handsome, I'm looking more like a tired old drag queen every day but am still passably attractive. I'm desperate for some fun. I haven't had fun in about twenty years."

"You know that I'm not much for fun, Shanna. And I'm certainly not about to abandon staff and move to Vegas."

Eva brought us our drinks.

"Staff don't need us. Half of them are looking for new jobs anyway. The other half are related to Tony."

"What about your kids? I thought you moved here to be closer to them," I said.

"I've given up. They treat me like a stalker. It's only a matter of time before they take out a restraining order. I've stopped caring, Trevor. I don't care anymore, I just *don't care.*"

I sipped my drink and regarded her. "It's not like you to give up. You want to escape the celebrities, don't you?"

"Honestly, no. While I sat in the theatre today and saw their displays of grief, I realized they're not actually that different from me. They're just beautiful and rich and famous, and I'm not—that's all. I also realized I fear the women—the young women—not the men. This could be a turning point."

"Congratulations."

"Fortunately, Scarlett Johansson wasn't there. Of all of them, I fear her the most." She crossed her legs and sat back, jabbing at the olive in her glass with a toothpick. "I've decided to see a counselor. I'm hoping that in finding a cure for my own fears, I'll gain a better understanding of my kids' fear of me. I have a theory it's all connected."

"I wish you luck."

She raised her glass. "Vegas or not, it's time we started exploring options. Do you want to work for Tony Cavalli the rest of your life? I also came across an ad for a bed-and-breakfast for sale in Vancouver."

"Now you're talking," I said. "I've always dreamed of opening up my own little place someday."

"You and every other hotel industry employee. Don't delude yourself, it's a lot of work. Me, I couldn't bear having to do everything myself. I prefer to rule my domain from above."

"I think it's the idea of not reporting to an owner that's most attractive," I said.

"Trevor, I've been through openings, acquisitions, mergers, expansions, and bankruptcies. Owners have different priorities than managers—like making a profit. Good hotel managers require humility, compassion, integrity, and respect. Most owners are driven by ego and greed. The despicable ones are no different from feudal lords. They derive pleasure from being feared and exalted by their subjects; it gives them an inflated sense of importance. The best hotels separate church and state: ownership does the deal-making and makes the tough decisions, and management runs the hotel and takes care of guests and employees. Owners often fancy themselves hoteliers, but rarely do they have the necessary qualities. Only in small establishments do dual roles work; no one works harder than a manager with a financial stake in the property. You, Trevor, would have some growing to do as an owner, but you'd do a wonderful job of managing your business.

As for me, I'm contemplating forgoing all responsibility entirely and applying for a job as a lobby hostess at the Regent. But I fear it might be too demanding."

"This hotel opened nine days ago, Shanna. I'm not ready to leave, nor should you be. You're the one who hoodwinked me into taking this job. The least you can do is stick around."

"Do you realize that Janie and Bernadina are this hotel's appointed heirs? As soon as he can, Tony's going to move us out and the relatives in. After all our hard work, that's who we'll leave our legacy to."

It was a sobering thought.

"How about that scene outside the theatre!" Shanna exclaimed. "I'm so glad they finally arrested someone who isn't on our payroll. I must say, I was suspicious of Bryce from the beginning. He's the obvious suspect."

I set my drink down. "Actually, I think they have the wrong person." I recapped my conversation with Bryce.

Shanna chewed on her olive, processing the details. "Okay, I think I got it. Bryce says Chelsea fired Moira because she wasn't happy with the publicity she was getting, and Moira reacted by killing her?"

"In a nutshell, yes."

"And we just hired this woman to represent us." Shanna swilled down the last of her martini. "Suddenly Kitty Caine isn't looking so bad after all."

"It's not too late. Tony still hasn't fired her."

"You don't think Bryce cooked up this story to divert suspicion from himself?"

"I believe him. He thinks Detective Christakos is totally incompetent, and I tend to agree."

Shanna frowned. "This makes my head hurt. We need more martinis." She stood up, waved to Eva, and then slinked down in her seat. "Guess who just walked in."

I discreetly checked the lobby. Moira Schwartz had wandered in, cell phone attached to her ear. She turned in a circle as though in search of someone, then went to the front desk. After a brief conversation, Janie pointed in our direction.

"Duck," said Shanna.

"Too late."

"Hiding here, are we," Moira said as she reached our table. "Now I know why I couldn't find you at Madeo. What did you think of the service."

"It was lovely," said Shanna.

I nodded. "Nice work, Moira. What brings you here?"

"Hold on, my phone's ringing." I hadn't heard it ring, but she reached into her purse and answered it. "Moira Schwartz Media Group . . . No, Miss Schwartz is not taking on new clients. No, she's not accepting names for a waitlist . . . Call her in the new year and"—her cell phone began ringing in mid-sentence—"Huh?" She looked over to me. "Stupid phone. I must have got cut off. Moira Schwartz Media Group, hello? No, Nigel. I told you, she's a fraud. I've never even seen her before." She hurried out of earshot.

"Strange girl," said Shanna. "You know, I dropped by the offices of Moira Schwartz Media Group in Culver City a couple of months ago to give her a copy of the contract. The group consists of one person—Moira—in a shabby shared office that smells like a men's locker room."

"Why am I not surprised?" I watched Moira. In a city full of actors, she claimed to be one of the few real people. Was she?

She came back to our table. "I gotta go."

"Can I ask you a question?" I said, emboldened by the martini. "Did Chelsea fire you the night of the party?"

Moira's jaw dropped. "Why would she fire me? I *made* her. Did that lying bastard Bryce tell you that? He'll say anything to save his ass. A lot of good that's done. I heard police arrested him after the service."

"Did you say you spoke with Chelsea's mother the night she died?" I ventured.

Moira scowled. "I was talking to *my* mother. Why are you—?"

"I thought your parents passed away ten years ago," I said.

"If you must know," Moira snapped, "I was adopted. My birth mother is alive and well, thank you very much. Any more inappropriate questions, Trevor?"

"That's it for now."

She let out a huff. "Don't forget about my event tomorrow. All the top entertainment media are coming. I'll introduce you around. It'll be a good opportunity for you to network."

On her way out, Moira stopped at the front desk to speak with Janie again, and then walked out the front door.

I turned to Shanna. "You know, the more I think about it, the more I'm starting to think Bryce is right about Moira. He asked me to help him. I feel guilty doing nothing. But how can I prove he's innocent?"

"Don't get involved, Trevor. Have confidence that if police arrested Bryce, they had good reason."

"I'm tired of sitting by while the detective bungles the investigation."

"Let it go."

"You're right," I said. "There's nothing I can do."

A half-hour later, on the way to my office to retrieve my house keys, I stopped at the front desk to ask Janie who Moira was looking for.

"Some lady named Loretta Maines," Janie replied. "She checked in this afternoon."

The name meant nothing to me.

As I was walking out the front door, a limousine pulled up, and a middle-aged, blond-haired woman in a black dress got out. I recognized her immediately as the woman from the service—the woman who had claimed to be Chelsea's mother.

"Good evening, Ms. Maines," doorman Doug greeted her. "Welcome back."

19

The Parent Trap

Monday morning, I arrived at work determined to put last week behind me and embark Hotel Cinema on its originally intended path. Only a few fans remained outside—no reporters, no angry protestors, only a handful of paparazzi who would likely become permanent fixtures. Shanna wasn't staked out in my office, waiting to deliver bad news. I walked into the operations meeting with a renewed feeling of optimism and sensed the same with staff. Ezmerelda was beaming again. Al Combs was grinning too, looking confident and proud. Even Dennis Claiborne appeared to be in good spirits.

In fact, the group looked *too* cheerful. Were they up to something?

As Shanna reported in on incoming groups, out of the corner of my eye I saw Dennis pass something to Rheanna under the table.

"What is that?" I asked, holding up my hand to stop Shanna.

Rheanna froze. "Um, nothing?"

Nervous giggles broke out across the room.

"Is that the *Spotlight?* I don't want to see that magazine at this meeting—or on this property—again." I looked around the table. "What's so funny?" Even Shanna was struggling to contain her mirth. I held out my hand. "Hand it over."

Rheanna's face turned scarlet. Slowly she slid the magazine toward me.

I snatched it up and inspected it. On the cover was a photo of Bryce outside the Kodak Theatre, under the headline BRYCE CHARGED WITH CHELSEA'S MURDER! "This is funny?" I said. In the upper right-hand corner was a photo of the blond, acne-scarred woman I saw climbing out of the limousine last night. The caption read IN THE SPOTLIGHT! MYSTERY WOMAN CLAIMS TO BE CHELSEA'S BIRTH MOTHER! Surely this wasn't what they were laughing about?

"Turn to page twelve," said Dennis.

I flipped through the magazine as bursts of laughter erupted around the room. On page eleven, I found a two-page photo spread. The left page read FUNERAL FASHION TRIUMPHS! and featured photographs of Cameron Diaz, Katie Holmes, and Jake Gyllenhaal arriving at the service, looking stylish and glamorous. On the right was the headline FUNERAL FASHION TRAGEDIES! To my horror, flanked between photos of Kitty Caine in her Mrs. Claus suit and a woman who looked like Bjork wearing a dress made of crow feathers was a full-length photo of me in a tuxedo jacket, tuxedo shirt, tan pants, pink socks, and flashing bow tie. The caption beneath read HEROIC HOTEL MANAGER TREVOR LAMBERT CAN'T SAVE THIS TRAGIC OUTFIT.

"Oh my *God*," I said, slapping the magazine shut.

The room exploded with laughter.

"No question marks on *that* headline," Shanna remarked, letting out a shriek of laughter.

My face felt like it was on fire. "In my defense, I ruined my tuxedo diving into the pool to save Chelsea. I had nothing else to wear."

I waited for them to settle, quietly tolerating their banter. After a moment, I'd had enough. "Is everyone finished?" They weren't. Even my loyal Ezmerelda couldn't contain her giggles. I looked back at the photo and felt a little tug at the corner of my lips. How could I take myself seriously in that clown suit? I broke into a grin and chuckled along with the others. "Hilarious," I said, sliding the magazine back to Rheanna. "Now put it away."

Ezmerelda jabbed her finger at the photo in the upper corner. "She is staying here. I see her this morning. Ms. Maines. Room 114."

"I entered her reservation on Saturday," Rheanna said. "Mr. Cavalli released a block of rooms he was holding for the celebrities he expected at the wedding. She was on the waitlist."

"Does this mean the mob is coming back?" Al asked, looking worried.

"I doubt it," Shanna said with confidence. "That woman is a fraud."

★ ★ ★ ★ ★

After the operations meeting, I closed my office door and picked up the phone.

"Hello, Dr. Rutherford? This is Trevor Lambert. I used to be a patient of yours?"

He was silent for a moment. "Yes, of course, Trevor. What can I do for you?"

"Remember my girlfriend, Nancy Swinton? She went in to see you a couple of times last year?"

"Of course I remember her. I was so sorry when I heard she was on that WWA flight."

"I need to ask you a question. Was Nancy pregnant?"

"Pregnant? No, not as far as I know. Of course, that information would be confidential between doctor and patient."

"I know, but considering she's … When she was in Salisbury, she was going to ask a doctor to call your office to have her test results forwarded. Do you know if she did that?"

"Oh no, that wasn't me. I only saw her once. I referred her to a specialist."

"A specialist? What kind of specialist?"

"A lung specialist. I assume she told you. The poor girl had the same lung disease that killed her mother. When I heard she perished in the WWA flight, I wondered if she wasn't better off."

★ ★ ★ ★ ★

Shanna opened my door and placed a copy of the *Spotlight* on my desk.

I didn't look up. "Haven't you had enough fun at my expense?"

She lingered by the door, half in, half out, as though suddenly shy. "There's an article about the Worldwide Airways flight in there. I thought you should see it."

"Why, Shanna? Why would I want to see it?"

She came in and sat down. "It speculates about the mystery woman who missed the flight." She hesitated. "Nancy is listed as one of the top three potentials. Trevor, if this story breaks into mainstream media, they'll start hounding you again."

"I warn you, Shanna, don't bring that trash into my office again."

"Fine. I'm sorry." She reached for the magazine but didn't leave.

I tried to focus on the arrivals list in front of me. But the doctor's voice kept echoing in my ears … *the same lung disease that killed her mother.* Nancy wasn't pregnant; she was dying. Suddenly everything she had said and done in the weeks before the crash—every inflection in her tone, every flicker in her eyes—took on new meaning. *Let's wait for the test results and see if I'm dying.* I needed time to think, but I was afraid to be alone with my thoughts. Why couldn't I bring myself to tell Shanna? She was a good listener. She cared. But I was struggling to hold myself together, and I knew if I told her I would lose control.

"I don't see a gorgeous, honey-haired, brainless waif in her, do you?" Shanna said, oblivious to my state of mind. She held up the magazine, open to a photograph of Loretta Maines. "She looks more like Moira, with that pale skin and bad hair. Then again, pack twenty years of hard living on Chelsea and reverse the plastic surgery and, yes, I suppose they could be related." With a sigh, she flung the magazine in the trash can. "I think I'm done with tabloids too. Lately I'm filled with self-loathing after I read them."

I could feel her eyes observing me.

"Mr. Greenfield called, quite upset to see you in *Spotlight* wearing his bow tie. I had to comp his room tonight to appease him." Another pause. "Are you okay, Trevor?"

"I think I need some time alone."

"I'm sorry I brought up Nancy. It was insensitive."

I gave a shake of my head but did not look up.

"Are you mad because I embarrassed you at the ops meeting?"

"You didn't embarrass me, my outfit did."

"I should have made you change."

"Yes, you should have. I would have looked less ridiculous in one of Mrs. Greenfield's pantsuits."

She smirked. "Now that I'd like to see. This place could use some comedy. It's been nothing but tragedy, drama, and farce since the day we opened."

"I'm glad I could provide some relief."

"Why are you taking yourself so seriously? You said yourself it's a mindless tabloid."

I pushed the report aside and sat back in my chair, folding my arms. "I think that's what's so embarrassing," I said. "I *was* taking myself seriously. Enjoying the attention, the role of heroic hotel manager, hotelier to the stars. I've always been so shy, and overnight I became a media star—and I liked it! I started believing my own press. When I saw that photo, I saw myself for what I was: a buffoon in a clown suit."

"It wasn't quite that bad…"

"I can't pander to the media, Shanna. It's not me. I value discretion and honesty. What am I doing surrounded by people like Tony Cavalli and Moira Schwartz, who value hype and exploitation and grandiosity? In this hotel, where facial validity holds more value than competence? This hotel is a nightmare production, and I've been terribly miscast. I don't belong here. I think I'd be better off at the Ritz-Fucking-Carlton."

I expected her to argue, but she gave a resigned sigh. "You're right, Trevor. Your talents are wasted here. I think you should resign and go back to Vancouver."

"You do?"

"I took the liberty of inquiring about that inn I told you about. It's called Graverly Manor. It's in a superb location in the West End and a steal of a deal. I think you should get a bank loan and buy it. You might want to change the gloomy name first—perhaps something like the Sunshine Inn?"

I was startled by how quickly she had switched gears. "What would you do if I left?"

"I had a long talk with your mother on the phone last night. She's been helping me through some of my issues."

"You realize she's a nurse, not a counselor."

"She's a wise woman. We had a breakthrough last night. I've come to realize that my phobia goes beyond celebrities to all young people. I yearn for youth, yet because I can't recapture it, I'm repulsed by it. I need to accept that everyone gets old—me, my children, even Scarlett Johansson will, eventually. Only misfortunate people like Chelsea never grow old, and who's better off? Your mother thinks my kids are picking up on my resentment—that I subconsciously channel it to them. I guess I'm saying I'll stay here in Los Angeles for a while. I'm not ready to give up on my children."

"I'm glad."

There was a knock on the door. Shanna reached behind her to open it.

Valerie Smitts was standing there. "A reporter from the *Daily Spotlight* is on the line, Trevor. He says it's urgent."

"Is it already starting?" I said, reaching for the phone.

"Yes, Mr. Lambert, it's Nigel Thoroughbred, how do you do. I'm calling in regard to one of your guests, Ms. Loretta Maines."

"I'm sorry, Mr. Thoroughbred, but I can't confirm who is staying here. Hotel policy. I trust you understand."

"I know she's there, you twit. I just got off the phone with her. She's agreed to do an interview with *Spotlight Tonight*, and I need you to extend her stay for one more night. *Spotlight* will cover all charges except alcohol. In fact, I want her mini-bar emptied. I need her sober. And kindly move her to a larger room on a higher floor. She complained that her room is noisy, and I need her to be happy. An upgrade would be most appreciated. Send her a gift basket, and charge it to our account. The poor woman hasn't eaten in days. But no booze, no cigarettes. Her voice sounds cancerous enough."

"I'm sorry, Nigel," I said, pressing the speakerphone button so Shanna could hear, "the hotel is completely sold out tonight."

"You *must* be able to do something. This is Chelsea Fricks' birth mother! I'd move her to our preferred hotel, the Peninsula, but she insists on staying there. She wants to be in the place her daughter lived out her last moments."

Shanna was waving for my attention.

"Can you hold for a moment, Nigel?" I pressed the hold button.

"I think you should take it," said Shanna, getting up and squeezing past me to my computer. "Al put a half-dozen rooms into service over the weekend, and Tony released that wedding block. I think we still have one left to sell." Her fingers raced across the keyboard. "Here we are: a deluxe pool-view room on the fifth floor. It's listed at $519. Charge him $989. *Spotlight* can afford it. Hold on, let me pull up her profile … here she is. Ms. Loretta Maines from Langley, British Columbia. Isn't that near where you're from?"

"Close."

"Oh dear, looks like she discovered the mini-bar. Maybe she *is* related to Chelsea. Why, the little vixen watched two adult movies last night. Perhaps we can sell that story to *Spotlight*."

I released the hold button. "Good news, Nigel. We can squeeze her in. We have a gorgeous deluxe pool-view room available on our penthouse level. I can offer a very special rate of $989."

"$989? That's outrageous. Don't we have a corporate rate with you?"

"Can you hold again, please?" I turned to Shanna. "The old windbag wants a deal. Should I tell him to shove it?"

"Trevor, he's not on hold."

I spun around. "Not funny, Shanna."

She shrieked with delight. "Tell him to take it or leave it."

I released the hold button. "Mr. Thoroughbred, I'm sorry, but it's the best I can offer. Should I ask Reservations to hold the room?"

He sighed. "Is it large enough for a camera crew?"

Shanna was flapping around the office, mimicking Nigel. I had to cover my mouth to contain my laughter. "You never said anything about an interview in the room."

"Loretta refuses to leave your hotel. I promised we would come to her."

I looked at Shanna.

She shrugged and mouthed, "Tony wants buzz."

"Fine, Nigel," I said. "You can hold the interview here."

"It's absolutely essential that no one finds out she's staying there. She thinks she's in danger. She's a skittish thing, a frightened little bird, and I don't want her flying off. I know you've had security issues."

"Not to worry, Nigel," I said. "I'll take care of arrangements personally."

★ ★ ★ ★ ★

A half-hour later, I knocked on the door of Room 114.

Loretta Maines answered with a bath towel wrapped around her torso.

"I'm terribly sorry, ma'am," I said, averting my eyes. "I'll come back."

"No, no, come on in," she said. "I'm just getting dressed. I'll be out in a sec." She hurried into the bathroom and closed the door.

I looked around the room. The bed was neatly made. A small, floral-patterned suitcase was placed by the door. "I'm sorry you found the room noisy," I called out, glancing at the locked window.

"I don't mind the noise," she said from the bathroom. "I'm just nervous about being on street level. Mr. Thoroughbred says he wants to give me star treatment, but I prefer no fuss." She emerged from the bathroom dressed in a grey workman's undershirt and baggy Wranglers. She was younger than I thought, about forty-five. A layer of blue eye shadow covered her eyelids. "Can I smoke up there?" she asked.

"There's a balcony," I said. "You'll also have more room for the interview."

"Don't even mention that interview," she said, pressing a palm to her forehead in a mannerism that reminded me of Chelsea. "Scares the heck out of me." She fished two one-dollar bills from her pocket and placed them on the pillow.

I was impressed. Even seasoned travelers rarely remembered to tip the room attendant.

"I used to be a chambermaid," she explained. "They have the hardest job—besides the manager, of course." She looked around. "Well, I think I'm ready. Who would have thought it'd take me an hour to get ready to move up a few floors?" She guffawed. Her teeth were greyish and uneven, yet the shape of her lips reminded me of Chelsea again. Her eyes were brown—Chelsea's natural color. Could this be Chelsea's real mother, the woman she had rejected because she was hoping for Sophia Loren? I realized she did look a bit like Charlize Theron's character in *Monster*, though thinner. "Gosh, where are my manners?" she said, holding out her hand. "Loretta Maines, pleased to meet you, Mr. Lambert."

Her hand smelled of cigarette smoke. "Please, call me Trevor."

"And you can call me Loretta. I've been called a lot worse." She guffawed again.

There was something likable about her. She was not quite small-town but suburban, friendly, and down-to-earth. I picked up her bag. She was traveling light.

"It was only supposed to be a one-nighter," she explained, pulling a macramé purse over her shoulder. "I'm gonna have to wear the same dress I wore to the service for the TV interview. Unless I go shoppin' on Rodeo Drive." More throaty laughter, followed by a fit of coughing. She pronounced "Rodeo" like the stampede, as I had done when I first came to Los Angeles.

I pulled open the door and gestured for her to go first. As we walked down the hall, I observed her awkward, lumbering gait and compared it to Chelsea's floating swish and decided they couldn't possibly be related. Then again, aside from her brief appearance on the pool deck, I had only seen Chelsea in movies and magazines.

We reached the elevator and stepped inside. I stood in front of the iris scanner and pressed the fifth-floor button.

"I read your welcome letter in the room directory," Loretta said. "You're from Vancouver? Maybe that's why I feel comfortable around you. It's hard to know who to trust in this town."

"You're from Langley?"

She shook her head. "I grew up in Oregon. I moved to Canada when I was seventeen. After … well, you know."

I raised an eyebrow.

We were alone in the elevator, but she felt compelled to whisper. "After I gave birth to Chelsea."

I searched her eyes, trying to decide whether to believe her. They twinkled like Chelsea's but were a bit crazed, revealing … what? I tried to read her emotions: fear … pain … deception? I couldn't tell. The similarities to Chelsea were eerie. Was she doing a spot-on impression? Not another actress. So many people had lied to me and deceived me in the past week, I didn't know who to believe anymore.

The elevator jolted to a stop on the fifth floor. "On your left, down the hall to Room 521," I said.

"I was wondering," Loretta said as we walked, "is it possible to make me anonymous? So if anyone comes looking for me, they won't know I'm here?"

"Of course. We can make you incognito or give you a pseudonym. If you're incognito, no one will be told you're here. If you use a pseudonym, only people who know it will be told you're here."

"Is that what movie stars do?"

"Some, yes. Sometimes they like to use silly names like Daffy Duck or Daisy Duke."

This amused her. "Oh yeah? What name did Chelsea use?"

"She didn't use a pseudonym," I said. "She checked in as herself. Sometimes the biggest stars do that, I'm not sure why." Shanna had a theory that B-listers did it even when there was no threat to security or privacy because it made them feel important. Tonight, a well-known rapper was due to check in under the seemingly innocuous pseudonym of Mike Hunt. Front-desk staff were tittering at the prospect of addressing him by name.

"I know what I want my name to be," Loretta said, eyes lighting up. "Maggie McKendrick."

"Who?"

"She was the mother in my favorite movie, *The Parent Trap*. The original, not that awful remake with Lindsay Lohan. Maureen O'Hara played her. I named Chelsea after Mrs. McKendrick's daughter, Sharon, who was played by Hayley Mills. For one day of her life, Chelsea was named Sharon. Now there's a bit of trivia for you." She lifted her finger to her lips. "But don't tell anyone."

"My lips are sealed. After you, Mrs. McKendrick."

Pleased, she stepped in front of the scanner. It paused for longer than usual, as though trying to decide if she was who she said she was, and finally beeped. The door clicked open.

"I'll update your name in the computer as soon as I get downstairs," I assured her. "That way, the media won't be able to harass you."

"Oh, it's not the media I'm worried about."

"Who, then?"

"Wow!" she exclaimed, surveying the room. "It's so pretty, I might not want to leave." Her eye caught a basket of goodies and bouquet of calla lilies on the coffee table. She withdrew a gift card and read it, pressing it against her heart. "Mr. Thoroughbred is *such* a kind man." She nosed through the gift basket. "I was hoping for a bottle of wine." Walking to the mini-bar, she pulled open the door. "Empty? Dang. I could sure use a drink."

A loud splash in the pool drew her attention to the balcony. "Mind if I have a smoke?" she asked, pulling a pack of du Maurier from her shirt pocket. I shook my head. She went to the door, moving a clump of hair away from her forehead with her index finger in another nervous, Chelsea-like gesture, and slid it open.

"My goodness, it's hot out," she said, pushing aside the curtain and stepping out. "Gosh, look at that, the pool's right there." She pointed to the opposite wing of the building. "Is that where she jumped?" she asked quietly.

"Yes."

She smoked in silence. "When I heard what happened, I was so upset. I wasn't close to her—only met her once—but she was my daughter, and I felt a powerful bond. I think she was terrified people would find out her real mother was a washed-up, trailer-park alcoholic." She turned to me. "I tried to respect that. I didn't say anything to anybody. It was my choice to give her up, not hers. Well, not so much *my* choice as my mother's. I was seventeen, broke, pregnant by some drifter." She flicked her cigarette butt over the railing.

Alarmed, I leaned over and saw it land in the pool, a small plume of smoke rising from it.

"I guess I shouldn't have done that," said Loretta, looking embarrassed. "Sorry."

"Why wouldn't they let you into the service yesterday?" I asked.

She took out another cigarette. "After I heard about Chelsea, I contacted her mother in Oregon to offer condolences and told her who I was. She hung up on me. Mrs. Fricks thought I told Chelsea she was adopted, but it wasn't me, it was Moira." She lit the cigarette and stared at the penthouse balcony. "When I heard there was going to be a service in Los Angeles, I got an advance from my boss, booked a flight, and bought a second-hand dress. I wanted to stay at this hotel because my baby died here, but it was sold out. I kept trying, and on Saturday a room came available. It was a lot of money, but I felt I needed to be here. I had no idea things would turn out this way."

She stubbed her cigarette out on the metal railing, leaving a smudge of ash, and tucked it back into the cigarette pack, pushing the pack into her shirt pocket. Leaving the door open, she plunked herself down on the sofa.

I felt I should leave, but she seemed eager to talk, and if I left Ms. Maines while she was in confession mode, I knew Shanna would never forgive me.

"I expected the service to be in a church, not a theatre," Loretta said with a laugh. "That was Chelsea's life: pure theatre. I planned to slip in and out without anyone noticing. Then I saw the cameras and the glitz and the glamour, and it scared the heck out of me. I tried to sneak past security, but they caught me. Thank goodness Mr. Thoroughbred rescued me. I was so upset that I told him who I was, and he personally escorted me into the theatre with his press pass. We sat right near the front. I cried the whole time. After, he took me to dinner at this beautiful hotel that looks like a castle."

"Chateau Marmont."

"I guess I got tipsy. My story came spilling out."

"Then he published it in the *Spotlight*," I said. "How did that make you feel?"

"I gave him my permission. He paid me generously. I feel bad, but I've been broke all my life. Chelsea's dead, and I don't feel compelled to protect anyone anymore. Tonight I tell the rest of my story on-camera." She shuddered. "Gosh, I'm so scared."

"There's more to your story?"

She nodded. "Today's *Spotlight* tells only half of it. But I'm sworn to secrecy. They made me sign papers. Watch the show, and you'll know everything." She went to the mini-bar again and pulled open the door. "Why isn't there any booze here? I need a drink bad."

"Mr. Thoroughbred wants you sober for the interview."

"Sober? Ha! I won't be able to do it if I'm sober." She took a few steps toward me and smiled, reaching up to touch my face. "Be a doll and call room service? Get us a bottle of good Canadian whiskey. I don't mind paying. You look like you could use a drink too."

"I'm sorry, I can't."

"When I drink, my lips get loose. There's no telling what will come spilling out of me."

I heard Shanna's voice urging me to stay. "Fine," I said. "One drink." I went to the phone.

★ ★ ★ ★ ★

After the room service attendant left, Loretta and I sat on the sofa and sipped whiskey on the rocks—or rather I took pretend sips while she took large gulps.

"If I knew Chelsea was going to kill herself, I never would have told her the truth," Loretta said. "I feel just awful."

"Kill herself?" I said. "Chelsea was murdered."

Loretta shook her head. "You shouldn't believe what the tabloids say."

"Who told you she killed herself?"

"Moira."

Moira the spin master. "How do you know Moira again? Through Chelsea?"

Her eyes looked troubled. "Moira's the one who found me on reunite.com."

"So it was you who Moira talked to on her cell phone that night?" I said.

"I talked to both of them."

"Moira *and* Chelsea?"

She nodded. She was calm and composed now. "Moira called me, and then she handed the phone to Chelsea."

"Do the police know this?"

A look of fright came over her. "Why? I've said too much, haven't I?" She set her drink down and sat back, creases of worry forming on her brow. A shaft of early afternoon light illuminated the cratered side of her face. "A detective called me the day after it happened. He wanted to confirm that I spoke with Moira that night."

"Did you tell him you spoke with Chelsea too?"

She closed her eyes. "No, I didn't."

"Why?"

Her eyes snapped open. "I wanted to protect her."

"From what?"

She was staring straight ahead. "From the tabloids. She swore us to secrecy. Moira and I both, we wanted to protect her."

"That doesn't sound like the Moira I know. Did she say anything about cocaine in Chelsea's suite?"

Loretta nodded slowly. "She flushed it. She didn't want it to get out that Chelsea did drugs."

"Chelsea didn't kill herself, Loretta. She was murdered."

She gave a hoarse laugh and broke into another coughing fit. "I told you," she said, pounding her chest, "you shouldn't believe what you read in the tabloids. That night she was so upset. I feel so bad for what I did. I thought she could handle it."

"Handle what? That you were her mother?"

She shook her head. "She already knew that." Her eyes grew distant.

I wanted to shake her. "Loretta, I was in the penthouse after it happened. There were blood stains on the carpet."

"Moira says she cut her foot. The tabloids tried to make it out like—"

"Someone stabbed her repeatedly."

She let out a small gasp. "It was all just gossip. Moira said …" She turned to me, eyes growing wide. "Who would do such a thing?"

"What did Chelsea tell you that night?"

"Oh, Lord." Loretta began to rock back and forth. "It can't be true."

"Loretta, did Chelsea say she fired Moira?"

"No, nothing like that."

"What did she say, then? You have to tell me."

"I promised not to say anything, and listen to me, spilling my heart out." She reached for the bottle and poured more whiskey into her glass. She was quiet for a moment, contemplative. Then she turned to me, eyes lighting up. "Hayley Mills was so good in *The Parent Trap*, wasn't she?"

"I didn't see it."

"Oh, you have to watch it! She's such a sweet-looking, innocent girl, yet *so* mischievous!"

I had lost her. She was babbling now, drunk. I stood up. "Loretta, I have to go."

"Don't go," she said softly.

"I'm sorry." I went to the door.

"You won't tell Moira I'm here, will you?"

"Why are you afraid of Moira? She wants to sell this story to *Spotlight* herself, doesn't she?"

"Oh, no. This is one story she doesn't want told at all."

★ ★ ★ ★ ★

I called Detective Christakos on his cell phone. "I think you need to have another chat with Loretta Maines."

"Moira's mother? I already talked to her. She's got nothing to say."

"Loretta Maines is *Chelsea's* mother—her birth mother. Haven't you seen the *Daily Spotlight* today? She's on the cover. She's staying here, and we just had a chat. She told me she spoke with Chelsea on the phone that night and something she said really upset Chelsea."

"You mean she spoke with Moira."

"She spoke with *both* of them. Loretta says she talked to Moira, and then Moira handed the phone to Chelsea."

"I talked to that dopey lady the day after Chelsea died. She's got nothing to offer but an alibi for Moira." He sounded out of breath. "I got my killer, I got my murder weapon, and I got my motive. Murder is rarely this tidy, Trevor. Don't ruin it for me."

"Hear me out, Detective. I just printed an activity report for Moira's room. It indicates that Moira left her room at 23:20, the same time Chelsea went back to her suite after leaving for only two minutes.

That's a full *two minutes* after Bryce opened his door. Moira didn't go back into her room after that. She's gone a full fifteen minutes until 23:35, when she knocked on Bryce's door and took him to her balcony. Where was she all that time?"

"I covered all this a long time ago, Trevor. She was in the hallway. She was worried about Chelsea."

"Wouldn't she have seen whoever entered Chelsea's suite, then?"

"Bryce followed Chelsea into the suite at 23:20, seconds before Moira came into the hallway."

"Then how did Bryce get back into his room undetected? And if Moira was in the hallway, how did she know Chelsea jumped into the pool? She told me she was in her room when she heard the splash. Furthermore, Loretta told me Moira said she flushed the cocaine down the toilet, yet Al saw it when he was up there the second time, although Moira claims she wasn't in the suite after he left it."

"I told you, Trevor," Stavros said, gasping for breath, "Moira's got an alibi. Her mother confirmed they were on the phone together the whole time. Bryce does not have an alibi."

"Remember how the eye scanner wouldn't work for Chelsea at check-in because she was wearing colored contact lenses? Al confirmed she was wearing them when he was in her suite the second time. She had them on when she jumped into the pool—I saw her green eyes myself when I pulled her out. How did she get the reader to work at 23:20 if she had her contacts on?"

"She must have taken them off. What are you getting at, Trevor?"

"It just doesn't add up."

"Bryce is a lying rat, and he's going to pay for what he did. End of story."

"Are you mad at him because they cut your part on *Modern Loving?* Is that it?"

"They cut my part?" There was a loud clatter, punctuated by grunts and curses. "Hello? Hello?"

"Are you chasing a criminal or something?"

"I'm at the gym. I fell off the elliptical. Gimme a sec."

I could hear him wheezing. "Detective, listen to me. Chelsea *fired* Moira that night. Loretta Maines is going on-camera in a matter of hours to tell the world her story on *Spotlight Tonight*. It's going to be very embarrassing for you if it turns out you've arrested the wrong person—*again*."

"I never arrested those other people! I took them in for *questioning*." He stopped talking to catch his breath. "If you think Moira's a murderer, why did you hire her?"

"It's a long story."

"Christ, Trevor. First you tell me to keep my hands off your staff, now you're telling me to go after them. Why do you care so much, anyway?"

"Because I'm tired of the lies and deceit. I want the truth, and I want justice."

"Well, listen to the heroic hotel manager! You think I don't want the truth? You must think I'm a really bad detective."

"I have my doubts."

"Stop messing where you don't belong, Trevor. As soon as I start telling you how to manage your hotel, you can tell me how to run my investigation. If I decide there's a reason to talk to Loretta Maines, I'll do it. Until then, butt out!"

"But…"

"I'm about to jump in the shower. Unless you want to join me, I'm gonna hang up."

20

The Truth Shall Set You Free

"It doesn't get any bigger than Ripley Van Vleet," Moira said.

"There's no one here, Moira."

"Trust me, they're coming. Ashton and Demi had some stupid charity event today. Most of the media went there first."

I looked at my watch. "I can give you this section for another half-hour."

She reached into her purse and pulled out her cell phone. "Moira Schwartz Media Group. Oh, hi, Nigel, where are you … Are you kidding me. She just did a movie with Jamie Foxx. Tom Cruise wants her to read for him. And you think you have a better story. Fine. Whatever. Your loss." She slapped her phone shut and stuffed it into her purse, slamming the purse on the cocktail table so hard I heard a crack.

I eyed the table. If she broke it, she was paying.

"Nigel Thorough-Bastard isn't coming," she said. "I've given that jerk so many scoops, and this is how he rewards me." She let out a roar of frustration. "It better not be about that psychopath who claims to be Chelsea's mother." She looked at me. "She checked out this morning, right?"

"Yes. Right." My eyes moved to the front door, fearing Nigel and his crew would arrive early for the interview and alert Moira to Loretta's presence.

Moira began pacing, reaching into her purse every minute or so to check her phone.

"I'm going to go back to my office," I said.

"No, stay. I want to introduce you to some key contacts. *Spotlight's* exclusive is over tomorrow, and we need to move into stage two of the campaign. I'm going to set up a bunch of interviews."

"I'm not doing any more interviews, Moira."

"Oh, yeah? We'll see what Tony says. Oh, here they come. Finally."

A half-dozen people charged through the doors, escorted by doorman Doug. Another four trailed behind, followed by several others. Within minutes, the lounge was busy with reporters from virtually every major entertainment news outlet. I was impressed.

Moira worked the room. "She's going to be hotter than hot. Blond bombshell with brains and brawn. Did you get that down ... R-I-P-L-E-Y ... Relax, she'll be here ... No, she's *not* going to be the next Chelsea Fricks. Tonight's about RIPLEY VAN VLEET, the blond bombshell with brains and brawn. Her movie co-starring Jamie Foxx will be out in December. Tom Cruise wants her in his next flick ... Huh? I told you, she's running behind. Take a pill ... I won't even dignify that remark by commenting. All I'll say is Loretta Maines is a con artist. CON ARTIST. I've never seen her before in my life. And rest assured, neither had Chelsea ... Don't forget to mention you saw Ripley at HOTEL CINEMA, the hottest new hotel in the entire world."

It was dizzying to watch. She didn't introduce me as promised, but I was happy to watch from the sidelines. I was still gun-shy around entertainment journalists.

At seven PM, Ripley still had not arrived. The media were getting restless, and so was Reginald Clinton, who needed the section back.

"I can give you ten more minutes," I told Moira.

She checked her cell phone again. "Where the hell is that little airhead?"

A reporter tapped her on the shoulder. "Bettz and I have to get to another function."

"Just wait a friggin' minute," Moira snapped. "She's coming. This is probably her now." She lifted her cell phone to her ear and wandered off.

The woman watched her go. "I didn't hear it ring, did you?"

I shook my head.

"Is she coming or not?" a man shouted at Moira's back.

All eyes turned to Moira.

Moira covered her ears and walked out of earshot.

A moment later, she was back. "She's not coming," she whispered in my ear. "Some bitch in the publicity department at Universal won't let her. Small technical issue regarding Ripley not being legally permitted to hire me. Stupid girl never told me."

I glanced over Moira's shoulder at all the expectant faces. "You better tell them."

"No way. You tell them."

"Why me?"

"You're the manager. You sponsored this event."

"I didn't sponsor this event, and I'm not going to tell them."

"Please?" she pleaded. "I can't." She clutched her chest as though having difficulty breathing. "They'll be furious. This is my reputation. Public speaking scares the hell out of me."

"It's hardly a huge crowd. I'll stay right here behind you."

She took a deep breath and turned to the crowd. "Hello, everyone. Yeah, um, so …" She drifted off, eyes wide, as though incapacitated by stage fright.

Thinking Ripley was about to be announced, a technician in the back switched on a spotlight.

Moira cowered back, covering her eyes. "Turn that light off!" she shrieked.

The light went off immediately.

She turned back to the group. "Ripley's not coming."

There was an enormous outcry.

"What a monumental waste of time!" cried the woman named Bettz.

"That's it, Moira," cried another. "This is the last time I come to one of your events."

"Without Chelsea, you're a nobody!"

As one, the group turned toward the door.

Moira looked crushed. "Wait!" she cried. "I have another story—a better one."

A few of them stopped and turned around.

"This is Trevor," she said, pointing at me, "Trevor *Lambert*, the general manager of this hotel. His fiancée died in that WWA crash last year. There's a story in the *Spotlight* about it today. Rumor has it she might still be alive. We may be interested in selling an exclusive."

"What?" I cried. "What the hell are you talking about, Moira?"

Several journalists were regarding me, curiosity piqued. For a fleeting moment, I considered cooperating. I could recapture that euphoric feeling…

Nancy's smiling face appeared in my head, her eyes flickering.

"It's not true," I said solemnly. "She's lying."

With a huff, they headed for the door. As I watched them go, I saw Loretta Maines walk in and stub out a cigarette in the ashtray by the door. I turned to Moira, hoping to distract her.

"I'm ruined," she said, knees buckling.

I caught her just before she hit the floor. Her eyes rolled back. Setting her down on my knees, I touched her forehead.

Her eyes fluttered open. "I think I'm gonna puke," she said. "I need to lie down."

I looked over my shoulder into the lobby. Loretta was at the elevator now. "I don't think we have any rooms," I said. I tried to lift her to her feet, but she remained sprawled over my knees. A number of people were staring. Loretta disappeared into the elevator. Heaving Moira up, I placed her arm around my shoulder and walked her to the front desk.

"Holy cow!" Janie Spanozzini exclaimed. "What happened?"

"I think she fainted. Do we have a room available?"

"Sorry, we're sold out."

"Go ask Valerie if there's a late arrival. Moira needs to lie down for an hour or so."

"Can't pay," Moira muttered.

"Don't worry, we won't make you pay."

She tossed her head from side to side. "Turn that spotlight off. It's blinding me."

"There's no spotlight, Moira. You're seeing things."

Janie returned to the desk. "Valerie says you can have Room 110 until nine PM, but not a minute lata."

"Perfect," I said. Loretta Maines was a safe four floors away—not that Moira looked to be much of a threat.

"Are they gone?" Moira asked, lifting her head to check the lounge.

"They're gone."

She stood up suddenly. "My purse. Where's my purse?"

At that moment, a server hurried over with it, handing it to her with a flourish and a smile.

She snatched it from him, peering inside it as though suspicious he had stolen something. Pulling out a pair of dark sunglasses, she slid them over her nose.

"My career is over," she lamented, slumping onto the front desk. "Those journalists will never trust me again."

Janie lifted the iris scanner. "Miss Schwartz, I'll need a quick scan to bring up your guest history."

"Fine." Moira lifted her glasses and leaned over the counter.

Janie took the scan and typed a few keys on the computer. "Weird. Um, Treva? Can you have a look at this?"

"What?" I hurried around the desk. "Try it again."

Moira sighed heavily but cooperated as Janie rescanned her. "Is this going to take long?" she said.

"See?" Janie said, pointing at the screen. Her scan had brought up Chelsea Fricks' profile.

"Must be some sort of glitch," I said. "Bring up her profile manually and check her in. I'll let her in myself." I went around the desk to gather up Moira and walk her to her room.

When we arrived at the door, I stepped in front of the scanner and pushed open the door. "Lie down and relax for a while," I said. "We'll need the room back in two hours at the latest. Someone will give you a wakeup call. I kindly request that you don't sleep past—"

She shut the door in my face.

★ ★ ★ ★ ★

Artie was at the front desk with Janie when I returned.

"Looks like things are getting screwy with the Opti-Scan system," he said.

"Uncle Tony's gonna freak when he finds out," said Janie.

"No, he's not," I said. "Because you're not going to tell him."

"He said it's my responsibility to keep him apprised of such mattas." She placed her knuckles on her hips defiantly. "Now that I'm a managa an' all."

Artie and I exchanged a look of surprise. "A manager?" I said, turning to her.

"Oops, I guess he hasn't told you yet." She smirked.

I felt the urge to leap over the desk and throttle her. Instead, I said, "Congratulations, Janie. You have a bright future ahead."

Artie came around the desk and took me by the arm. "Let's go call the Private-Eye rep," he said.

As we walked off, Janie stuck her tongue out at me.

"There goes the future of Cavalli Hotels & Resorts International," I muttered.

"Don't let her get to you, Trevor," Artie said, unlocking the security office.

A minute later, we had Murray Kopinski from Private-Eye on speakerphone.

"This is a strange one," said Murray. "I dialed in, and the only explanation I can offer is the front desk agent mistakenly took Schwartz's eye scan last Friday and attached it to Fricks' profile."

"Valerie Smitts wouldn't make a mistake like that," I said. "And that doesn't explain the Cavalli incident."

"That one's a bit puzzling too. There's no activity via the connecting doors—they were bypassed. Think he scaled the balcony and got in through the door?"

"Impossible," I said.

"Then somebody's lying," said Murray. "A person can't enter a room twice without leaving. At Private-Eye Corporation, we stand by our product."

"There's no way the scanner confused Lorenzo and Enzo?" I said.

"Uh-uh." Murray was silent for a moment. "Did you say these guys are twins?"

"Yes."

"Maybe that's it. No two irises are the same, but identical twins could be an exception. To be honest, I've never encountered this before. The version you guys bought is medium- to low-res. In theory, I suppose, the twins' irises could be similar enough that the system confused them."

"You're telling me we paid $200,000 for a *low-grade* system?" I said, alarmed by how much I sounded like Tony.

"Don't blame me," said Murray, "blame your owner. He downgraded it to save money. But I wouldn't worry. It's not like identical twins are that common. I can pretty much guarantee you'll never encounter this issue again."

"You better be right," I said.

Artie reached for the phone and disconnected.

Something was bothering me. "Artie, have you ever seen the movie *The Parent Trap?*"

"Yeah, I took my daughter to see the remake a couple years ago."

"What's the premise?"

"Let me see … two girls are separated at birth, and they plot to reunite their parents."

"Twins?"

"Yep, twins."

★ ★ ★ ★ ★

As I hurried past the front desk on my way to Moira's room, Janie called out, "Your motha's on the phone."

"Tell her I'll call her back."

"She says it's urgent. She sounds real upset."

I stopped. "Fine. I'll take it in my office. Has the *Spotlight* crew arrived?"

"Uh-uh. They called to say they're running late. They'll be here in a half-hour."

I picked up the phone. "Mom, what's up?"

"Trevor, I have the most disturbing news. It's about Nancy."

"What is it, Mom?"

"Remember that gate attendant with Worldwide Airways—Lydia Meadows? Well, I met her for a cup of coffee at LAX before my flight on Friday."

"Mom, you promised to drop this matter."

"You may have no interest in solving this mystery, but I do. I asked Lydia if she recalled Nancy—anything at all I could pass on to you to remember her by. She couldn't. I guess I can't blame her, with 133 passengers on that flight. She had heard about Suzan Myers and feels terrible for misleading her family all this time. She insists she remembers a young lady she thought was Suzan running to the gate minutes after the plane departed. She said she must have fallen asleep and not heard herself paged. She looked tired and sickly. Lydia gave her Suzan's boarding pass and told her to retrieve her bags and go to ticketing. The woman walked off, and no one ever saw her again. That's

400

all she was able to tell me. My flight was departing. I thanked her and gave her my number."

"This is why you're calling me, Mom? To dredge up information I already know?"

"I'm not finished. Well, Lydia just called. She said she'd been thinking about our conversation all weekend. If it wasn't Suzan she gave that boarding pass to, who was it? After the crash, Lydia told investigators that the woman's accent sounded American rather than Irish, but the family was dismissive, saying Suzan wanted to lose her Irish accent and was probably practicing. Lydia logged onto the WWA-0022 memorial website and looked up Nancy's photo. She was shocked by the similarities to Suzan. She told me it was unlikely—but not impossible—that she mixed up the boarding passes. She said if it hadn't been Suzan in the waiting lounge, it would explain why she hadn't responded to the pages or picked up Suzan's luggage."

Blood was pulsing through my neck. "Mom, this is crazy," I rasped. "What are you trying to tell me?"

"Coincidentally, a videotape Dexter Lee from the flight commission sent me of passengers boarding arrived in the mail today. You can see one of the standby passengers, a dark-haired woman in a white dress who I'm certain is Suzan, approach Lydia, accept a boarding pass—probably Nancy's by accident—and flash her passport before heading through the gate. Lydia takes only a cursory glance at it. A few other standby passengers board. Lydia pages someone repeatedly, no one arrives, and they close the gate. Then another dark-haired woman approaches Lydia. A minute later she walks off, visibly upset. The footage is grainy, but I'm positive … Trevor? Are you there?"

I grabbed my collar and wrenched it away from my neck. "What is she wearing, Mom?"

"She's also wearing a white dress. It's similar to Suzan's but decorated with flowers. It's hard to tell, but I think they might be fleurs-de-lis."

I crumpled to the floor.

"Do you realize what this means, Trevor? Nancy didn't board the flight. She could still be alive!"

I gripped the phone, caught between the longing to believe her and the urge to fling it across the room. "Why, Mother? Why do you torture me like this?"

"*Torture* you? I beg your pardon?" She made a series of high-pitched sounds to express her outrage. "All I want is for you to be happy. I've always known in my heart she was alive, and I know you have too. You can't move on until you know the truth. Those hangups—maybe they're her. She might have amnesia. She found your number in her purse, and she doesn't remember who you are. She—"

"*Stop.*"

"Why, Trevor? Why don't you want her to be alive?"

"Don't you understand?"

"Understand what?"

"If Nancy is alive, she abandoned me."

"Treva?"

I looked up to see Janie in the doorway. The receiver fell from my hands.

"Whatcha doin' on the floor?"

"Trevor?" Mother's voice called out. "Are you there? I think we need to hire a private investigator."

"I think I mighta done somethin' stupid," said Janie.

I hauled myself to my feet and steadied myself on the desk. "What, Janie? What did you do now?"

"I gave Miss Schwartz access to Miss Maines'—I mean Miss McKendrick's—room."

"You *what?*"

"She said she needed to brief Miss Maines before the shoot. I thought it'd be okay. Then I remeba'd Miss Maines changed to a fake name and Miss Schwartz didn't use it, and I thought, 'Uh-oh, Janie, you mighta done something real stupid.'"

"I gotta go, Mom," I said into the phone.

"But Trevor, we need to talk about this."

I silenced her by setting the receiver on its cradle.

★ ★ ★ ★ ★

"Trevor!"

Shanna Virani rushed up to me as I crossed the lobby to the elevator.

"What is it?" I asked, punching the call button. "This is *not* a good time."

Her face looked stricken. "I—I don't know how to tell you this … Someone is here to see you."

"Who? Who wants to make my life more miserable now?"

"Darling, please." She reached for my hand. "This is important."

"It'll have to wait. I'm dealing with an urgent matter."

She glanced over her shoulder. "I don't think it *can* wait."

"Loretta Maines is in grave danger," I said. The elevator door opened, and I stepped inside.

"Wait! Trevor. This is more important."

"I'll be down in a minute."

As the elevator door closed, I saw Shanna walk toward a dark-haired woman seated by the glass fireplace. I felt a tug at my heart.

The door closed, and she disappeared.

★ ★ ★ ★ ★

I lifted my hand to knock on Loretta's door but stopped when I heard what sounded like an animal growling inside, followed by a cry of pain. I banged on the door. "Let me in! It's Trevor!" Sidestepping to the scanner, I waited for the beep and pushed the door open.

The room was dark except for a sliver of light from an opening in the blackout curtain. The balcony door was open. I could hear the sounds of splashing in the pool, children laughing. The air was heavy with cigarette smoke.

"Hello?" I called out, straining my eyes in the darkness.

There was a muffled response from the bed.

"Loretta?" I grappled for the light switch and flicked it on. Moira and Loretta were lying on the bed, legs entwined. Moira was pressing a gun against Loretta's temple.

"Are you crazy, Moira?" I cried. "Put that gun down."

"Get out of here, Trevor," Moira snarled. "This is a private family matter."

"She said she's going to kill me and make it look like suicide!" Loretta cried.

"Shut up!" Moira growled and smacked her in the head with the pistol.

Loretta yelped. Blood poured down her ear, dripping on the white sheets.

"Jesus, Moira," I said, taking a step toward her. "Leave her alone!"

Moira aimed the pistol at my stomach. "Stop, or I'll shoot."

I stopped.

"Now I have to kill you both," Moira said wearily. She gestured toward a chair. "Sit."

I moved to the chair and sat down. Moira kept the pistol trained on me. I closed my eyes, trying not to think of a bullet ripping into my guts.

I've always known in my heart she was alive, and I know you have too.

Part of me wished she would pull the trigger.

"Why do you have to kill us?" I asked Moira.

"You think I'm going to let this bitch go on TV and tell my secrets? My own mother?"

"You mean Chelsea's mother."

"*My* mother," snapped Moira.

I turned to Loretta. "Which are you? Chelsea's mother or Moira's mother?"

"Both," she replied. She touched her ear and regarded the smear of blood on her hand in awe. "Chelsea and Moira were twins."

"Shut up!" Moira cried, lifting the pistol.

Loretta cowered back, raising her hands to shield herself.

"Leave her alone!" I shouted, rising to my feet.

Moira pointed the pistol at my face. "One step closer, and I'll shoot you in the eye. Then we'll see if that fancy eye-scanner works."

"Be careful, Trevor," Loretta said, letting out a sob. "She's crazy." Casting a wary look at Moira, she reached for a cigarette from the night table and lit it. "Moira's adoptive parents died years ago in a car crash," she said, exhaling a cloud of smoke. "A few years ago, she decided to find her real parents. She found my profile on reunite.com."

Nancy didn't board the flight. She could be still be alive!

"They look so different," I said.

"Now, yes," said Loretta. "But if you look at old photos before Chelsea got all that work done, you'll see how similar they are. If

Moira cared about her looks, she could be just as pretty." She turned to Moira. "Right, honey?"

Moira ignored her. She pointed the gun at herself and peered inside the barrel.

My eyes searched the room. The door was a few feet away, but Moira would shoot me before I reached it. And I couldn't leave Loretta. I looked for an object to throw. The gift basket contained nothing of substance. I could hurl the flower vase or the whiskey bottle. The bottle was closest. It was half-full, heavy enough to send the gun flying out of her hand. If I missed, Loretta and I would be shot dead.

Why, Trevor? Why don't you want her to be alive?

"Did Chelsea know you were twins?" I asked Moira, stalling.

Moira gave a shake of her head like a fly was buzzing around it.

"Moira was afraid it would drive her away," Loretta answered, her frightened eyes moving back to Moira. "At first, I didn't tell Moira about her twin either. We both had such high hopes for our reunion, but there was no connection. Moira seemed so lonely, so desperate for someone to love, that I decided to tell her. I hoped if she could find her twin, they might have more in common. I didn't know where she was or who she was or even if she was alive. I only knew that the young family who adopted her had lived in Portland, Oregon. Moira became obsessed with finding her. She emailed me every few days with more questions." She reached up to touch Moira's cheek. "You wanted to find your sis, didn't you, Susan?"

Moira swatted her hand away. "Touch me again and I'll shoot your tit off."

Loretta turned back to me. "She's still Susan to me. My little girls, Susan and Sharon."

Moira pointed the gun around the room, from the lamp to the light switch and over to the television and stereo, mocking pulling the trigger and mouthing the word "bang" like a child. She aimed at the sprinkler head above me. I silently urged her to shoot it, knowing it would set off the hotel's emergency system. But instead she moved it to Loretta's big toe.

Loretta moved her foot and used the sheet to wipe blood from her face. "Moira tracked her twin to Los Angeles. She was living in New York at the time, working as a publicist for a cigarette company, but she had always wanted to live in LA, so she moved. At the time, Chelsea's career was just starting to take off. Moira got someone to introduce her at a nightclub, and Moira helped her escape the paparazzi that night. They got friendly, and Moira convinced Chelsea to let her plan Chelsea's twenty-first birthday party. Moira didn't tell her it was her birthday too. Chelsea wouldn't have cared anyway." She looked over to Moira. "Right, Susan? It was always about Sharon, wasn't it?"

Moira didn't respond.

Loretta turned back to me. "Chelsea was pleased with the results, and Moira convinced her to hire her as her publicist. The two became close. Chelsea's fame skyrocketed, in part thanks to Moira. Meanwhile, Moira tried to work up the courage to tell Chelsea they were twins. But Chelsea's parents had never told her she was adopted. Moira broke that news and offered to help her seek out her real mother. Obviously, that was easy. After a few months, Moira got up the courage to tell Chelsea she found her mother. Moira made me promise not to tell her they were twins or that she and I had met. She wanted to take things slowly.

"As I told you, the meeting didn't go well. I was not the beautiful, glamorous woman Chelsea had hoped for. She made me promise not to tell anyone she was adopted, and then she broke off all contact. I was heartbroken, but I understood.

"After that, Moira decided never to tell Chelsea. But then *Blind Ambition* came out, box-office revenues fell far short of expectations, and Chelsea became convinced she was going to disappear into obscurity. Desperate for another big story to get her back in the spotlight, she started flirting with the idea of leaking the adoption story. Moira was horrified. If the media found out about her mother, inevitably they would dig further and find out about her twin sister. That would put the spotlight on Moira. She has a social phobia, you know. She makes a living out of exploiting other people but can't stand attention herself. She'd rather die—or kill—than be the subject of such scrutiny."

"Shut up, Loretta!" Moira shouted, turning the gun to her face.

Loretta cowered back but bravely persisted with her story. "Moira refused to cooperate. Chelsea threatened to find a publicist who would. She fired you that night, didn't she, Susan? Your own sister … How did that make you feel?"

"I'm warning you," Moira barked, jabbing the gun at her. "I'll fucking blow your brains out." She was fighting back tears.

"In a desperate attempt to save her job and to salvage their relationship, Moira revealed the truth: that they were twin sisters. Chelsea didn't believe her. She called her pathetic for making up such a stupid story. A huge fight ensued. Moira stormed back to her room and sulked, and then called me on her cell phone. She convinced me to talk to Chelsea and confirm it was true. Moira walked the phone over and knocked on Chelsea's door. She wouldn't answer. Then a miracle happened: the door clicked open. The scanner thought you were Sharon, didn't it?"

Moira didn't answer. Loretta stubbed out her cigarette and lit another. "In the suite, Moira handed the phone to Chelsea, and I told her it was true. Chelsea went ballistic." Loretta craned her neck to look up at Moira. "She turned the tables on you, didn't she, Susan? She called you a freak, a lesbian, every horrible name you could imagine. She threatened to go to the tabloids, to tell the CHELSEA'S INCESTUOUS LESBIAN TWIN PUBLICIST! story."

"I'm not a lesbian!" Moira shouted, bursting into tears. "I loved her like a sister!"

"How did you feel," Loretta continued, "hearing Chelsea threaten to tell *your* secrets the way you've been selling hers for years?" She turned back to me. "Then the phone when dead, and I didn't hear any more."

Moira began banging the gun against her head, making herself bleed.

"A few hours later, Moira called to say Chelsea killed herself," Loretta continued. "I was devastated. She made me promise not to tell anyone about the conversation, about our relationship. 'We have to protect Chelsea,' she said. Even when the detective called, I kept my word. Truth is, I was protecting myself too. I felt awful for driving Chelsea to suicide. Now I know Moira grabbed a knife and stabbed her to shut her up. Didn't you, Susan? Sharon jumped off the balcony to save her life."

I thought back to Detective Christakos's original theory. He was right about love, but it was sisterly love, and he was right about money, although it played a minor role. Addiction played the biggest role, but not addiction to drugs. Publicity—Chelsea's addiction to it and Moira's fear of it—had driven Moira to murder her. Maybe the detective was smarter than I thought.

Moira let the gun fall at her side and convulsed with sobs. "I miss her so much. I hated her, but I loved her too. I didn't want to kill her."

Loretta put down her cigarette and reached up to caress Moira's face. "After that, Moira pretended I didn't exist. I decided to come down here for the service anyway. When I met Nigel Thoroughbred, I was so angry at Moira I agreed to tell my story. Tonight, I'm going to tell the other half. I'm going to tell the world about Chelsea's twin sister. And you can't do anything about it, can you, Susan?"

"You bitch!" cried Moira, lifting the gun and slamming it down on Loretta's face.

Loretta cried out in pain and stabbed Moira in the eye with her cigarette. Moira shrieked and pistol-whipped her. The cigarette flew out of Loretta's hand.

I lunged for the whiskey bottle, aiming it at Moira. She turned the gun on me. Loretta rolled over and reached for the lamp, heaving it down on Moira's chest.

Moira let out a groan. Pushing it away, she leapt to her feet, standing on the bed and jabbing the gun at Loretta. "You fucking cow!" she cried. "I'm going to kill you!"

"Don't!" I shouted. I hurled the whiskey bottle at Moira. It struck her forehead, sending her flying off the bed. The bottle shattered against the headboard, spraying whiskey over the sheets.

Loretta rolled off the bed and ran toward the door.

Moira scrambled back onto the bed, pointing the gun at Loretta. "Move and I'll blow your head off!" she screamed.

Loretta froze. She turned to Moira with a pleading look. Suddenly, Moira shrieked. The sheets had caught fire at her feet. She leapt off the bed. Her dress was on fire. She grabbed a pillow and smacked it against herself, wailing in pain.

While Loretta watched her daughter, looking like she wanted to help her, I ran to the door and pulled it open. "Run!"

Loretta tore her eyes from Moira and dashed out. I went to follow her. Moira cried "Stop!" Dropping the handle, I turned to face her.

She trained the gun on my head and pushed me away from the door, slamming it. Blood was gushing from her forehead.

"You are *so* fired, Moira," I said.

"Too late. I quit."

My eyes darted around the room. The bed was on fire. Flames were licking the wall. Soon the entire room would go up in flames.

The balcony.

There was a loud bang on the door. "Open up! Police!"

Moira reached behind her and locked the door. "I won't let you tell my secrets, Trevor," she said, moving the gun to my head. "I'll kill you first. Then I'll find Loretta, and I'll kill her too."

There was another bang at the door. Moira glanced over her shoulders and I reached out and knocked the gun from her hands. She cried out and dove to the floor to retrieve it. I dashed across the room and onto the balcony. My only hope of survival was to jump. I leaned over to gauge how far I'd have to leap to reach the deep end of the pool.

It would be a stretch.

"Don't move!" Moira cried from behind me.

Scrambling onto the railing, I looked over my shoulder and saw her rushing toward me with the gun.

I leapt.

A shot rang out while I was in mid-air. Like Chelsea Fricks days before, I arched into a dive. My head struck the surface of the pool, feet slamming against the concrete deck. I plunged under. Was I shot? Opening my eyes, I took stock of my body. No blood swirled around me. I felt no pain. I stayed underwater until I could hold my breath no longer. Swimming toward the edge of the pool, I broke the surface.

Moira was leaning over the railing, pointing the gun at me. Black smoke billowed behind her.

I ducked under again. Another shot rang out. And another.

Then silence.

I rose to the surface, gasping for air, and opened my eyes.

A dark figure was leaning over the balcony railing. "You okay, Trevor?" Detective Christakos called out.

"I think so," I called back.

Behind him, the curtains exploded in flames. "Here I come!" he yelled, climbing onto the railing. He leapt, plunging into the water beside me.

I looked up for Moira. She was slumped over the balcony railing, shot in the head. The balcony was engulfed in flames.

"Trevor, it's me."

I turned to see the thin, dark-haired woman from the lobby crouched down at the edge of the pool. Shanna stood behind her, hands pressed against her face. Behind them, Nigel Thoroughbred and a camera crew burst onto the deck.

I waded toward her. *It couldn't be...*

As I drew closer, she held out her hand. Her arm was emaciated. She was gasping for breath. That crackling sound ... her lungs. She pulled off her sunglasses, and her sallow eyes flickered in the torch-light.

The truth is in the eyes.

I heard a thud. Moira had fallen onto the pool deck, dead.

Tony Cavalli and Kitty Caine rushed onto the scene.

"Oh my God—fire!" Kitty shrieked. "Someone call 911!"

"My hotel!" Tony wailed, falling to his knees.

A bright light illuminated the deck. As Hotel Cinema went up in flames and its cast of characters arrived to take their final bow, *Spotlight* was catching the drama on film.

I pulled myself from the water and took the wasted figure in my arms, burying my nose in her lovely dark hair.

"How could you abandon me?" I asked her.

"I didn't. I set you free."

Let's wait and see. The fear in her eyes…fear she is dying. The heartache…the thought of her suffering destroying me like her mother's suffering had destroyed her father. *I would have done anything to spare him that pain.* In England, the doctor delivers the fatal diagnosis. She can't bring herself to tell me over the telephone. She agrees to come home early. The missed flight, the crash, the boarding pass—an opportunity to spare me the pain, to stage her death. On impulse, she slips away from the airport. She returns to her grandmother's house to die quietly, but she is tormented by guilt and remorse. She longs to hear my voice. Her health deteriorates. She reads about Suzan Myers and sees me on *Spotlight Tonight*. Fearing the tabloids are about to break the true story, she decides she must tell me herself.

Nancy Swinton has come to say goodbye.

★ ★ ★ ★ ★

THE END

Acknowledgments

My sincerest gratitude goes to my mother and editor, Marcia Craig, and to my readers Bonnie Craig, Suzanne Walters, and Katrina Carroll-Foster. Thank you also to Brett Blass of Hotel Roosevelt for his insight into managing a Hollywood hotel. And my heartfelt thanks to my friends and colleagues at Opus Hotel for making every day a privilege and a pleasure.

About the Author

Daniel Edward Craig began his career in the hotel industry in 1987 and has since worked for luxury hotels across Canada. Most recently, he was vice president of Opus Hotels and general manager of Opus Vancouver, world-renowned for exemplary service, cutting-edge marketing, and celebrity sightings.

Originally intending to pursue diplomatic service, he holds a bachelor's degree in international relations and has studied modern languages, new media, film, screenwriting, and acting. Today, he works as a writer and consultant in Vancouver.

In his leisure time, Craig likes to travel, practice yoga, and enjoy a healthy lifestyle. He is particularly passionate about hotels, having stayed at—and managed—some of the best in the world. Visit him at www.danieledwardcraig.com, where his popular blog provides a frank, entertaining look at issues in the hotel industry.

WWW.MIDNIGHTINKBOOKS.COM

From the gritty streets of New York City to sacred tombs in the Middle East, it's always midnight somewhere. Join us online at any hour for fresh new voices in mystery fiction.

At midnightinkbooks.com you'll also find our author blog, new and upcoming books, events, book club questions, excerpts, mystery resources, and more.

MIDNIGHT INK ORDERING INFORMATION

Order Online:
• Visit our website www.midnightinkbooks.com, select your books, and order them on our secure server.

Order by Phone:
• Call toll-free within the U.S. and Canada at
  1-888-NITE-INK (1-888-648-3465)
• We accept VISA, MasterCard, and American Express

Order by Mail:
Send the full price of your order (MN residents add 6.5% sales tax) in U.S. funds, plus postage & handling to:

Midnight Ink
2143 Wooddale Drive
Woodbury, MN 55125-2989

Postage & Handling:

Standard (U.S., Mexico, & Canada). If your order is:
$24.99 and under, add $3.00
$25.00 and over, FREE STANDARD SHIPPING

AK, HI, PR: $15.00 for one book plus $1.00 for each additional book.

International Orders (airmail only):
$16.00 for one book plus $3.00 for each additional book

Orders are processed within 2 business days. Please allow for normal shipping time. Postage and handling rates subject to change.

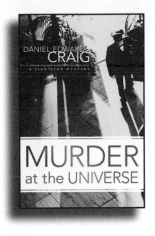

Murder at the Universe
A Five-Star Mystery
Daniel Edward Craig

For thirty-six-year-old Trevor Lambert, life revolves around work. As Director of Rooms at the luxurious and ultra-modern Universe Hotel in New York, he radiates dignified professionalism and high-end hospitality. But when Trevor inadvertently escorts VIP guest Brenda Rathberger—the cantankerous executive director of the Victims of Impaired Drivers conference—past the dead body of the hotel's owner, Trevor's perfect world implodes. Police believe a hotel executive may be responsible and their suggestion that alcohol may have been involved encourages Brenda to use the controversy to grandstand her cause. She joins forces with celebrated TV anchor Honica Winters, who exposes the sordid details on national television.

With his dear coworkers under suspicion and his treasured guests turning on him, it's all Trevor can do to protect everyone, particularly his sweet and lovely duty manager, Nancy. In the resulting clash among pampered guests, harried employees, and militant protesters, Trevor struggles to find the killer and to preserve the dignity of the Universe.

978-0-7387-1118-8 • 5³⁄₁₆ x 8 • 480 pp. • $14.95